STALIN'S FINAL STING

A Joe Johnson Thriller

ANDREW TURPIN

The Write
Direction
Publishing

First published in the UK in 2019 by The Write Direction Publishing, St. Albans, UK.

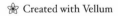 Created with Vellum

WELCOME TO THE JOE JOHNSON SERIES!

Thank you for purchasing **Stalin's Final Sting** — I hope you enjoy it!

This is the fourth in the series of thrillers I am writing that feature Joe Johnson, a US-based independent war crimes investigator. He previously worked for the CIA and for the Office of Special Investigations — a section of the Department of Justice responsible for tracking down Nazi war criminals hiding in the States.

The other books in the series about his various war crimes investigations are all for sale on Amazon. In order, they are:

I also have a second series, featuring former MI6 operative **Jayne Robinson** (who also appears in the Johnson books). This series so far comprises:

If you enjoy this book, I would like to keep in touch. This is not always easy, as I usually only publish a couple of books a year and there are many authors and books out there. So the best way is for you to be on my Readers Group email list. I can then send you updates on the next book, plus occasional special offers.

If you would like to join my Readers Group and receive the email updates, I will send you, **FREE** of charge, the ebook version of another Joe Johnson thriller, *The Afghan*, which is a prequel to the series and normally sells at $2.99/£2.99 (paperback $11.99/£9.99).

The Afghan is set in 1988 when Johnson was still a CIA officer. Most of the action takes place in Afghanistan and Washington, DC.

To sign up for the Readers Group and get your free copy of *The Afghan*, go to the following web page:

https://bookhip.com/RJGFPAW

If you only like paperbacks, you can still just sign up for the email list at the above link to get news of my books and forthcoming new releases. A paperback version of *The Afghan* and all my books is for sale at my website, where you will find large discounts on bundles of my books. I can currently ship to the US and UK:

https://www.andrewturpin.com/shop/

Or if you live outside the US and UK you can buy them at Amazon.

Andrew Turpin, St. Albans, UK.

This book is dedicated to Alexa, an enthusiastic student of Russian history, and Ross.

"Because Afghanistan has long been a crossroads, famous conquerors such as Alexander the Great, Genghis Khan, Timur Lane, Babur, Nadir Shah Afshar, and the British have invaded it, but the Soviet invaders have surpassed all in the systematic killing of its people and the destruction of their land. They did so at a time when nations had never been so loud in support of peace, and never so loud in opposition to war. Among the governments of the world, the Soviet government was the loudest in all this, as well as in its trumpeting of the rights of the toiling people, an instance of truly Orwellian doublespeak."

Afghanistan: The Soviet Invasion and the Afghan Response, by M. Hassan Kakar, University of California Press (1995)

PROLOGUE

Tuesday, March 15, 1988
Kabul

A jolt of pain from his broken ribs and bruised kidneys shot through Javed Hasrat as he jerked awake. He felt the concrete floor beneath his body shake as an explosion blasted through the cellblock in which he was lying, causing a spike of agony in both eardrums.

Javed momentarily closed his eyes, his confusion born of the three previous sleepless nights during which he had been tortured naked by Soviet intelligence officers and their Afghan thugs with electric shocks, wooden batons, and a whip.

Now he hauled himself to his feet, white flashes appearing in front of his eyes from the pain that gripped his rib cage.

Another explosion hammered through the building. The bang, together with a sliver of white light that pierced the cell through the rectangular barred window, was followed by a series of piercing screams outside and shouting from other neighboring cells.

Through his semiconscious state, Javed's first thought was that this was the start of another KGB torture routine. Then he realized that the explosions were from rocket-propelled grenades.

Javed glanced around. The three other men who were sharing his cell remained lying on their burlap mats, too broken to move, despite the din.

He tried to stand tall enough to see through the eight-inch-square barred opening three-quarters of the way up the door of his cell in block one of Pul-e-Charkhi prison. There was a piece of sheet plastic partly covering the gap, in a vain attempt to keep out the cold. But every time he pushed up on tiptoes, the agony was too great and he sank back down again, breathless and feeling broken. Smoke wafted in through the unglazed window, causing Javed to cough and masking the stench of urine and excrement from the bucket that stood in the corner of his cell. More pain around his ribs caused him to lose his breath for a few seconds.

The sound of gunfire echoed from outside the cell window, interspersed with two more RPG explosions and more deep guttural screams. They were followed by raucous shouts in an excitable deep voice.

"Allahu akbar!" Again they came. "Allahu akbar! Allahu akbar!"

Somewhere inside Javed, the mujahideen's traditional battle cry triggered a surge of hope. A minute later, there was more gunfire, this time from inside the prison. Javed could hear it as it echoed down the corridor outside his cell.

What is this?

From outside the cell came the sound of running footsteps, heavy boots clattering on the concrete floor. There was a jangle of keys and a metallic scratching sound as one of them was inserted into the lock of his cell.

Finally, a click, and the door swung open. There were two men standing there in the gloom. The one in front, holding the keys, was wearing a prison guard's blue-gray uniform with a flat peaked cap and a frozen stare, clearly terrified. The one behind, an Afghan holding a pistol that was pointed at the guard, wore a dark gray *shalwar kameez*—a traditional long linen shirt and baggy trousers—a black sleeveless jacket, and a black *chitrali* cap.

The Afghan pulled the guard back out into the corridor and shoved him hard in the back with the butt of his gun, sending him sprawling onto the floor. Then he pointed the gun at the guard and pulled the trigger twice in quick succession, shooting him through the back of the head with both rounds.

"Which of you is Javed Hasrat?" the man in the *chitrali* cap asked in Pashto.

"Me."

"Good. We are taking you and a few other men out of here," the man said.

From outside, there was another huge explosion that rocked the building in which they stood, followed by more gunfire.

"Who are you?" Javed asked.

"I will tell you later. A friend of your friends."

"What about these other men?" Javed asked, pointing at the others, who were now sitting, silently staring at the dead guard and the Afghan.

"No time. Just you. Let's move." The Afghan walked out, beckoning Javed to follow.

Javed, his injuries tearing at the inside of his rib cage and stomach, forced himself to walk down the corridor, its white paint peeling, and past other cells with metal barred doors to the right and the left. Their footsteps echoed from the bare concrete walls, ceilings, and floors. Then they passed through a heavy steel barred gate, which was half open, and turned left down two flights of stairs.

"We walk as fast as we can and straight, across the yard and through a black metal bar gate directly ahead," the Afghan said when they reached the ground floor.

As Javed exited the cellblock into the dusty light of early morning Kabul, he saw a scene of total carnage. The bodies of at least a dozen guards were strewn in a line across the yard to his left. They all had bullet wounds to the head. It appeared as though they had been lined up and shot.

Three other dead guards lay to the right, together with four prisoners, all of whom had blast injuries; one had lost both his legs below the knees. Pools of dark red blood were spreading across the ground next to them. The smoking remains of a gray prison van, its bodywork ripped apart by a rocket or grenade, stood next to the high stone wall with its coiled razor-wire topping that formed the perimeter of Pul-e-Charkhi's interior exercise yard.

In the background, Javed heard sirens wailing outside the prison wall, and an alarm was squawking incessantly.

He did as instructed and walked across the uneven crushed stone exercise yard toward the black pedestrian gate, feeling all the while as though he might pass out from the pain in his ribs. He looked to his right, where the mushroom-shaped concrete security observation tower loomed high over the prison below, then over his shoulder at the gray mono-lithic mass of the cellblocks behind him with their bicycle-spoke structure, each block running out from a hub in the center.

There came a gunshot, followed by the unmistakable

whine of a bullet above his head, followed by another. The Afghan pushed him in the back. "Run," he shouted.

Javed broke into a jog, expecting at any moment to feel the impact from the next round. But he reached the heavy steel barred gate, which the Afghan pushed open. It led through the internal perimeter wall, which was more than a meter thick, to an external security buffer zone, also surrounded by a thick wall that was similarly topped with coils of razor wire.

Forty meters ahead of him were the twin square three-story stone turrets of the main prison entrance and the tall black gates, one of which was leaning open at a drunken angle, its steel bars and panels bent into a tangle. Far behind them, the snowcapped Hindu Kush mountains towered into the pale blue skies.

Six mujahideen men dressed in Pashtun clothing, two of them carrying Kalashnikovs and two with RPG launchers, ran past them and out of the gate.

Near the gate on the inside of the entrance were three gray prison vans, a mujahideen holding open the rear door of one of them. Three other mujahideen stood nearby, watching.

"Get in the back of the van," the Afghan behind Javed snapped. "Quick. We need to get out of here."

That was when Javed noticed the devastation just outside the main gate. Nine guards lay dead next to an old green Afghan police pickup truck that lay on its side, a huge hole in its windshield, the bent hood half open, most of the cab now nothing more than a tangle of metal and all four tires shredded. It appeared to have been blown apart. Another police car stood a few meters farther away, its door panels riddled with large bullet holes, all its windows smashed and two officers visible in the front seats, slumped motionless. Incongruously, the red light on its roof was still rotating, its siren shrieking.

Next to the cars was a crater from which stones and earth had been scattered over a distance.

Javed gritted his teeth, his broken ribs digging into something inside his chest as he bent to climb into the van and sat on a padded bench seat that ran down the right side wall. Four other men, all dressed like Javed in *shalwar kameezes*, were on the bench seats on either side of the van. They looked at each other, not needing to speak. That could come later; it was too early to be confident. They were not safe yet.

Within seconds, the rear door was slammed shut, followed by the two front doors. The engine revved hard, and with a squeal of tires, it shot forward with such force that Javed had to hang on to the exposed roof struts to prevent himself from being thrown backward.

Javed glanced through the back window with its crisscross steel bars as the van turned right out of the prison gates and then sped along Pul-e-Charkhi Road north across the dusty gray plain, past the flat-roofed houses of Dekhuda Dad, over the Kabul River and onto the main highway running east out of the capital toward Nangarhar Province.

But the van only traveled half a kilometer along the highway before swinging sharply left into another housing area. There it braked to a halt. The back doors were flung open, and Javed and the others were bundled out and into the backs of two battered white Toyotas that were standing waiting, their engines running.

As the car in which Javed was now sitting accelerated up the road, he glanced behind him; a man was pouring gasoline from a can into and over the prison van.

It was three days since he had been seized by the KGB bastards in Jalalabad, following a covert meeting with the American CIA agents Joe Johnson and Vic Walter. Now, only a couple of hours after he had thrown himself on Allah's mercy after another interminable night of torture, Javed glanced upward and prayed through the fog of his pain and his all-encompassing exhaustion that this escape was going to work.

PART ONE

CHAPTER ONE

Tuesday, May 28, 2013
Kabul

Joe Johnson peered out of the window and gripped his armrest as the Ariana Afghan Boeing 737 banked to the right and hit an air pocket, causing it to bump sharply as it descended. Below, Johnson could see the toy town cars and trucks buzzing along the Kabul-Nangarhar highway leading east out of the capital; a tarmac strip etched in gray against the pale terra-cotta landscape.

He glanced at Jayne Robinson, who sat next to him in the aisle seat, reading an article in *The Economist* about how investment bank Silverson Renwick was running a program to encourage more Afghan women into business. She had one slim jeans-clad leg up at a right angle, her bare foot resting on the seat. It was always either *The Economist* or *Vogue*. Johnson smiled inwardly at her divergent choices in reading material.

The one-hour flight from Mazar-i-Sharif had been delayed by ninety minutes, much to Johnson's annoyance. They were now going to be late to the evening reception at the US embassy, which was due to start at six o'clock. He had been looking forward to the presentation organized by the Afghan Ministry of Mines and Petroleum about the opening up of gas and oil resources to foreign investment, not because of the subject matter but because he expected to see at least a few familiar faces.

He had also received two intriguing but vague calls the previous week from a British investment banker, Frank Rice, about some potential investigative work in Afghanistan and had arranged to meet him at the reception to chat more. Rice wouldn't go into detail on the phone and insisted on speaking face-to-face. He hoped that Rice would still be around when they arrived.

Johnson finished the *Newsweek* magazine profile of Kurt Donnerstein, the US secretary of energy, that he had been reading. Donnerstein was giving the keynote speech at this evening's reception—yet another reason why he was irritated to arrive late. His star had risen steadily under Barack Obama's presidency, and he was now seen as a dead certainty for secretary of defense if Hillary Clinton ended up president of the United States in 2016.

Donnerstein had a reputation as one of the toughest nuts inside the Democratic Party. He was throwing his weight behind Afghanistan's initiative to bring foreign investment into their oil and gas sector. Doubtless he was hoping that a few US companies might benefit from such a move, Johnson mused.

As the aircraft descended further, Johnson looked out the window over the city that had battled so hard, and in vain, to retain security and normality in the face of constant waves of Taliban attacks in recent years.

They were now quite low in their approach to Kabul International Airport. His attention was caught by a black car racing westward toward Kabul along the two-lane divided highway, swerving to overtake other vehicles.

From somewhere ahead of the car there was a large puff of black smoke, and a truck appeared to jackknife and roll over. The car swerved to avoid the truck. Then Johnson noticed another puff of smoke, this time from a minibus ahead of the fast-moving car, and a second later the minibus erupted in a ball of orange flame.

The aircraft passed directly over the highway as it came in to land, causing Johnson to lose sight of what happened next.

He turned to Jayne. "I've just seen a couple of serious smashes on the highway down there," he said, jerking his thumb downward. "Looked like there were explosions on the road or something. Clouds of black smoke coming up and a minibus caught fire."

Jayne looked up. "Probably normal for Kabul," she said in her whiskey-low voice.

"Didn't look normal."

She shrugged. "Maybe a car bomb or RPG attack—they happen all the time."

Nothing much fazed Jayne. And it was true—there had been a continual string of attacks by the Taliban and other insurgent groups on American military and civilian vehicles. These tended to involve vehicles packed with explosives or rocket-propelled grenades fired from ambush points along the road.

For both of them, it was their first visit back to the region since 1988. At that time, Johnson had been a CIA case officer in the Directorate of Operations' Near East Division, working out of the Pakistani capital Islamabad with occasional covert sorties across the border into Soviet-occupied Afghanistan. He had applied for the role inspired partly by disgust at the way the Russians had carried out a virtual genocide across the country. The posting, which began in June

1986, was his first overseas role with the CIA, which he had joined in 1984. Jayne, also based in Islamabad, was an officer for the British Secret Intelligence Service, otherwise known as MI6—she had also been Johnson's girlfriend for a short while.

Now their roles were somewhat different. Johnson was a freelance investigator, specializing in war crimes, and Jayne had worked with him on several projects. Both had come to Afghanistan for an exhausting series of interviews, presentations, and meetings over the previous two days in Mazar-i-Sharif about a potential consultancy contract with the International Criminal Court. The ICC was considering a full-scale investigation into war crimes committed in Afghanistan by all sides during the current ongoing conflict—not just the Taliban and other factions but also US, British, and other NATO military forces—since 2003, when Afghanistan joined the ICC. The contract, if secured, would involve running a significant portion of the research work required.

Although confident, they both now had to wait a couple of weeks to find out whether they would win the contract. Privately, Johnson agreed with the many human rights campaigners who argued that the scope of the proposed inquiry was too narrow. He and the campaigners thought that the Afghan government should extend investigations into human rights abuses back to 1978, when the Soviet army invaded the country. But that was never going to happen.

Johnson popped a mint into his mouth as the aircraft touched down on the Kabul runway. While the plane was taxiing toward the terminal building, the pilot made an announcement over the intercom in the same respectable albeit heavily accented English he had been proudly deploying at intervals during the flight.

"I have some unfortunate news for passengers who are

traveling onward by road into Kabul city center. We have just been informed there has been a security incident on the highway outside the airport. There may be delays while the authorities deal with the situation. I would like to apologize to all of you for this. There will be updates available when you get into the terminal building. Thank you for flying with Ariana Afghan Airlines."

CHAPTER TWO

Tuesday, May 28, 2013
Kabul

The windshield of Yuri Severinov's black Porsche Cayenne 4x4 had a spiderweb of cracks where it had been hit by flying debris, and the driver's side wing panel was heavily dented where it had clipped the bumper of another car.

Severinov accompanied his Afghan chauffeur and his head of security in Afghanistan, Ivan Lvov, who had been in the car along with his close protection bodyguard, on a quick inspection of the damage. The vehicle was now parked behind a maintenance hangar at Kabul International Airport.

He knew he was lucky to still be alive. Thankfully, the chauffeur, a highly skilled driver, had managed to avoid a minibus slightly ahead of him that had been hit by some explosive device on the highway heading toward the airport. Severinov guessed it had most likely been a rocket-propelled grenade. That had come just after his driver had miraculously avoided a jackknifing truck that also appeared to have been hit by an RPG.

Severinov was certain that the two missiles were not intended for the minibus or the truck. They were aimed at his Porsche. The distance between the two strikes was at least three hundred meters, and his was the only vehicle close to both of them. It was no coincidence.

It was likely that he had been saved by the speed at which his chauffeur had been driving, making it difficult for whoever had launched the missiles to aim accurately. So he had survived, and several other innocents had undoubtedly died.

Severinov shook his chauffeur's hand and nodded his head in acknowledgment. "Thank you. You did a good job," he said in Pashto, because the Afghan spoke virtually no Russian.

He surveyed the damage once more. "Take the car and get it repaired," Severinov said. "Then get it back to Sherpur as quickly as you can. I will need it on my next visit."

"Of course, sir," the chauffeur said. "You have been watched over by Allah today, that is certain."

Severinov stifled a grin and ran his fingers through his wiry dark hair, now heavily mottled with gray and receding down both sides. "Yes, of course. He watched over us both very well. Off you go."

Two months earlier, Severinov had bought a new nine-bedroom, four-story, luxury villa on a hillside in the Sherpur Cantonment area—known among US expatriates as the Beverly Hills of Kabul—a kilometer or two west of the embassy district. It would be perfect if he needed to live in the city in the future, which he anticipated would be the case. There was enough space there for him and his staff, although unlike many other Russian oligarchs, Severinov tended to travel with a minimal number of assistants. Lvov, who had his own suite of rooms at the villa, had installed an array of high-tech security devices, including infra-red intruder detection alarms and eye-retina and fingerprint entry systems.

At around the same time he had bought a safe house— actually a small concrete and brick business unit on a site protected by a high brick wall and razor wire—from a fellow Russian entrepreneur. It was just off the Kabul-Nangarhar highway in northeastern Kabul, only about four kilometers from the airport. It was ugly, and the previous owner had been only partway through converting it into a residential property, so it still had piles of building materials scattered around the site and was unfinished. But it was secure and it was all Severinov needed. He wouldn't be living there, so its condition didn't matter much.

Despite its poor state, the property blended well into its surroundings, and Severinov considered it unlikely to attract attention, which was a principal reason he had chosen it, along with its proximity to the airport. It was only a kilometer to the east of the sprawling Camp Phoenix US military base, which in Severinov's view reduced the chances of it being a target for the Taliban.

Severinov headed around the side of the hangar and onto the apron, where his leased $50 million Bombardier Global Express private jet was being prepared for the trip back home to Moscow. Lvov, who was busy on a phone call, followed. The Global Express was Severinov's main aircraft, particularly for longer trips. He also had a smaller Cessna Citation. Both were normally kept at Moscow's Vnukovo Airport, only eleven miles south as the crow flies from his expansive home near the banks of the Moscow River in the Gorki-8 district.

Nodding at a security guard who stood at the bottom of the aircraft steps, Severinov climbed into the cabin, slowly removed his jacket, and asked the steward to pour him a vodka.

Lvov, who had now finished his phone call, caught up with

him. "Sir, I've just been speaking to a contact in the Afghan police. I thought I'd better report what happened on the highway to him—off the record, of course. But I did not anticipate this: he now wants to come and speak to you. But I've put him off. I said we were leaving soon."

Severinov turned to face him and paused for a moment before answering. "Why the hell did you want to report it to them? You know I want to keep a low profile in this country. I don't want to get involved in this. I'm not talking to their police people if I can help it. Definitely not."

Lvov nodded, running a hand through his short blond hair. "Sorry, sir, I shouldn't have called him. I'm glad I at least put them off, sir."

The steward returned holding Severinov's chilled vodka, his usual Beluga. It hadn't quite been the outcome he had expected when he had headed out of Kabul earlier that day for a couple of meetings. The first was with a top-level source he had cultivated inside the Afghan government machine who was now helping him prepare for a giant and audacious bid for a stake in the oil and gas production projects that the Afghanistan government was opening up to international investment. The second was a quick chat over chai with an old informant of his dating back to his KGB days in Afghanistan.

Assuming that he had actually been the target of the attack on the highway—and all his instincts told him that was a correct assumption—the puzzling question that remained was, why?

True, at home in Russia, his huge wealth as an energy oligarch, his status as a close ally of the Russian president Vladimir Putin, his political ambitions, and his ruthless business methods meant that he did have a number of opponents, some of whom might be pleased to see the back of him.

But it had been a long time since he had engaged in any

meaningful activity in Afghanistan—twenty-five years, in fact, dating back to his time as a KGB officer. So what had just happened didn't seem to make any sense.

* * *

Tuesday, May 28, 2013
 Kabul

The sun had just set as Johnson and Jayne strode across the small plaza toward the US embassy's modernistic sandstone chancery building, past the manicured flower beds, decorative lawn, and trees. They headed through the entrance, inset into an enormous glass frontage beneath a concrete canopy.

Johnson's first reaction on seeing the expanse of glass was that it must be an irresistible target for Taliban bombers, despite the extensive security checks required to get anywhere near it. Indeed, there had been a couple of attacks in the previous couple of years, resulting in casualties, although none to embassy staff. He was surprised there hadn't been more since the new building's opening in 2006.

A familiar figure stepped forward to greet them as soon as they passed through the door.

"Better late than never," said Sally O'Hara, assistant chief of mission at the embassy, who had invited him and Jayne. "Come through. You've missed Donnerstein, unfortunately. He's made his speech and gone to the airport already. But there's a lot of other people I'd like you to meet."

"Yes, I'm sorry. Nothing we could do," Johnson said. "We got held up in Mazar for ninety minutes, then there was the Taliban attack out on the highway, which meant we couldn't get out of the airport for half an hour. Crazy. Were the speeches and presentations recorded?"

O'Hara, a serious-looking slim woman with a gray bob cut, nodded. "Yes, they were. I can arrange for you to see the video if you like."

"Yes, that would be good. Thank you. You're getting a stream of VIP visitors through here at the moment, aren't you?"

"Yes," O'Hara said. "It's crazy busy. We've got a lot of investment bankers here. There's Richard Lorenzo, the Silverson Renwick chief executive, over there." She pointed to a bespectacled figure talking to three other men near the stairwell. "He's meeting local businessmen and is also speaking here tomorrow as part of Silverson's women-in-business initiative. And next week Paul Farrar is in town. He's got meetings with Karzai and then both he and Lorenzo are speaking at a big security conference in Delhi immediately afterward."

Farrar was the US secretary of state and had been pushing the Afghanistan president, Hamid Karzai to keep American troops in the country beyond the scheduled end of the NATO combat mission in 2014.

"It sounds hectic. Do you know if Frank Rice is still here?" Johnson asked. "I was supposed to meet with him."

"Yes, I saw him not long ago," O'Hara said. "He was enjoying a scotch. Come on. You'll both need a drink after that long delay."

She led Johnson and Jayne through the reception area toward the central atrium. Johnson could hear the clinking of ice cubes in glasses and the murmur of conversation before they entered the room.

There was a crowd of at least two hundred people gathered in the ground floor area at the foot of the central stairwell, overlooked by the internal office windows and landings of the floors above. At the front, there was a heavy wooden lectern, placed on a red carpet, from where Donnerstein had presumably made his speech earlier.

But now the group of diplomats, energy industry executives, Afghan government representatives, and other expatriate hangers-on were getting down to the real business of the evening—schmoozing.

O'Hara caught the arm of a tall, slim man with a gray crew cut and a tanned face who was passing them in the other direction.

"Joe, I'd like to introduce you to Seb Storey before he leaves us," O'Hara said. "Actually, Lieutenant Colonel Seb Storey. He's in charge of the US Army operation down in the Khost-Gardez Pass—it's his job to keep it open. You might have a few things to talk about. Seb, this is Joe Johnson. He worked in Afghanistan years ago, and now he's talking to the ICC about a war crimes investigation here."

Storey looked Johnson up and down. "Just as long as you don't investigate us," he said with a serious face. "We play it straight."

"I'm sure you do," Johnson said. "Good to meet you. You've got quite a task on your hands, keeping the Taliban at bay down there. I'd like to have a chat at some point. I think you'd have valuable insight into the issues we're dealing with."

Storey nodded. "Sure. Not now, though. I need to run. One of my staff officers can set something up. Sally here has my contact details—Sally, can you give them to Joe?"

O'Hara nodded. "I'll get them to you tomorrow," she said to Johnson.

"Give me a call anytime," Storey said. "Although you might need to be patient. The Taliban keep blowing up the cell phone towers. Enjoy the evening." He turned and left.

As they edged across the cream stone floor, inset with a yellow, blue, and black pattern, Johnson spotted Rice heading in their direction, wearing the same striped shirt and tie as in the photograph he had emailed a couple of days earlier.

Rice, a London-based investment banker for Brownhill & Co., a small operator that specialized in the global oil and gas sector, was holding a scotch. He shook Johnson's hand and then Jayne's as she introduced herself.

"I'm sorry we were late," Johnson said. "There was a security alert outside the airport on the way in."

"There always is," Rice said, scratching his fleshy cheek. The three of them spent a few minutes chatting about the security situation and the difficulties it caused expats in going about their day-to-day business. It was the usual embassy cocktail party routine.

Johnson glanced around to ensure nobody was paying them too much attention or eavesdropping. "So," he said to Rice, "what did you want to talk about?"

"It's all focused around the huge potential of Afghanistan's oil and gas reserves," Rice said, sipping his scotch and looking alternately at Johnson and Jayne. "The most recent assessment is showing massive, and I mean massive, potential. There's 1.6 billion barrels of oil potential and 16 trillion cubic feet of gas, plus another half a billion barrels of natural gas liquids. Look at that lot and it's a big asset. Development of it has hardly scratched the surface. There's billions and billions of dollars at stake here. We can discuss the precise details of what I might like you to do if we sit down privately."

During their previous phone conversations Johnson had already run through his background. He had detailed his history working for the CIA in Pakistan and Afghanistan in the late 1980s, followed by a long stretch through to 2006 at the Office of Special Investigations (OSI), the US Nazi-hunting unit that was part of the Department of Justice. He had also explained how he had subsequently set up his own business as a private investigator with a focus on war crimes and had worked closely with Jayne, giving some of her background as well.

"I've been doing some more research of my own since we last spoke," Rice said, "including reading press coverage about some of your cases. I was impressed."

Johnson nodded. Rice seemed well informed, which Johnson expected but still felt was a good sign before he went into business with someone. "Jayne's played a big part in those investigations. She's former MI6, from your patch in London."

Jayne took the cue to give Rice a little more background about herself, briefly mentioning her early MI6 days and her decision to leave the service and go freelance in 2012, when she started working regularly with Johnson.

Rice looked thoughtful. "Interesting. Well, here's the deal. I'm looking at this Afghan gas and oil investment project on behalf of a US client, and given your background, I'd like you to do some in-depth research on some of the potential rival bidders. Deep background stuff, political as well as financial checks. You'd have to sign nondisclosure agreements and so on before I can tell you anything further. It needs to be confidential. Is that something you might consider?"

Rice hadn't mentioned the investment project or the need to sign NDAs when they had last spoken. Working for an investment banker wouldn't be his number one choice, although he had a good knowledge of their requirements. Furthermore, he couldn't see how working for such an organization would have any relation to his core war crimes work. He glanced at Jayne, who gave a small shrug.

"I'm not sure," Johnson said, turning back to Rice. "It doesn't sound like my normal type of work. We can have a conversation about it, though, if you'd like."

"Right," said Rice. He checked his watch and looked around the room. "Listen, why don't we see if we can get a meeting room here for twenty minutes now. I've got a couple of NDA forms in my briefcase. You can sign those and we can get things moving straightaway. If the project or terms don't suit your needs, no harm done and I'll look elsewhere. Is that okay?"

Johnson nodded. "Yes, I understand. Jayne, what do you think?"

"Yes, that's fine with me," Jayne said.

Johnson pointed at O'Hara, who was nearby. "Ask Sally. She'll find a room for us."

Rice headed over and spoke to O'Hara for a few minutes, then returned to say that she could provide a room. "I'm just going to have to get confirmation from my London office that it's okay to enter into preliminary discussions with the two of you," he said. "It's just a final check of both your credentials. Why don't you mingle and socialize while I do that. I'm guessing it will take about an hour."

Johnson glanced at Jayne. This would be a final sign-off on the due diligence that Rice had done earlier, he assumed. Johnson nodded. "Yes, that's fine with us."

As soon as he had gone, Johnson murmured to Jayne, "I think he's checked me out already. There's no way he'd be talking about signing NDAs so quickly otherwise. He probably just needs to verify your story."

Jayne nodded. "I know. But let's go with it. Could be interesting."

"It's interesting that the Afghans are opening up the gas market to foreign investment with all this Taliban activity still going on," Johnson said. "It's going to be quite risky. I mean, a well-placed RPG into a gas production or distribution facility or pipeline is going to reshape the goddamn Hindu Kush if they're not careful. Some investors might not be too eager to get involved."

An hour and a quarter later, after Rice said he had

received clearance from his London office, the three of them were sitting around a table in a small room on the first floor of the embassy. The internal window looked out over the party in the atrium that they had just left. Only a few people had left, and those remaining were getting steadily louder and more drunk.

Johnson and Jayne signed the nondisclosure agreements that Rice produced from his bag, and he slid them back into a plastic folder with a satisfied sigh.

"Right," Rice said, propping his elbows on the table, hands clasped together. "Here's the score. My client, a US private equity company called Haze Investments, is hot on Afghanistan. They've got several medium-sized oil exploration companies in their portfolio and now want to move up a league. They've come to me for advice because I know Afghanistan, up to a point. What they need is some intelligence on their potential rival bidders; they want to know what they're up against so they can tailor their offer accordingly. But we're struggling a little to get the information we need on two of the other parties who are interested in getting into bed with the Afghans."

"Who's handling the process for the Afghanistan government?" Jayne asked.

"The Ministry of Mines and Petroleum is leading it," Rice said. "So the minister there and his officials are responsible, but one of their people, the head of financial transactions, is running the process for them."

"So who are the bidders you're interested in?" Johnson asked.

"First, the Chinese," Rice said. "There's a couple of state-owned companies, could be either of them who lead it, but it's basically the Chinese government plus whatever partners they can bring in. They'll be into it because they won't like the idea of the Russians getting back into Afghanistan. But

I've got a guy in Shanghai who's doing the due diligence on them. You don't need to worry about the Chinese."

"So who else, then?" Johnson asked.

"There's a Swiss-based investment company—you might have heard of them. ZenForce Group," Rice said.

"No, I've not heard of them," Johnson said.

"They're extremely private. Into oil and gas trading, and they are increasingly buying up production companies and exploration businesses. They've got a front man, the managing director Rex Zilleman, who's American, now based in Zürich, where the company's home is. There are others involved, we believe, but we don't really know all the details."

It all sounded far too corporate, complex, and not remotely interesting to Johnson. "Is there anyone else?" he asked.

"The other one is a Russian, a crony of Putin's," Rice said. "He's an oligarch—a billionaire, maybe a multibillionaire. But he's very secretive. He's got strong interests in energy and has the funding to basically buy whatever he wants. A group of oil fields fell into his lap somehow—as they seem to in Russia— during the 1990s, and Putin has supported him. Since then he's used the resulting cash flows to snap up all kinds of assets, ranging from gas fields to pipelines and power stations in various parts of the world, and now a few exploration companies. Apart from that, we don't know a huge amount."

The idea of doing some research on an oligarch seemed slightly more appealing, but the oil and gas sector? Johnson knew little about it, and it was just too removed from his normal field.

"So you want to know more about this guy," Johnson said. "Makes sense, but I'm not sure if poking my nose into Putin's toilet is my thing, really. Frankly, it's not my scene."

Rice leaned back in his seat and adjusted his open-neck shirt. "I'll do it on your usual terms," he said, "plus a special circumstances fee that will reflect the security situation here in Afghanistan and the people you may be dealing with on the Russian side in particular. I can negotiate. My client is paying so there is flexibility."

"What you're trying to say," Jayne interrupted, "is that it's bloody dangerous."

"Let's be honest, there are security risks. I want to ensure that's reflected in the payment," Rice said, scrutinizing Johnson. He wasn't smiling. "What do you think?"

"Like I said. It's not my scene," Johnson said. "I'm a war crimes investigator."

"Well, actually, I have reason to believe one of the parties involved might be of particular interest to you, then." Rice raised an eyebrow.

"Who?"

"The Russian."

"What's his name?" Johnson asked.

"Yuri Severinov. Runs a business called Besoi Energy. Haze is thinking that if a Russian rival is trying to get involved in Afghanistan, they might be able to leverage the history between the two countries. I mean, Russia occupied Afghanistan from 1979 to 1989. If this guy has any skeletons in his cupboard dating from that time, then, well, you know . . . " Rice's voice trailed off and he raised his hands expressively.

They were obviously thinking of playing slightly dirty if the opportunity arose. "You think he might have skeletons?" Johnson asked.

"Possibly. In the '80s, he worked for the KGB here in Afghanistan."

The KGB? Severinov? Johnson had to stop himself jerking upright in surprise as he made the connection. Instantly, his mind flashed back to 1988, to running for his life from a remote Afghan village as two Russian Hind helicopter gunships closed in.

"You've heard of him?" Rice asked, his gimlet eyes scanning Johnson's face.

"Indeed," Johnson said, grimacing a little. "I've heard of him. Oh, yes."

CHAPTER THREE

Wednesday, May 29, 2013
Moscow

Severinov tried to relax as his driver negotiated the smooth stretch of black tarmac driveway through the trees and up toward the imposing facade of the Russian prime minister Dmitry Medvedev's private residence in the luxurious Gorki-9 district.

But after less than four hours' sleep following his flight back from Kabul, and then an early morning call from Medvedev's urbane personal assistant Mikhail Sobchak summoning him to Gorki-9 before he could even eat breakfast, relaxation was proving elusive. He had made do with eating a couple of bananas in the car en route.

He scanned the array of eight Roman-style pillars that decorated the front of the symmetrical white three-story building, then looked up at the slate gray dome that topped the roof.

This *dacha*, on the south side of the Moscow River, was

one of many occupied by the rich and famous in the so-called Rublevka area, just off the Rublevo-Uspenskoye highway, around eleven miles west of the capital. The property had previously been occupied by former president Boris Yeltsin until he had resigned in 2000.

It was Severinov's first visit to Medvedev's home, although the two had met several times at the Kremlin and at the Russian White House—the main government building and Medvedev's official workplace.

Severinov's black Mercedes Maybach came to a halt outside the front of the house, and a doorman moved smartly forward to open the rear door for him, nodding deferentially as Severinov stepped out. His close protection bodyguard got out of the other side of the car and walked briskly around to join him.

He screwed up his eyes in the glare of the late spring sunshine. The heat, combined with a slight nervousness about the meeting, caused beads of sweat to form on his forehead.

Severinov was now worth many billions of dollars, thanks in part to the patronage of Vladimir Putin and Medvedev, former head of the Russian oil and gas giant Gazprom. In contrast to their battles against other oligarchs, the pair supported the acquisition by Severinov's business, Besoi Energy, of three underperforming state oil and gas fields for peanuts, debt-free.

Severinov gave them a shake-up, installed new management, and turned them around. The resulting tidal wave of cash that flowed into his bank accounts enabled him to pay off the modest acquisition cost within two years and then purchase a whole raft of other energy assets, both in Russia and abroad.

A key factor behind Putin's support was Severinov's background. His father, Sergo, had been a fiercely loyal Russian, a hero of the Second World War—the Great Patriotic War as the Russians called it. He had then spent seven years working for Josef Stalin as a close bodyguard and an enforcer who became known for his brutal methods of extracting information from reluctant interviewees. Once, after a night of drinking vodka, his father confided that his favored technique was to use a rubber truncheon and a spring-loaded steel rod to systematically break leg and arm bones.

Severinov also had links to Putin through the KGB. After studying economics at Moscow State University, Severinov joined Russia's main security agency in 1980. He was based in Berlin, where he became fluent in German and English. Putin, a KGB officer from 1975 to 1991, had worked in the Leningrad and Dresden bureaus. The two men occasionally cooperated on Cold War operations.

So far, Severinov's parentage, his links to Stalin, his shared KGB background with Putin, and his care in operating his business had carried some weight. Nevertheless, things weren't quite the same as they had been. Putin remained mindful of old connections and friends but had forged strong links with new people and brought in new methods and attitudes, and Medvedev likewise. Severinov knew his currency with both men had been somewhat debased over the years and was aware that whatever he had could be taken away at the president's whim.

Sobchak had told him that Medvedev wanted to further discuss bidding plans for the exploration and production assets owned by the Afghanistan government. It was the type of large, heavily politicized strategic deal that Putin and Medvedev took a very close interest in.

The truth was that Severinov held Medvedev in some awe, partly because of his vast knowledge of the oil and gas sector but also because of his power.

Sobchak, dressed in a smart black suit, held open the

imposing front door of the house for Severinov and his body-guard as they entered the entrance hall. He shook Severinov's hand and apologetically indicated toward the airport-style X-ray scanning machine to his left.

Once Severinov and his bodyguard had passed through the device, he immediately saw Medvedev, a slightly stocky man with dark, receding hair and a straight, even slightly downturned mouth, step forward to greet him.

"Yuri, greetings," Medvedev said. "How are you? I heard about your narrow escape in Kabul. Damned Taliban."

"Greetings, Prime Minister," Severinov said. "Yes, the Taliban are everywhere still. It's irritating, but I try to stay positive. If we're going to do business in that country, we have to work around them."

Medvedev, wearing a white cotton shirt with gold cuff links but no tie, led him through a set of black double doors and along a red-carpeted corridor to the door of his private office, and Sobchak brought up the rear. Severinov indicated to his bodyguard to wait outside.

Once in the reception suite outside his office, Medvedev turned around and faced Severinov. "I have a special guest who will also be joining us for the meeting," he said.

Before Severinov could ask who that might be, Medvedev opened the door and walked into the dark oak-paneled office. There, sitting in a chair next to the desk, was Putin. Severinov did his best to remain cool and collected. A double-header involving both the president and the prime minister was not what he had been expecting. *Dermo.* Shit. Were they taking Afghanistan this seriously? Clearly they were.

Severinov walked across the light oak floor, interleaved with strips of dark wood to form a diamond pattern, and shook the president's hand. As on the previous occasions when he had met Putin, his hand felt as though it had been through a crusher.

The president, unsmiling and unblinking, made no attempt at niceties. It wasn't like the old days. "Sit down," he said.

Severinov, not daring to take his eyes off Putin, lowered himself into one of the ornate dark wood chairs decorated with gold leaf, its padding lined with heavy blue material. Medvedev sat in the other chair, a large Russian flag drooping from a pole behind him.

"We both want to speak to you because we are concerned about what happened in Kabul," Putin began. "It was careless of you. I'm not going to ask for an explanation, but that story was all over the damn television news in Kabul, and of course, international media followed up, including some of the useless asshole journalists around here."

My God, that idiot Lvov and his police briefings, Severinov thought, fresh beads of sweat breaking out on his forehead.

Putin stroked his chin. "What was my core, most important instruction to you when I set you this task in Afghanistan?"

"Mr. President, sir, you said you wanted to keep everything very low-key," Severinov said.

"Yes. I did. And being so careless as to leave yourself open to an RPG attack on the main highway is hardly low-key, is it?" Putin spat.

"No, I have to agree, but—"

"What kind of surveillance detection did you follow before and during that journey, can I ask?"

Severinov should have expected this. Putin took the concept of shouldering personal responsibility for security measures extremely seriously, no matter the capabilities of his support staff.

"It wasn't thorough enough," Severinov said. "I would like to apologize for that. It was an error that won't be repeated."

"No, it won't," Putin went on. "This oil and gas investment in Afghanistan is one of the most important strategic moves we currently have on our books. If we don't secure it, the Chinese will. And we simply cannot allow that. Russia failed using outright military muscle in Afghanistan in the 1980s. Now we are taking a different approach. If we control Afghanistan's natural resources, we control the country. What's more, it will enable us to strengthen our ties with Kabul at a time when they are absolutely sick of having the Americans and the British stomping all over the country. They can't stand Obama. And I've put you in personal charge of this project because I trust you."

"Thank you," Severinov said.

Medvedev tapped his fingers on the desk. He was going to have his say too. "We've canceled twelve billion dollars of debt the Afghans owe us, we've sold them a massive amount of weapons and ammunition, and Hamid Karzai is keen to build bridges with us as an alternative to Washington. We can help them—we're experts in oil and gas. They want us in, and it's your job to make sure it becomes a done deal."

Putin nodded in agreement, then leaned forward over the desk's mirror-like, polished surface and thrust his face toward Severinov's so that the two were no more than half a meter apart, eyeballing him. "I am personally looking forward to traveling to Kabul to sign this deal. I want it to be seen as part of Russia's attempts to build much better relations with Afghanistan."

Not the reality that you want to use it as a strategic move against the Chinese and the Americans, Severinov thought.

"Yes, I understand," he said. He knew that Putin and Medvedev had both seen the briefing paper he had written on the Afghanistan opportunity, including a short assessment of the likely rival bidders. It had been a difficult paper to write, partly because information on the rivals had been hard to obtain—particularly the Swiss group ZenForce. Apart from their managing director, Rex Zilleman, his knowledge of the key people behind ZenForce was sketchy at best.

Putin sipped from a glass of water that stood on the desk in front of him. "Do not misunderstand me: I want you to not only be extremely careful but also extremely ruthless. I don't want to hear about things going wrong or people getting in your way. Tell me—you worked in Afghanistan in the 1980s, so I'm assuming you did things we wouldn't want to be made public now. Is that risk being managed so this deal isn't threatened?"

"The Afghan government knows nothing," Severinov said. "My role in the 1980s was impactful but below the radar. And there are no records anyway."

The KGB files relating to his time in that country—some of which he himself had written—had all been destroyed when the Soviets withdrew in 1989.

"Good," Putin said. "If anyone does get in your way, you take whatever measures you need to take. We've got the tools. But I don't want any more publicity like we've just had. Do you understand? If necessary, you can call on the SVR or our special forces to ensure things stay quiet. Got it?"

Severinov felt his stomach flip over inside him. "Yes, sir." He could see where this was heading.

"If needed, we can start with a social media blitz to discredit rival bidders," Putin went on. "That can be done at arm's length—a disinformation campaign. But I don't need to tell you any of that."

Putin glanced at Medvedev and leaned forward, eyeballing Severinov again. "While you're here, there's another job I also want you to think about, and that's Andrei Fedorov, seeing as he is an old friend of yours."

"Yes, that's a bad business, sir," Severinov said.

Putin had done his homework. Andrei Fedorov was indeed one of Severinov's oldest friends. Fedorov was an illegal, deep-cover spy who had been operating in the United States for the previous twenty years under the guise of his day job as a translator and technical writer for an electronics company. But he had been imprisoned six months earlier in New York City after being convicted of being a handler for a number of highly placed agents in the US government and intelligence services machine. He had consistently fed back priceless information to Moscow over those two decades without detection but had ultimately fallen into a trap laid for him by the CIA after one of his agents at Langley informed on him.

"Bad indeed," Putin said. "And we need a solution. Fedorov is a good man and I want him back. I'm thinking in terms of a prisoner exchange. But at present, we have no bargaining chip to offer. I need ideas from somewhere, and the worthless idiots at the SVR have so far come up with nothing. You can keep that in mind."

"I will, sir," Severinov said.

"However, Fedorov would be a bonus. The main task on your plate is the oil and gas deal. And let me tell you this," Putin said, lowering his voice a fraction. "I respect your pedigree—I always have, you know that. But if you fail, don't take your wealth and status for granted. The SVR might take an interest too if things reflect badly on Russia—and on me."

Severinov grimaced. Threats from Putin were not to be taken lightly. And he knew exactly what was meant by *an interest*. The SVR, Russia's intelligence agency that was successor to the KGB, might have moved on in many of its working practices but not in terms of some of the subhuman techniques used to interview and extract information from those out of favor.

* * *

Wednesday, May 29, 2013
  Kabul

Johnson stumbled down the narrow mahogany staircase of
the three-bedroom villa he and Jayne had rented, walked into
the kitchen, and flicked on the kettle. Thoughts of Rice and
Severinov had been spinning around in his head since he had
woken, and he needed to think everything through.

Severinov. He had never met the Russian, but the name
sent a shiver through him.

In 1988, Johnson had come under fire from a pair of
Soviet Mi-24 helicopters—dubbed Hinds by the US military
and intelligence services—in an Afghan village, Hani. The
raid prematurely terminated a secret meeting with a
mujahideen contact whom Johnson was cultivating, Javed
Hasrat.

A few weeks later, he had again sneaked over the border,
this time with his CIA colleague Vic Walter, for another
covert meeting with Javed at a safe house in Jalalabad. But the
meeting was similarly aborted after they were alerted to an
imminent raid by the KGB.

Both forays had been arranged by Johnson's chief informant at that time in Pakistan's ISI intelligence agency,
Haroon Rashid. Fortunately, Johnson and Vic managed to
escape safely back to Pakistan, but Haroon later discovered
that Javed had been captured by the KGB in Jalalabad and
thrown into the snake pit that was Pul-e-Charkhi prison.

And both times, it had apparently been Severinov who
had coordinated the raids on the Soviet side.

So to have heard from Rice that Severinov was now an
oligarch running a major Russian energy company had come
as a surprise, to say the least.

Johnson had already arranged a long overdue and much

anticipated reunion for later that day with Haroon, who was flying in from Islamabad. The pair hadn't seen each other since 1988. The plan had originally been for a casual catchup to talk about old times. Now, however, the news that Severinov was again involved in Afghanistan would add a new twist to the meeting. It would be fascinating to hear what Haroon made of it all.

Johnson finished making his coffee and walked through to the living room of the villa, a slightly run-down property with peeling green paint on the doors and the window shutters, just off Wazir Akbar Khan Road. It was less than a kilometer from the US embassy in a secure area protected by security guards and barriers at both ends of the street. It was definitely a safer and more anonymous option than staying in a hotel such as the Intercontinental or the Serena, which were both under constant threat of attack by suicide bombers or rockets launched from nearby. It was also better than the temporary accommodation pods, made from converted shipping containers, inside the embassy compound that many of the staff lived in.

Johnson found it easy to see why long-term expatriates suffered from cabin fever during their postings to Kabul; it was compulsory to get around by armored car, even for the shortest of journeys. His favorite pastime in foreign cities—wandering around by himself on foot—was extremely risky here.

Only the previous month, one of the US embassy staff, a woman in her mid-twenties, had been killed by a Taliban car bomb.

Johnson turned on the television to find a national news bulletin underway on the ATN channel. He could understand most of what the newscaster was saying—his Pashto, learned while working for the CIA in Islamabad, had become rapidly less rusty, even in the brief time he'd been back in

Afghanistan. He sat at the table, nursing the hot mug of coffee in both hands, and listened. The segment concluded with an interview with the Silverson Renwick chief executive, Lorenzo, carried out through an interpreter, about women in business.

Just as the bulletin ended, Johnson's phone rang. It was Sally O'Hara with the contact details for Storey that she had promised to him during the embassy party. After scribbling down the email address and phone number, Johnson asked her if the embassy had picked up any updates about the previous day's RPG attack near the airport that he had witnessed from the airplane window.

"We've had a few updates from police," O'Hara said. "Apparently fifteen schoolchildren and a truck driver died. All Afghans."

"Fifteen?" Johnson said incredulously.

"Yes. The minibus and the truck were both definitely hit by rocket-propelled grenades. That's been confirmed. But we're hearing that police believe they were hit accidentally and that the real target was a black Porsche owned by a Russian oligarch on his way to the airport, which got away untouched."

"Do you know who the Russian is?" Johnson asked.

"I've not heard a name, but I was told that he was in Afghanistan in connection with the oil and gas reserves sale. I'll let you know if we hear any more later on."

"Thanks, Sally, I'd appreciate that." He ended the call.

A Russian oligarch. There weren't exactly going to be too many Russian oligarchs in Kabul linked to the oil reserves sale, that was for sure. It had to be Severinov.

Johnson picked up his laptop and did a Google search for Severinov, which threw up a number of references to him in the context of energy deals, links to Putin, and photographs showing a muscular-looking figure with short, graying black hair that was receding. There was nothing about his KGB background, of course.

"You're up early," a voice said from the doorway. He looked up. Jayne was standing there, her white robe falling open at the bottom, showing almost all of her right thigh.

Jayne had changed very little physically from when they had first met in Islamabad. They had both been heavily involved with their respective intelligence agencies in plotting to supply weaponry to the mujahideen rebels in their fight against the Soviet military. Their affair back then, short-lived as it was, had seemed almost inevitable. Equally inevitable, looking back on it, was the negative reaction of Johnson's boss, the subsequently disgraced Islamabad station chief Robert Watson, who deemed it a security risk.

Even now, Johnson had some feelings for Jayne, who occasionally accused him of not knowing what he wanted from her. Maybe she was right. But since they had started working together again, their relationship had remained professional.

"Too much on my mind," Johnson said. "So I got up to make some coffee. Listen, I just had a chat with Sally at the embassy."

He told her about the Russian connection to the RPG attack and the obvious conclusion that the target was Severinov.

Jayne walked across the room toward him. "Yes, it must be him. I still find it hard to believe how a KGB officer becomes an oligarch. That's modern Russia, I guess. He must have made a ton of enemies on his way to the top."

"Yes, but likely in Russia, not Afghanistan."

Jayne shrugged. "Don't know. Does the Severinov angle make you interested in Rice's proposal?"

"I'm interested in Severinov, not Rice's money."

"But you're looking doubtful."

"My old OSI boss always said never to trust a money man, because their heart's always in the wrong place."

"Get Rice checked out, then."

"Yes, I will."

"Could be an interesting job, though," Jayne said. "We've got some free time while we wait for the ICC decision. We could do it. Why don't we chat with Haroon about it later. He might have a view." The reunion with Haroon was due to take place over lunch.

"Sure, we'll chat with Haroon," Johnson said. "But I don't know. I also need to decide whether to stay here or head home while we're waiting for the ICC decision."

As a single father with two teenagers at home in Portland, Maine, Johnson was always weighing up his responsibilities and the amount of time he spent away working. His investigation trips tended to be spaced several months apart, but they usually lasted for a few weeks. It was difficult. Jayne, almost three years younger than Johnson, had never married or had children, but she always saw his point of view. She nodded, silently communicating her understanding.

"I do keep asking myself whether I should be here at all," Johnson said, "let alone chasing after someone who's been on the wrong end of an RPG attack."

CHAPTER FOUR

Wednesday, May 29, 2013
  Moscow

Severinov remained silent, deep in thought, as his driver
negotiated the way back from Medvedev's home to the
Rublevo-Uspenskoye highway, the A106, that cut through the
Gorki-9 area, otherwise known as Barvikha. The meeting
with Medvedev and—to his horror—the president had left
him in a slight state of shock. He knew exactly why he was
feeling this way. It all came down to fear. Fear of losing what
he had worked for: his possessions, his money, his property.
His status.

His own *dacha* lay about eight kilometers to the west in
Gorki-8, also on the Moscow River. The property, which he
had bought in 2006 for the equivalent of $30 million, was on
around seventy-five hectares of land, roughly thirty soccer
fields.

It contained a house with seventeen bedrooms, a thirty-
meter indoor swimming pool, a fully equipped gymnasium,

and a ballroom. There were two helipads and a garage complex able to take up to sixteen cars, as well as a multilevel heated outdoor swimming pool, a man-made lake filled with water pumped from the Moscow River, a tennis court, and a golf driving range. The landscaped gardens had uninterrupted views down to the river.

After his meeting, Severinov was tempted to head home, have a swim, and relax with a chilled vodka on his terrace.

But he knew he needed to take action. So instead, he instructed his driver to turn left, in an easterly direction. He gave an address and then sent a quick text message to check that the person he wanted to visit was at home. He received an instant affirmative reply.

If there was an investigation to be done, and possibly a lethal hit to follow, then he knew exactly the man to do it.

Ten minutes later, the Maybach pulled into the driveway of another secluded property behind a tall, green-painted wall and an electric gate on Myakininskaya Ulitsa street, a quiet, potholed lane on the fringes of Moscow. The house, just a couple of hundred meters from the river, was far smaller than his previous stopping point but nevertheless luxurious by most Russian standards.

Vasily Balagula was one of a few friends Severinov still had that dated back to his time in Afghanistan. They were both tough, uncompromising, and sometimes unscrupulous survivors. Others had died during the war there or had subsequently met untimely ends while carrying out various deeds of dubious legality in various dark corners of the globe. Two, Severinov regretted to say, were killed while carrying out jobs that he himself had paid them to do.

Now he was about to put a proposal to Vasily. And he knew the amount of money that he was going to offer would make the job irresistible.

The electric gate slid silently open, and the Maybach

glided through before coming to a halt next to an ornamental fountain near the front door.

Vasily emerged from the door, a large grin on his face. He always reminded Severinov of a gorilla, not just because of the thick mat of dark hair that covered his chest but also because of his physique. He had an almost perfect barrel chest and forearms to match, both of them tattooed with images of twisting pythons.

A former Spetsnaz special forces operative during his time in Afghanistan, Vasily had also done a stint in the KGB before that, and after the withdrawal from Afghanistan, he was the ringleader on a variety of dirty jobs for the Russian military, including during the 2008 invasion of Georgia. Severinov never asked how many bodies he was responsible for; he knew it was a lot.

Vasily had taken retirement from the regular special services after that and instead had gone freelance. Severinov was one of his main clients.

Severinov instructed his bodyguard to remain in the car with his driver and went inside with Vasily, who poured two generous measures of neat, deeply chilled Green Mark vodka. Severinov needed a drink after his encounter in Gorki-9.

As he started to explain why he had come, Vasily interrupted. "I know what you want."

"What do you mean, you know?" Severinov threw back his first vodka in one gulp and held out his glass for a refill.

"I saw the TV news, from Kabul."

Mother of all evil, has this gone everywhere? Severinov thought. He tried not to roll his eyes.

"Good guess. I need to know who carried out the RPG attack, and unless they were genuinely targeting someone else —which I am certain can't be the case—I want them buried. Simple." He went on to explain the nature of the ultimatum he had just received from Putin and Medvedev.

Vasily did a double take. "You're not joking. *Putin* gave you the order?" he said as he topped up Severinov's glass.

"Correct. Well, he actually gave me two orders."

"What's the other?" Vasily asked.

Severinov paused. "Fedorov. He wants a prisoner exchange."

Vasily shook his head. "Two easy jobs, then. Afghanistan's a small enough place. I'm sure we can track down whoever launched the RPGs, no problem. Maybe the Americans and the British troops there will give us a hand. There's enough of them. And as for the prisoner exchange, maybe we'll find a couple of US spies hanging around in the coffee lounge at the Russian embassy who'll be happy to volunteer."

Severinov didn't smile. "Very funny."

"Seriously, though," Vasily said, "do you have any idea who might be behind the RPG job?"

"None. Everyone I can think of is dead. Although I do have one starting point. I have a couple of old friends, contacts, among the mujahideen who I looked after very generously during my time there. I could put them back on the payroll, so to speak."

Severinov told Vasily about Sandjar Hassani, whom he had met in Kabul the previous day. Hassani was a Pashtun tribesman from the village of Wazrar in the Khost-Gardez Pass whom he had cultivated during the 1980s and had turned into a prime source of top-class information about the mujahideen, the ISI, and the CIA. Hassani had consistently and profitably betrayed all of them during the Soviet occupation and had never been caught. He had made a significant contribution to Severinov's beloved Motherland and the push to protect her interests in Afghanistan.

The highlight had been the trapping of a mujahideen commander, Javed Hasrat, in Jalalabad. Severinov had had strong reasons for wanting to catch Hasrat and had been looking forward to torturing him in Kabul's Pul-e-Charkhi jail.

"So did you torture this Hasrat?" Vasily asked.

"I gave him a beating, and so did my team. But I had planned to do a lot more. There was a mujahideen attack on the jail a couple of days later, before I could get there to finish the job properly. They were trying to get some of the prisoners out."

"Ah, yes, I remember it. So he died or escaped?"

"Died, apparently, along with many others," Severinov said. "The prison authorities said a lot of them were blown apart in their cells but that none escaped. There were so many body parts that they couldn't identify most of them. It was a pity in some ways. I'd have enjoyed dragging out the process for a few days longer and making the bastard suffer a lot more."

"Hassani's a clever man," Severinov went on. "He was wasted, stuck in those tiny villages farming and tending goats, and he realized that eventually. He got into telecoms and works now for the mobile phone companies as an engineering manager. He's still well connected. Maybe he can help me out again, after all these years."

Severinov downed his second vodka. "And I've got a new mole too. Very new."

Vasily looked surprised. "Really?"

"I can't talk about that one," Severinov said. "Other than to say she is very much higher up the tree than Hassani."

"*She?*"

"Yes, she."

Severinov wasn't going to give any more details. His mole, in the Afghanistan energy ministry, was an important source of critical information for the bid for the Afghan oil and gas assets, and he wasn't going to put his relationship with her at risk.

"Interesting. Well, I'm keen," Vasily said. "I haven't had a lot of action recently, so tell me when I can get started. We'll need to decide whether we take the low-key approach, where I just handle this myself alongside you, or bring in the others."

Vasily often worked as part of a team of six, all ex-Spetsnaz, who had carried out a lot of freelance operations together over the years.

"I think we'll start with just you. We can think about bringing some or all the others in if needed. And we need to start immediately. I've got Putin threatening me with an SVR vacation if I fail."

* * *

Wednesday, May 29, 2013
  Kabul

Haroon Rashid, known to Islamabad-based CIA officers of 1988 vintage only by the code name MILLPOND, was one of the best operators Johnson had ever worked with. He had provided the CIA with a stream of important ISI inside information about Russian military activities inside Afghanistan.

To have survived more than four decades in the boiling political cook pot of the ISI, through nights of mass backstabbings and betrayals, and to have served two masters through a good chunk of that time, spoke volumes for both his slickness on the street and his professionalism, not to mention his ability to deal with stress.

The Pakistani, who had retired from the ISI three years earlier at the age of sixty-four, had refused to meet Johnson in any café, restaurant, or hotel in Kabul, believing them all likely to be under surveillance. Instead he came to the villa Johnson and Jayne were using, arriving after taking a two-hour surveillance detection route.

"Joe, I'm black, as you used to say in the Agency," Haroon said as his opening gambit, indicating with a wave of a hand behind him that he had no tail. "But two hours. I can't do that at my age. It's killed me. I've been through every shop and down every alleyway this side of the airport."

Johnson laughed. "Old habits, eh?" He briefly embraced his old working partner.

The thin grin hadn't changed in two and a half decades, although the hair was now pale gray, bordering on white, as was the thin mustache, and the lines on his face had deepened into brown ravines. His twig-like physique was also the same. Johnson felt he was constantly in danger of snapping in half.

As Johnson poured some chai, Haroon scrutinized him, then Jayne in turn with his shotgun-barrel black eyes. "So, what are you here in Kabul for, then?" he asked. "Not a holiday, I assume."

"No, not exactly." Johnson told him briefly about the ICC consultancy contract and then outlined the proposal that Frank Rice had put on the table.

Haroon raised his eyebrows. "Who's the oligarch?"

"You might remember him. Yuri Severinov. Now one of Putin's puppets."

Haroon fell back in his chair, eyeballing Johnson as he did so. "*Severinov?* That bastard. Well, at least I can tell you about him properly now." He grinned at Jayne. "Sorry, I'm using your English swear words."

"What do you mean, you can tell me properly?" Johnson said, ignoring the attempt at a joke. "I know Severinov organized the raids on Hani and Jalalabad that nearly killed me. Is there more to it?"

"Yes, there's more."

"Go on," Johnson said.

Haroon wrinkled his face as he recalled the details. "Severinov was working against the mujahideen I put you in touch with, Javed, and against others in the K-G Pass. It was Severinov who was organizing all the Hind gunship attacks on the Afghan villages, the huge massacres. I would have told you at the time but couldn't."

This is getting interesting, Johnson thought. "He was coordinating all that shit?" he asked.

"Yes. The Soviet bombings. Genocide, you could call it, in those poor villages."

During the Soviet occupation, the Hinds ran amok among villages all over Afghanistan, terrorizing the inhabitants with their cannons and machine guns, forcing those inhabitants still alive to flee into Pakistan and beyond.

"Why couldn't you tell me?" Johnson asked.

"We were trying to recruit him."

Johnson raised his eyebrows. "Now you tell me. I should have known."

"It was actually one of my bosses who was trying. I knew it wouldn't work; I had a gut feeling he was too much the patriotic Russian, and I was right."

Johnson gave a wry smile. "If you couldn't recruit him, you should have buried him."

"If I'd had my way, we would have," Haroon said.

There was a short silence. "And Javed. Did you ever find out what happened to him?" Johnson asked.

"He got out of Pul-e-Charkhi. I discovered that many months later, long after you had left Islamabad."

"He *escaped?*"

"The muj rocketed the prison and got quite a few prisoners out, including Javed. I heard there was a big cover-up and that the prison authorities told the Russians the missing prisoners had been killed."

"Interesting. And then what?"

Haroon sipped his chai. "I heard Javed went back to his village, Wazrar, but after that, I don't know. He cut off contact with me. He likely thought I was behind the leak to the Russians that trapped him in Jalalabad—and nearly trapped you. Which I wasn't."

"I know," Johnson said. "I'm convinced it was Robert Watson who leaked it to the KGB. But we had no proof."

After fleeing the Jalalabad meeting, Johnson, Vic, and an Afghan guide were pursued by a gunman. Johnson caught a bullet on the top of his right ear, leaving him with a lifelong scar. After that, they had ended up in a gun battle in an abandoned warehouse. Johnson shot the gunman dead—he turned out to be Leonid Rostov, one of the KGB's top intelligence officers in Afghanistan.

The trio had fled back through a mountain gorge over the border to Pakistan, using a combination of mules and pickup trucks. But there was an ensuing diplomatic row over Rostov's death—not least because Pakistan's president, General Zia, had expressly forbidden CIA officers from operating in Afghanistan or having links with mujahideen, insisting it all be carried out through the ISI. This, coupled with Johnson's affair with Jayne, gave Watson the excuse he needed to orchestrate his dismissal from the CIA later that year.

"We at the ISI all thought Watson was corrupt," Haroon said.

"Yes. What happened to him last year confirmed it."

"I heard," Haroon said.

Watson had proved to be one of the most crooked long-term CIA operators in living memory. It had emerged during Johnson's investigation the previous year into a Yugoslav war criminal that Watson had for years been skimming off large sums of money by coordinating under-the-counter arms sales from Croatia to Syrian rebels. He had also profited immensely from the import of Iranian arms into Bosnia during the early 1990s. After the revelations, Watson had fled DC, abandoning his CIA job and his house in Virginia, and had not been heard of since. The Agency managed to keep news coverage of the incident to a minimum as they launched a massive manhunt, but the trail had gone cold quite quickly. Watson—known to most of his colleagues as Watto—might have been corrupt, but his tradecraft was impeccable.

"Seeing Watson in prison is still at the top of my wish list," Johnson said. "But for now, we've got more immediate work to do."

Jayne leaned forward. "Speaking of which, Haroon, are you still in touch with your network, your sources who were plugged into Russia and the KGB?" she asked.

"I try to be. We meet up fairly often, so yes. Why?"

"Maybe you could help us out here," Jayne said. "You could perhaps try to get your contacts to check out Severinov."

The Pakistani nodded. "It is possible. I will make inquiries. Some people in my network are still well connected in Moscow."

They talked for another hour or so. Haroon told them how for the latter five years of his working life he had given up his covert duties for the CIA after his wife had pointed out that she would like to enjoy having him at home during his retirement rather than see him in the visiting room of a prison in Rawalpindi.

He also declined the usual offer to highly valuable CIA agents of a retirement property in a secure location of his choosing. Instead, he preferred to stay in his modest villa in a suburb of Islamabad, only a short distance from his beloved

Rawalpindi Cricket Stadium.

But he did have a bank account in the Cayman Islands that was now stuffed full of US dollars to reflect the work he had done.

Haroon then had to leave for a meeting with another old agent of his. He was planning to stay in Kabul for several days and to catch up with a few other contacts before returning to Islamabad, but he and Johnson agreed to stay in touch and meet again.

The ISI veteran had taken one step out the door of the villa when he suddenly turned around. "I was just thinking."

"What?" Johnson asked.

"About you never having properly nailed Watson. It was a pity you weren't able to keep that photo of Javed's from Jalalabad," Haroon said. "That would have buried him properly. Remember it?"

Johnson exhaled. "Don't remind me. Dynamite." Retirement definitely hadn't dulled the Pakistani's memory.

In Jalalabad, Johnson had learned from Javed that Watson appeared to have been privately selling Stinger missiles to some other mujahideen leaders. Indeed, Javed and his colleague Baz had shown Johnson a photograph of Watson and another man handing Stingers over to some rebel fighters. The picture had even pinpointed the location: next to a bridge identifiable by carved wooden eagles mounted at each end, several kilometers into Afghanistan on a mountain route from Pakistan. Johnson recognized the bridge because it was on the same route that he and Vic had taken en route to Jalalabad.

Unfortunately Javed had not allowed Johnson to keep the photo. He thus had no proof of Watson's illegal dealings—it would have been his word against Watson's, and in that conflict there would have been only one winner.

The more recent revelations about Watson's illegal activities in the former Yugoslavia had solidified Johnson's conviction about his arms trading in Afghanistan.

"Maybe you should try to track down Javed?" Haroon said. He put his hands on his hips and looked Johnson squarely in the eye.

Is he challenging me? "I've thought about it occasionally over the years," Johnson said. "I just never had the time."

"But now you do have the time. Don't you?" With that, Haroon turned and left.

CHAPTER FIVE

Wednesday, May 29, 2013
  Kabul

The tall red propane gas cylinder rolled off the back of the truck and smashed onto the dusty sidewalk, breaking a paving slab and sending fragments of cement flying into the air. Javed Hasrat and his friend Baz, both standing no more than a meter away, jumped back just in time to avoid it.

Javed's first thought was that the thing might explode. He skirted around the device, which now lay on its side next to a rusting wheelbarrow full of bananas and oranges that a street seller was peddling to passersby.

The bearded truck driver, standing on the back of his vehicle, waved an apologetic hand at Javed.

"Stupid son of a donkey," Javed said, turning to point an accusing finger at the driver.

Seconds later he was forced to sidestep again between two stalls offering fake watches and jewelry as a moped headed straight toward him, seemingly out of control.

Just as they returned to the sidewalk with its jagged, uneven concrete slab surface, Javed shook his head at two young beggar boys who ran up to him holding out their hands, as they did almost every day. It was all fairly typical of his routine stroll down the road to fetch his favorite bread, yogurt, and eggs.

Javed and Baz continued for another twenty meters along Qala-e-Fatullah Road, past a row of dilapidated small shops selling cigarettes, crockery, and cooking utensils. Then they turned right down a side street, Street Nine.

There were two properties that Javed was using in Kabul. One was a villa on Street Ten in the Taimani area that he had rented since his return to the city in 2005. This was the address he gave to his employers at the Ministry of Mines and Petroleum and for any other official purpose. It was listed under his alternative name, Kushan Mangal, which he used for work purposes as a security measure, given the level of hostility among the Taliban, Russians, and others toward mujahideen, past and present.

The second property was a house on neighboring Street Nine that had belonged to his brother Mohinder until his death two years earlier and where Javed was spending most of his time. He wanted to keep the two separate for several reasons, including that he didn't want any unexpected visits from government officials to Street Nine. Anyway, his intention was to sell his brother's property once his work in Kabul came to an end.

As had become his habit on the way back to either property, particularly the one on Street Nine, Javed checked carefully that he wasn't being followed. He paused and lit a cigarette as he stood under a tree, offering one to Baz, who also lit up. While doing so, Javed had a good look up and down the street in both directions. He had retained the paranoia from growing up in a country dominated by fear of intelligence service surveillance and had learned countersurveillance techniques during his time in the mujahideen.

Street Nine was far quieter than the hustle and chaos of Qala-e-Fatullah Road. The road had been remade recently, transforming it from its previous potholed condition. A few new trees had been planted along the curbs, and several of the high walls that separated the villas and apartments from the street had been painted white. Most properties were residential, with a few small businesses alongside them, including a medical clinic, a restaurant, and a dentist. It was quiet and anonymous, which was the way Javed liked it.

Eventually, satisfied that nobody was following, he led the way to a flat-roofed house painted in a terra-cotta color and set back from the sidewalk. It had a curved ornate wooden balcony that ran around the outside of the property at the upper-floor level and a matching barrier on the flat roof to create an outdoor roof patio.

There was a wall, three meters high, that ran across the full width of the property, with a metal pedestrian gate built into it, also three meters high, next to the house, and a matching vehicle gate to the right.

"Let's get the coffee on and talk business," Javed said. "We need to decide quickly what we're going to do after what happened yesterday."

It was the first time he had voiced anything approaching criticism of Baz, who had been cursing himself since the double miss with his shoulder-fired RPG launcher on the Kabul-Nangarhar highway the previous day.

Javed led the way through the pedestrian gate and the heavy front door, which he closed behind them as they entered. He turned the key and fastened two large brass bolts.

In the driveway was parked a black Toyota Hilux pickup

that had formerly belonged to his brother, who had run a carpentry business prior to his death. At the back of the pickup, his brother had installed a false bed made from marine plywood, creating a cavity that was designed to conceal his tools from thieves. However, Javed had recently put the cavity to another use: it was perfect for ferrying RPGs around Kabul without detection. Once covered with tarpaulins, the base, which was covered with old cement dust, spilled oil, sand, and other detritus, was almost undetectable, barring the closest of inspections.

The two men continued into the kitchen, where Javed placed his purchases on the counter and turned to face Baz.

"I said twenty-five years ago that I would get him eventually and have my revenge. And I will. What happened was unfortunate. Normally there would have been a lot more traffic, we know that, and he would have been going more slowly. It wouldn't have been a problem. It was bad luck. Don't blame yourself."

"We'll try again," Baz said. "But what do we use next time? If we want to guarantee catching him in traffic, that means doing it in the city, where there's more security forces. It's risky."

"I agree," Javed said. "But what's the alternative? I've thought it through carefully—I would love, really *love*, to get up close and make the bastard suffer so I could see it in his eyes. But that would be even more risky. And anyway, we know we're not going to get near to him, given his security. I don't have a sniper rifle, and I wouldn't be good with it anyway. Neither would you. So the only other option is—"

"Stingers," Baz interrupted.

"Stingers? No," Javed said. "I was going to suggest some kind of car bomb."

"Why not Stingers? He's got his own private aircraft. We know that now. We could just take it down. It's not going to be a case of killing hundreds of people; it would just be his private jet. You could easily get Mahmood to tell you when Severinov's plane is coming in."

Mahmood Marwat, who had a senior role in Afghanistan's air traffic control, was a former mujahideen colleague of both Javed and Baz from the 1980s.

Javed pursed his lips. "I don't know."

"You've still got several left. It would mean we could operate out of the city. It would be much safer."

It was a fair point, and Baz was correct. He did have several Stingers left, together with gripstocks, sights, and battery coolant units, all stashed in a cave in the Sulaiman Mountains north of Khost, not far from the Pakistan border.

"Are they still going to work, though?" Javed asked. "The BCUs are the issue. I thought they were only viable for a few years? They've been there since '88."

The battery coolant units were small, single-use circular devices that were screwed into the base of the Stinger's grip-stock. They provided the power to fire up the missile's infrared homing device a few seconds before launch. They also contained pressurized argon gas that cooled the infrared system. Each missile was supplied with a pack of three BCUs.

Baz shook his head. "I've talked to a few people who think they'll be fine. Remember Royan?"

Javed nodded. He did remember Royan, who was a Tajik and thus in the minority in the mainly Pashtun region where they had all lived. He had been a rival mujahideen commander in a neighboring valley.

"He also has some Stingers stored somewhere," Baz said. "He tested two a year or so ago, and I know for a fact they worked perfectly. Anyway, there's three per missile, so if one doesn't work, we have plenty more. I think the rumors about their limited shelf life is just American propaganda. They obviously don't want them in circulation."

Javed grinned. "That's true, no doubt about it. How did Royan test them? I hope he didn't shoot down a US chopper."

"Not quite. But he did shoot down an American drone. They've been using the drones in the valleys around here to keep tabs on the Taliban. He took one of those out."

Javed grimaced. "That's not good. I'm sure the Americans were furious."

"Yes. It caused an uproar. They knew the drone had been hit by a missile but didn't know it was one of their own Stingers, of course, and they presumed it was the Taliban who'd done it. Anyway, the point is, the missile worked fine."

Javed and Baz Babar had been friends since childhood, when they had grown up in the village of Wazrar. Their parents had made sure they were well educated. Both had gone to university in Kabul, and they had fought together as mujahideen rebels against the Russians during the 1980s. The Stingers, acquired from the Americans via the Pakistan intelligence service, the ISI, had been a key part of their armory. Between them, they had taken down more than fifteen Russian Mi-24 gunship helicopters.

But since the Soviet occupation had ended in 1989, their paths through life had been very different. Baz had remained in Afghanistan, working as a civil engineer on various roads and infrastructure projects, including the Khost-Gardez Pass.

After the death of his wife, Ariana, and their eight-year-old daughter, Hila, in a devastating Mi-24 attack on their village by the Russians in early 1988, Javed had secured asylum in the United States, mainly because of assistance he had given to the CIA. He had been accompanied by his two remaining daughters, Roshina and Sandara, now forty-one and thirty-nine, respectively, and mothers themselves.

Their move to the US followed Javed's ordeal at Kabul's

Pul-e-Charkhi jail after he had been trapped by the KGB. Baz had somehow managed to avoid capture.

Once in the States, Javed ended up in Houston, where he worked for a series of exploration companies, producers, and investment consultancies in the oil and gas industry.

But Javed had never forgotten the KGB officer who, together with his underlings had broken his fingers, kicked in his ribs, electrified his testicles, and wrecked his kidneys.

He had found out the name of the Russian, Yuri Severinov, from his mujahideen network, which also informed him that it had been Severinov who had orchestrated the Hind attacks on the villages in the K-G Pass that had killed his wife and daughter.

Although Javed had moved to the United States, the deeply ingrained Pashtun tradition of *Nayaw aw Badal*— revenge and justice—was tattooed on his core as firmly as if it had been put there with a branding iron.

It was a blood feud of the highest order—avenging the death of his wife and daughter. His determination to achieve it had always been there, but as time went on and the distractions and challenges of dealing with life in another culture took over, his focus had become diluted.

However, Javed's experience, coupled with his Afghan background, eventually led headhunters to approach him in 2004 for the role of the head of financial transactions for the Afghanistan Ministry of Mines and Petroleum.

Javed decided to take the job, accepting a sharp cut in salary for the chance to work in his home country again. When the government decided to open its oil and gas fields to foreign investors, Javed ran the process. And then, unexpectedly and not long after the bidding had gotten underway, Severinov appeared in Kabul. Now he was some kind of tycoon, trying to buy into the very same oil and gas assets that Javed was responsible for selling.

His desire for revenge had been instantly rekindled.

After the RPG failure, maybe now, with some downtime while he was waiting for the oil bid process to move to the action stage, he should put himself in a position to ensure the next attempt succeeded.

Javed emerged from his own thoughts and noticed that Baz was staring at him. He began to speak slowly.

"Maybe you're right," Javed said. "Perhaps we should consider Stingers. But how are we going to get them back here?"

"Fetch them with mules from the cave, then bring them here in the pickup—under the false bed, like the RPGs. Simple."

"What if they get found at checkpoints?"

"They won't. We won't get that kind of detailed search unless you give them a reason. We're not on any watch list. And we bribe our way through the police checkpoints anyway, if necessary."

"Okay," Javed said, a doubtful note in his voice.

"There's one thing that worries me," Baz said. "Are you sure Severinov doesn't know who you are?"

"I don't know," Javed said, a little hesitantly. "I've only been face-to-face with him twice when he came in for briefings. He's not shown any sign of it, but then he wouldn't, would he, being ex-KGB? I only met him briefly when he tortured me in '88, and I looked very different then."

Javed now had only a stubbly, short beard and was bald and bespectacled. Twenty-five years earlier he had worn a long beard, had a thick head of hair, and was significantly slimmer.

"Let's hope not," Baz said. "The other thing is, if we do decide to use the Stingers, it's going to be very difficult to plan an attack. We'll need to keep track of where Severinov is, what his movements are, and when he's flying in and out."

"That's all fixed," Javed said.

"What do you mean?"

"Well, all of the people who came in for briefings on the oil and gas sale had to hand their phones in. All of those phones now have tracking devices built into them, mostly in the new batteries the security team put in. And the same goes for the sale prospectus documents they took away with them. They've all got trackers built into the spines. As long as Severinov has his phone on him, or his prospectus in his briefcase, I'll know where he is at any time."

Javed took his phone from his pocket, tapped on the screen until a map appeared with a blue dot in the center, and showed it to Baz. "Look. He's just west of Moscow right now, in a house next to the Moscow River."

* * *

Wednesday, May 29, 2013
Kabul

After Haroon had gone, Johnson realized that although he felt very much of two minds about taking on Rice's proposal, almost unconsciously he was being sucked in.

He had to admit, he did find the Russians fascinating. He had studied Russian history during his time at Boston University and had learned to speak fluent Russian as well as German while getting his PhD on the economics of the Third Reich at the Freie Universität in Berlin.

Now Haroon's new revelation about Severinov coordinating the village helicopter attacks had added a new spin to the story. Could the man really have been a big league war criminal?

"What are we going to do if we get evidence of Severinov's crimes—can we have him prosecuted?" Jayne asked.

"I'll upturn every stone," Johnson said. "But whether the ICC prosecutes or not, it will trash his reputation and put him out of the race for the oil reserves and probably every other international deal he might ever want to attempt in the future."

Johnson needed more information to help him make a final decision. At least he had made a start with his inquiries into Severinov. Next would be ZenForce Group, the Swiss investment fund, and its managing director, Zilleman. Maybe Vic, who was still working at the CIA in Langley, Virginia, along with their former colleague in Islamabad Neal Scales, also now at Langley, could help him with that one. They could quietly check out Rice and his client Haze's credentials at the same time. Vic and Neal could get access to a large number of information sources that Johnson couldn't.

Johnson reached for his phone and rang Vic's number, using the encrypted connection the pair of them habitually employed for their conversations.

"Guess where I am?" Johnson asked when Vic answered.

"How the hell should I know?" asked Vic in his trademark low-pitched voice.

"Kabul. Apologies in advance, Vic, but I could do with some help."

"You're always asking for frigging help."

Vic Walter, his most trusted CIA colleague when they were stationed together in Islamabad, had remained a close friend, as had Neal. Both of them were now among the Agency's Directorate of Operations' longest-serving employees. Vic's current role had a strong focus on Afghanistan and involved supplying intelligence to the special activities division, which concentrated on covert and deniable attacks on Taliban and other insurgent groups.

When Johnson needed a little assistance on one of his investigations, which usually involved extracting information on individuals from CIA files, Vic did his best to help, though it very much went against Agency rules.

Johnson, who was sitting at a table in the living room of the villa in Kabul, quickly outlined the proposal that Frank Rice had put to him.

"I'm a little skeptical about doing this. The risk factor is quite high," Johnson said. "But I was discussing it with Jayne, and I thought I'd check it out."

"What do you need?"

"First, I want you to check out Rice himself, and his client Haze," Johnson said. "I need to know they're trustworthy before I work with them."

Next, Johnson told Vic about the opaque investment company ZenForce Group and its managing director, Rex Zilleman. "He's originally American, I'm told, now in Zürich. Can you see if there's a file on him and if any of your contacts at the NSA can get any phone intercepts? I'd like to know what Zilleman and his company do, who else is working with him, what businesses they have stakes in, and who their investment clients are, if possible."

The National Security Agency was focused on collating so-called signals intelligence, with communications at its core, particularly phone, email, and internet traffic.

"You're not asking too much, then," Vic said. "I mean, I don't have a day job to do, so I've got tons of time on my hands, of course."

"Sarcasm's the lowest form of wit," Johnson said.

"It's all you deserve," Vic said with a chuckle. "Yes, I'll see what I can find on all of them. How are things at the embassy there?"

"They're busy and stressed," Johnson said. "A lot of movers and shakers coming through, bankers, politicians.

There was Donnerstein yesterday, of course, as well as the Silverson Renwick chief executive, and then Paul Farrar's here soon—Afghanistan seems to be right at the top of his agenda."

"Yes, I know," Vic said. "He's hot to keep our troops there as long as possible. I've been doing some work on the wider security implications of that, coincidentally."

"By the way, I saw Haroon Rashid earlier," Johnson said. "He flew in from Islamabad to see me specially."

"MILLPOND? How is he? He must be retired now, no?"

"He is. But he's like me: he can't let go and he still seems well connected. So he's going to do a bit of work for me, chasing down the Russian I mentioned, Severinov, and his company, Besoi Energy."

"Severinov. I still can't believe he's resurfaced. They're all coming out of the woodwork," Vic said.

"They are. Speaking of people coming out of the wood-work, have you heard anything more about Watto?"

"No, nothing," Vic said. "They're still looking for him, although it's gone a bit quiet on that front. They think he may be in South America somewhere, probably Brazil or Argentina, under a false identity, of course."

"Haroon suggested trying to track down Javed and see if he's still got that photo of Watson with the Stingers," Johnson said.

"Good luck with that, buddy."

"I know, I know."

After ending his conversation with Vic, Johnson toggled over to his email app and wrote a brief note to each of his children. Carrie was sixteen and Peter would soon be fifteen. Both of them were home in Portland, where his sister, Amy, and her husband, Don Wilde, were taking care of them, as was normally the case when he was away over-seas on a job. They didn't have children of their own and enjoyed doting on his. All of them were worried about him in Afghanistan, so he tried to keep in touch as often as possible.

Amy, at fifty-two, was a couple of years younger than Johnson. She had been an invaluable help ever since Johnson's wife, Kathy, had died from cancer in October 2005 at the age of just forty-six. They had only been married for eleven years. The following year Johnson had given up his job with the Office of Special Investigations and moved the family from DC back to Maine to run his own investigation business.

Johnson dispatched the emails and walked to the kitchen, where Jayne had set up a makeshift office on a small round breakfast table. She had also been busy, using a secure cell phone to speak to one of her former colleagues Alice Hocking, who was based at the UK's Government Communications Headquarters base in Cheltenham. Alice occasionally helped Jayne with off-the-books background checks on people and organizations when needed.

"Any luck?" Johnson asked.

"Yes, Alice is getting some background on Zilleman, hopefully," Jayne said. She clasped her hands behind her head. "She's going to double up on what you've asked Vic to do and see if there have been any useful email or cell phone intercepts. It might be the case if he's involved in major investment opportunities with energy companies, given the national security implications in that sector. We'll see."

GCHQ was responsible for collecting online, digital, telephonic, and other communications-based intelligence to complement the work of MI6 and its domestic equivalent, MI5. It made sense to ask them to run checks to back up whatever Vic's people at the NSA might uncover.

"The one thing Alice did pick up, though," Jayne said, "is that Zilleman still spends a lot of time in the US. Usually in DC or New York, according to a first glance at the phone records she accessed. Her first comment was that his client base of investors is probably there—rather than Zürich."

* * *

Wednesday, May 29, 2013
Washington, DC

Robert Watson pulled his faded gray baseball cap down over his face, adjusted his glasses, and walked past the French restaurant and the elegant red-brick facade of the John Wesley African Methodist Church on Fourteenth Street NW. He turned right into the sunshine that streamed down Corcoran Street NW and then, after passing the church's main entrance, stopped and leaned against the wall.

He pulled a phone from his pocket and made an imaginary call that lasted around thirty seconds. During the animated "conversation" that followed, he made a careful final check for any sign of coverage. There had been none during his surveillance detection route around DC, and he was confident he had not been followed. But Watson could not afford to make a single mistake.

Following his escape from Virginia to an apartment in Vila Madalena, a neighborhood in western São Paulo, in the wake of the fiasco surrounding the Yugoslav arms-to-Syria revelations, Watson had not previously ventured back to the States. He was now, for all intents and purposes, Dirk Leman, a sixty-seven-year-old retired teacher from San Francisco who was enjoying a slower pace of life in Brazil.

Ironically, his cover story had been assisted by the natural inclination of the CIA to clamp down on media coverage about his disappearance the previous year, worried about the sensitivity and the embarrassment factor.

But now he had been obliged to break cover to make this trip. One reason was to extract a large amount of money from two US savings accounts that were listed under false names. A second was to reclaim his original birth certificate from his lawyer, who he knew would turn a blind eye to his status. The other was to hold detailed discussions about Project Peak, a forthcoming, potentially highly lucrative multibillion-dollar oil and gas investment project in Afghanistan, and finally decide whether to press ahead with it.

The Leman legend, or cover identity, was an old one he had created privately some years earlier rather than an official CIA one. He had all the documentation he needed to run it effectively, including a birth certificate, a passport, a driver's license, and credit cards. All he needed to do to fit the profile was don a pair of tortoiseshell-framed glasses and let his hair grow so it had a shaggy, unkempt look.

For Watson, it was almost like being an operative again after years in senior management roles at Langley.

Eventually, Watson ended his pretend call, pocketed the phone and, with a slight limp, slipped down an alley that ran alongside the church.

The limp had been acquired following a gun battle in late 2001 in the caves at Tora Bora, twenty-five miles southwest of Jalalabad, near the Pakistan border, when he had damaged a knee ligament while on an ultimately unsuccessful CIA National Clandestine Service hunt for Osama bin Laden, along with members of the US Army 5th Special Forces Group.

About fifty yards along the alley, just past the church, Watson clicked open the latch on a tall wooden gate, slipped into the backyard of a house, and shut the gate behind him.

The property was one he had visited a couple of times before for meetings with EIGER and Rex Zilleman. The house actually belonged to a friend of Zilleman, who had flown in from Zürich.

The three men had worked together intermittently for years on a number of clandestine investment projects. Originally, it was just Watson and EIGER; then they had joined forces with Zilleman in the late '90s after realizing their agendas were similar while working on an arms deal in Iraq.

Watson opened the rear door of the house and stepped inside, turning the key in the lock and fastening bolts at the top and bottom of the door once he had done so. He turned and was about to head for the living room when the figure of EIGER stepped out into the hallway ahead of him.

"Robert, nice to see you again," he said in a low voice.

Watson strode over and shook hands. He had christened him with the code name EIGER a few years earlier.

"Yes, good to see you," Watson said. "I hope you're keeping safe?"

"Yes, just about. Come this way. Rex is waiting; then we can talk business. I don't have very long."

Watson liked EIGER because although he had never been a professional intelligence operative, he certainly behaved like one. There was little chance of him causing their venture to be torpedoed because he'd been careless.

They walked into a small living room, where Zilleman was waiting, papers spread out in front of him on a table next to a coffeepot and three cups. He stood and greeted Watson, then poured the coffee for all of them.

Zilleman sipped his drink. "What I'd like to do is get some soundings from you, Robert, before we press the button on Peak. I'd like to be slightly clearer on how you think the Chinese will react when they realize that we, the Russians, and others like Haze are all bidding. Will they come in with a high offer at the outset? If they do, I want to be ready to hit straight back with a knockout number."

"I think they will," Watson said. "I think they'll see this just as strategically as the Russians do. Putin is probably going to want to do this under the radar and hope nobody notices. He'll probably try to characterize it as just another part of Russia trying to have a friendly, helpful relationship with Karzai and his government. I mean, we know better. The Chinese won't let that pass easily. They'll probably try the same tactic but also use some fairly aggressive guerrilla PR activity to remind everyone of Russia's track record in Afghanistan."

Zilleman opened his laptop and spent the next forty minutes showing EIGER and Watson a series of documents detailing the production potential of each of the gas and oil fields that the Afghanistan government was including in its sale prospectus. Then he opened a spreadsheet that illustrated the prospective financial returns should each of them be developed to full production.

EIGER whistled softly at the numbers. "Looks damn good. So it may be better to go in high from the outset?" he asked.

"Yes," Watson replied. "You want the Chinese to know that we're taking this very seriously and we're in there to win it."

"So we're looking at north of $11 billion," Zilleman said.

"Yes," Watson said.

EIGER also nodded. "Go high," he said. "Gas and oil are the new guns and bombs as far as Afghanistan is concerned. That's where we'll make our money in the future."

"You're right," Zilleman said. "Any other issues?"

The three of them had a general discussion about the security situation in Afghanistan and the implications should they be successful in winning the bid.

"Any other obvious threats facing us?" Zilleman asked.

EIGER folded his arms. "There's the obvious one—which

I guess has always been there—that my cover gets blown," he said. "That would be terminal."

"True," Watson said, nodding. "But that's been the case with every deal we've ever done, and it's not been blown yet. We've got my cover to worry about too, now, of course."

The three men had worked together for many years and had done many deals, mainly in the arms industry, none of which had leaked.

"Let's make sure it doesn't get blown," EIGER said. "I want to get hold of a list of all American and British officials, including intelligence and security services, who are currently in Afghanistan and to check through it for any potential or obvious threats. I don't mean regular army; I'm talking diplomats and known spooks."

"That could be a long list," Zilleman said.

"I know. But we should do it. I can't request it, obviously, so one of you will have to. Robert, do you still have ways to get that information?"

"Yes," Watson said. "I can't get it directly, but I have someone who can get it for me, hopefully by tomorrow morning. You're right, it's worth checking if there's anyone there who we think might disrupt things for us."

EIGER leaned forward. "If there's someone in that bracket, we'll have to find a way to sideline them. That'll be your job, Robert."

CHAPTER SIX

Thursday, May 30, 2013
Kabul

Johnson sat bolt upright and turned his head away from the monitor screen that he and Jayne were viewing in a small meeting room at the US embassy. "Can you rewind that back to where the main part of Donnerstein's presentation finishes, please," he asked the technician who sat next to him, operating a laptop. "There's something I need to see again."

Sally O'Hara had finally arranged for Johnson to view the video recordings of the briefings on the Afghanistan oil and gas investment project that he had missed two days earlier.

While the technician was sorting out the video, Johnson glanced out the window. It was only quarter past nine in the morning, but the sun was blazing from a typical cloudless Afghan sky. The office overlooked a sprawling expanse of shipping container accommodation units across the road. Hundreds of US embassy staff lived in the pods, which were surrounded by sandbags for blast protection, during their assignments in Kabul. The embassy was spread across two sites, on the east and west sides of Bibi Mahru street, connected by a thirty-meter tunnel.

He had heard the staff referring to the container housing units as hooches, a reference to a thatched hut. Kabul was a tough posting for diplomats. Although they made the best of it with their own internal social life, movement was severely restricted given the ongoing risks. Everyone seemed to talk only about their next trip back home.

"There you go, Joe, ready to go again," the technician said. He pressed play, and Johnson looked up at the monitor screen on the wall.

There was Donnerstein, a tall, perma-tanned, thickset man with muscular shoulders, finishing his talk about the massive opportunity for Afghanistan to create great wealth from developing its oil and gas assets. He stressed the parallel opportunity for those willing to take the risk of investing. Johnson focused hard as Donnerstein brushed a hand through his neatly groomed gray hair, stepped away from the lectern, and moved off to his right, where the video showed him in conversation with another man, who looked like an Afghan.

The Afghan, in a sharp suit and tie, was gesticulating as he spoke. At one point, he twirled his index finger around rapidly in repeated circles in front of him, as if to emphasize something he was saying or indicate that something needed to be done quickly. At the same time, he was nodding his head. The sound feed did not pick up anything of what he was saying, but there was something in the twirling hand gesture, the nodding head, and the man's appearance that took Johnson back twenty-five years.

Then he remembered what Rice had said about the Ministry of Mines and Petroleum's bid process.

One of their officials, the head of financial transactions, is running the process for them.

Johnson turned to Sally, who was standing behind him, also watching the video footage. "Who is that man talking with Donnerstein there?" he asked, pointing at the screen.

"That's the government official who's managing the oil and gas sale," Sally said.

"Do you know his name?"

"Not sure. I can go and check, if you like. Why, do you know him?"

"I'm not certain. Possibly. If you could check, that would be great," Johnson said. Sally opened the door and disappeared.

"I think it's the same guy," Johnson muttered.

"The same as what?" Jayne asked.

"The consultant who Donnerstein was talking to on the film there. I think he's the mujahideen commander I met in Jalalabad and Hani in '88—Javed Hasrat. He told me then he had worked in energy, for the Afghan state electricity utility company."

Jayne raised an eyebrow. "Really? You think it's the same guy?" She looked skeptical. "Why do you say that?"

"I don't know how, but it's that hand-twirling gesture he was doing," Johnson said. "I remember him doing that like it was yesterday at both those meetings I had with him. You know, just when he wanted to emphasize something he was saying or indicate we needed to get moving with something."

The adviser in Sally's video had a stubbly beard and was wearing a suit, whereas the Javed Hasrat who Johnson knew in 1988 had a full black beard and was wearing a *shalwar kameez* when they last met in Jalalabad. Nevertheless, Johnson had a sudden conviction that he was correct.

Javed Hasrat had, moreover, facilitated the biggest triumph of Johnson's CIA career in Islamabad. He and his colleague Baz, working under Johnson's direction, shot down and captured a Russian Mi-24 gunship helicopter in the

Kurram Agency, a V-shaped piece of Pakistani territory that jutted into Afghanistan, about thirty-five miles southwest of Jalalabad. The Hind had been at the top of the CIA's wanted list in terms of technology, and the operation earned Johnson a congratulatory telegram from the CIA director at Langley. Unfortunately for Johnson, the triumph was completely soured by the catastrophic foray into Jalalabad that occurred at around the same time.

Johnson looked up as Sally came back into the office. "His name is Kushan Mangal," she said.

Johnson pressed his lips together. "Okay, thanks for checking."

"Sorry," Sally said. "Not your man."

"Maybe not," Johnson said. "Do you know where he lives or where his office is?"

"I've no idea where he lives. I assume he's got an office at the Ministry of Mines and Petroleum at Abdul Haq Square," Sally said. "It's less than a mile away."

Johnson turned to Jayne. "You know what. I'm going to make sure about this. I think he would be worth meeting, just to be certain," he said. "I'll see if it's possible to fix something."

Jayne stood and made the same twirling circular gesture with her hand that Kushan Mangal had been making in the video. Johnson laughed. That was what he liked about her: she had a sense of humor and was still able to get on with the job. Both were critical in this kind of environment.

"You don't like leaving stones unturned, do you?" Jayne asked.

"No. You know me."

"Anyone would think you were a virile young twenty-eight-year-old again, not fifty-four."

"I don't like the implication that because I'm fifty-four I'm not virile," Johnson said with a mock frown. "Are you putting me to the test, Jayne Robinson? Come on, let's see if we can get a meeting. Then we'll know."

* * *

Thursday, May 30, 2013
  Kabul

The armored car that had picked up Johnson and Jayne from the US embassy took precisely four minutes to get to the Ministry of Mines and Petroleum offices, a drab gray concrete building about three hundred yards south of the busy traffic circle at Abdul Haq Square with its five lanes of vehicles flowing in a predictably chaotic fashion amid a cacophony of car horns, yelling, cursing, and general road rage.

The traffic circle, named after a mujahideen commander who battled the Soviets in the 1980s, was populated by a variety of street vendors selling everything from shoes to kebabs, with a number of money changers hustling passersby for their business from their vantage point beneath a few pine trees. Three traffic cops were fighting to keep control of the chaos.

Nearby was an array of other Afghan government buildings, such as the Ministry of the Interior and the KHAD intelligence agency. Next to the circle was a tall tower block, which O'Hara had pointed out to Johnson as the place from where a group of hard-line Taliban militants had launched a concerted and prolonged assault on the US embassy and other buildings two years earlier, using RPGs and other weapons.

Johnson and Jayne, who was wearing a blue *hijab* to cover her head and neck as she normally did when in any public areas of Kabul, made their way into the security check area of the Ministry of Mines and Petroleum's offices. They were required to produce passports plus one other form of identification, and then there were personal and bag searches, which seemed focused on checking for explosives.

Once cleared, they were allowed through into a waiting room. The decor was typical of government buildings in Kabul: cheap plywood brown doors, a gray cement floor with a crazy paving pattern, and ineffective lighting.

A glass display case on the wall contained photographs of all the senior civil servants in the department. Faded curtains hung at the windows, and the only other wall decorations were badly framed photographs of Hamid Karzai and the current minister of mines and petroleum.

Johnson had telephoned from the US embassy to try to speak to Kushan Mangal. He had gotten through to his secretary, had given his name, and after she had said he was too busy to speak on the phone, had requested a short introductory meeting instead. He told her that he was working as an adviser to the International Criminal Court and wanted to build a picture of the economic damage that Afghanistan had suffered from Taliban attacks on energy installations. None of it was true, but Johnson felt he had no viable genuine excuse for requesting a meeting and was therefore justified in fabricating one.

The secretary had confirmed a thirty-minute slot for five o'clock. Now, though, the man on the front desk told Johnson that Kushan was unavailable and that instead the meeting would be with the deputy minister, Safia Joya, together with one of her advisers. Johnson grimaced; it was typical of his experience with Afghan bureaucracy.

He and Jayne waited nearly half an hour before the deputy minister, a slim, pretty, middle-aged woman wearing a navy blue *shalwar kameez* with a pale blue *hijab*, appeared through a set of half-glazed swing doors. She appeared unbriefed, slightly confused, and had no adviser with her, so Johnson had to explain that they had originally been scheduled to meet Kushan Mangal, as well as the reason for the meeting.

"You would not have had a meeting with Kushan," Safia said firmly. "He has decided to take some vacation for a few days. I do not know why that meeting with you was scheduled."

"Vacation? While this oil sale is going on?"

She shrugged. "This is a quiet period. Nothing is happening while we wait for the bidders' presentations."

"Do you know where he's gone?" Johnson asked.

"No. He called to say that he was going to be away for a few days, out of Kabul, and did not give a reason."

"We'll have to try another time, then," Johnson said. "He was recommended to me, but I don't know him. What's his career background?"

Safia hesitated, as if unsure whether to give the information, but then said, "He worked in electricity, then he left after the Soviet occupation and went to a few of the big oil companies in the United States in jobs that involved investing in oil and gas exploration. We knew all that experience would be very useful for us when he joined eight years ago. He is good and knows the industry. He is also good on the finance side."

He worked in electricity. Javed had worked in electricity too.

In 1988, when Javed agreed to try to capture a Hind for the CIA, he had stipulated that in return he should get US passports and permanent residential visas for himself and his children, together with air tickets to New York. That was when he told Johnson that he had a background with an electrical utility. But although Javed had delivered the Russian chopper, he had then been captured in Jalalabad before arrangements could be made for the passports and visas to complete the deal. Johnson had then left Islamabad without hearing from Javed again.

If this *was* him, he must have gotten the US visas and the refugee status somehow.

"Which day is he due back?" Jayne asked.

"I am not sure which day, exactly. This bid process is nearing its conclusion. He will be back before that—in two weeks we reach the final stage, when the bidders will have to make their presentations to the minister, myself, and the rest of the team in person. That will be critical."

"Do you know where Kushan lives?" Jayne asked.

Safia looked at her blankly. "Of course we have his address," she said. "I am not giving you those details, though. They are private."

"Well, could I ask his assistant or leave a message?" Johnson asked.

"That is the best option."

"Okay, I'll do that. Where does his assistant sit? Upstairs somewhere, I assume?"

"Yes, she is on the third floor," Safia said, "but she will not be there now, and I cannot let you go up there, anyway."

"Thanks, I'll call her tomorrow," Johnson said. "Also, do you know who Kushan worked for in the US?"

"I am sorry, I cannot remember," Safia said. She glanced at her watch and stood. "I need to go. I have a meeting. The security guard will see you out." She shook hands and left.

Johnson stroked his chin and caught Jayne's eye. "You know what? It would be a terrible waste to have gotten all the way through security into the building and not make use of our time."

Jayne grinned. "Yes. I was trying to think of a reason not to slip up the stairs and look for his office, but I can't. Maybe we might find his address or phone number there."

CHAPTER SEVEN

Thursday, May 30, 2013
Kabul

Johnson and Jayne moved into the corridor of the Ministry of Mines and Petroleum and waited near the elevators at the bottom of the stairwell while having a casual conversation about their favorite film stars. In the meantime, they kept a close watch for internal security patrols. There appeared to be none, although a security officer did appear through the swinging doors that led to the reception area, walked to a nearby toilet, and went inside.

"Let's take the stairs," Johnson said. He turned, took his phone from his pocket, and adopted one of his favorite strategies: pretending he was on a call in the hope that it would dissuade anyone from challenging him while he was in an area he shouldn't be. Jayne did likewise, and the two of them climbed past the first and the second floors.

A series of people passed them on the way down, mostly Afghans carrying small backpacks and briefcases. A couple turned and stared, but nobody challenged them. Everyone was heading home for the evening.

Johnson checked his watch. It was now nearly quarter past six.

On the third-floor landing, there were sets of double doors to both the right and the left. Johnson, spotting that the decor to the left appeared more luxurious than the right, chose to go that way. "He's senior, so I guess he's got a nice office," he said.

An expanse of open-plan office cubicles, all around two meters square with desks and ancient-looking computers with old-style bulky monitors, stretched away in all directions, most of them unoccupied. There were piles of paper, books, staplers, pens, and notepads everywhere. Almost everyone had gone home. However, there were two late workers still there. Johnson strode purposefully up to one of them, a man who looked to be in his thirties and was glued to his computer screen.

"Hello, I'm looking for Kushan Mangal's office, please, or his assistant's desk," Johnson said in Pashto. "I have a delivery for him." He raised his bag slightly so the man could see it.

The man looked up and raised his eyebrows. "Do you know him?" he asked, furrowing his brow and fixing Johnson with a stare.

"No. But I have some documents he requested."

The man turned to Jayne. "And what about you?"

Jayne, who had also learned to speak fluent Pashto while in Afghanistan with MI6, said, "We work together."

The man put on a quizzical expression but pointed. "He sits over in the corner office, there. His assistant sits in the cubicle just outside."

"Thank you."

Johnson, followed by Jayne, turned to walk in the direction the man had indicated. He had taken two steps when he felt a sharp tug on the back of his shirt.

"Stop," Jayne hissed. "Look."

Johnson looked toward the office they were aiming for, and then he saw why Jayne had pulled him back. Sitting just twenty yards away from them, in Kushan's office, on a chair next to a filing cabinet, was a woman in a blue *shalwar kameez* and a pale blue *hijab*: Safia Joya.

She had her back turned and was rifling through papers in the filing cabinet, one of which she took out and began to read. Johnson watched for several seconds, making a mental note of the drawer from which she had taken the paper.

"Let's get away from here," Johnson murmured. "We can come back when she's gone." As they turned to go, he could see Safia holding her phone above the paper. Was she photographing it?

They walked at a normal pace to the other end of the office and out through the double doors through which they had entered. Leading off the landing area, adjacent to the elevators and the stairwell, were three meeting rooms. All of the doors were open and the lights were off.

"In here," Johnson said. He slipped into the center meeting room ahead of Jayne, then pulled down a blind to cover the half-glazed window, but he left a crack at the bottom. "She'll have to come out this way, so let's watch."

Johnson pulled a chair up and positioned himself so he could glimpse through the crack.

"We're absolutely going to get killed if we're found in here," Jayne said.

"For God's sake, Jayne. We'll just say we had a meeting scheduled with Kushan and that he still hasn't turned up. Now shut up and let's just keep watching."

A couple of minutes later, the two men who had been

working in the office area came out together and walked down the stairs. But there was still no sign of Safia.

After another ten minutes, Johnson stiffened and lowered his head slightly as Safia appeared.

"She's just walked out," he murmured to Jayne. "Now she's pressed the elevator button and she's waiting."

There was another pause, probably only of about thirty seconds but which felt much longer to Johnson. Then Safia entered one of the elevators and the doors closed. He turned to Jayne. "Gone."

They waited another couple of minutes, then Johnson opened the door. "Come, let's go."

They walked back through to the open-plan office, which was now deserted. Johnson strode purposefully to the door of Kushan's office and tried to open it. It was locked.

Johnson swore. "She must have locked it when she came out."

"Well, did you bring your tool kit?"

"Yes, I've got the tools. The question is whether to use them in here."

It was almost a rhetorical question. Since starting private investigation work, Johnson had gotten into the habit of always carrying around a small tension wrench and a couple of rakes that would fit into his wallet. They had been useful several times: Jayne had seen him in action using them.

Johnson examined the lock, which was of the standard pin tumbler variety. He looked around. The office was definitely empty, and there was no sign of internal security cameras, but then, he didn't expect to find such equipment in an Afghan government building.

If he was going to do it, he needed to work quickly. "Jayne, just watch the office. I'll have a go at it," he said. He took his wallet from his pocket and removed the small tension wrench and pair of rakes.

Johnson inserted the small end of the L-shaped tension wrench into the bottom of the key hole and, using his left hand, applied a little pressure to the handle until he felt some resistance. Then he selected the shorter rake with three ridges and with his right hand inserted it at the top of the key hole. Johnson repeatedly pushed and pulled the rake in the keyhole, applying some upward pressure as he withdrew it each time.

Despite varying the amount of pressure with the tension wrench slightly, the lock wouldn't budge. "Shit, damned thing," he said.

He pulled the wrench and the rake out and started again. This time, he managed to get the amount of torque he was applying to the wrench just right, and eventually, as each of the spring-loaded pins were pushed up by the rake, he was able to open the lock.

"About time," Jayne said. "You're losing your touch."

He replaced the tools in his wallet and pocketed it.

"Right," Johnson said. "I'll go through the filing cabinet. See if you can spot anything with an address or phone number on it in the assistant's cubicle."

Unlike all the offices and cubicles on the third floor, Kushan's office had no papers, books, or other paraphernalia lying around. It was spotless. Johnson went straight for the second drawer down in a gray filing cabinet, the one he had seen Safia extracting a document from earlier, while Jayne moved outside and began sifting through a pile of documents on the assistant's desk.

There were a few hanging files in the drawer containing documents and folders. Johnson removed some documents from one of the files at random and glanced through them. They were publicly available International Energy Agency reports on Afghanistan's oil and gas reserves. Nothing of interest there. He replaced them and tried another. This time they were investment bank analysts' reports on the oil and gas sector.

Johnson spent the next few minutes going through each of the files, now working more systematically. There seemed to be nothing personal and nothing confidential. Perhaps Kushan kept the crucial ones elsewhere. But in that case, why had the deputy minister been in his office going through his papers?

"There's nothing here," Jayne said from outside the door.

Johnson continued going through the hanging files. The second from last one had just one sheet of paper in it, which he removed.

It was a curriculum vitae, printed on both sides of the single sheet, with a name at the top that caused Johnson's eyes to widen abruptly: Javed Kushan Mangal. He knew that many Afghans had double first names.

The CV showed he had briefly attended a school in a place called Wazrar and then another in Khost, followed by universities in Khost and Kabul in the 1970s. It stated that he belonged to the Mangal tribe and gave a home address on Street Ten in the Taimani area of Kabul, together with the name of his home village, Wazrar, but no street name.

Johnson turned the sheet over. Next came a list of employers: it stated that he worked at the Afghanistan national electricity utility, DABM, followed by a spell with an energy company in Khost until 1989. There was a gap until 1991, when he had begun work with Dark Star International Oil and Gas, based in Houston, Texas. That role had lasted until 2004, and the next job listed, as head of financial trans-actions with the ministry in Kabul, began in 2005.

There was no cell phone number listed, but right at the bottom of the second side of the paper was a Hotmail email address.

Johnson stared at the email address for a moment and

frowned. It was hasratj56@hotmail.com. Surely that confirmed it, but then again, the last name at the top of the CV, Mangal, was wrong.

"Jayne, come here a moment," Johnson called over his shoulder.

Jayne came into the office and he handed her the CV. "What do you make of that?"

She scanned down both sides of the sheet. "Looks like it might be him, doesn't it? Compound first name, Javed Kushan, then he's using his tribal name as his last name."

"Ah, yes, of course. The tribal name. And the email gives it away. Hasrat. It's him. Got to be."

"I think so."

Johnson took out his iPhone and used it to photograph the CV, then replaced it in the file.

He quickly ran through the other documents. There was nothing else of interest. He closed the drawer and checked the drawers of the desk. There was only a collection of the usual office paraphernalia: pens, staplers, notebooks. The computer on the desk looked archaic. He doubted that Javed ever used it; presumably he had his own laptop.

"Better get out of here," Johnson said. He turned and walked out of the office. Jayne followed and closed the door behind them. It clicked shut as the lock re-engaged.

"I'd be interested to know what our friend Safia was searching for in there," Johnson said.

Jayne shrugged. "Yes, indeed."

As they left through the swinging doors, the man who had originally pointed them toward Javed's office came back in, carrying a sandwich. He stared at them. "Did you find Kushan's desk?" he asked.

"Yes, thanks," Johnson said, not breaking his stride. "We dropped the delivery off." Without looking back, he continued across the landing and down the stairs, Jayne right behind him.

"I *knew* it was him as soon as I saw him on that video," Johnson said. "Now we just need to go find him. I'll send him an email for starters, and we'll go check out his house."

Five minutes later, they were sitting in the rear of the embassy car, en route to their villa.

Johnson glanced at Jayne. "What do you think?" he asked.

She folded her arms. "First, I was impressed that the Afghans are happy to promote women into that type of ministerial job. And what do I think about our task? I think you're going to do this job for Rice. Otherwise you'll die wondering."

Johnson nodded. "Yes, you're right. I'll confirm it with Rice. We could get Haroon to work with us. His face fits into the crowd, unlike ours. He's not an obvious target for the Taliban on the street, like us."

"I think that's a good idea. He'd enjoy it."

Johnson leaned back in his seat.

Javed and Severinov. This is just intriguing.

He took out his phone and sent a short text message to Rice. *We're on board. We'll do your job.*

Johnson turned back to Jayne. "Step one. If we're going to do this properly and start picking up evidence against Severinov, we need to track down Javed."

"Agreed," Jayne said. "If he's on vacation out of Kabul, maybe we should go and try his home village. These guys usually gravitate back to where they came from. They all have a big extended family."

She was right, as usual, Johnson thought. "The village is on his CV—Wazrar, in the K-G Pass. But let's find his Kabul house first."

"The K-G Pass? Better pack our flak jackets," Jayne said. She wasn't smiling.

CHAPTER EIGHT

Thursday, May 30, 2013
Moscow

More than two-and-a-half thousand miles northwest of Kabul, Yuri Severinov sat at his desk overlooking the Moscow River and studied an email he had just received on his phone. It made for interesting reading.

The note, sent from a private email address, contained a photo attachment showing a document: a curriculum vitae for the man handling the Afghanistan oil and gas exploration investment round, Kushan Mangal.

Severinov had only met Mangal in person twice, when he had gone into the ministry for briefings. He was a Westernized Afghan, with only a stubbly beard rather than a full-length one, and spoke English with an American accent. But there was also something about the man. Severinov's old intelligence officer's instincts had picked up on the way Mangal looked at him with a certain emotion in his eye that he was trying but failing to hide. Was it recognition, envy, or simply instant dislike? Severinov hadn't been sure, but he had felt that he should find out.

Therefore, Severinov had requested the CV and other background information on Mangal as part of the usual thorough preparation and planning process he went through on all Besoi Energy's major acquisitions, of which there had been several. That was how he had grown the business, which had begun with three huge oil and gas fields in western Siberia but now encompassed oil and gas production in Kazakhstan, a 40 percent stake in a gas pipeline from Turkmenistan to China, a large refinery on the Black Sea coast, and gas-fired power generation facilities in Thailand, China, and the Philippines. Overall, it had generated a profit of $1.4 billion in 2012.

His financial analysis and business development teams were all going through the potential future performance numbers for the Afghan assets, but Severinov liked to do his own homework and then test his conclusions against those of his staff.

But apart from the numbers, he wanted to know as much as possible about the people who were running the process so that he could tweak his bid and get his proposals in line with their particular prejudices and interests. He also needed as much detail as possible on his rival bidders. Given the laser-like focus that Putin and Medvedev had on the Afghanistan project, he didn't want to leave anything to chance.

The sender of the CV had written a short note. *I am attaching the document you asked for. I hope this helps.*

Severinov tapped on the attachment, enlarging the two-page image so he could read it properly on the small screen.

At the top was the name Javed Kushan Mangal; then came details of schools attended in Wazrar and Khost and universities in Khost and Kabul. There was the name of his tribe, Mangal, and an address in Kabul.

His employment record showed he had worked in the US

for some time. That would explain his accent and his Westernized appearance, Severinov thought.

Severinov scanned the document to the end, where an
email address was listed. He read it slowly out loud to
himself: hasratj56@gmail.com. He scrolled to the name at the
top of the CV, then back to the email address again.

"Javed Hasrat, Wazrar," breathed Severinov, as he realized.
"So that's who you are. My God. I thought you were dead."

He paused, then yelled out loud at the top of his voice to
the empty study, banging his hand down on his desk, "*Ni
khuya seb!* No fucking way! You bastard."

He stood and walked around his office, kicking the carpet
as he went. Eventually he calmed himself, sat down, and read
the rest of the note.

> *If you were thinking of contacting Kushan, you need to know
> he has gone on vacation for a few days. I don't know where.
> Also, this might not be relevant, but an American named Joe
> Johnson and a British woman Jayne Robinson came to our
> offices today for a meeting scheduled with Kushan. I met
> them instead. Johnson said he was doing some research work
> for the International Criminal Court and needed to speak to
> Kushan. He is also linked to the US embassy. Regarding your
> query about the Swiss bidders, ZenForce, I do not yet have the
> detail about the key people involved on their side but am
> hoping to get it soon. I will be in contact again soon.*

Severinov put his phone down and leaned back in his seat.
His recruitment of Safia Joya was continuing to pay dividends
and had been easy enough to negotiate: her monthly salary as
an Afghan government minister, equivalent to $2,100, made
the money Severinov was offering too much of a temptation.

Now, among the other inside information she had
provided about the bidding process, which would give

Severinov a major advantage against the competition, Safia had unwittingly come up with a gem of much greater interest.

Severinov's mind went back to the events of 1988. Then he was working in Afghanistan as an officer in the KGB's Line PR unit, which was responsible for military intelligence and active operations.

A key part of his role was to prioritize and assign targets for the fleet of Mi-24 gunship helicopters that the Soviet 40th Army operated in Afghanistan. The main priority was to blitz villages from where mujahideen were believed to be operating.

Much of his focus was on the Khost-Gardez Pass, the tortuous, twisting mountain highway between the two strategic towns of Khost in the south, just a handful of kilometers from the Pakistan border, where the Russians had a large military base, and Gardez to the north.

From 1979 onward, when the Russians invaded Afghanistan, the K-G had always been controlled by the mujahideen. But then, in late 1987, the Soviet 40th Army launched Operation Magistral, using thousands of troops and brute force to finally gain the highway.

To keep control, the Russians launched frequent forays, both airborne and on the ground, against mujahideen bases and villages.

In January 1988, Severinov had signed off on an attack on the village of Wazrar. He had learned from Sandjar Hassani that there were several mujahideen in the village. The attack had succeeded and the village had been pulverized. But just a few minutes later, two of the three Mi-24s had been shot down by mujahideen using Stingers. The crew of one of those helicopters had subsequently met a particularly grisly fate at the hands of the mujahideen.

Even now Severinov couldn't bring himself to talk about the incident.

Hassani had subsequently informed Severinov that the man who had shot down the helicopter and killed the crew had been Javed Hasrat, assisted by Baz Babar. Further intelligence from Hassani led Severinov to capture Javed in Jalalabad and throw him into Pul-e-Charkhi jail. But then had come the raid on the jail by mujahideen, in which—so Severinov had been originally told—Javed had died.

Now, twenty-five years later, it emerged that Javed had not died and was in fact working in an important role for the Afghan government to help sell off its oil and gas exploration assets.

For Severinov, as a highly ambitious KGB officer, Operation Magistral had been a major opportunity to make a name for himself. The intelligence he gathered was a key factor in the Soviet success. It also directly paved the way for a promotion back to the murky, shark-infested waters of Berlin in 1989—the place where he had thrived in his previous KGB posting.

After leaving the KGB when it was replaced by the SVR in 1991 as the Soviet Union broke up, he worked for oil and gas companies as a foreign affairs and security director. During the '90s he was allocated shares in some of those companies, which flourished under the economic reforms brought in by the new Russian president, Boris Yeltsin. Severinov was one of the lucky few who earned a fortune and forged strong contacts in Russia's political community.

It was during that time that Severinov's KGB background, his growing business profile, and his political interests brought him to the attention of senior people in the Russian economic and government machine. Most crucially, he renewed contacts with Yeltsin's successor as president, Vladimir Putin, and won the trust of Putin's *siloviki*, the group of mainly former KGB and military men who took charge of Russia, particularly Medvedev. Severinov subsequently set up Besoi Energy, and his financial and material reward had been huge.

He often felt that the long hours and intense focus on his business life had come at a cost, however. Despite several relationships—including his current lover whom he kept a close secret—Severinov had never married nor had children. Maybe, he sometimes worried, there was truth in the accusation leveled at him by one of his girlfriends—that the brutality of his time in the KGB had rendered him incapable of behaving as a loving husband should.

Sometimes, he reflected to himself, he would have swapped all of his acquired wealth for the incident in January 1988 to have been unwound and reversed.

Severinov snapped out of his thoughts. It was a pity that Safia hadn't obtained the detail on ZenForce that he wanted, but the contents of her email had taken him several steps forward.

Most immediately, Safia had raised two big issues in his mind. The first was, what should he do about Javed Hasrat? The second was Joe Johnson. He remembered the name from his time in Afghanistan working for the KGB. Hadn't Johnson been CIA?

He reached for his phone and did a Google search.

A minute later, Severinov was staring at Johnson's website. He was an investigator, specializing in war crimes, based in Portland, Maine, who had worked as a Nazi hunter for the US Office of Special Investigations in the past and was now running his own business.

That was him. In 1988, Johnson, as a CIA agent in Islamabad, had recruited Javed as his mujahideen agent inside Afghanistan. The two of them had been meeting in a safe house in Jalalabad as Severinov, acting on intelligence from Hassani, arrived at the location near the Kabul River and the airport.

But Johnson had gone and Severinov had trapped only Javed. Soon after, it emerged that Johnson had shot dead Severinov's boss Leonid Rostov in a nearby warehouse while escaping.

Needless to say, Johnson's website mentioned none of that. It didn't even mention his CIA background.

If Johnson now wanted to speak to Javed as part of some work he was doing for the ICC, as Safia was indicating, then what would Javed tell him, and where would he stop? If it were the ICC, then it must be something to do with war crimes.

Severinov's imagination, which was always active, went into overdrive. Might Johnson also start digging into Severinov's background? And if he found things that Severinov didn't want made known—all the villages and their populations destroyed during Operation Magistral, for example—and went public, what might be the outcome in terms of reputational damage to him and to Russia? To Putin?

The timing did not look good. He had visions of a stream of allegations being made public about his role in Magistral, angering the Afghans and thus flattening his bid for the oil and gas fields.

Am I overreacting?

He didn't know the answer to that question. But he certainly wasn't going to just sit and wait for the time bomb to explode. He was going to have to do something. In his experience, attack was the best form of defense.

He glanced up at a framed quotation that hung on his office wall, written in fading ornate Russian cursive handwriting on yellowed paper.

It read, "Be a bee that stings for the Motherland: be busy, be dangerous."

In all four corners of the print was a large black-and-white image of a Russian honeybee, and underneath was an attribution: Josef Stalin. The print had been one of his father's possessions, and Severinov hung a small replica of it in all the various properties he owned, including the safe house in Kabul.

Next to it was a black-and-white photograph of Stalin, taken in his later years.

Severinov gazed first at the photograph, then at the framed quotation. He had used the quote as his motivation for years—right from the start of his career in the KGB and through the building of his business empire. But whenever any of his visitors asked about its origins, he had always avoided answering.

He decided he would ask Lvov to go and check out the Kabul address on Street Ten listed on Javed's CV and also would start to think about how to tackle Johnson.

Severinov's phone beeped twice. He looked at the screen. There was a warning message: *Battery Low.* That was slightly odd, he thought. The phone was only four months old, and already the battery life was dwindling. True, he used it a lot, but it should perform better. He made a mental note to ask his head of IT to test it.

PART TWO

CHAPTER NINE

Thursday, May 30, 2013
  Wazrar, Khost-Gardez Pass, Afghanistan

Javed groaned as the black Toyota Hilux pickup rounded a hairpin bend. Fifty meters ahead of them, the segment of smooth black tarmac ended and the highway turned into the same old rough, stony, rutted gray surface that he had always remembered.

"I thought this was just too good to be true," Javed said to Baz as the vehicle bumped off the end of the tarmac and onto the dirt section, shortly after they had begun their descent from the pass's highest point at 2,900 meters. The noise level in the cab rose dramatically as stones thrown up by the Toyota's tires continually pinged into the wheel wells.

Baz, who was behind the wheel, shrugged. "They've still got another thirty-five kilometers of highway to pave. Most of the Khost and Gardez ends are done; it's mainly in the middle."

He steered left to overtake a gaudily painted and heavily

overloaded truck that was battling up the steep slope in first gear, throwing off a dense cloud of dust and stinking diesel exhaust fumes.

The Khost-Gardez Pass, running more than one hundred kilometers between the cities of Khost and Gardez, had been a rough dirt route for as long as Javed could remember, apart from a few poorly maintained gravel and tarmac sections. It used to take trucks all day to navigate, and that was assuming there were no rockfalls, mudslides, or storms to hold vehicles up further.

A project funded by the US Agency for International Development had been paving the route since 2007, although progress had been far slower than hoped, partly due to flooding but mainly because of corruption, bribery, and continual attacks on the project by the Taliban. Javed had been told that project costs had more than doubled from the original $69 million budget.

The Toyota rounded another hairpin. A group of US soldiers, all carrying semiautomatic rifles, were standing next to a barrier in the center of the highway constructed from two armored vehicles and some orange cones. One soldier raised his hand in a signal to stop. To their right were four Afghan National Army soldiers. Baz braked to a halt.

It was the fourth US-operated checkpoint they had come across. Normally, Javed enjoyed chatting with US servicemen, but during this journey he had shown his Afghan passport and shied away from conversation, sticking to his native Pashto rather than his American-accented English, acquired in Houston.

After checking their passports and quickly searching the Toyota, the soldier, whose face was caked in dust and sweat, waved them through. The dirty plywood bed at the rear of the truck merited only a cursory glance.

As they moved off, Javed clicked onto the cell phone

monitoring app through which he was keeping track of the various bidders in the oil and gas investment process. The NDS, the Afghan National Directorate of Security, had installed the trackers, partly at Javed's request but also because they wanted to keep a close eye on those interested in the country's strategic energy assets.

The first one, in Zilleman's phone, was located in Washington, DC. No surprise there, Javed thought. The guy was American, after all, and seemed to split his time between Zürich and the US capital. The location of the second, belonging to Severinov, was also unsurprising. He was still in Moscow, at a location a few miles west of the capital, near the Moscow River. Javed checked the others. None gave any cause for concern.

He logged out of the app and was about to put his phone back in his pocket when an email alert showed on his screen. He opened it.

Hello Javed, you might remember me from Jalalabad, 1988. I know what happened there, and I've felt guilty about it ever since. I understand you are currently in Kabul. I too am back in Kabul for a while. I called your office and arranged a meeting via your assistant, but I was told on arrival that you were on vacation. It would be good to meet up again.
Regards,
Joe Johnson

Javed looked out the windshield. *First Severinov and now Joe Johnson.* It was more than odd that after two and a half decades, both had popped back up into his life. During his time in the US he had considered trying to get in touch with Johnson but had never followed through. He resolved to reply as soon as time permitted; it would be interesting to meet again. Perhaps it would help to explain whether these resur-facing specters of his past were connected.

It was just as well that he hadn't been staying at his own rented house in Kabul, Javed thought. If Johnson was on his tail and desperate enough to try to arrange a meeting at his office, it wouldn't be a great surprise if he had also tracked down his address on Street Ten.

The Toyota lurched hard to the left as a wheel hit a pothole, dragging Javed's attention away from Johnson's email and back to the highway, which was carved out of a rocky, khaki-colored mountain slope, almost completely devoid of greenery. To their left, cliffs climbed six hundred meters into the dazzling blue above. To their right, an almost vertical one-hundred-meter drop descended to the river, which tossed and smashed its way southward along the valley floor toward Pakistan.

It was prime hunting country for the Taliban and its offshoot groups of guerrilla insurgents, such as those led by Jalaluddin Haqqani, who were fighting the Afghanistan government and its US-led military supporters from NATO countries. It seemed like such a long time since Haqqani had been a high-profile leader of the mujahideen, someone whom Javed had respected until the leader had switched his alle-giance to the Taliban in 1995.

The mountainous territory around the Khost-Gardez route, with its myriad of hidden trails, paths, and passes, provided the Haqqanis with easy opportunities to sneak over the border from their Pakistan bases and launch rocket attacks on the various US military camps and convoys.

"It seems like everything has changed, but nothing has changed," Javed said. "In the '80s it was us against the Russians. Now it's the Taliban."

"Most people hate the Haqqanis," Baz said. "But they're all scared. So they keep their mouths shut. We will need to be mighty careful going up to the cave. We're quite likely to run into some Taliban or Haqqanis along the way."

They had agreed that on reaching Wazrar, they would rest at Baz's family compound—or *qalat*—on the edge of the village, where he, two cousins, and their extended families all lived in a small cluster of houses. Baz's wife, Nazia, and their three grown-up children were away in Khost visiting her sister, but the rest of the family was around.

Once they finalized their plans and preparations, they would continue by mule into the mountains up to the cave where Javed's remaining Stingers and RPGs were stored. Baz had assured him they were still there, all intact, as he had checked on them periodically.

Baz negotiated the Toyota through a Z-shaped bend and past a convoy of four trucks. "Almost there," he said, glancing at Javed.

Javed nodded. "This feels odd, coming back to my roots, without the rest of them." He didn't need to say any more. Baz knew he was referring to Ariana and Hila.

"Yes," Baz said. "One day you need to bring Roshina and Sandara."

Javed's two remaining daughters had never again set foot in the land of their birth after the three of them had left for Pakistan and then the United States in 1990.

Javed knew exactly when he would see the view he had been so eagerly awaiting. They rounded an outcrop that jutted out into the highway, and there, across the other side of a gorge, tucked up against the sandy brown mountainside that towered behind them, he saw a row of flat-roofed mud-brick homes.

As they drew nearer, he could see the village had expanded somewhat since his departure. The cluster of brown houses, a hundred meters or so back from the river-bank, now had a few smarter green- and cream-painted buildings among them. The homes that had been destroyed by the Russians had all been rebuilt, and the four ancient trees that marked the center of the village were still there.

Five and a half hours after leaving Kabul, they had arrived at the northern fringes of Wazrar. Baz turned left off the highway and continued up a narrow lane.

At the top of the lane, Baz steered through a gate into the area where the four homes belonging to his extended family stood, including those of his brother, Noor and two cousins. All were built from mud bricks and were enclosed in a single large courtyard by a thick wall that provided some security and protection from the hot sun in summer and the freezing winds of winter.

Javed had a sudden sense of going back in time. He climbed out of the Toyota. The first sound he heard, in the distance, was a faint but distinct whine, followed by a bang: mortar fire. He turned to Baz, who was removing his bags from the rear seats, and pursed his lips.

Baz caught the expression on his face. "Welcome home," he said. "Nothing's changed, as you can hear."

"I want to go and see the grave first," Javed said, ignoring his friend's comment.

"Sure," Baz said.

They walked out the gate and turned right, heading farther up the track until they came to the community grave-yard where the bodies of Ariana and Hila had been buried so long ago, their graves dug north to south as is the Pashtun custom, their faces turned toward the Kaaba, the sacred mosque in Mecca.

Javed stood silently for a couple of minutes at the foot of the two graves, gazing down at them. The mortar fire had stopped, and the only sounds were the distant cries of chil-dren and the whistling of the wind.

"I will have my revenge, Baz," he finally said in a level tone.

* * *

Thursday, May 30, 2013
   Kabul

The Olympic-sized open-air swimming pool stood on top of the parched brown mount of Bibi Mahru Hill, less than a mile northwest of the US embassy. It was empty, with just a few puddles of rainwater lying on the bottom, far below the five diving boards that hung uselessly overhead.

Haroon had suggested walking up the hill after agreeing enthusiastically to Johnson's suggestion that he stay in Kabul for a while and help him and Jayne with their investigation.

"Why have you brought me up here?" Johnson asked. He looked down into the pool, feeling a little exposed out on the hillside, so far from the safety of the villa or the embassy. Small groups of men were hanging around, staring at them, and piles of rubbish and what looked like debris from building sites lay everywhere. Two youths sat on an abandoned car tire, smoking, and some younger boys were playing cricket with a tennis ball and a bat made from an old plank.

"I have brought you here because I want to put this job into context," Haroon said. "This pool shows you the ambitions the Soviets had for their occupation of Afghanistan—and it reminds me of the disgust I have always had for the way they operated."

Haroon gazed down through the smog over the city below, wiping the sweat and dust from his forehead. "They killed about two million Afghans during that time. I feel like I have got unfinished business with them. This pool is symbolic. They built it thinking they would hold the Olympics here. Instead, they were forced out, and the Taliban used it as a place to execute their prisoners. They shot them inside the empty pool and pushed others off the top diving board to their deaths on the concrete below."

Johnson pursed his lips. "Maybe the Russians also have unfinished business."

"Yes. I think they still want control of this country—but by another route. That is why they are bidding for the oil and gas fields."

"But the oil bid doesn't explain why Severinov is being targeted for assassination," Johnson said.

He furrowed his brow. Since his discovery earlier that day that both Javed and Severinov were in Kabul and involved in the oil and gas sale process, his mind had been buzzing. Now there seemed to be only one logical answer.

"If Javed was involved in the attempted hit on Severinov, as seems possible," Johnson said, "then it's most likely some sort of revenge mission linked to the destruction of the villages. Javed's a professional energy industry guy now, not a mujahideen or a street thug, so he would need a good reason."

"Like I said yesterday," Haroon said, glancing at Johnson, "track him down and find out."

Earlier, Johnson, Jayne and Haroon had visited the Street Ten address on Javed's CV but had drawn a blank. The property, a renovated white-painted two-story villa that was set back from the street behind a tall wall, had been locked up with no sign of occupation. The windows were all closed. When they asked a neighbor, they were told that the owner hadn't been seen for a couple of days. It appeared that Javed had left town, as Safia had suggested.

Johnson told Haroon that he had decided to take a trip to Wazrar to try to track down Javed.

Haroon pursed his lips. "Good idea. Just be careful driving down there."

"There's a big US and Afghan army presence on that route. It should be okay."

"I think it would be better if I come with you, Joe," Haroon said. "I speak the language better than you and know the people and the country."

With some relief, Johnson accepted the proposal. It made absolute sense.

Haroon casually checked all around him, as he had done continuously during their entire walk up the winding dusty footpath that climbed from the city streets through a few rows of emaciated trees that were barely clinging to life.

"If you're going to get proof of Severinov's wrongdoing in the '80s, you'll need documentary evidence," Haroon said.

"Except there won't be any," Johnson said.

Haroon shrugged. "Probably not."

"Could there be anything of help?"

Haroon paused for a few moments. "The only possible source I can think of would be the old KGB files, and they don't exist anymore."

"The *KGB* files?"

"The KGB country files from the '80s—the KHAD was responsible for keeping them here in Kabul," Haroon said. "All the detail would have been in there, if they hadn't been destroyed."

There was no doubt it would all be in there, Johnson thought. The KGB and KHAD officers recorded everything —they had to. Not just about their opponents, their agents, and their informers, but about each other.

"I'm sure you're right," Johnson said. "The KGB would have destroyed the files when the Russians pulled out of Afghanistan."

Haroon nodded. "Yes. Transporting them would be too risky."

Johnson put his hands on his hips. "Is it worth double-checking? It would be good to be sure."

"I think we'd be wasting our time," Haroon said. "Although I do know who might tell you what happened to them."

"Who's that?"

"Someone I tried to recruit in 1987, the old head archivist in the KHAD, an Afghan. His name was Abdul Akbari. I used to call him 'the keeper of the secrets'—he was in charge of the KHAD and KGB files here. He had the confidence of the top men in Moscow—I think because he provided such top-quality information. He had an office near the Dar-ul-Aman Palace, down in a basement where his vaults of files were kept." Haroon pointed to the southwest of the city.

"I remember you speaking about Akbari at one of our meetings in Islamabad," Johnson said. "Did you recruit him in the end?"

"No, although I think he was tempted. I met him twice—I took a big risk—and felt he always had an underlying sympathy for the mujahideen and what we in the ISI and you Americans were trying to do against the Russians, whom I do not think he liked. I never heard him say anything in support of the invasion and the occupation. I always had the impression he was taking money from the KGB but had no loyalty to them, although he must have been doing an outstanding job to keep his position. He also seemed to hint that he might be willing to supply us with information if the time and the terms were right. So it was worth a try—it might well have worked if I had more time."

Johnson removed his pack of Marlboros from his pocket and offered them to Haroon, who took one. Johnson put a cigarette in his mouth, flicked his lighter, and then lit first Haroon's, then his own.

"What happened to your man Abdul, then?" Johnson asked.

"I heard he fled Afghanistan, like so many others."

"Where to?"

"I have no idea," Haroon said. "But I doubt it was done legally. Not unless he was going to spill his secrets in exchange for something. And as I told you, I tried to get him to do that and did not get anywhere. So he probably told a sob story to immigration officials somewhere in the world about how the Russians had hounded him out of his village and got asylum. He is probably sitting right now in a bar in Rio de Janeiro or somewhere, sipping a whiskey."

"He's not going to be much use to us, then," Johnson said. It was likely, he thought, that Akbari had simply vanished amid the tidal wave of six million Afghans who had fled to Pakistan, Iran, and then to other countries all over the world during the Soviet occupation of the 1980s and the Taliban terror from the 1990s onward.

"No, not much use. He probably got himself a fake passport like everyone else and started a new life," Haroon said.

"Would he have been responsible for destroying the files?"

"I would assume the Russians did all that," Haroon said. "There must have been mountains of them. They would not trust anyone else to do it."

That was a certainty, Johnson thought. He glanced around him again as three men walked past. A couple of boys were flying kites at the other side of the pool.

"I think we've spent long enough here," Johnson said. "I don't like to be in one place for too long in this city, not with the threat level as it is."

Haroon nodded. "Agreed. I think we should walk back." They set off back down the track.

Johnson mulled over what Haroon had said. He could now try asking Vic or Neal to do a trace on Abdul Akbari, but if he had left under a false passport, the archivist's real name would be a dead end.

"Who would have supplied a fake passport to someone like Abdul?" Johnson asked. "There couldn't have been many high-quality passport forgers in Kabul at that time."

Haroon stopped and faced Johnson. "That is a good question. There were actually a few who were on the ISI payroll whom we used when we were smuggling people out of Afghanistan. I will dig out their details. It was a long time ago, but it is worth a try."

CHAPTER TEN

Thursday, May 30, 2013
Washington, DC

The cheap burner phone rang only a couple of minutes after Robert Watson had sat down on the bench. He had bought the device an hour earlier and had given the number to only one person. He knew who it was.

"Yes," he said in his gravelly voice, shaped over the years by a steady flow of nicotine, whiskey, and coffee.

"Are you in place?" the caller asked.

"Yes, the runway's clear." Watson glanced around him, as if to reassure himself that the green light he had just given EIGER was in fact the correct signal. There was indeed nobody else in sight.

"Good. I'm in the parking lot. I'll walk down there. See you in five minutes." The call ended, and Watson put the phone back into his pocket.

The meeting place, at Great Falls Park, next to the Potomac River in Washington, DC, was one Watson had used occasionally during his CIA career when he needed to make covert calls to any one of his several unofficial contacts around the globe. Now he needed to be doubly careful, given his fugitive status in the US.

Almost unconsciously, Watson patted his jacket pocket, where he was carrying his Dirk Leman passport.

Since getting involved in ZenForce Group's bid for the Afghanistan assets, Watson had, as usual, checked whether there was anyone linked to opposing potential investors with whom he had a history. In the particular world that he inhabited, it was almost inevitable that familiar faces would pop up. He had a system of grading them according to likely threat, using a traffic light mechanism.

However, in the case of this particular project, there were very few players previously known to Watson.

One such person was the Russian oligarch Yuri Severinov, with whom Watson had an arrangement in the 1980s. Watson had been on the KGB payroll then for a while, and both men had taken a cut of the proceeds from fiddling a US scheme to buy back unused Stinger missiles that had been supplied to mujahideen leaders. They combined their information about which mujahideen had weapons. Then Severinov sent two of his tame Spetsnaz guys on nighttime raids of the mujahideen camps, killing the tribesmen and confiscating the weapons, thus allowing him and Watson to cash in on the repurchase.

Since then, Watson and Severinov had bumped into each other occasionally but knew that each had enough knowledge to bring the other down, so they maintained a mutual standoff.

Watson had gone one step further, though—enabling him to double his returns. The mujahideen whose names Watson handed over to Severinov for targeting by the Spetsnaz were the same ones to whom he had earlier, equally fraudulently, sold Stingers via a back door route. All such missiles were meant to have been routed to the mujahideen via the ISI. As far as Watson was aware, Severinov knew nothing of this doubling-up.

All in all, the illegal trade in Stinger missiles had been a massive cash cow for Watson. He had pocketed more than two million dollars—not something that his bosses at Langley had ever been aware of. He assumed that Severinov had done almost as well.

Now Watson was unsure whether Severinov would have discovered his involvement as an adviser to ZenForce Group, which was a bidding rival to Severinov's Besoi Energy. Either way, although Severinov was a threat in the business sense, Watson wasn't particularly concerned in the personal sense: Severinov got a green light on the traffic light system.

There was one other individual whose presence Watson had become aware of and about whom he was now going to brief EIGER. He leaned back on the bench and waited.

Soon he spotted a figure walking along the path from the direction of the parking lot. EIGER, wearing a pair of thick-rimmed glasses and a tweed cap, had arrived. In the nearly thirty years that the two men had worked together, EIGER and Watson had almost never met twice in the space of two days—normally their meetings were many months apart. But since it was highly likely that this could be his last trip to the US for some considerable time, Watson had decided to make it a face-to-face meeting, which in any case he viewed as generally safer than using electronic communications.

EIGER sat next to Watson on the bench.

"What do you have?" EIGER asked, forgoing any attempt at the usual pleasantries.

The bench, at the side of a hiking path, was a good distance from any bushes, significantly reducing the risk of hidden eavesdroppers. There was also significant cover noise from the river waters below, which would help mask their voices if long-distance microphones were being used as part of any surveillance. Still, Watson was confident there was none of that. He was black, of that he was certain.

Watson ran his hand through his shaggy white hair, then removed a sheet of paper from his pocket and unfolded it. The sheet contained a list of American nonmilitary nationals known to be working in Afghanistan.

"We have a problem," Watson said. His bony, wrinkled finger traced through the list of names and their respective passport numbers and dates of birth until it came to rest about three-quarters of the way down the page. He tapped vigorously on the name shown at that point.

"This guy is the problem," Watson said, adjusting his tortoiseshell glasses.

EIGER leaned over to look at the sheet. "Where did you get this list?" he asked.

Watson couldn't resist a smile. "Let's just say it came from a contact in the State Department."

EIGER grinned. "The State Department. Of course. Very good. Anyway, continue. Who's the problem?"

"Joe Johnson. He's a war crimes investigator. Former CIA, used to work under me. He's the bastard who's responsible for me now being in exile. He uncovered a Syrian arms deal that I was running out of Croatia last year, and I had to make a sharp exit from the US. Well, there was a bit more to it than that, but that's basically it."

"So what's he doing in Afghanistan?"

"According to the State Department list, he's visiting the International Criminal Court, holding talks about a potential investigation," Watson said.

"Why's he going to be a problem in Afghanistan?" EIGER asked. "He's not likely to latch onto what we're doing—he's on a completely different task, isn't he?"

Watson snorted. "You would think so. But based on past

experience, the story could be different. I think part of the problem is that I had him fired from the CIA in Islamabad. He botched an operation inside Afghanistan. Anyway, he doesn't seem to waste any opportunity to get his teeth into me. He's sharper than he seems. He's working with a British woman, Jayne Robinson, who's ex-MI6. The two of them had an affair in Islamabad. That's another reason he was fired."

This more than explained why he had Johnson marked down as a red light in his file.

EIGER leaned his tall frame back on the bench and folded his arms. "So you've got two ex-spooks with some sort of grudge against you. I only get worried if it impacts my day job. Otherwise, it's immaterial. But I'm assuming that you can take care of that?"

Watson remained silent for a few seconds. "Yes, don't worry. I'll take care of it."

"And what about the Russians?" EIGER asked. "How dangerous are they?"

"As rival bidders, they're dangerous. They'll be very interested in the sale because Putin and his crew will see it as strategic," Watson said. "In the personal sense, I don't think so."

"Right. Have you briefed Zilleman?" EIGER asked. "He's arranging the financing today. The money is coming into Zürich this afternoon from Hong Kong, so we'll be good to go as soon as this deal can be tied up."

"I will do so later."

"Good, make sure you do. If we've got more than $11 billion at stake, we can't afford for things to go wrong, can we?"

* * *

Thursday, May 30, 2013

Wazrar

A flurry of dust, caught by the wind, flicked into Sandjar Hassani's eyes, and he reflexively turned his head sideways. He was on his way back home from a secluded place near the burial ground in Wazrar, where he had gone to just spend time quietly thinking about his two eldest children, both boys.

He hadn't seen either of them for eight years. Both had long fled from Afghanistan to Pakistan, and from there, one had moved on to the United Kingdom, the other to Germany. One day they would return, he hoped.

Although he often visited his thinking spot, as he called it, the route he had taken back to his house was not his normal one.

Sandjar, a skinny man with a craggy face that looked as though it had been chiseled from stone, had decided to take the somewhat circuitous route down past Baz Babar's property out of curiosity. He had been more than intrigued to see Baz back in his home village, arriving in a black Toyota pickup truck earlier that day with another man in the passenger seat whom he didn't recognize, although it had been hard to see through the glare reflecting from the windshield.

His cell phone beeped as a text message arrived. Two months earlier, Sandjar mused, that wouldn't have been a possibility in Wazrar. But like many rural areas of Afghanistan, Wazrar now finally had a cell phone mast, perched on a concrete plinth on a hilltop just outside the village—in fact, Sandjar had helped to install it.

Since 2004, he had worked for Afghan Wireless, the cell phone company partly owned by the Afghan Ministry of Communications, as a tower technician, carrying out installations and upgrades of cell phone masts. The work was mainly in Paktia Province, where Wazrar lay, and neighboring Khost Province, on the border with Pakistan.

The job had in many ways made it worth spending four years studying physics at university in Khost in the 1990s, after the Russians had departed. But though the role was secure, the salary was low, and Sandjar was responsible for supporting an extended family of sixteen people.

More immediately worrying, he had two younger sons who had remained at home and were now on the verge of getting married. The Afghan tradition of paying a bride price meant Sandjar was facing two enormous bills: the family of one bride was demanding 600,000 afghanis, or roughly $8,500, the other 750,000 afghanis, or $10,500.

Therefore, he had felt compelled to find other means of earning money. Almost by default, he had fallen back on what he was good at and what he had long ago realized was valuable currency in that part of the world: trading information.

During the Russian occupation, Sandjar had been recruited by Soviet intelligence. His main handler, a KGB officer named Yuri Severinov, had rewarded him well for supplying information about mujahideen operations in the Khost-Gardez Pass.

He had been surprised to find that after the occupation, when the Soviets were long gone, Severinov had maintained contact, even if it was infrequent. Indeed, he had had a brief meeting with him only a few days earlier in Kabul, where Sandjar had gone to attend a two-day telecom technicians update course.

The burst radios he had used in the old days to keep in touch with Severinov were long gone; now cell phones made things much easier.

Sandjar no longer worked for the Russians, of course. Instead, he supplied valuable information to the Taliban about cell phone masts and installations. Taliban leaders had ordered the phone companies to turn their masts off at night so nobody could inform the security services if they spotted a Taliban military unit on an operation against US forces.

If the phone companies refused to comply, the Taliban simply blew up the masts. Sandjar was able to tell them exactly how to do that at a minimum cost and with minimum effort. He also told them which providers were turning off and which weren't. So far the Taliban had paid him more than $5,000.

Sandjar continued walking down the hill until he drew level with Baz's family compound, where he spotted the black Toyota pickup, parked outside. The air was still and hot, and Sandjar caught the faint sounds of a low-pitched conversation that was taking place on the other side of the tall mud-brick wall that enclosed the four homes in the compound. He stopped to listen.

There were three male voices taking part in the conversation, which Sandjar could only pick up intermittently. He heard them discussing the condition of the Khost-Gardez highway that ran through the village and how much more work was required to complete the paving that was ongoing.

In order to hear better and see who was there, Sandjar moved around the property to a gate that led into the courtyard on the side nearest the track. Now he was much nearer to the men. He applied his eye to a narrow crack between the wall and the gatepost and looked through.

All three men were sitting around a low table on the far side of the courtyard.

One of the men was Baz. The second was his brother, Noor, who Sandjar also knew well. But the third threw Sandjar initially. He wasn't clean-shaven, but his beard was only a little longer than a stubble.

Like the others, the man was speaking Pashto, but the

voice was quite slow, as if the speaker was occasionally searching for words. Was this the man who had been in Baz's Toyota?

Sandjar watched the trio for a few moments, straining to pick up the conversation, his mind whirring. Then he realized with a jolt of surprise who the third man was. Quite apart from the missing beard, the face was broader and bespectacled, the hair was far shorter and tidier, and the demeanor seemed less manic. But he knew that it was Javed Hasrat. He hadn't seen him since 1988, when he had been captured by Severinov and then briefly had reappeared in the village a few weeks later. Quickly, though, he had vanished again, this time taking his two remaining daughters with him.

On that occasion, Sandjar had not been the one who supplied the intelligence that led to Javed's capture; he had never found out who did. However, Sandjar had previously given Javed's and Baz's identities to Severinov, who had requested the names of the men who had shot down two Russian Mi-24 helicopters and killed the surviving crew members.

Sandjar had felt quite guilty for a few years about taking Severinov's money for that piece of information. Later, when the Russian asked him on one occasion if anybody in the village had heard what had happened to Javed, he replied no, adding that everyone assumed he had died in prison. Severinov had seemed content with the answer and never mentioned it again.

Sandjar looked back through the crack in the gate. Although the men were keeping their voices low, he could just about make out what was being said. The conversation had moved on from the state of the highway, and Baz was asking Javed something about when he was planning to head into the mountains.

"Saturday," Javed said. "I'll need three mules to carry the hardware. Can we get those?"

"Yes, no problem," Baz replied.

"Good," Javed said. "I suggest you stay here. I'll go with Noor. We'll take Hashim and Kabir with us, and then I'll radio you when I'm on the way back. At that point, you can bring the truck to the meeting place. I'm definitely not walking three mules back into the village with those things on board for everyone to see."

There was silence for a time.

Then Baz spoke again. "I'm just going to fetch a couple of things from the Toyota." He stood and began walking toward the courtyard gate behind which Sandjar was standing.

Sandjar quickly ducked around the corner and ran behind another wall that belonged to the neighboring property; then he headed down a narrow alley that led back to the main road. From there, he continued walking down the track toward his own home, about a kilometer away.

When he arrived, he sat and ate dinner with his wife, Laila, his sons, and four of their cousins. Unusual for him, he was subdued and untalkative during the meal of vegetable and chive-filled dumplings, topped with tomato and yogurt sauces.

Afterward, he sat out alone on his patio until much later than normal.

What should I do? he asked himself.

It was past eleven o'clock. The night air was going cold, and the stars shone like a finely detailed painting above him. By then, he knew what he was going to do. The temptation of earning a significant chunk of money was just too much—and he knew Severinov always paid properly if the information was valuable enough.

He slipped his phone from his pocket and checked the

reception indicator. Four bars. The Taliban had left the towers alone that night. He tapped in a message.

> *Hello Yuri. It was good to see you in Kabul. I have some news.*
> *A mujahideen Javed Hasrat who you know from 1988 is here*
> *in Wazrar. He is staying with his old friend Baz Babar. I*
> *thought you would be interested. Sandjar.*

Sandjar's finger hovered over the "send" button three times. And three times he withdrew it. Finally, he decided to sleep on it and make up his mind in the morning.

CHAPTER ELEVEN

Friday, May 31, 2013
Moscow

It was still only five thirty in the morning when Severinov woke. As usual, he leaned over, grabbed his iPhone from his leather-covered bedside table, and checked his messages. There was only one, from Ivan Lvov, to say he had been to check out the Street Ten address for Javed, but it had appeared to be unoccupied. There was no sign of him and no vehicle parked there. He was going to keep the property under further surveillance.

Severinov put the phone down again. Usually, his first waking moments in his king-sized four-poster bed were spent thinking through his business priorities for the day.

Today, though, he had something more personal on his mind. He picked up a folder that was lying next to him on the bed and removed a densely typewritten report on two sheets of faded yellowing paper. He had removed the folder from his safe the previous night and had been intending to read through the report before he went to sleep. But he had somehow just drifted off.

Now he decided to read it before getting up. It had been many years since he had last looked at it—but now he felt he needed to do so again for reassurance that he should not doubt his own motives.

MEMO

35th OVP Independent Helicopter Regiment (Military unit 57723)

1st Squadron—based Jalalabad

Ref: X6720PR

FROM: Captain Yegor Malevich (Commanding Officer)

TO: General Lieutenant Boris Gromov, Commander, 40th Army, Kabul

SUBJECT: Death of 2x Mil Mi-24 helicopter crews —Flight 19

LOCATION: Wazrar, Khost-Gardez Pass, Saturday, January 2, 1988

PERSONNEL: Deceased Crew Members Aircraft 1: Nikas Shalamov (pilot); Dmitry Shukshin (weapons systems officer); Georgy Matrosov (technician)

Deceased Crew Members Aircraft 2: Ioseb Grigorovich (pilot); Leonid Gogol (weapons systems officer); Konstantin Herzen (technician)

INCIDENT SUMMARY: Flight 19, consisting of three Mil Mi-24 helicopters, departed Jalalabad Airfield 07:30 and landed at Khost Airfield 08:05.

The flight departed Khost 10:45 following Jalalabad base orders for preplanned operational strategic strike on known mujahideen bases in Wazrar and Balak villages, Khost-Gardez Pass.

Multiple inhabitants of Wazrar/Balak were known from KGB intelligence sources to possess Stinger/RPG weapons.

*Flight 19 assigned altitude 12,000 feet and initial flight path
270 degrees, instructed to follow highway from Khost heading
west then north into the Khost-Gardez Pass. The flight operated in V-formation, Aircraft 1 leading.*

*Strike on Wazrar village executed by Flight 19 and was
successful. All targets destroyed with Gatling guns and
autocannon.*

*Flight 19 left Wazrar at 11:19 on a course for Balak. At 11:22,
the pilot of Aircraft 3 (surviving member of Flight 19)
reported seeing anti-aircraft ground-to-air missile fired from
a location approximately one mile north.*

*The missile, suspected to be a Stinger FIM-92, struck the lead
Mi-24, Aircraft 1, destroying it. Debris from Aircraft 1
struck Aircraft 2, disabling the rear rotor. The pilot of
Aircraft 2 succeeded in executing an emergency landing on the
highway that runs through the Khost-Gardez Pass.*

*The crew of Aircraft 3 had visual confirmation of the crew of
Aircraft 1 exiting the helicopter. The pilot of Aircraft 3 took
the decision to climb to 12,000 feet out of range of further
Stinger missiles. He set a course back to Khost Airfield. He
reached the airfield at 11:41.*

There was another paragraph, headed Supplementary
Information Received, but Severinov couldn't face reading
that again. It reported the ensuing mutilation and killing of
the surviving crew in the second Mi-24. The episode had
been typical of mujahideen who captured Soviet military prisoners and then subjected them to prolonged and extremely
agonizing torture.

The full report, which Severinov also had a copy of in his
safe, was far longer, at fifty-two pages, but he didn't want to
read that, either. There was too much gory detail.

Immediately, he had a mental flashback to that day. The
call that had come in from General Lieutenant Gromov at

40th Army headquarters to tell him the news. The rocky helicopter ride to Khost and the trip in an armored car to the military mortuary. The white-coated officer pulling back the sheet.

Severinov fought to stop the anger rising inside him as he read.

A few minutes after he finished, his phone beeped. He grabbed the device and checked the message that had just arrived. It was from Sandjar Hassani in Wazrar.

"Shit," he said out loud as he read it. So, Javed was not only alive, but he had disappeared on vacation from his Kabul office and now had turned up in his old home village. That would explain why there was no sight of Javed at the Kabul house.

Severinov immediately tapped out a reply to Sandjar.

Thank you, my friend, that is helpful. What is he doing in Wazrar?

An hour later, a message came back.

Javed planning trip into the mountains with mules on Saturday. Bringing something back. During the war he stored weapons (Stingers?) in cave near Wazrar. I think there is a connection.

Severinov's first thought took him back to the RPG attack on the highway heading to Kabul Airport three days earlier. It must have been Javed. Now what should he do?

There seemed only one obvious answer, and to achieve that, there were two options. One was simply to delegate it to Vasily Balagula and to keep his own hands clean. That was his modus operandi and undoubtedly the logical thing to do. It would also be the option that his personal head of security and close protection bodyguard would try to insist on.

But somewhere deep inside him, Severinov knew that for his own peace of mind, he needed to be there himself if the circle of justice was finally to be closed off—he needed to deliver the coup de grâce personally. Forget the advice from his staff. *Be a bee that stings.*

He picked up his phone and dialed Vasily.

When his former Spetsnaz friend answered, Severinov went straight into a detailed list of instructions for two jobs that he wanted Vasily to join him in carrying out—urgently. The first related to Javed Hasrat, the second to Joe Johnson.

* * *

Friday, May 31, 2013
 Kabul

The list of potential passport forgers that Haroon supplied was a short one. There were just three names on it. Johnson had been expecting a few more.

"This line of inquiry could be over more quickly than I thought," Johnson said to Jayne, who was sitting on the other side of the dining table in their rented villa.

"And that's if they're all still around," Jayne said. "Might be a long shot."

The details attached to the names were also brief. First was Din Khan, who was the owner of a private commercial printing company. The others were Ali Jadoon, who ran a book publishing business, and Gul Shah, a graphic artist.

Haroon added in the email that it would be better if he went along with Johnson, with Jayne staying at the villa, as three would be too many for what was meant to be a low-key visit.

"Fill your wallet with afghanis and dollars," the note added. "We'll need plenty of baksheesh. Cooperation unlikely." That was a given. Johnson smiled: he had just finished reading a report from the embassy estimating that nationally, such bribery payments totaled over $2.5 billion a year, equivalent to a fifth of the Afghan economy.

"We'd better get started," Johnson said.

An hour later, after collecting Haroon from the small guesthouse where he was staying, Johnson's driver, Omar, was parking their armored silver Toyota Hilux pickup outside Din Khan's printing business on Andarabi Road, next to the Kabul River. The truck blended seamlessly into the environment. Nearly every vehicle in Kabul seemed to be a Toyota: the cars were mainly white Corolla sedans, and the pickups were mainly Hiluxes. All were covered in a thick layer of light-colored dust.

Johnson handed over two bundles of bank bills to Haroon, one containing dollars, the other afghanis, and gazed out the car window. The two-story printing business shop front was narrow, and the door windowpane had a large crack running from top to bottom. A steel security grill was raised three-quarters of the way to the top, and a faded cardboard sign in Pashto displayed in the window indicated the shop was open.

On the other side of the road, behind a low concrete wall, the subdued brown waters of the Kabul River meandered past extensive piles of plastic bottles, waste cardboard, abandoned metal, and other flotsam and jetsam that lay on mudbanks on both sides of the water. Several young boys and old men were sifting through the debris, occasionally placing items they thought sellable into plastic bags.

As soon as Johnson stepped out of the car onto the sidewalk, the dust and smog triggered a coughing fit. Kabul's air quality really was unbearable.

Once his eyes had become adjusted to the gloom inside the shop, Johnson realized that the frontage was deceptive. The shop stretched back a long way and became gradually wider toward the rear.

He followed Haroon to a plain wooden counter that ran

down one side of the interior. Immediately Johnson noticed a small man at the other end of the counter wearing circular wire-rimmed glasses, a wispy gray beard, and a *chitrali* cap who was dealing with a customer. He took a brown envelope from somewhere under the counter and passed it to the customer, who handed him several bank bills in return, which the man swiftly counted and stuffed into a drawer. The customer nodded and walked out. There was no receipt, no record of the sale.

Once the customer had gone, the man walked along behind the counter toward Haroon and greeted him with a restrained smile of recognition and a formal, clipped greeting.

"Hello, Din," Haroon said. "It's been such a long time. It's good to see you again, my friend. Can I introduce a friend, Joe Johnson?"

Din Khan didn't look particularly pleased to see Haroon. He nodded toward Johnson and shook hands in a quick, slightly nervous manner, then turned his attention back to Haroon. "What can I do to help you?"

"It's a long story," Haroon said, "but going back to the late 1980s, do you remember a man called Abdul Akbari? He worked for the KHAD."

Johnson watched Din's face intently. After considering the question for a few seconds, Din nodded. "I do remember Akbari a little," he said.

Quickly, Haroon launched into a whispered explanation in Pashto of what they were looking for. They had a high-speed back-and-forth debate that Johnson tried to follow. Din explained the difficulties involved in sourcing old information, and Haroon asked Din how much money he wanted to be permitted to go through his records. Then Haroon counted out a handful of dollar bills and pushed them over the counter. As Din pocketed the bills, he spoke rapidly then shook his head vigorously.

Din suddenly disappeared to the rear of the shop, leaving them alone.

"He was speaking too quickly for me to follow," Johnson said. "What did he say about the records?"

"Yes, he does have records of what he supplied, all written in a ledger, but he's not sure where it is. He says he needs time to put his hands on it. And he does remember Akbari, but he can't recall actually doing a job for him, although there were a lot of such jobs at that time, and it was twenty-five years ago, so you wouldn't expect him to. He's promising to try to check. We'll have to give him a few days, he says." Haroon shrugged.

"What's it going to cost?" Johnson asked.

"Probably eight thousand afghanis if he comes up with the goods, but he wants it in dollars. I've given him fifty bucks so far just to pay him for his time spent searching."

Johnson quickly calculated. Eight grand was about $115. Din returned, shook hands with Haroon and Johnson, and held the door open for them as they left. He looked as though he was in his late fifties and probably wasn't the type to put up a major fight if backed into a corner, but you never knew. If he had survived in business in Kabul this long, he must have someone powerful on his side, either physically or politically.

The next stop was Gul Shah's graphic design studio, about a mile from Din's shop and sandwiched between several other arts-related businesses in a small courtyard near Abdul Haq Square. The studio was on the second floor of a converted warehouse and required Johnson and Haroon to climb a rickety external fire escape to reach it.

Haroon knocked on the solid black metal door. After a short wait, it swung open and there stood a man whose proportions were diametrically opposed to Din's. Gul was immensely obese, to a degree that made it visibly difficult for him to walk, and although Haroon tried to engage him in a friendly conversation, his monosyllabic responses and body language told Johnson all he needed to know within the first thirty seconds: Gul Shah seemed unlikely to be of any help. But he at least invited them in.

Johnson and Haroon sat on stools next to a bench on which three iMac computers stood, while Gul remained standing. The building had high ceilings and bare brick walls. Again Haroon went through his explanation of what he was seeking.

"Did you know Abdul Akbari?" Haroon asked.

Gul shook his head. Johnson saw the faint outline of a pistol beneath the linen waistcoat he was wearing above his *shalwar kameez*. He very much doubted that the graphic designer would be particularly quick on the draw if it came down to that, though of course he hoped he wouldn't have to test out his theory.

A few minutes later, Johnson and Haroon were making their way back down the fire escape. "Was he always that helpful?" Johnson asked.

"I only met him twice before," Haroon said. "The second time, I heard he shot his deputy manager just a few minutes before he saw me. You'd never have guessed. His face never changed. What you have to bear in mind with these guys is that it's quite likely they were doing work for both sides during the Soviet occupation. They wouldn't want to get on the wrong side of anybody, and because they were good at what they did, they were useful to everyone. That's most likely why they're so cagey, even now. They're survivors."

The third man, Ali Jadoon, owned a book publishing and printing warehouse just south of the airport in a small business park. He snorted when Haroon brought up Akbari's name.

"I was in a different building then," Ali said. "But I

remember him—a nasty son of a mule, like all the KHAD people who were close to the KGB. He came in once. He wanted a new Afghan birth certificate and a French passport. I could do neither, because my machinery was broken at the time. He started off by offering me more money, but then he got angry and shouted at me, but it made no difference. Sorry, I don't know if he got the work done somewhere else."

"Who else might he have used?" Haroon asked.

"There were two other guys, Gul Shah and Din Khan, who did my type of work. They're both still around in Kabul. Go and ask them."

Afterward, as they stood in the parking lot, Johnson felt they had made at least some progress.

"It's not Ali," Haroon said. "Let's give Din a few days to find his records. Hopefully he'll come up with the goods."

"At least we know what Akbari wanted," Johnson said. "But I hope we're not on a wild goose chase here—do you really think he's worth the effort?"

Haroon paused. "Possibly not. It's a long shot. And regarding the forgeries, yes, we know now what he wanted. But we need the name in which the documents were issued. Without that, we're stuck."

"I saw that Gul had a pistol under his waistcoat," Johnson said. "Jayne and I both need one too before we go to Wazrar, probably on Sunday. I'm certainly not going along the K-G Pass without a weapon. Is there anyone here who might supply one and some ammunition? I'd need a Beretta M9, ideally, and Jayne a Walther. Can you help with that?"

Haroon scratched his head. "I do know someone. I'll take care of it."

* * *

Friday, May 31, 2013

Langley, Virginia

Vic was always anxious about using the National Security Agency for non-CIA jobs. It was strictly prohibited, of course, but like Neal and one or two of his other colleagues, he occasionally slipped the odd private request into the massive workstream that flowed in and out of the NSA's huge offices complex in Fort Meade, Maryland.

When the response took some time to come back, his anxiety levels rose as he began having visions of some senior supervisor scrutinizing the request he had submitted, finding it suspicious, and then escalating it up the chain of command.

The request that Vic had submitted on behalf of Johnson was for a trace on all phone, email, and internet traffic involving Rex Zilleman. The fact that Zilleman was an American made his request all the more dicey, since the NSA was strictly forbidden by law to monitor US citizens for any reason. The risk and potential consequences were a big step up from simply taking a peek in the CIA's vast files.

Finally, late on Friday evening, just as Vic was about to head home from Langley to his smart red-brick house on the corner of Sherier Place NW and Manning Place NW, in the Palisades suburb of DC, an email popped up in his personal account from his contact Steve at Fort Meade.

Vic had been about to shut down his PC. Instead, he opened the short report and the attached spreadsheet and scrutinized the contents.

The sheet consisted of an analysis of communications involving Frank Rice and his client Haze, which showed a lot of international traffic but nothing warranting concern. That corroborated Vic's own research at Langley, where there was no file on Rice.

The report also contained full details of the phone

numbers that Zilleman had called and emails that he had received and sent from his three different accounts over recent weeks. There was a cross-check of the phone numbers to which the connections had been made.

The NSA, Vic knew, would have collected all the data by tapping into the myriad of cables that connect mobile networks across the globe, both in the United States and elsewhere.

The report found nothing out of the ordinary apart from calls to and from two cell phones that appeared to be throw-away burner devices. The cross-checks had shown that twenty-four hours after the calls had taken place, the SIM cards had been deactivated and the phones rendered untrace-able—they had disappeared from all networks and could not be found by triangulation, GPS, or Wi-Fi. To have one call to such a device would be classed as unusual; to have two raised a red flag at the NSA.

The assumption was that the batteries and SIMs had been removed from the corresponding phones, which was very typical of the behavior seen among criminal elements or those engaged in other activities that they wanted to keep undercover.

Zilleman received or made the calls using his normal cell phone from a variety of locations, including Zürich, Washington, DC, and London. One of the other parties using the burner phones was located in the Brazilian city of São Paulo, where the device had been bought, and another in DC.

Vic wrote a quick thank-you note to Steve and asked him to continue monitoring Zilleman's cell phone, with a specific focus on calls to or from throwaway devices. He wanted as much information as possible about those devices' locations and where they were purchased.

Then he forwarded the report to Johnson.

CHAPTER TWELVE

Saturday, June 1, 2013
Wazrar

The three mules flicked their tails continuously to try to rid themselves of flies as they climbed their way slowly up the narrow gray dirt track that led out of Wazrar. By eight o'clock the sun was high in the sky, and the exertion was making Javed sweat.

Noor walked at the front, turning decisively at each of the myriad forks in the path along the way; he had no need of a map. Meanwhile, Javed remained at the rear of the convoy to ensure the mules kept moving.

With them were two of Noor's nephews, Hashim and Kabir, aged eighteen and nineteen, respectively, who were acting as lookouts and, if necessary, messengers who could relay details back to Wazrar if cell phone coverage via the recently installed masts proved problematic. The two youngsters said little. Just like Javed, Baz, and Noor had been at that age, they were extremely fit, thanks to the amount of time they spent on foot among the mountains.

The group had set off just after seven thirty after finalizing their plans with Baz. He remained in Wazrar and was to take the Toyota to a shed behind a cousin's house four kilometers north at a remote spot just off the Khost-Gardez highway. Once they had collected the Stingers from the cave, Javed and Noor would then return to the pickup truck and load the missiles beneath the false bed before driving it to Javed's brother's house in Kabul. Meanwhile, Baz would walk back to the house in Wazrar.

There was a lot to do, including checking that the Stingers and RPGs were still in good order after such a long period lying in the cave.

They would keep in touch using a pair of Motorola SRX 2200 walkie-talkies that a Wazrar villager had acquired from a group of Taliban found shot dead on a mountain near the village. The radios were not always reliable in the mountains but were far better than cell phones, despite the recent installation of new masts.

Noor told Javed that because the radios were military-grade devices, he guessed the Pakistan intelligence service may have supplied them to the Taliban, with whom they were widely suspected of being complicit.

As they left the village, Javed, anticipating that they would lose their cell phone connection soon after heading into the mountains, checked his tracker monitoring app. Zilleman was still in DC, but Javed's stomach muscles contracted involuntarily as he realized that Severinov appeared to be on the highway heading south of Kabul toward Gardez—the same route that he and Baz had taken two days earlier. The blue dot that showed his location was moving slowly down the highway. He was obviously in a vehicle.

Why is the Russian back in Afghanistan? Javed wondered. There was no obvious answer, but the speed and unexpected nature of Severinov's movements underlined the difficulties he was going to face in taking him down.

As they walked, his mind went back two and a half decades to the last time he had taken this route. Little had changed. The track was perhaps broader and more worn than he remembered. He was glad to see there was no sign of the opium poppy cultivation that had caused such problems in some areas of Afghanistan in the early 2000s.

Even Noor, now aged sixty-one, looked almost as nimble and slim as Javed remembered him to be in his thirties, although his hair had gone quite gray and his face was far more creviced.

They continued steadily upward. Where the terrain flattened out from time to time, there were always expanses of cultivated land, split like a patchwork quilt into informally shaped small areas of vegetation and grazing land. The track lay parallel to the broad stream that ran a few meters below.

The farming carried out here was very limited in commercial terms and was more designed to feed extended families.

After about four kilometers, the cultivated green area ended, and the track climbed more steeply into a barren, arid brown landscape.

Noor stopped, holding up his hand. He took the halter of the lead mule and guided it off the path and behind some bushes to the left, where he crouched on his haunches. Javed did likewise.

"What's up there?" Javed whispered.

"Taliban or Haqqani's people," Noor said.

Eventually Javed spotted the tiny figures on the mountainside across the other side of the valley walking in single file along a path, almost invisible against the khaki-colored earth behind them.

A firecracker splattering of gunfire broke the silence, coming from farther away to their right.

"Shit, I think those are Americans—firing at the Taliban," Noor said. "There they are." He pointed. Yet again, it took Javed several moments to see the dark figures huddled up against a rocky outcrop. Noor was correct—US soldiers.

The Taliban or Haqqanis immediately began moving back toward where they had come from and then disappeared behind some boulders.

"We need to be very careful," Noor said. "Those Americans sometimes come up here from their base a few kilometers away—Wilderness, they call it. Don't want them mistaking us for Taliban. Two guys from the village were caught like that last month. They had Taliban firing at them from one direction, they ran the other way, and then they were being fired at by American soldiers. They were lucky to get away alive."

Javed knew about Firebase Wilderness, which was one of several outposts operated by US and Afghan army forces to try to ensure security along the K-G Pass. He had read reports about the base coming under mortar and rocket fire from Taliban or Haqqani insurgents from time to time.

"Not good timing for us, midsummer," Javed said. That was when the rebels were always most active, when the passes and pathways were clear of snow.

"No, it's not the best for us," Noor said. "I came up here a few weeks ago when there was still some snow on the ground, and there was no sign of Taliban."

While they were waiting, Javed saw three gray wolves emerge silently from behind some rocks and walk across the path, only 150 meters from where they were hiding. They vanished as quickly as they had appeared. It was the first time he had seen such animals since the 1980s.

Javed also checked his cell phone tracker monitoring app

again, but there was no coverage now. They were too far into the mountains to get anything other than a sporadic signal.

The two men, together with Hashim and Kabir and their mules, waited behind the bushes for another half an hour before Noor and Javed judged it safe to move on.

Soon they reached the part of the path that Javed had always hated on his previous visits: a segment where it became no more than a ledge on an almost sheer rock face, a steep drop of more than one hundred meters falling away to their right. One false step would mean instant death, but it was the only way to get to their destination.

Javed wasn't especially afraid of heights, but even he was forced to walk as far to the left as he could, pressed up against the cliff wall. The mules seemed to have no such issues and plodded sure-footedly onward.

A couple of kilometers farther on, they finally stood under a rock overhang. It was the spot where, twenty-five years earlier, Javed had arrived with Baz and four heavily laden mules, each carrying four FIM-92 Stingers; a cargo of weaponry that in 1988 had been worth well in excess of $1 million. Over the years he had occasionally wondered to himself why he hadn't simply sold the missiles and set himself up for life. But back then, the cause and the fight seemed the most important thing of all. It was a fierce patriotism that overrode all material considerations.

As he had continued to do during their journey, and with special care following the near-encounter with the Taliban and the US Army, Javed stopped and did a final check for any kind of surveillance. But as previously, there was nothing. In truth, it was unlikely that Taliban would find their way to this spot; the cave was near the edge of a cliff and was a long way off the various paths and trails that crossed the mountains. One of the villagers in Wazrar had originally come across it while searching for some lost sheep and had happened to casually mention it to Javed. There was simply no reason for anyone to be there, which was why he had chosen it.

"Shall we go in?" Noor asked.

"Yes, all looks good," Javed said.

Noor took two strap-on headlamps from his backpack, put one on his head and turned it on, and handed the other to Javed, who did likewise.

They led the mules beneath the overhang and through a natural fissure in the cliff face, behind which was a cave. The overlapping geometry of the rock surface around the fissure left the entrance virtually impossible to detect until one was almost on top of it. The gap was only just wide enough for the mules.

To Javed, the cave looked unchanged from his last visit. It was larger than he remembered, stretching about thirty meters back from the entrance and perhaps twenty meters wide. After glancing around, he looked at Noor. "Let's get the hardware out and have a look at it, shall we?"

Before doing so, Noor instructed his two teenage nephews to keep a careful check on both sides of the valley below the cave. Hashim was to take responsibility for the southern side, Kabir the northern side. "If anything moves within four kilometers of this cave, I want to know about it," Noor told them. They both nodded and headed off.

"Are they good?" Javed asked after they had gone.

"They are excellent," Noor said. "We use them as an alarm system for the Taliban if we are out in the mountains and need to know if we're getting into a dangerous situation."

"That sounds like a risky role."

Noor looked slightly nonplussed, as if he hadn't considered the risk factor. "A little. But they're quick and almost invisible, and they've not let me down yet. You can rely on them."

Javed, reassured, walked with Noor to the back of the

cave and slipped through another much narrower fissure into a cavity deeper inside. Noor clambered up on a couple of rocks and levered himself up to a ledge that was above head height.

"They're all still here," Noor said. He reached over, and Javed heard a scraping noise as he pulled the first Stinger across the rock surface toward him.

A second later, Noor carefully passed him a one-and-a-half-meter fiberglass launch tube, tightly wrapped in heavy-duty clear plastic sheeting and secured with insulating tape. Javed grasped it in both hands—it was heavier than he recalled—and lowered it to waist level, where he held it for a few moments, his hands spaced wide apart, cupping it beneath. The plastic sheeting was covered in a deep layer of gray dust. He brushed a little of it off with his thumb to reveal the familiar dull green surface beneath the plastic wrapper. The breakable glass disks at either end of the launch tube were intact.

Holding the missile brought back mixed memories: the camaraderie and triumphalism of successful operations, the shared danger, the exultation of destroying the enemy. But also, grim thoughts about the devastation wreaked by the Russians they had been aiming at. His wife and daughter, long gone.

"How many shall we take?" Noor asked.

"Nine Stingers," Javed said. "That's more than enough. We can put three on each mule. We'll take two gripstocks and the BCUs, and the six RPGs and two launch tubes that are left here as well." He carried the Stinger tube through to the main cave and placed it carefully on the floor before returning to take the next from Noor.

Twenty minutes later, all the equipment, similarly protected by clear plastic, was lying on the floor of the main cave. Javed unwrapped one of each item and took them outside so he could examine them in the daylight.

"These all look in remarkably good condition," he said, squatting down and running through his own mental checklist as he ran his hands around the components. The fact that the missiles themselves were in hermetically sealed tubes meant there was every likelihood they were still in perfect working order. But the BCUs too, which had been his biggest worry, looked fine.

"Yes, it's cool and dry in there," Noor said. "It's like keeping them in a fridge."

Javed looked up at him. "Let's hope it's done the job, then. I'm not going to test them. There's too much chance of being spotted and caught before we're even out of the valley."

Javed removed the Motorola radio from his backpack and flicked it on to text message mode. The device was capable of sending messages up to two hundred characters long. But Javed wasn't going to need that many.

He quickly tapped out a two-word missive to Baz.

All OK.

He wasn't going to run the risk of communicating in anything other than coded language. The US Army would almost certainly be monitoring all frequencies, and quite likely, the Taliban too. He pressed send.

Soon after, a crackle of gunfire erupted from somewhere across the other side of the valley, followed a few seconds later by another volley of shots from a position farther west.

"Taliban again," Noor said. "Probably the same lot we saw earlier."

"I'm certain they weren't tracking us, though."

"They weren't, but if we move from here, the chances of them spotting us rises. I think we should stay and sleep here, then head back tomorrow."

"Agreed," Javed said. He picked up the Stinger components and carried them back into the cave, where he rewrapped them. "We can't risk Taliban or the Americans finding us with a load of Stingers on the mules."

* * *

Saturday, June 1, 2013
  Kabul

Johnson ended the forty-five minute Skype call with Carrie and Peter and put his phone down on the table. His two teenagers had been understandably worried at the news that their father was going to be traveling through dangerous areas of a country far from home about which they knew little, other than what they'd seen in the news. And that wasn't reassuring.

He had attempted to downplay the dangers and instead talked about the fascinating history of Afghanistan and the beautiful mountainous countryside he would be traveling through. But it wasn't cutting much ice, he could tell. Even the family dog, Cocoa, seemed subdued and spent the whole call lying on his mat in the background.

It was difficult as a single dad, trying to ply his trade, follow his passion, and earn enough to keep his family solvent without having to resort to boring hometown investigations in which he had little interest. Johnson often called it his own personal trilemma.

He picked up the Beretta M9 semiautomatic from the table. The familiar shape felt reassuring in Johnson's hands. He didn't ask Haroon where it had come from, nor about the Walther PPS that he had obtained for Jayne.

He ran his hands over the sleek black casing, and then he took the magazine out and racked the slide back. There was no live round in the chamber. The fifteen-round magazine was full, as were the two spare magazines that Haroon had brought along to Johnson's villa.

Meanwhile, Jayne was checking the Walther over. She seemed similarly happy: preparations for their journey from Kabul to Wazrar early the following morning seemed to be on track.

Haroon grinned, looking alternately at Johnson, then Jayne. "Will those do?"

"Yes, good for me," Jayne said. "Thanks a lot."

"And me," Johnson said. "Don't let me ever say you ISI people aren't resourceful."

Haroon laughed. "In this part of the world, being resourceful is the first skill you learn when you pop out of the womb, Joe." He slipped his hand beneath his jacket and pulled out a Heckler & Koch P2000 semiautomatic. "Couldn't bring mine on the plane so I got myself one too," he said with a smirk.

Johnson nodded in approval.

"I've also emailed both of you a photo," Haroon said. "It's a picture of Wazrar in 1988, after it had been blitzed by a bunch of Russian Hind helicopters. Have a look."

Johnson took out his phone and clicked on the email that Haroon had sent. The attached photograph, a scanned copy of a slightly dog-eared print, showed a collection of mud-brick houses that had been almost entirely demolished, their walls fallen in and roofs collapsed. People were sitting in the dirt next to them, weeping.

He looked up at Haroon, who pointed toward the photo. "Shocking, isn't it?" Haroon said. "Someone sent me a copy of that picture years after the war was finished, but it made me think we were right to help the mujahideen. You'll see the difference when you go. They've rebuilt the village."

"The Pashtun spirit," Johnson said.

Jayne leaned over his shoulder to look at the photograph. "Pity they can't rebuild lost lives," she said.

Johnson turned back to his list of tasks. Another tool he had added to his collection in recent months had been micro tracking devices, roughly thirty-five millimeters square and only eight millimeters deep. He had used them to good effect to track a terrorist sniper rifle on its journey across the Atlantic on a previous job in Northern Ireland.

That success had underlined to him the potential of such devices for personal security. At only a few hundred dollars each, they were well worth the investment.

He had commissioned a contact in New Hampshire who specialized in covert tracking to create a tiny cavity in his rubber shoe sole into which a tracker could be inserted when necessary. Jayne had required little persuasion to also have one installed in a pair of her walking shoes. The trackers, with a battery life of around two weeks, could be monitored anywhere in the world using an iPhone app.

Johnson removed the insole from his right shoe and, using the blade on his Swiss Army Knife, he slowly levered out a finely cut segment of the honeycombed rubber midsole beneath, revealing a shallow cavity in the heel. He slipped a tracker inside, then replaced the rubber segment. He took Jayne's shoe and installed one in hers too. Then they both synchronized the trackers with their phone apps so both could be monitored from either device.

Johnson gave Omar, the driver, three backpacks and other mountain gear borrowed from the US embassy to be loaded onto the Hilux along with water, dried food, and three jerry cans of spare diesel. Then he called the ICC office in Kabul to let them know his travel plans, in case they needed to contact him regarding the investigation contract, and that they should allow for potential delays in replying to messages, as cell phone reception would be unpredictable.

Next came a meeting with Frank Rice at the Serena Hotel, where he was staying, to brief him on progress so far and to ensure he was on board with their plan to track down Javed and investigate Severinov—and just as importantly, to ensure that he was prepared to underwrite the cost.

Rice was happy to do so. He rapidly grasped the significance of the apparent linkages between Javed's and Severinov's present and past roles and the importance to his own investment decisions of getting to the bottom of those. To his mind, if there was a possibility of uncovering damaging revelations about rival bidders that might give him and his client a big advantage, he was 100 percent behind it. In the context of a potential multibillion dollar investment, the charges for a driver, the Hilux rental, Johnson and Jayne's daily rate, a payment to Haroon, and other incidental costs were insignificant.

Given Rice's commitment, Johnson had been relieved to receive the report from Vic, giving the British investment banker and his client a green light.

Next, he and Jayne briefed Haroon on developments since their meetings with the three passport forgers on the Friday morning. They had spent the following twenty-four hours working on plans for the trip to Wazrar, and Johnson wanted to make sure Haroon was comfortable with everything.

Johnson was also insistent that for security reasons, the US embassy was kept in the loop, and they had spent some time with Sally O'Hara to get her up to speed with their plans.

Because of the number of Taliban and Haqqani attacks in the Khost-Gardez area, O'Hara initially tried hard to dissuade them from traveling there. But after realizing that wasn't going to work, she suggested that Johnson get in touch with Seb Storey, the US Army lieutenant colonel to whom she had introduced him at the US embassy reception the previous week.

It made sense. Storey was located at Firebase Wilderness, an army command post midway along the Khost-Gardez highway—roughly fifteen kilometers from Wazrar. From a security point of view, it would pay to try to get Storey onside. Johnson's only concern was that he might end up being hamstrung by the US military machine and prevented from doing what he wanted to do: finding Javed.

Johnson wrote a short email to Storey, which he copied to Jayne, outlining his plans and suggesting they try to arrange a meeting while he was in the vicinity.

Finally, he decided on one final visit to the address he had for Javed on Street Ten, just to make sure.

CHAPTER THIRTEEN

Sunday, June 2, 2013
Wazrar

It was almost eight o'clock in the morning as Baz made his way up the hill from the small shop in his village, carrying the bread and yogurts that he had just bought for his breakfast.

There had been no rain for more than two weeks, and the early summer sun had dried out the surface of the Khost-Gardez highway, turning it to dust. Every time a truck passed through the village, it threw up a dense cloud of gray particles that smothered everything, from vegetation to houses and vehicles.

A group of children ran past him, playing in the street, as they seemed to do every day at the moment. Their school had been closed for the past three days, since the Taliban had thrown a grenade into the building—thankfully while it was unoccupied—and caused extensive damage. It would probably take another two weeks of repair work before it could reopen.

As he arrived back at his house, he felt the Motorola radio hidden beneath his *shalwar kameez* vibrate in his pocket. Immediately his heart rate rose a little. He had agreed with Javed and Noor that they would keep any communications to an absolute minimum and use only text messages unless in a real emergency. They all knew that radio frequencies were monitored by the US military and quite possibly by insurgent rebels too.

But Javed and Noor were to let him know, using brief, cryptic language, whether the Stingers were in the cave as expected and whether they looked in usable condition.

This could be good or bad news.

He shut the door behind him, placed the bread and yogurts on a table, removed the radio and, using the LCD screen, scrolled to the message in-box.

All OK the message said.

Baz breathed out. He clicked on reply and sent a two-character response: *ok*.

Then he placed the radio in a drawer beneath the kitchen table and closed it. He didn't want any of his extended family to see it if they happened to walk in; they knew little of what his extracurricular activities involved. And as the patriarch of the extended family, since the death of his and Noor's father, Feroz, in 2001, Baz was conscious of trying to set a good example for the younger members of the family, particularly his own children.

Baz checked his watch. He had no idea what time Noor and Javed would actually leave the cave, but it didn't really matter; the Toyota was in place, ready for them farther up the valley. He would wait to hear from them again.

He filled his kettle with water and set it to boil. There was little else to do but have a cup of chai and wait. He turned on a black radio set that stood on the table and settled down to listen to a news program.

Then, behind him, he heard the door latch click.

Baz whirled around, just in time to see two men, both clad in charcoal gray *shalwar kameezes* and wearing black ski masks that covered their mouths and noses, slip through the door and move fast toward him.

"Don't move, stay still, and do what I say," the first man said in basic, heavily accented Pashto.

One of them was holding a gun, the other a long knife.

* * *

Sunday, June 2, 2013
  Wazrar

Severinov walked around the plain wooden chair that stood in the center of the darkened kitchen. He repeatedly smacked the rubber truncheon that he was holding into his open left palm.

In the chair, his hands lashed to the wooden arms, feet similarly tied to the chair legs, was Baz. A ball of rag was stuffed into his mouth, and a steady trickle of blood coursed from his nose down over his upper lip, staining the rag crimson.

"Tell me exactly how to get to that cave," Severinov said in Pashto, his voice level and menacing. "You've got ten seconds." He patted the Makarov pistol stuffed into his belt and began to count slowly downward. "*Ten, nine, eight . . .*"

With each number, he smacked the truncheon into his palm. When he got to two, Baz shook his head a little, the whites of his eyes showing in the gloom.

"*. . . one, zero.*"

Baz shook his head again.

Severinov stood and stared at the Pashtun for a couple of

seconds. It had been quite some time since he had been up close and hands-on like this with an interrogation victim. He had almost forgotten how it felt: the adrenaline rush, the sense of power. The fact that Baz had been involved in the shooting down of the helicopters in 1988 in the K-G Pass added to his satisfaction.

He bent down, raised the truncheon, and smashed it hard into Baz's right shin just below the knee. Baz's head jerked back in agony as his tibia splintered into three pieces, one of which was pushed sideways so that it protruded out through the skin on the inside of the upper calf. He issued a muffled scream through the gag and then another, his face contorted and purple like a rubber mask on Halloween night.

It was a technique that Severinov had learned from his father, Sergo, who had occasionally enjoyed telling his teenage son tales of extracting information about plots against his boss, Josef Stalin, during the 1940s. Stalin had ordered confessions, so Sergo, who had no option but to comply, made sure he had obtained them, whether true or not. He had proved himself good at his job. In turn, Severinov himself had deployed similar techniques during his stint in Afghanistan with the KGB in the '80s, although then the victims were mainly mujahideen who had been captured by the Soviet 40th Army.

"Just nod if you'd like to tell me where the cave is, and I'll remove the gag so you can talk," Severinov said.

Baz's body sagged into the chair. Severinov watched it sink with approval. That was always a good sign. He turned to Vasily, who was keeping watch, a Makarov in his hand.

"He'll talk soon," Severinov said, switching to Russian. "We'll just keep going until he starts squealing."

Vasily nodded in approval. "Do another countdown. He'll break."

Severinov began another lap around the chair, like a

prowling lion around a wounded buck. "Okay," he said. "Left shin this time. Tell me, Mr. Babar, where is the cave? I know you have a map that shows the route."

Sandjar had told him that Baz had a map somewhere in his house that showed the precise location of the cave in the mountains.

Again Severinov began to steadily smack the truncheon into his left palm as he walked and counted. "*Ten, nine, eight . . .*"

But Baz didn't budge. He just shook his head as the countdown finished. Again, Severinov bent down and this time smashed the truncheon into his prisoner's left shin, with a similar outcome to the right, although this time, the broken fragments of bone did not pierce the skin.

"You stupid bastard," Severinov said in Russian, this time raising his voice. Without any further warning, he smashed the truncheon down onto Baz's right hand, which was fastened in position on top of the wooden armrest. The blow instantly flattened and broke Baz's thumb joint and the first two knuckles. Again, Baz's head jerked back in a spasm of agony, this time with his eyes closed.

Sandjar had told Severinov that Baz was a tough nut, but his comment had been made in passing. He certainly hadn't said he would be this difficult to break. *These damn Afghans. How the hell do they breed them like this?* Severinov wondered to himself.

"Let's try a little knife work," Vasily suggested.

"Yes. Pass it here."

Vasily picked up the fifteen-centimeter hunting knife that he had bought upon their arrival in Kabul and handed it to Severinov, who held it up in front of Baz's face. "We're going to start with your fingers, and then I'll move on to your toes. One at a time."

Severinov smacked the flat of the knife against Baz's

pulped right hand a couple of times to check if there was any reaction. But Baz remained silent and still.

Suddenly Severinov turned the knife over, placed the blade against Baz's right little finger just above the knuckle, and pressed hard downward, using both hands together for added power. The finger severed after a couple of wiggles of the blade and fell on the floor. Immediately, blood began to pour from the wound.

"Are you going to tell me where the cave is?" Severinov asked. "I'm sure you have a map."

Now Baz looked as though he was about to slump into unconsciousness. His head lolled sideways and his eyes closed. Severinov slapped him hard, first on the right cheek, then on the left.

"Threaten to cut his throat," Vasily said. He was watching intently now, seemingly enjoying the process.

Severinov carefully pointed the sharp tip of the knife right under Baz's chin and pricked him with it slightly, just enough to draw a thin trickle of blood.

"You see this knife? It can take your life with one tiny flick of my wrist," Severinov said. "I'm going to push it up against your artery, like this." He moved the knife to the carotid artery that was visibly throbbing on the right side of Baz's neck and pushed the blade into the skin next to it. Now Baz's eyes were bulging, his mouth hanging slightly open, and he stared at Severinov, clearly in shock. Meanwhile, blood continued to pour from his severed finger.

The silence in the house was broken by a loud rattle at the external door behind Severinov, followed instantly by the shrill, high-pitched scream of a child. Severinov flinched at the noise, and as he did so, the razor-sharp blade of his knife pushed a fraction, just enough to cut into Baz's carotid.

The incision was a small one, but it was enough. Blood

immediately gushed out in a thin, fine spray, all over Severinov's chest just a few centimeters away.

The door behind them slammed shut and Severinov swiveled around. "Who the hell was that?" he demanded.

"A kid," Vasily said. "He's run off." He noticed the blood squirting from Baz's neck and his voice rose. "What the hell have you done? You've cut his neck. I said threaten him, not kill him."

Severinov ignored the comment. "Did the kid see us?"

"Yes, of course he did. Why the hell do you think he screamed?"

"Shit," Severinov said. "He's going to tell someone." He turned back to look at Baz, who had passed out. "This guy's bleeding like crazy now."

"Well, you stuck a knife in his throat—"

"Shut up, asshole," Severinov interrupted. He wiped his hands down the front of his *kameez*, which was splattered with Baz's blood. "He was telling us nothing. Maybe he didn't even have a map. We need to get out of here. I don't want a horde of angry Pashtuns coming in here after us."

"What are we going to do, then?" Vasily asked.

"Leave the bastard—he's useless," Severinov said. "He deserves it, anyway. Let's get to Sandjar's house. He'll have to guide us to the cave as best he can. He's not 100 percent sure where it is."

Vasily threw his head back. "Okay. This is all becoming shit now."

Severinov picked his bag up from the floor and put the knife in.

Maybe I should have brought Lvov along as well, he thought. *A third person standing guard outside would have headed the kid off. Too late now.*

He took the Makarov from his belt and flicked the safety off. "Let's move."

CHAPTER FOURTEEN

Sunday, June 2, 2013
  Kabul-Gardez Highway

The fifth police roadblock on the Kabul-Gardez highway was the final straw for Johnson.

The roadblocks, with their red and white concrete barriers funneling long lines of trucks and cars through the inspection points, were manned by lethargic-looking officers who only seemed energized when drivers, bored of negotiations, finally furnished them with the obligatory bribe in order to be on their way again.

At the fifth one, however, Johnson's US passport and Jayne's British one came under particularly long scrutiny. The policeman wrote down both their passport numbers on a notepad, then took the documents to the office.

Despite Omar's warning to remain in the pickup because of the risk of being robbed or worse, Johnson got out. He had been fighting the temptation to smoke, but now his anxiety was mounting. He gave in and lit a Marlboro while they waited, politely declining the wares of the dozen or more hustlers who descended on him, touting everything from *chitrali* caps to soap and socks.

Ten minutes later the policeman returned, demanding forty dollars before they were allowed to progress.

It seemed odd to Johnson. If the officer was only after a quick bribe, why take the passports away and waste time that could be used for extracting a payment from the next driver?

By the time they reached Pol-e Alam, capital of Logar Province, the roadblock count had risen to eight, and Johnson's cigarette count was at five.

Omar spent most of the journey south from Kabul navigating a path between overladen trucks that swayed alarmingly in a strong wind, moped riders and cyclists who seemed equally incapable of steering straight, the ubiquitous yellow and white taxis, and a myriad of cars of varying vintages.

The 170-kilometer route initially followed the Logar River valley, with its mishmash of small cultivated fields combining to form a narrow strip of quilted green across an otherwise parched landscape. The river, which flowed northeast to eventually join the Kabul River near the capital, was almost a permanent fixture to the left of the road as they continued south.

But from Pol-e Alam onward, they left the river valley behind. The land became more mountainous, brown, and treeless, with no birds in sight. This was a remote, stark part of Afghanistan that neither Johnson nor Jayne had seen before. Their activity in the '80s had been covert and, with the odd exception, such as Johnson's foray into Jalalabad, mainly restricted to the areas bordering on Pakistan.

Once through Gardez, another dust-filled town, Johnson checked the map. It was around fifty kilometers to Wazrar, and quickly they found themselves on the fairground switchback ride of a highway that formed the Khost-Gardez Pass.

Omar cursed his way past the sharp corners and the slow-moving trucks, and then let out a further stream of expletives when the road turned from tarmac to gravel just after yet another Afghan police checkpoint. Here the vegetation was nothing more than the occasional blob of green scrub on a khaki blanket.

Five hours after leaving Kabul, they finally pulled into Wazrar village. Johnson immediately realized there was some detective work to do: there were more houses than he expected, perhaps three or four hundred at least, and he didn't know exactly where Javed's family home was or even if he still had one here.

Haroon got out and tried asking several locals but was met with blank, unhelpful stares. Eventually, he found a man pushing a bicycle up the hill who pointed vigorously toward a group of houses up a track farther along the hillside.

"They are all at Baz's house," he said as he got back into the Hilux. "That *qalat* over there."

A group of about twenty people was gathered outside the compound, which Johnson could see comprised four houses. As they pulled up outside, a slender, gray-haired woman wearing a long green *kameez* emerged through a gate, clutching her head and crying. She was supported by two younger women, both also weeping, and a man.

The older woman sat on a large blue plastic fuel drum outside the gate and bent over, her head down near her knees, now weeping openly. A few of the other people went to her and placed their hands on her back, trying to comfort her.

Two men dressed in white, one carrying a bag, came running up the track from the main highway, going around the corner and through the gate.

"This doesn't look good," Jayne said, adjusting her customary blue *hijab*. "We'd better go and see what's going on in there."

CHAPTER FIFTEEN

Sunday, June 2, 2013
   Wazrar

"You're going to have to take us, whether you like it or not. And we need to go now," Severinov said. He folded his arms and looked around Sandjar's darkened living room.

The house was one of the smartest in the village, constructed mainly of concrete blocks rather than mud like most of the others. But nevertheless, it was sparsely furnished: the living room, badly painted in a shade of mustard yellow, had only a few brown wooden chairs, a burlap rug, some maroon cushions on the floor around the edges of the room, and two long, low tables in the center. The laptop computer on the table was the only sign of modernity.

Sandjar shook his head. "I have told you, I am not sure where it is. That's why we needed Baz. It is thirty years since I've been there. I might be taking you the wrong way."

Severinov pushed his face close to Sandjar's. "I don't care. Get your boots on. We need to go. We're already way behind." He pointed his Makarov right between Sandjar's eyes. "Do you understand, or would you like me to make it a little clearer still?"

At that point, Sandjar appeared to realize he was out of options. He grimaced and began strapping on his boots.

After removing their ski masks, Severinov and Vasily had driven the two kilometers from Baz's house to Sandjar's in the gray double-cab Ford Ranger pickup rented under a false name at Kabul Airport.

To Severinov, who realized that Javed must be ahead of him by some distance, every minute now counted. His urge for revenge was one thing, but the prospect of Javed getting his hands on a clutch of powerful weapons was another. And it was also a matter of time before Baz's body was discovered, which would trigger a manhunt.

"Where do we start from?" Severinov asked. "And not the village."

The question elicited a shrug from Sandjar, and Severinov pointed his pistol in the Afghan's face again.

"You're right. We can't walk through the village," Sandjar said eventually. "They hate Russians around here. If I get spotted helping you, they'll kill all of us."

Severinov and Vasily were both carrying forged letters of authority from the United Nations that showed that they were part of an international antidrug enforcement team carrying out checks across rural Afghanistan. But Severinov knew the letters, put together at short notice by Lvov, would not stand up to any detailed scrutiny.

"You'd better start thinking of an alternative," Severinov said, his voice now rising.

"There's a place two or three kilometers south of the village," Sandjar said. "We can leave your pickup there. We walk from there and go east along a track that runs into the mountains. I'm just worried about the Taliban—"

"You'd better make sure we don't run into the Taliban," Severinov interrupted. "But if we do, we're ready." He nodded at Vasily, who was putting an AK-47 rifle and two rocket-propelled grenades into one large backpack and an RPG launcher and three missiles into a second.

The bags also contained night-vision infrared goggles and spare magazines for the rifle and the Makarovs, plus water bottles and snacks. They had brought all the weaponry from Severinov's safe house in Kabul in a locked crate marked as sensitive scientific equipment for use as part of their antidrug work. It had only come under scrutiny at one of the check-points, and they had talked their way through that without a search.

The rifle, missiles, and the launcher, all of them almost a meter long, were sticking way out of the backpacks, and Vasily had to adjust the specially adapted head covers to conceal them as best he could. Eventually, he finished and stood, put one backpack on himself, and handed the other to Severinov, who strapped it on.

"Let's go," Severinov said, stuffing the Makarov into his belt.

Ten minutes later, Vasily had parked the Ranger behind some boulders a few hundred meters off the highway south of Wazrar. After checking carefully, Severinov was content that the vehicle was indeed invisible from the highway, although it would be in plain sight to anyone on the mountainside. The spot where they had parked was, however, well away from the village, and there seemed to be no obvious reason why anyone would stop there.

"We go from here, up that track," Sandjar said, pointing up a steep slope that led east. Severinov looked. There was a faint line across the scree that marked where others had walked. But this was clearly not a well-used path.

* * *

Sunday, June 2, 2013
Wazrar

Johnson took an involuntary step back when he walked through the door. There, tied to a wooden chair that stood in a pool of blood, was a man he hadn't seen in twenty-five years.

Baz's head lolled sideways and his clothing was soaked in blood, which continued to trickle from a wound in his neck. His severed finger lay on the floor next to his chair.

The two men dressed in white, local medical workers of some sort, were heatedly discussing whether to call for a doctor.

Don't waste your time, Johnson thought.

He turned to the woman behind him who was standing next to Jayne and Haroon, her shoulders hunched, arms folded, weeping uncontrollably, her tears leaving dark stains down the front of her green *kameez*.

This was Baz's wife, Nazia, whom he had seen crying outside the house upon their arrival.

"I'm so sorry," Johnson said in Pashto. "Let's go to the other room." He led her through to a living room and helped her sit, crouching next to her so he was at the same level.

She was understandably suspicious of this American stranger and demanded to know who he was. Johnson explained quickly that he was an old friend of Javed's, dating to the '80s, when they had worked together against the Soviet occupiers. He showed her his US passport.

"Did you find your husband's body?" Johnson asked.

"No, my grandson came to the house and saw him," Nazia said. She turned and pointed toward a boy, aged about ten, who stood in the doorway, his head bowed, avoiding eye contact. "He saw two men in black attacking him with a knife and guns. Then the boy ran and got help. I have only just arrived back here from Khost, and I find my husband dead." She burst into tears again.

Johnson waited a moment for her to settle. "I am sorry. It is important to ask questions because we need to try to find the men who have done this," he said. "But if you don't feel able to answer questions now, I can talk to you later."

He waited silently as she continued to cry and took a handkerchief that Jayne offered to wipe her eyes, the rims of which were now bright red.

"I will talk to you now," she said eventually.

Johnson breathed a sigh of relief. "That's good. Do you know what your husband was doing yesterday?"

"Yes, he had Javed here. Now Javed and Noor, Baz's brother, have gone into the mountains."

"He told you this?" Johnson asked.

"Yes, we spoke on the cell phone," Nazia replied.

"Why have they gone into the mountains?" Johnson asked.

Nazia looked away and said nothing.

"I really need to know," Johnson said. "It may be important to explain what has happened."

"I c-cannot . . . I cannot tell you." Now Nazia was stuttering.

"Take your time, Nazia," Jayne said. "Can we talk to the boy?"

Nazia hesitated. "I think so, yes. You must."

Johnson beckoned the boy over and explained that he wanted to find the men who had killed his grandfather. "Can you describe the men? Were they Afghans? Were they from the village?" he asked.

The boy then also began crying, and Johnson had to wait again. Eventually, the boy composed himself. "They were not

Afghans. They spoke another language I didn't recognize. They had black hair and they looked different, although they were wearing *kameez*."

Johnson nodded. This felt like a jigsaw puzzle, but one or two pieces were starting to fit together and make sense. "Did the language they speak sound something like this?" Then he spoke a couple of sentences in Russian.

"I think so, yes. Not English, and not any other language I have heard on the radio," the boy said, pointing at a black radio on the table. "It was like you just said."

Johnson turned back to Nazia. "Listen, I think these men who killed your husband were Russian. Can you just tell me, please, I am asking you, why Javed and Noor have gone into the mountains."

Nazia looked at the floor, then looked behind her to see who was there. "They have gone to fetch some weapons."

"Some weapons? Guns you mean?"

"No, not guns. Missiles, I think."

"*Missiles?* You mean rockets or grenades or something?"

"Maybe. They are old Stinger missiles." Nazia sank back into the chair and covered her face with her hands. "Please, please. I don't want to get them in trouble."

Johnson struggled to keep the surprise from showing on his face. *Stingers?* Surely they weren't relics from the mujahideen stocks the CIA had supplied all those years ago?

"I think they are in trouble already," Johnson said. "They're in danger from the men who killed your husband. Can you tell me why they want the missiles?"

Nazia put her head in her hands, staring at the floor. She just shook her head.

"I need to try to stop them. Do you know where they are fetching the Stingers from?"

"It's a cave," Nazia said. "But I don't know how to get to

it. I have never been there. I know it is several kilometers from here. It's a long and difficult walk."

"Is there a map? Can you show me roughly where it is?"

Nazia raised her head. "A map?" She shook her head. "I need some water. I'm going to the kitchen." She stood and headed toward the kitchen door. Johnson made to follow, but she turned and said, "No, I'll go. You wait here."

Johnson nodded and sat again. He watched as she closed the kitchen door behind her. Seconds later, he heard a loud scraping noise from behind the door.

A minute later, there was another scraping noise, and then the door opened and Nazia emerged, carrying a cup of water in one hand and a folded piece of paper in the other. She sat down, drank the water, then unfolded the paper. It was a printed map.

"Here," she said. "Baz kept it hidden. It shows where the cave is. Look here." She stabbed her finger on a circle drawn in blue ink.

Johnson took the map from her and studied it. It was large-scale and had a route marked with the same blue pen, leading from a point outside Wazrar to the location marked by the circle. It looked to be around ten kilometers, by his rough calculations.

He turned to Jayne and Haroon. "We can give this a go. What do you think?"

Jayne nodded. "We have to." Haroon also signaled his approval.

"Two of Baz's sister's boys have gone with Noor and Javed to help," Nazia said. "But there is another nephew, Imran, who can go with you. He knows where this cave is. That will help."

"Thank you," Johnson said. "That would be very helpful."

Nazia wailed out loud again, then tried to apologize to Johnson. "I am sorry," she said. "We should be burying my husband today. But how can we do that with Noor and the boys and Javed out in the mountains? They do not even know what happened."

"Why would you bury him so soon?" Johnson asked.

"It is our custom. But we can wait." She wiped her eyes, which were leaking tears.

Another thought stirred at the back of Johnson's mind.

"Nazia, I have another question," he said, after allowing her a moment to catch her breath. He told her briefly about the covert meeting with Baz and Javed in Jalalabad in 1988 and the outcome of that.

"Did Baz or Javed ever have a black-and-white photograph of an American man giving a Stinger missile to some mujahideen?" Johnson asked. "They showed it to me, and I often wondered what happened to it. It's very important."

The photograph of Robert Watson had been taken in a place several miles into Afghanistan on a smugglers' route from Pakistan's Mohmand Agency. It showed several other missiles on a mule cart and another unidentified tall Western man, also holding a Stinger, from a company called Kay Associates. Johnson had spotted him visiting Watson at the CIA station in Islamabad a few weeks previously, but had been unable to find out his name. On the back of the photograph was the single word TENOR, written in capitals, which Johnson assumed was a code name.

Another tear trickled down Nazia's face, but she wiped it away with Jayne's handkerchief. "No, I never saw anything like that. But Baz told me that when Javed was caught by the KGB and put in Pul-e Charkhi, they took all his possessions, his papers, his identity card, everything he had on him, and he never got them back."

Johnson nodded. "Thank you Nazia. You have been very helpful," he said. "I am sorry to have to ask all these questions at such a difficult time."

He stood and turned to Jayne and Haroon. "We should get moving. We have work to do if we're going to catch up with Javed and Noor. I think Jayne should stay here and act as backup. I don't want all three of us stranded out there if something goes wrong."

He fished out the piece of paper on which he had written contact details for Seb Storey and passed it to Jayne. "Here, you can contact Storey at the army base if you need help."

Jayne started to protest but Johnson insisted. "No," he said. "Haroon speaks the language best and knows the region. It's better that he and I go, especially if we're faced with Taliban out there as well as these goddamn Russians, if they've gone in that direction."

CHAPTER SIXTEEN

Sunday, June 2, 2013
  Sulaiman Mountains

The firefight between the Taliban insurgents, holed up in a stronghold to the south, and the US Army in the neighboring valley had continued until late into Saturday night and then resumed at first light on Sunday morning. Gunfire and explosions echoed from the rocky mountainside at regular intervals.

Javed and Noor decided to sit it out in the cave until the battle was over. It was fairly typical of the scrapping that had continued in the area for years as US forces tried to keep the region clear of rebels and the Khost-Gardez highway open.

Every couple of hours or so, one or the other of Noor's nephews would pop back into the cave with an update, have a snack and some water, and then disappear again.

Javed considered telling the boys to be careful not to put themselves in a risky situation, but he knew they would take that as a personal insult.

By two o'clock in the afternoon, the gunfire had stopped, and Javed and Noor decided they should load up the mules with the Stingers, RPGs, and associated equipment so they were at least ready to go once his nephews gave them the all-clear. Javed was keen to get on the road back to Kabul as swiftly as possible.

They spent half an hour loading up the animals, who like most mules, stood with an air of world-weariness. They always reminded Javed of a particularly sullen-looking taxi driver he had often used in Houston. The missiles and other equipment were carried in special canvas holders that were slung across the mules' backs, balanced carefully on either side.

When they had completed that task, both men sat on a rock near the entrance to the cave and waited.

At half past two, Hashim hurried into the cave, out of breath. "There are three men coming up that valley," the boy said, his eyes wide. "One is Sandjar Hassani. The others, I do not know. They are not Taliban, not soldiers, and not Afghans. They are speaking another language—maybe Russ-ian. I heard them."

"*Sandjar?* Are you sure? And they're speaking *Russian?*" Javed asked.

"I am very sure," Hashim replied. "It is him. And yes, I believe it was Russian. They're dressed in black and carrying backpacks with what looks like some kind of gun or weapons inside."

"How far away?" Javed asked. His thoughts immediately went to the GPS tracker in Severinov's phone, which had shown him heading south of Kabul on the highway toward Gardez.

"Probably three kilometers. They were looking a little lost and arguing between themselves. Then they stopped and were eating food, but I don't know how long for."

Javed looked at Noor. "What is Sandjar doing with two other men? I don't like the sound of this," he said. "Does Sandjar know where this cave is?"

"I seem to remember him coming a very long time ago," Noor said. "Before you put the missiles in there. We could just kill all of them—ambush them."

"No," Javed said. "They may be armed, and anyway, I don't want to do anything that could draw in the Taliban—I have to assume they're still out here somewhere. If we start a fire-fight, we'll be asking for trouble. We'll just get out of here down the other path that runs down the northern valley and back to the Toyota that way. It will be safer."

He picked up his backpack and shouldered it, as did Javed, just as Kabir arrived back.

A few minutes later, the group was heading out. This time, rather than turning right out of the cave in a westerly direction to return the way they had come, Noor led the group east for a short distance and then cut around to the north, on a circuitous route back.

* * *

Sunday, June 2, 2013
Sulaiman Mountains

It may have been the adrenaline, and possibly because he had been making a real effort to run and keep fit over recent months, but for the first few miles of their trek into the mountains, Johnson was surprised at how well he coped with the rapid pace set by Baz and Nazia's nephew Imran. Staying away from cigarettes at home had made a definite difference. He resolved to try harder to do likewise while working overseas as well.

The heat caused Johnson and his companions to stream sweat, and the dust from the bone-dry mountain path irritated his nose as he walked, but he felt stronger than he had expected. Haroon, who was wiry and fit for his age, also seemed untroubled by the often steep terrain through the mountains above Wazrar.

Imran did not need the map that Nazia had provided, although at intervals, when they stopped to drink water from the bottles they were carrying, he did use it to point out to Johnson where they were.

"There was fighting here last night and this morning between the Taliban and the Americans," Imran said. "But they have all gone now."

"Are you sure?" Johnson asked in Pashto.

"Yes, we know they have gone," the youngster said. Johnson didn't ask how they knew, but there was certainly no sign of fighters from either side along their route. Nevertheless, he kept a strict routine of checking for any kind of surveillance or hostile presence.

Despite his initial energy, four hours after leaving Wazrar, Johnson was starting to feel fatigued. The downhill sections, in particular, were proving tough on his knees, while his thighs were aching from the climbs. It was with some relief when, not long after negotiating a particularly vertigo-inducing narrow path along an almost vertical rock face, Imran stopped as they rounded a rock pillar. He pointed at a cliff face about half a kilometer ahead of them on the other side of a gorge. "There. See that overhang? That's where it is."

"Good work," Johnson said, taking another sip of water. He looked at the youngster closely. "When did you last come here?"

"About four years ago, with Noor."

"Did you go into the cave?" Johnson wanted to ascertain how much Imran knew about what was hidden in there.

"No, Noor did. He asked me to stay outside to just keep a lookout for Taliban."

Johnson nodded.

Fifteen minutes later, the three of them were standing beneath a canopy-like piece of rock that jutted out from the cliff. Beneath it, just visible now that they had gotten up close, was a fissure in the cliff's surface.

"It's in there," Imran said. He looked down at the ground. "I can see they must have been here very recently. See the mule prints and footprints."

Johnson looked, and faintly visible on the stony surface were marks that could have been made by a mule. Clearly, Imran's eyes were better trained than his.

"I'm going with Haroon to take a look inside," Johnson said. "Can you keep a watch out here?"

Imran nodded. "No problem."

Johnson and Haroon strapped on their headlamps and walked through the narrow gap in the rock that marked the cave entrance. Johnson could see why they had chosen it: the cave was enormous inside, bigger than a basketball court, yet almost undetectable because the fissure in the rock that formed the entrance overlapped to conceal it.

Johnson immediately smelled dung, and sure enough, the headlamps revealed piles of droppings that mules—presumably belonging to Javed and Noor—had left behind. Here on the dust floor of the cave, the hoofprints and the footprints were much more obvious than they were outside. There were two paper bags behind a rock, both containing bread crumbs.

Evidently the two men had only very recently departed. But now there was no trace of them. Johnson suggested to Haroon that they search it carefully.

Johnson worked his way around the right side of the cave, Haroon the left. After a couple of minutes, the Pakistani called Johnson. "Here, there's another gap through here. Looks like there's another cave at the back."

Johnson walked over. Another narrow fissure at the rear of the large cave led to a smaller space. They went through and spent some time examining the ground with their head-lamps: there was nothing of interest.

However, there were rock ledges and recesses above head height. Johnson used natural hand- and footholds in the rock face to lever himself up and directed his headlamp farther upward. On the right side of the cave there was nothing. He twisted around to face the other way, changing his footholds carefully, and looked across toward the left side.

That was when he saw it. On top of a ledge on the other side of the cave, pushed three or four feet back from the edge, was the outline of a long, straight-edged object. Johnson stared at it.

"See something?" Haroon said, looking up at him.

"Think so. I'll just check it out," Johnson said. He stepped down to the ground and crossed the cave floor to the other side.

He again levered himself up using a rock as a foothold until he could see onto the flat ledge in the rock surface. As he raised himself, it became evident that there wasn't just one object. Lying in a neat row, side by side, were seven green tubes, all about five feet long, covered in clear plastic wrappers.

"What's there?" Haroon asked.

"You're not going to believe this," Johnson said. "There's a bunch of Stingers. All in their tubes."

The Pakistani grinned. "Well spotted. I wouldn't have seen them. But if Javed and Noor have been in here, they've probably taken some with them. Is there any launch gear?"

"No gripstocks, no BCUs, nothing." They both had a good

knowledge of the components required to launch the missiles.

"Let's not waste time," Haroon said. "Imran can go and track where they've gone. Leave those tubes."

As always, Haroon was talking sense. Johnson stepped down to the cave floor. "I agree. There's no time to waste."

They had just moved back into the main cave and were walking toward the entrance when from outside came the muffled sound of a gunshot followed by a long, piercing shriek of agony, then another gunshot and a thud. Then there was silence.

CHAPTER SEVENTEEN

Sunday, June 2, 2013
  Sulaiman Mountains

"If you have guns, throw them on the ground now, then come out slowly, with your hands above your head," the man's voice shouted. It was a deep, guttural, heavily accented form of Pashto, spoken slowly by someone who was definitely a non-Afghan.

Johnson and Haroon looked at each other, both weighing their options. "Russian," Haroon said softly. Johnson nodded and mouthed a silent curse to himself.

"If you don't come out, I will throw a hand grenade in there," the voice came again. Now the Russian accent was more distinct.

Johnson shrugged and motioned with his hand to Haroon that they should do as instructed. The Pakistani nodded. Johnson had to assume that given the gunshots and the scream, the grenade threat wasn't a bluff.

He put his Beretta on the floor and walked toward the

cave exit, hands raised above his head. Haroon did likewise with his H&K and followed.

The bright glare of the sun blinded Johnson for a moment. Then the first thing he saw was Imran's body, lying facedown a couple of yards away, with blood pouring from a bullet exit wound in the center of his back and another in his left shoulder. His clothing was soaked red.

Johnson looked up, and ten yards farther back were three men, two dressed all in black, the other in a gray *shalwar kameez*. One of the men in black was pointing a Kalashnikov straight at him, the other doing likewise with a handgun.

"Not Javed," the man in the *shalwar kameez* said in Russian, a note of surprise in his voice.

"No," the man holding the pistol said, also in Russian. "Who are these people?"

He looked at Johnson and switched to Pashto. "Who are you?" he demanded.

It was at that point that Johnson recognized the short, receding gray-black hair and the handsome Russian face that he had seen in photographs. The man with the pistol was Yuri Severinov—the man he was supposed to be investigating, the owner of Besoi Energy.

Given that Johnson had a wallet in his pocket with a credit card and a couple of other items identifying his name, he could see little point in playing games. "I'm Joe Johnson," he said.

In truth, he felt somewhat bewildered. What the hell was it about this Russian billionaire oligarch and the target, Javed, whom he was obviously pursuing, that had driven him from his life of luxury out onto the side of a bleak Afghan mountain, miles from anywhere, holding a pistol?

"And who are you?" Severinov said, indicating at Haroon with his gun, which Johnson could now see was a Makarov.

"Haroon Rashid."

"From where? Are you a Pakistani?" Severinov asked.

"Yes, I am."

The barrel-chested man next to Severinov, holding the AK-47, looked menacing to say the least, like some sort of professional hit man. Which he clearly was. Johnson glanced down at Imran's lifeless body.

Severinov spoke to his colleague in Russian, telling him to go into the cave and check if Javed or anyone else was in there and to also look around carefully for any heavy weapons, guns, or ammunition.

Johnson understood the Russian perfectly but decided not to show it—it might be useful if he could eavesdrop. He was pleased that Haroon also showed no sign of comprehension. The man with the AK-47 walked to the cave entrance, removed a flashlight from his pocket, and disappeared inside.

Severinov turned back to Johnson and this time spoke in English. "What *are* you doing here? If you are also looking for Javed, just explain to me why. You Americans—you just can't help yourselves, poking your noses in where you're not wanted. Do you not think you have caused enough problems in this part of the world, provoking extremists and jihadists and suicide bombers?"

Johnson said nothing. It wasn't worth wasting his breath on such a hypocrite.

Severinov took a step forward and eyeballed Johnson. "I know all about you, Johnson—you worked with Javed and the *dukhi* scum here in the '80s, didn't you?"

Dukhis was the Russian word for "ghosts," a tag that the Soviets applied to all the mujahideen during the occupation.

"You gave them the weapons they needed to massacre hundreds of my comrades, you and your CIA rats working with those worthless Pakis," Severinov continued.

"You're Yuri Severinov, aren't you?" Johnson asked.

Severinov ignored the question. "I should have killed you

in Jalalabad," he muttered, almost to himself, before continuing. "I'm asking you again—why are you looking for Javed? Are you working with him again? And what is he doing with you?" He indicated toward Haroon.

"We're doing nothing that's going to impact you," Johnson said. "You're wasting your time."

Severinov exchanged glances with the Afghan in the *shalwar kameez*, who had stood silently watching. Johnson didn't miss the exchange. The Afghan was complicit—he had doubtless sold Severinov the information that had brought him up here.

The Russian with the AK-47 eventually returned, carrying Johnson's Beretta and Haroon's H&K. "There's these two pistols but nobody in there and no sign of any other weapons," he said in Russian. "There's definitely been people and mules in there recently—there's shit on the floor and food wrappers."

"They must have taken the weapons," Severinov said.

So they know about the Stingers, Johnson thought.

Severinov stood for a moment, visibly thinking, then spoke again in Russian. "Vasily, get that boy's body in the cave. Put it out of sight and kick dust over the blood. Then we have to get these two out of here. I'm thinking they might be useful to us. Empty their pockets and tie their hands behind their backs."

The man who Johnson now knew to be Vasily dragged Imran's body into the cave, then reemerged a couple of minutes later. After kicking dust over the trail of bloodstains that now led to the cave entrance, he removed Johnson's wallet and phone from his pocket and took out the SIM card.

Then Vasily did the same to Haroon. He put the two pistols, the wallets, and the phones and their SIMs into his backpack and removed a length of blue climbing rope, which he cut into two pieces. He lashed first Johnson's hands behind his back, then Haroon's.

Severinov stood and watched as Vasily carried out the work. Then he spoke to the Afghan in Pashto. "Can you track where the mules went? Or can you follow any footprints?"

The Afghan walked along the path, away from the cave, studying the ground in both directions, heading west toward the village, then east away from it. Then he came back, shaking his head. "The ground is too rocky and the trail is not obvious. I can see some signs that they went east, but the prints then disappear. We could waste a lot of time. I'm not a tracker."

"All right, then," Severinov said. "We will go back to the village and look for Javed from there."

He instructed the Afghan to lead the way back, then pointed his Makarov at Johnson and spoke in English again. "You. Follow on. I will be behind you, so if you try anything, you'll get a bullet. Understand?"

Johnson just nodded.

* * *

Sunday, June 2, 2013
  Sulaiman Mountains

Severinov's first instinct after working out who Johnson and his Pakistani friend were had been to shoot them, leave the bodies for the wolves and the jackals he had seen on his walk up through the Hindu Kush mountains, and then immediately get back on the trail of Javed, his main target.

He cursed the delay caused by the death of Baz; if it hadn't been for that, and if they had taken Baz at gunpoint as their guide, Severinov estimated they would probably have reached the cave at least an hour earlier. Maybe they could have even arrived before Javed had left. Now it seemed foolish to do anything that would slow them down further.

But then, after thinking it through, the words of Putin at his meeting at the Rublevka mansion suddenly came back to him.

. . . Fedorov is a good man and I want him back. I'm thinking in terms of a prisoner exchange. But at present, we have no bargaining chip to offer . . .

Suddenly, Severinov's opportunistic mind saw that here he had a chance to not only neutralize a war crimes investigator who was a potential threat to him, his reputation, and therefore to his chances of success in the Afghan oil and gas investment process but also, maybe, to exchange him for Fedorov.

It seemed a long shot, and the fine details of how it might be done eluded him. But he trusted himself to think of a solution. He always did.

As he walked at the back of the line of men trekking back over the tortuous mountain paths toward the Khost-Gardez highway, Severinov's mind was elsewhere, trying to get two steps ahead.

That was what his father, Sergo, had instilled in him. "One step ahead, and you'll be cut down by the man behind. Two steps and you're safe," echoed his father's voice in his head. He had usually added that that was how he had navigated the shark-infested waters surrounding him during his seven years working for Josef Stalin. His mother, Olga, had used similar rhetoric, but she seldom talked about Stalin.

His parents had met while working for the Russian leader. Olga Orlov, as she was known before marrying, had been a cook at Stalin's *dacha* in the Kuntsevo District just outside Moscow for eight years, from 1944 until 1952—a year before

Stalin died. She got used to having her meals tested for poison by Stalin's team of tasters.

Sergo began work at the *dacha* in 1945, after an outstanding career in the Red Army during the Second World War, in which he spent most of his time fighting against the Germans and was decorated with the Order of the Red Banner. He remained part of Stalin's inner security circle until 1952.

The couple had gotten together in 1948, when Olga was thirty and Sergo thirty-six, and had married in 1950. Yuri was born seven years later. Severinov often had to try to wipe some of the difficult moments in his parents' marriage from his mind, but they somehow stuck it out and died within nine months of each other in 1994, before they could see their son start to succeed in his post-KGB business life.

After two hours spent walking under the baking sun, Severinov needed a drink. Never mind that the Pakistani, who looked to be in his sixties, was visibly wilting, and Johnson also looked tired. He ordered a halt for water at an ice-cold stream that ran down the side of a north-facing scree slope and sat on a rock to think. Meanwhile, Vasily stood guard with his AK-47 pointed at Johnson and Haroon as they drank and splashed themselves.

There was little doubt in Severinov's mind that Javed was likely to attempt another attack on him. His assumption was strengthened by the fact that Sandjar had been certain there were other weapons, possibly Stingers, in the cave and that they had now disappeared.

And if Javed was to attempt another attack, then most likely he would be heading back to Kabul in order to carry it out.

Perhaps the best option would be to get Johnson and Haroon back to the safe house in Kabul, near the airport. Perhaps there might then be a way to smuggle them, using his private jet, from there to Moscow. If Johnson were, say, to be discovered trying to break into some government official's mansion—maybe even Medvedev's—and accused of spying, there might be scope to engineer the exchange that Putin wanted. It was exactly the type of exchange that Russia and the US had carried out on many occasions before.

Alternatively, Severinov could somehow "discover" through one of his sources in Afghanistan that Johnson, like many of his American nongovernmental organization colleagues before him, had been kidnapped by the Taliban or the Haqqani network. That would be plausible. Then he could offer to lead the push to have him released via those same sources in exchange for Andre Fedorov's return to Russian soil?

Maybe that might also be a viable solution.

Whatever the answer he ultimately came up with, it seemed that keeping Johnson secured in Kabul would at the very least give him trading options.

Importantly, it would also put him out of harm's way until the oil and gas stake sale process was safely concluded in Severinov's favor. The Pakistani Haroon would have to go with him, given he had witnessed everything. He would then be dispensable.

Severinov felt confident that he could distance himself from any allegations of kidnapping—the Kabul safe house had been bought for cash in a false name, which gave him anonymity and deniability.

Vasily, who had been walking at the front of the single-file convoy, moved to the back and joined Severinov, both of them keeping their weapons ready for use if needed. Thankfully there had been no sign of Taliban so far.

"What are we going to do with these idiots?" Vasily asked, nodding toward Johnson and Haroon.

"Wait," Severinov said. "Drop back. These two may speak

Russian." They slowed until they were walking forty meters behind the others. "I'm thinking the Kabul safe house," Severinov said.

"Good idea," Vasily said. "If Lvov temporarily takes care of them at the house, then you can take care of the oil bid, and I can continue searching for Javed."

"Yes, I want Javed dead. I'm guessing he'll head back to his house in Kabul. We'll get him there."

"Yes, don't worry," Vasily said. "But you've never said exactly why."

Severinov waved his hand dismissively and looked in the other direction. "It's a revenge issue that goes back a long time," he said.

"And you can't tell me more?"

"No."

"Why's that?"

"I swore an oath," Severinov said, glancing at his colleague.

Vasily hesitated, his mind almost visibly ticking. "An oath? Who to?"

"To the leadership."

"Ah, I see," Vasily said.

Severinov knew that Vasily understood what he meant and not to ask further questions.

An hour later, the group arrived back at the Ford Ranger, which, slightly to Severinov's surprise was where they had left it.

"Truss them up; they'll have to go in the back," Severinov said to Vasily, gesturing toward the hard-top cover over the back of the double-cab pickup. He lowered his voice to a whisper. "And gag them. I don't want them shouting out while I'm bribing my way through the police checkpoints."

PART THREE

CHAPTER EIGHTEEN

Sunday, June 2, 2013
Washington, DC

The text message that went from Robert Watson's burner phone in Washington, DC, to a similar device in an office just off Abdul Haq Square in Kabul was short and succinct.

The message followed a couple of days of hard thought by Watson, who had been struggling to work out a strategy to neutralize any potential threat from Johnson to EIGER and Zilleman's investment project in Afghanistan. The simplest approach—and one that Watson had generally adopted to good effect across his entire career—was to get someone else to do his dirty work for him.

I believe US national Joseph Johnson is "undertaking espionage work for the US in Afghanistan." He may be claiming to work for the International Criminal Court. Johnson is ex-CIA. He is understood to be traveling outside Kabul. Suggest you apprehend for as long as possible and interrogate. My usual terms.

Watson then followed it up with a second text message

containing Johnson's passport number from the list he had obtained from his mole within the State Department.

The recipient of Watson's messages was Mohammed Burhani, executive assistant director in Afghanistan's National Directorate of Security, the intelligence agency that was formed in 2002 to succeed the KHAD. He was third in command of the agency, which was headed by the director, Asadullah Khalid. Watson knew that Burhani would understand exactly the meaning behind the quotation marks in his message—he could picture him grinning as he read it.

Burhani, like virtually all of the senior people in the NDS, was a graduate of the old KHAD school of intelligence gathering. And Watson knew very well that like many of his Afghan government colleagues, he was paid so little that the chance of earning some extra cash for carrying out a task that had little risk was difficult to turn down.

The previous day, Watson had made a telephone call to the office of the ICC in Afghanistan, posing as a business associate of Johnson who needed to contact him urgently.

The ICC official to whom he had spoken informed him that Johnson was traveling around the country and that his precise location wasn't known. But that was enough information for Watson's purposes.

Burhani was a man whom Watson—after considerable effort, much risk, and a not-insignificant initial payment— had gotten to know during his time as Islamabad station chief in 1988. Burhani at that time was much further down the chain of command at the KHAD. Watson had put him on his payroll in return for snippets of information about KGB and KHAD activities in Afghanistan.

Most notably, he had earned his money in 2009 when Watson, then running the CIA's Pakistan drone strike program against insurgents along the Pakistan-Afghan border, paid Burhani to detain a man who Watson believed had knowledge that four particular Taliban targets were about to be hit and was poised to warn those in the camps.

Not long after Watson had sent his message about Johnson, a reply came back from Burhani.

That is not a problem. If Johnson is traveling outside Kabul it is easier. I will make alert regional offices to arrest at police/army roadblocks and will update you with progress. Will try to hold in jail one week then deport and refuse future visa applications. There are other "options" available.

Watson smiled to himself. He didn't know for certain what Johnson's agenda in Afghanistan was, but if history was anything to go by, his presence didn't bode well for Watson's current plans. So deportation after a week in custody would be an ideal scenario. With any luck it would be long enough for Johnson to get a good beating or two in whichever prison the NDS decided to detain him. It would not be a pleasant experience, of that Watson was sure.

If that didn't work, then Burhani's "other options" might need to come into play.

* * *

Sunday, June 2, 2013
  Wazrar

For the sixth time in an hour, Jayne checked her cell phone. There was still no signal, either for data or voice traffic. From her position sitting on the floor cushions, she glanced across at Nazia, who had been tearful all day and yet had to try to help her relatives make arrangements for her husband's funeral.

"It seems to take them several hours to get the towers going again if the Taliban have forced a local engineer to turn them off," Nazia said, rubbing her red-rimmed eyes with the back of her hand. "They take them at gunpoint and make them do it. But if they've actually blown up the tower, it can take far longer—days or weeks."

Jayne tugged at her *hijab*. She had been trying all afternoon to use the monitoring app on her phone to check where Johnson was. It was frustrating because the GPS tracking device inserted into Johnson's shoe had been operating perfectly when he had left with Haroon and Imran.

She had watched a blue dot on her cell phone map move slowly eastward into the mountains from Wazrar. But then, suddenly, just after lunchtime, it had vanished.

Without a data connection, there was no chance. The landline phone was also dead because the Taliban had cut the cables farther down the valley the previous week, Nazia told her.

"You'll just have to wait for them to switch the cell phone network back on," Nazia said. She seemed resigned to the disruptions, which were just another example of how daily life was taken hostage by the insurgents.

"It's really frustrating," Jayne said. Her Pashto, like Johnson's, had rapidly regained its fluency while in Afghanistan.

"Yes. It is everything from transport and food supplies to fuel, electricity," Nazia said. "You learn to live with it. This is making it hard to arrange for my husband's funeral."

However, it didn't require a cell phone network for news of Baz's death to spread through the village. Everyone knew. Two men had arrived with a kind of wooden cot, which they placed in the courtyard outside the house.

Baz's body had been lifted onto the cot, with his big toes tied together and his eyes closed, his face carefully aligned so that it faced toward the Kaaba. Then a constant stream of visitors had come in during the afternoon, chiefly women who sat in a circle around the cot and alternately chanted and wept. Nazia frequently joined them, sometimes beating her face and chest with both hands in anguish.

The sight made Jayne feel as though she was seriously intruding on the family space at a time of immense grief, which in turn made her occasionally tearful.

She forced herself to focus on the task at hand, which was trying to ensure Johnson's and Haroon's safety. Her level of concern mounted when one of Nazia's cousins came to the house to pick up something and mentioned that a large squad of US and Afghan soldiers had been seen heading into the mountains just north of Wazrar. The assumption was that the Taliban were active and that the military had gone in to try to track them down.

Finally, after nine o'clock in the evening, her phone burst into life with a string of six text messages from various friends and contacts. The network was back on.

Quickly, she logged onto the GPS monitoring app and waited for it to load. Even with a signal, the 3G data transfer rate was painfully slow. After a couple of minutes, a map loaded, and then finally a blue dot appeared.

To Jayne's surprise, the dot was in the center of a yellow highway. She quickly reduced the scale of the map so she could see where it was. Then she sat up straight.

"Shit!" she said, involuntarily. "How the hell . . ."

The dot wasn't located in the mountains east of Wazrar. Instead, it was on the highway north of Gardez, heading in the direction of Kabul, at least an hour away from where she sat.

This was so far off the plan that they had pulled together that she was certain something was wrong. Johnson would definitely have tried to call or send her a text to let her know about such a drastic change, and in any case, he would have had to return to the village before moving on.

Jayne immediately tried to call Johnson's cell phone. But

all she got was the usual recorded message. *The phone you are calling is unobtainable. Please try later.*

Was Johnson alone? Was Haroon with him? What happened to Imran?

Her options, she quickly realized, were limited to probably one immediate course of action. That was to call Lieutenant Colonel Seb Storey at the number Johnson had given her.

She dialed the number. The phone rang, but Storey's cell phone went to his voice mail, which had a recording advising callers to ring another number if it was an emergency and he wasn't available.

She tried the second number.

"Hello, Wilderness," said a man with an American accent. "Staff Sergeant Chris Thollen speaking."

Jayne briefly introduced herself and asked for Storey, explaining the circumstances succinctly.

"I'm sorry," Thollen said, "but the lieutenant colonel's in the operations room right now. We've got something very urgent going on that he needs to take care of. It's all hands on deck here and will be for the next few hours. I'll have to ask him to call you back, but it may be in the morning."

* * *

Sunday, June 2, 2013
 Kabul

It was just before midnight on Sunday when Javed finally rolled into Kabul after an exhausting five-hour solo drive from just north of Wazrar. He had been forced to go it alone because Noor needed to remain in Wazrar and help with the arrangements for his brother Baz's burial, which was now scheduled for noon the following day.

Their journey back from the cave had been a long one. Upon arriving at the Toyota that Baz had left in the shed for them north of Wazrar, they had been met by Noor's somber-looking cousin, who had given them the bad news about Baz's murder at the hands of the black-clad perpetrators.

Noor had crumpled in a heap on the floor upon hearing about his brother. Javed's stomach had turned in knots.

The killers were obviously the same Russian-sounding men who had been spotted heading toward the cave in the mountains. *Severinov?* It had to be him.

The other piece of news supplied by Noor's cousin was about the arrival in Wazrar of the American investigator Joe Johnson and his British colleague Jayne Robinson. That was utterly intriguing. He had asked the cousin to repeat Johnson's name to make sure there was no mistake. And then he had been told that Johnson had set off into the mountains accompanied by a mysterious Pakistani and Imran.

First an email from Johnson and now he also showed up in Wazrar. What was the guy doing? After receiving Johnson's email, Javed had assumed it was coincidence that both he and Severinov had resurfaced at around the same time.

But maybe this was no coincidence.

For most of his drive back from Wazrar to Kabul, Javed felt both tearful and torn.

He very badly wanted to attend Baz's funeral, but he knew that if the Russians, guided by Sandjar, were on his tail, the risks in remaining anywhere near Wazrar were too high. Not least of his considerations was that if there was a firefight, it would very likely result in collateral damage to a large number of innocent villagers, which was the last thing he wanted to be responsible for.

Johnson, however, was a different story.

If Johnson was now pursuing Severinov—and it was Javed's gut feeling that that was why he had ended up in Wazrar—then he would in principle like to meet up. He had clicked with Johnson in a fundamental way in those couple of covert meetings they had had in '88, both of which had ended badly at the hands of the Russians through no fault of their own. Their agendas against the Soviet occupation forces had been similar.

But at the same time, Javed also had a strong sense of caution. If Johnson was a war crimes investigator, it was hardly likely that his current intentions toward Severinov were going to be aligned with Javed's own thirst for revenge. More likely, he wanted to get him in court. He could therefore easily cause problems.

In any case, how he was going to engineer a meeting with Johnson now was something he was struggling to work out. Maybe that would have to wait.

During his drive back to Kabul, Javed's resolve to achieve revenge, first for his wife's and daughter's deaths and now for Baz's, hardened into a simmering rage that he struggled to shake off. He knew it wasn't a good thing—he needed a clear head to think straight—but there was too much bubbling around inside him to do that right now.

Javed turned the Toyota off Qala-e-Fatullah Street onto Street Nine, stopped and opened the gate to his brother's old house, and then parked out of sight of the locals who were still wandering up and down the street outside, despite the hour.

He was relieved to have made it back. He had been forced to heavily bribe his way through a few police checkpoints in order to avoid his pickup being searched. Thankfully, in contrast to the journey to Wazrar, there had only been two US Army checkpoints, and neither had caused any concern—

they were looking out for Taliban and seemed relieved to wave him through when he appeared to be nothing more than an ordinary carpenter.

Javed unloaded his cargo of nine Stinger missiles, two gripstocks, and the BCUs, all of which had been hidden under the false bed of the pickup, and took them inside, together with the six RPGs. He would store them in a hidden cupboard in his basement. Step one of his plan was complete.

CHAPTER NINETEEN

Monday, June 3, 2013
  Kabul

Johnson groaned as the Ford pickup turned a sharp left and bumped over a pothole, causing him yet again to bang the back of his head on the vehicle's floor. He didn't know where he was, but his best guess from the length of journey and the conversations he had overheard at police checkpoints was that they were back in Kabul.

For five and a half hours he had lain horizontal, his ankles trussed tightly together with thin rope, his arms likewise tied to his sides like an Egyptian mummy's, with a piece of rag stuffed in his mouth and secured with insulating tape.

The first part of the journey in particular, over the rough, unsealed section of the Khost-Gardez highway, had caused his head, the base of his spine, and his elbows to vibrate and bounce repeatedly against the thin mat that separated him from the metal floor. Now his head felt as though it had been pressurized from within; it was severely bruised at the back since there had been no way of supporting himself to stop it banging every time the vehicle hit a pothole or rut, of which there were many.

From the muffled groans coming from Haroon, lying two feet to his left, Johnson could tell the Pakistani was in similar discomfort. The Russians had stopped only once, pulling off the highway and removing Johnson's and Haroon's gags briefly to give them a quick drink of water. They had been given nothing to eat.

Johnson had initially pinned his hopes on being discovered through a routine search at one of the police and army checkpoints. As previously, there had been delays at most of the checkpoints.

He clearly heard Severinov negotiating bribes at some of them as they passed through. He also heard him mentioning he was working on an antidrug enforcement program for the United Nations. *Bullshit.* Some checkpoints took longer than others to resolve, but Severinov was obviously being sufficiently generous, because there were no searches.

A short distance farther on, the pickup came to a sharp halt, and there was a protracted metallic scraping noise, which sounded to Johnson like a gate being opened. Then the pickup drove on over some bumpy ground before coming to another halt.

Eventually, the hard cover over the back of the pickup, a few inches above Johnson's head, was lifted. It was dark, but there was an orange glow from the city lights that dimly illuminated his surroundings. This was definitely Kabul.

Severinov's colleague Vasily appeared above him, his face silhouetted against the glow behind him. He untied the rope binding Johnson's ankles and pointed a pistol at his chest.

"Get out, stand up," Vasily said in English. He didn't offer to untie Johnson's arms, so he was forced to shuffle his way on his backside to the end of the pickup and then let his legs swing down to the ground. Both feet were so numb that he had no feeling in them, with the result that he almost fell over when he tried to put his weight on them.

"Walk that way," Vasily said, indicating across the yard with his gun, which Johnson could now see was a Makarov. It was a large site littered with cinder blocks, piles of sand, old bricks, and other building materials, with a building in one corner that looked unfinished. Johnson did as he was told. Ahead of him, Severinov unlocked the door of the building and stood to one side as Vasily marched him through at gunpoint.

Johnson found himself in a kind of hallway with a rough concrete floor and unpainted, pink plastered walls. Somewhat incongruously, a framed print hung somewhat crookedly on the wall ahead of him, showing a quote attributed to Josef Stalin written in decorative Russian script.

"Be a bee that stings for the Motherland: be busy, be dangerous," it said. It was the only decoration in sight. Johnson was not familiar with the quote.

"Down the stairs," Vasily said, jabbing the barrel of the gun hard into Johnson's back.

Johnson walked down a set of stairs to the left of the entrance hall and found himself in a narrow corridor.

"Stop," called Vasily. He opened one of the doors to the left, stood back, and ordered Johnson into the room.

The small windowless basement room, with a bare concrete floor, had a thin foam-rubber camping mat in one corner, with a blanket, a bucket, and a plastic bottle full of water. The room was illuminated by a single bare low-wattage light bulb dangling from a cord.

"You are staying here. Don't try anything, otherwise . . . " Vasily didn't finish his sentence but waved his Makarov in the air. Then he ordered Johnson to strip naked. Once Johnson removed all his clothes, including his socks and shoes, the

Russian went through the pockets of his pants, carefully examined his belt, and then started to check his shoes. Johnson forced himself to remain calm as Vasily removed the insoles from his shoes and first looked inside them, then put his hand inside and felt around.

This is it, game over, Johnson.

But Vasily threw the shoes on the floor and ordered Johnson to get dressed again. Without waiting, he then walked out, shut the heavy wooden door, and turned the key in the lock, leaving Johnson feeling thankful that the lighting in the room was dim and the tracker had gone undetected.

Five minutes later, Johnson heard footsteps in the corridor outside his door and Vasily giving instructions, obviously to Haroon. He heard another door open and then the sound of a key turning in a lock. Haroon was being similarly incarcerated in the room next door.

"Bastards," Johnson said out loud. He kicked the gray cement floor.

* * *

Monday, June 3, 2013
Washington, DC

Watson sat back in his chair in the anonymous house he had rented in Dirk Leman's name on Bath Street, Springfield, half an hour's drive southwest of DC. He studied the text message that had just arrived on his burner phone from Mohammed Burhani in Kabul.

Have received data from police sources re Johnson. Passport seen yesterday June 2 at five police checkpoints Kabul-Gardez and at one checkpoint northern end Khost-Gardez highway. After that, nothing. He is traveling with Jayne Robinson (British), Haroon Rashid

(Pakistan) + Afghan driver. Suspect he still in Gardez-Khost area. Did not pass through checkpoints at southern Khost end of highway. Will notify if more information received.

To Watson, it seemed immediately clear that something was going on. If Johnson was doing something for the ICC, then the Khost-Gardez Pass was one area where he might focus, given all the killings by Taliban and Haqqani networks in the south of the country, near the Pakistan border.

But the K-G Pass remained a very dangerous area to be. Surely Johnson would stay in the main towns of either Gardez or Khost? He seemed to have gone off the radar somewhere between.

The pass was an area that Watson had known quite well during the late '80s, when he had gone off piste in the same region for very different reasons.

The other additional piece of information was that Johnson and Robinson had a Pakistani traveling with them. That also seemed odd. He recalled that Johnson had developed some good sources within Pakistan's intelligence service during the '80s.

There was no obvious reason to be worried. But Watson had a well-honed survival instinct that had kept him intact through any number of very tough situations over the years.

Now that same primeval survival instinct that had made him such a skillful intelligence officer was sounding alarm bells somewhere at the back of his mind.

What was the best advice he could now give to EIGER and Zilleman about what ZenForce should do? He stared out the window across the street at the park opposite. The parking lot was gradually filling up with cars carrying families, kids, young couples, and dog walkers. It was all a world away from the scenes he imagined in southern Afghanistan.

He should at least run the new findings past EIGER.

Watson slowly tapped EIGER's number into his burner

phone. After he answered, Watson ran through the detail he had received from Burhani.

"What concerns me is that Johnson is spending time in an area that's sensitive to us and is with an unknown Pakistani. It might be innocent or it might not be, I don't know," Watson said. "Listen, we could just walk away from Project Peak now, live to fight another day, and find something else in a less difficult part of the world, and that—"

"Why?" EIGER interrupted abruptly. "It most likely is all completely innocent. Think how long it's taken us to prepare for this bid—months, years. And think about the rewards if it comes off. We could almost double the size of ZenForce in terms of asset value. If we get to the stage where it looks as though it's all going to shit, then we can reconsider, but we're nowhere near that situation. Are we, Robert?"

Watson hesitated. "No, we're not in that situation right now," he said. "But on the other hand, I don't want to take unnecessary risks."

"I'm glad you agree with me," EIGER said. "Let's press ahead until we see something that tells us to do a U-turn. There's too much at stake." He hung up.

Watson slowly put the phone down on the table. Maybe EIGER was right. Maybe Burhani's people would yet pull Johnson in for questioning. Maybe, maybe, maybe.

CHAPTER TWENTY

Monday, June 3, 2013
   Firebase Wilderness, Afghanistan

A cloud of gray dust flew into the air as Lieutenant Colonel Seb Storey removed his combat helmet and sunglasses and brushed his hand down the front of his uniform. "*Russians?*" he asked. "That seems very unlikely. If he has actually been taken, it's more likely to be a Taliban kidnapping. It's got all the hallmarks and we should know; we've had to rescue a few victims in the last three or four years." Storey frowned and stroked his chin between his thumb and forefinger as he studied Jayne's face carefully.

"I think it has to be the Russians," Jayne said. Her strong gut feeling was that it was the same people who had so brutally murdered Baz. She described what she knew about Baz's death and the perpetrators.

"Listen," Jayne said, placing both hands on her hips, "I can't be completely certain who's got Joe, but I do know where he is. We need to go get him."

An hour earlier, after finally getting through to Storey on the phone and briefly explaining the situation, Jayne had been picked up from Baz's house in Wazrar by three US soldiers in an armored car. They took her a few miles up the Khost-Gardez highway to Firebase Wilderness, a fortified army outpost, not much bigger than an American football field, comprising a collection of a few dozen temporary huts and shipping containers built into the stark gray scree slopes of a small ravine. The base was surrounded by blast-proof barriers topped with razor-wire.

The army units based there, currently led by Storey, were tasked with providing security to the construction crews building the highway and also training Afghan National Army soldiers. They had frequently come under rocket bombardment by Taliban and Haqqani forces on the surrounding hillsides.

Jayne took out her cell phone, clicked onto her GPS monitoring app, and showed Storey where the transmitter built into Johnson's shoe was located, not far from Kabul Airport.

She knew that a United States' citizen who had apparently been kidnapped should be a priority for a US army unit. But it seemed that in practice, she would have to convince a stressed and skeptical-looking Storey. Flanked by Staff Sergeant Thollen—the same man Jayne had spoken to on the phone—and a sergeant, Dave Randall, he rattled through a series of questions.

Storey wanted to know how they had come to be in Wazrar and why Johnson had gone into the mountains with Haroon and Imran. Jayne was forced to go more deeply into the historic background to the situation than she had intended, explaining the linkages between Johnson, Javed, and Severinov and how they had become involved.

"The bottom line is, Joe and I believe there's been a series of war crimes committed by these people in the past," Jayne said. "But if we don't act quickly now, there'll be another. And instead of Joe doing the investigating, he'll be the victim."

Storey looked out the window of the hut where they were sitting. A pair of mobile 105mm howitzers, mounted on wheels, stood outside, and beyond them three helicopters, one a Chinook, the others Black Hawks, stood idle on a flat stretch of scree. Groups of soldiers in combat uniform walked purposefully past.

"I hear what you're saying, but why the hell you guys came out here alone is beyond me," Storey said in an even tone. "My soldiers are putting themselves on the line every day in highly dangerous territory. You should know not to do this without making proper arrangements with the authorities, including us. Now you're asking me to tell my guys to take more risks to rescue your friend Joe, all as a result of your stupidity?"

Thollen, an athletic-looking man with a dark crew cut, nodded vigorously.

Jayne paused. She could see his point. They should have kept Storey informed.

"I appreciate that, and I know that extricating civilians from a kidnap situation is not part of your normal day-to-day routine," Jayne said, glancing at both men alternately. "But I'm sure it should be top of your list right now. This is urgent. And as for what we're trying to do, well, you're helping ordinary Afghans who are being disrupted now by insurgents and terrorists, and we are trying to get justice for those who suffered the same thing twenty-five years ago. Except then it was Russians who were shooting the shit out of the Afghans, not the Taliban."

Jayne leaned back in her chair. She didn't want to keep talking; she just wanted them to take some action.

Storey nodded. "Give me a minute. I need to go and put a

call in to the general's office in Kabul. He needs to be in the loop on this." He stood and walked through into a neighboring office, closing the door behind him.

A few minutes later he returned. "The boss is in a crisis planning meeting. He'll get back to me as soon as he can. Shouldn't be too long."

Jayne groaned inwardly.

"Just tell me what you're hoping to achieve with this Russian," Storey said, glancing impatiently at his watch. "You can't take him to the international court for something that happened here in the '80s. You're wasting your time—and you're wasting ours." He gestured toward a bunch of soldiers who were loading rifles and RPG launchers into a collection of armored cars.

In the distance, Jayne could see a cloud of dust that was being thrown up by an armored car or other vehicle that was speeding toward Wilderness along the track that led from the Khost-Gardez highway.

"The ICC may not want to take him to court, though let's leave them to decide that," Jayne said. "But you can ruin people's reputations by telling the truth about them. The media love stories like that if the perpetrators are now in positions of power."

Storey shook his head. "You realize we're stretched to the limit here without having to handle your problem. I've spent the last two days in firefights against a bunch of trigger-happy terrorists whose only objective in life is to blow us back where we came from."

"I can see that," Jayne said.

"And I'm going to have to try to explain what you were doing here to the general. He's under extreme pressure and is going to be furious."

Shit, she thought. *Just get on with it. Every minute counts.*

Then she had an idea. She took out her phone, clicked on

the email containing the photograph of the devastation at Wazrar in 1988 that Haroon had sent to her and Johnson, and showed it to Storey.

"Send him this photo. This is what the Russians did to Wazrar," she said. "Just so you know. And I'm guessing a kidnapped US citizen will become big media news very quickly back home. It'll go right up the political agenda. Even more so if he dies."

Storey gave a slight nod as he studied the photograph. "Appalling," he said. "I tell you what: email that to me, and I'll send it to the general. That explains more than words will about what you're doing here."

Jayne immediately forwarded the photo to Storey. A few minutes later, his phone beeped as a message arrived, and he disappeared into the other room.

She heard the faint sound of Storey's voice from behind the closed door. Outside, a group of soldiers jumped into a Guardian M1117 armored security vehicle, which shot off.

Five minutes later, Storey reappeared. "The boss has seen your picture. I've explained everything to him. He's told us to get on with planning a rescue operation."

* * *

Monday, June 3, 2013
  Kabul

The razor wire that topped the ten-foot-high walls surrounding the building in Kabul looked new to Johnson. There was no chance of getting through it, even if he managed to scale the walls, which were possibly rough enough to allow some hand- and footholds. And the black metal gate was also topped with razor wire.

But in the daylight, during the ten minutes that Vasily allowed him out in the yard for exercise at gunpoint, Johnson was at least able to work out where he was. The intermittent roar of jet passenger aircraft passing low overhead and the orientation of the mountaintops—the only things visible over the wall apart from the top half of a nearby block of apartments—gave him enough clues.

This building, which seemed more like a business unit or workshop than a house, was in northeastern Kabul, maybe a couple of miles southeast of the airport. Not that knowing his location was going to help much, he thought.

The yard looked considerably larger in the daylight than in the faint glow of night. The plot was perhaps fifty yards long and maybe forty wide, with the building, made from concrete pillars infilled with brick, positioned in the northeastern corner. There was not one scrap of green vegetation to be seen, only gray dust and piles of sand, cement, and gravel. The hum of traffic told him that he might be near the Kabul-Nangarhar highway. His mind went back to the RPG attack on the highway he had witnessed from his aircraft window the previous week.

Johnson also realized that the property was only a mile or so from the giant US Army base, Camp Phoenix. From the yard, he could hear the frequent sound of helicopters descending and ascending as they came into and out of the base. That was doubly frustrating: there, almost within reach, were the men who could extricate him from this mess.

"That is enough, get back inside," Vasily ordered, waving his Makarov in now familiar fashion. He ushered Johnson through the door, where Severinov stood waiting.

Johnson stopped and stared at the Russian. "What is the point in keeping me here? What do you want?" he asked Severinov. "Let me know and I'll see if I can help."

"There's a lot of point," he said, a faint smirk on his face.

"For the time being, you're out of action, you can't do any damage. And you'll have other uses in the future. You might even get to go home, if your government plays ball. You might become the spy who came in from the cold, as they say —the CIA spy."

His face now straight, Severinov added, "But if they don't, well . . . " His voice tailed off and he shrugged.

"What do you mean?" Johnson asked. "And if they don't play ball?"

"Never mind," Severinov said. "But I'll tell you this much: people think the Cold War is finished but it isn't. It has never been over and probably never will be. There's just been a lull in hostilities. Vladimir Putin hates you lot and so does all of Russia. You don't understand the Motherland and all that it stands for."

"You're living in the past," Johnson said. "Just like you were when the Soviet Union invaded Afghanistan in the first place. That was a mistake—trying to revive the Great Game."

"That's where you're wrong," Severinov said. "Russia's been great in the past and will be again. We won the Great Patriotic War and we'll ultimately win the new Cold War. The occupation of Afghanistan in 1979 was about defending the interests of the Motherland—the Afghan Communist government there. You watch—we'll do it again."

"Where?" Johnson asked.

"The Crimea would be a good start," Severinov said. "We'll have it back, and maybe sooner than you think. Now, just get down those stairs and back into your room."

He nodded at Vasily, who prodded Johnson in the small of the back with his gun.

Johnson lurched forward and walked down the stairs and into the room. Vasily turned the key in the lock behind him.

It felt to him as though the clock had just been turned back twenty-five years. Once again, it was all about Russia and the United States, with Afghanistan as the battleground. He looked down at his shoe. All he could hope for was that the modern technology buried in the heel was working as intended.

* * *

Monday, June 3, 2013
  Kabul

The vagaries of the Afghan cell phone network and internet system had plagued Javed ever since his return to his home country. If it wasn't the Taliban blowing up the towers and their antenna, it was power failures or computer systems breakdowns.

In any case, once he had revived himself from his journey back from Wazrar with a strong coffee, Javed's thoughts were far from his cell phone. They were about 170 kilometers away, to be precise, in his home village, where he knew his old friend Baz was being laid to rest.

At just before noon, when the burial was due, he washed, then took out his prayer mat, laid it carefully in the direction of Mecca, sank to his knees, and murmured, "Allahu akhbar." Then he began a long prayer. He pictured the washing of the body, the candles, the procession to the village graveyard, the prayers, the distribution of alms, or *Iskat*, to the poorest villagers. Then he wept.

It was almost an hour later when he rose to his feet again. *What am I doing here instead of there?* he asked himself.

Having had no data on his phone for two days, not since leaving Wazrar for his walk into the mountains with Noor and the two youngsters, Javed half-heartedly checked it at just after two o'clock. By then, service had been restored, so he logged onto his GPS tracker service.

Javed had to check the map carefully to be certain of what he thought he was seeing: the tracker was located about eight kilometers away to the east, on the other side of the airport, just off the main Kabul-Nangarhar highway.

Taken by surprise, Javed refreshed the screen again, just to be sure. There was no mistake. He scratched his head, of two minds about what to do. He momentarily thought about loading a couple of RPGs into the back of the pickup and blasting whatever building Severinov happened to be in off the face of Kabul immediately.

But then he thought better of it; such a hasty move wasn't a good idea, especially at this hour of the day. Without a carefully thought-out plan, there was every chance he would end up being spotted by some Afghan or American security patrol. The site was quite near to Camp Phoenix, the US Army base, which made it doubly sensible to take a cautious approach. He would rather just go and check it out and work out whether an attack under cover of darkness was viable.

Javed went to the Toyota and hid his Browning 9mm Hi-Power in an underfloor cavity beneath the front passenger seat. Half a minute later he was on his way out the gate of his brother's house.

It took him over half an hour to negotiate his way through the usual Kabul traffic chaos. Eventually he located the site where Severinov appeared to be.

All he could see from ground level was a tall concrete wall, at least three meters high, topped with thick razor wire. Even the gate, a solid black metal unit, had razor wire above it.

Not wanting to be too obviously interested in the property, Javed drove past once in each direction, then cut onto a side street that ran parallel to the one in which Severinov was located and parked to think through what to do next. Here he was almost directly beneath the flight path into the airport, which was about two and a half miles away; every so often a jet passed low over his head on its way in to land. Three military Chinook helicopters buzzed in overhead and descended rapidly into Camp Phoenix.

Across the road he saw a five-story block of apartments, which was the only building taller than two stories in the vicinity. Maybe there was a way to see over the site from there?

He moved the Toyota up an alleyway between two workshops near to the apartment block where, barring the most careful of checks, it was out of sight of the street.

Javed put on a pair of sunglasses, got out of the truck, and walked purposefully across the street and into the apartment block, which had no security door. He then began climbing the exterior concrete stairs that ran up the left side of the building. Each floor had its own security door, giving access to a corridor from where the apartments could be accessed. But Javed found that the stairwell continued beyond the fifth floor and up onto the flat roof of the block. Two laundry lines had been strung up between pairs of metal poles that had been bolted to the concrete roof. The lines were fully laden with kids' clothing. At the far end of the roof was a small shelter consisting of corrugated sheeting mounted on four poles, with a couple of rusty old bicycles chained beneath it next to some wicker laundry baskets.

Above, the clatter-clatter of another helicopter grew louder. Javed looked up. It was another US Army Chinook. Presumably that was also heading into Camp Phoenix.

Javed walked to the edge of the roof closest to the property where Severinov's tracker was located, using the clothing on the line as cover. Now he had a good view down over the entire plot, which was about 120 meters away. To his surprise, it looked like a building site. There was a building there, but

—typical of so many construction sites across the city—it was not finished, and there were piles of bricks, sand, gravel, and other detritus everywhere. Was this really the kind of property that a Russian oligarch would purchase? Javed thought it highly unlikely—unless there was a specific purpose. His aerial view confirmed that the entire site was secured by the three-meter concrete wall topped with razor wire. Next to the house, a gray double-cab pickup was parked.

As he watched, he noticed a US Army armored vehicle drive slowly up the street past the house, then turn left and head toward the highway. That type of patrol was routine across the city.

Above him, the Chinook was now hardly moving, its twin rotors creating a noticeable downdraft, its engine noise deafening. Then its engine pitch rose, and it moved rapidly off to the north, in the direction of Bagram, the US military air base that was about forty kilometers away.

It didn't take Javed long to decide on a course of action. The obvious thing to do was to wait until nightfall, then return to the apartment block roof with an RPG via a more circuitous backstreet route to avoid the security patrols. Then he could pump a couple of missiles straight into the property below. It would be easy. He could get down the stairs afterward and away down the highway. That would destroy the house, pulverize the Russian, and avoid the complications and uncertainties involved in using the Stingers to bring down Severinov's aircraft, particularly as he wasn't 100 percent sure whether the Stingers were still functional.

Everyone would assume it was just another random Taliban attack.

CHAPTER TWENTY-ONE

Monday, June 3, 2013
  Firebase Wilderness

Storey bent over the three aerial photographs he had printed and stabbed his index finger at the first. "We can fast-rope a couple of guys into the site from one of the Black Hawks." He gestured through the window toward the helicopters out on the landing area. "Or, even better, we can just land the chopper if there's enough space. We'll take the other Blackhawk too, with a team to secure the site perimeter. I'm minded to go myself on this job."

"*You* are going?" Jayne asked. She was surprised that a commanding officer would get involved in a hands-on operation such as the one they were now discussing.

Storey was still looking at the photos. "I don't like asking my men to do things I don't do myself," he said. "I could ask the guys at Phoenix or Bagram to do it, but it's only forty-five minutes away from here, and I need to go to Phoenix anyway. We'll go. It's easier."

He turned to Thollen, standing next to him with Randall. "Isn't that right, Staff Sergeant?"

Thollen nodded. "Yes, sir. We lead from the front here. It's a slightly different way of doing things, but it works well in this environment."

The lieutenant colonel had swung quickly into action after his discussion with his boss about the possibility of launching a rescue operation. Her emailed photo and comments about the likely media and political storm if Johnson died had clearly done the trick, Jayne thought.

Using satellite photographs, Storey had quickly identified the property where Johnson's tracker device was located: a building on a plot just off the Kabul-Nangarhar highway.

He had then requested a set of high-definition aerial photographs from his counterpart at Bagram Airfield, just outside Kabul, who had sent a Chinook overhead with a cameraman on board. He had also sourced some ground shots of the property from another senior officer he knew well in Kabul, who had arranged a drive-by of the property. Jayne was impressed that the pictures had been emailed to him within an hour and a half.

"Can you give me a photo of your friend Joe?" Storey asked. "Headquarters is asking for one, for the record."

Jayne emailed him a picture of Johnson that she had on her phone, taken on their previous operation together in Northern Ireland.

"If you're going in there, what's the risk to Joe?" Jayne asked. "Won't the Russians hear the choppers and maybe do something stupid?"

"You'd be surprised," Storey said. "The Black Hawks are fairly quiet, and quick, and there's so many choppers over Kabul anyway people don't even notice them anymore. We'll be in there before they realize it. Don't worry. We're trained for this type of operation—we rescued a journalist who was kidnapped by the Taliban from a similar compound six months ago."

Storey paused. "The only possible hiccup is whether the general gives the plan the green light. He needs to sign it off."

Jayne nodded. "Will you get it?"

The lieutenant colonel shrugged. "I think so. I'm also informing the US embassy. I don't want them complaining that they haven't been kept in the loop. And I need to get an all-clear from the Afghan army HQ as well. Should be a formality."

"As long as it's kept quiet from the bloody media," Jayne said. "The last thing we want if we're carrying out an investigation is a ton of TV and press coverage."

"I'll do my best," Storey said.

"And I'd like to come on the chopper too," Jayne said. "That okay?" She felt that she should definitely be on hand to help exfiltrate Johnson from the building in Kabul.

Three other staff officers who were working at a desk in the corner turned round and glanced at Jayne, clearly surprised at her request.

Storey hesitated. "It's not normal for us to allow civilians on such operations."

"I've done this sort of thing several times before on MI6 operations. Joe and I are looking for evidence on Severinov, and I don't want to miss anything critical."

Storey pressed his lips together. "Okay, I guess I'll make an exception. I don't want you with us when we're breaching the building, though. There might be a firefight, and I don't want to take responsibility for you taking a bullet."

Jayne nodded. "That's fine."

"Good. We're aiming to get the birds in the air within the next hour. I don't want to waste any time. You're fortunate that the Taliban seem to have gone a little quiet over the past twenty-four hours. It's given us a small window where we can spare some resources. So, just to warn you, if something blows up here and we need the choppers, we'll have to scrap the rescue operation."

* * *

Monday, June 3, 2013
  Kabul

Severinov spat on the floor in front of Johnson and wiped his mouth. "You will have to stay here for the next couple of weeks at least while I'm doing my negotiating."

He decided it would be amusing to play with the American's head by giving a slight hint of what his plans were without revealing his full hand. There was the obvious possibility that Washington wouldn't play ball and agree to a prisoner exchange for Andrei Fedorov, so he didn't want to put himself in a position where it might appear his scheme had failed, especially if word of that filtered through to Putin. No, he would keep it to himself for as long as possible.

"If I were you, I'd behave. Both of my friends here"—he indicated with his thumb toward Vasily and his security chief Ivan Lvov, who had also joined them—"have been given full authority to shoot you dead if you try anything that's going to cause a problem. Do you understand?"

Johnson said nothing, and Severinov walked out of the basement room where he was incarcerated, followed by Vasily and Lvov, who locked the door carefully.

What Severinov really wanted was to give Johnson some of the same treatment he had handed out to Baz in Wazrar prior to his death. The thought of using his truncheon on Johnson's shins and hands was quite appealing. *Stings for the*

Motherland. But he knew that inflicting that kind of damage on the American could wreck his chances of exchanging him.

Severinov led the way back up the stairs and into a room that had been set up as a rudimentary kitchen. He had taken every precaution to check for surveillance on the journey back to the house from Wazrar and was fairly satisfied that his tactic of bribing his way through every checkpoint by offering as much money as it took had ensured that the Ford Ranger's details and plate number had gone unrecorded by the Afghan police. But he couldn't be certain—all it would take for the whole thing to go disastrously wrong would be one officer who decided for the hell of it to insert his details into the system, despite pocketing the cash.

So therefore, the best thing would be to get the rented Ford Ranger back to the rental office as quickly as possible, thus giving him deniability. If it all blew up, he would simply blame Lvov. Severinov needed to get back to Moscow immediately for a Besoi Energy executive committee meeting scheduled for later that day.

The biggest problem was he had made no further headway with his plans to take revenge on Javed. The guy had vanished out in the mountains east of Wazrar, and Lvov had seen no sign of him in Kabul at the address on Street Ten that was listed on his CV. If he didn't show up there, it wasn't immediately obvious how Severinov was going to track him down. But he was confident he would find a way; if nothing else, their paths would inevitably cross if they both continued to play a part in the oil and gas investment process. But for the next few days at least, he would have to put Vasily and Lvov in charge of the search.

Severinov had gone to a lot of trouble to ensure that there was nothing in the safe house that could be linked to him, including destroying the framed Stalin quote that had been on the wall. Even Vasily and Lvov only had burner phones. He had also told Lvov to leave his passport and other identification documents in an underfloor cavity in the Sherpur apartment, where they were unlikely to be found.

As a safeguard, Severinov instructed Vasily to remain at the Sherpur apartment, where he could act as a backup in case something went wrong at the safe house and could call in periodically to check everything. The two properties were only a twenty-five minute drive apart, and Vasily could use another pickup that was garaged at the apartment.

Severinov returned to another room where he had stored his belongings and threw them into a travel bag, then walked through to the kitchen to speak to Lvov. He instructed him to contact the crew of his Bombardier jet, which was parked at the airport, and tell them to prepare for takeoff within the next hour.

"I'm out of here," Severinov said to Lvov. "You've only got one task here, and that's to keep Johnson and the Pakistani under close guard and safe. If you can manage that until I close down the operation, there's a big bonus in it for you."

He turned to Vasily. "You need to call in at least twice a day and check that things are okay. And in between, you need to keep a close check on the Street Ten address."

The big Russian nodded.

"I don't know why you don't just shoot those two worthless idiots and throw them in the river," Lvov said, indicating downstairs with his thumb. "What possible use are they to you now?"

Severinov had decided not to confide in either man the details of his prisoner exchange plans for Johnson. The fewer people who knew about his intentions the better.

"Just do as I say," Severinov said.

"Yes, boss, no problem," Lvov replied with a sigh.

Severinov picked up the keys of the Ford and beckoned to

Vasily. "I'll drop you back at Sherpur on my way to the airport. Come on." The two men headed out the door.

* * *

Monday, June 3, 2013
  Kabul

At just before six o'clock, Javed was ready to head back to the apartment block. He had three RPGs and a tubular steel launcher in a large backpack hidden under a tarp in the back of his Toyota Hilux, while his Browning was stuck in his belt.

Before leaving, he checked that Severinov's phone was still at his target site. The blue dot on the map was reassuringly stationary.

This time, he chose a longer route that took him in a loop north of the airport through a series of backstreets and rat runs and back down toward the apartment block, thereby approaching it from the north, not the south as he had previously. It was a route guaranteed to avoid security roadblocks.

Forty minutes later he was edging down Tajikan Road, which led into Russia Road. Quite appropriate, Javed thought, as he then turned left a couple of blocks north of the Kabul-Nangarhar highway, did another set of stair-step turns onto the highway, and continued eastward until he reached his destination.

He pulled into the same alley he had used before, across the road from the apartment block, and paused for a few moments. This felt like the old days all over again: him against the Russians. More than twenty-five years since the death of his wife and young daughter, he would finally have his opportunity for revenge.

The street was quiet, but Javed spent a few moments

carefully double-checking that nobody was watching him. Then he took the backpack from beneath the tarp and walked the few meters to the staircase that led up the side of the apartment block. He climbed to the roof, which was deserted. The washing that had hung on the line earlier had been removed, and the bicycles had disappeared from beneath the small shelter.

He placed the rucksack up against one of the poles that supported the laundry line and walked to the edge of the roof, from where he had a clear view down into the yard surrounding the house below. This was going to work perfectly.

Javed retreated back beneath the shelter, concealing himself as best he could. He took the launcher, the optical sight, and one of the green missiles with its black warhead from his rucksack and clamped the sight onto the launcher. Then he crouched and, holding the launcher upright, inserted the missile, twisting it counterclockwise until it locked into place.

He shuffled to the edge of the flat roof, took up position, and carefully studied the building below. The best option seemed to be to try to aim at the largest window at the rear of the property, which faced toward him and to which he had a good line of sight. He guessed that the chances of him getting the missile on target and through the window were no more than fifty-fifty, but it gave him a focal point. He lowered himself into a prone position; there was no cover on the flat roof, so he figured that lying down would make him as invisible as possible to anyone glancing up from below.

He moved the safety switch on the trigger housing to off and rested the launcher on his right shoulder, holding the barrel grip with his left hand and steadying himself by planting his elbows on the concrete roof surface.

Carefully, Javed pressed down with his right thumb on the

hammer lever behind the trigger so it was fully cocked, then settled down and applied his right eye to the shield at the back of the telescopic sight, which he lined up on the exact center of the window. From this distance the window almost filled the frame.

Javed moved his right index finger onto the trigger and consciously slowed his breathing in order to keep the weapon as steady as possible. It all took him back to the '80s, when he had gone through this routine almost daily from the mountainsides and gorges up and down the Khost-Gardez Pass, aiming at Russian armored vehicles and tanks.

Slowly, inexorably, keeping as still as he could, he began to pull his finger back on the trigger.

There was a loud metallic click as the hammer pinged into the firing pin. But instead of the expected whoosh and large puff of smoke as the missile screamed away, nothing happened. The booster didn't ignite, and the missile remained in the launcher.

"*Shit,*" Javed said.

He recocked the hammer, eased himself back into his firing position, and took aim again. Gradually his finger pulled the trigger backward. Another loud click as the hammer was released, but again, the same result. It misfired for a second time.

Javed swore again. He raised himself to a seated position and flicked the safety back on, then checked that the round was properly seated in the launcher. It appeared to be, but something had caused the misfires. He slowly removed the round and checked the firing pin. There was a clear mark on it, so the hammer had definitely struck home both times. Perhaps the fault was with the round and he should try another one.

He pulled the rucksack toward him and was about to remove another warhead when from below there came the sound of a diesel engine starting. He looked up to see the gray pickup moving toward the black gates of the compound, which were swinging open.

At that point, Javed stiffened and swore out loud again. Was Severinov in the vehicle or still in the house? He fumbled in his pocket and took out his phone to check the location of the tracker device, almost dropping it in his rush.

As the Ranger accelerated out of the gate and onto the street, the blue dot appeared on the map on his screen. It was moving steadily away from his location. Javed looked skyward and silently cursed long and hard in his native Pashto.

He decided he would just have to sit and wait until Severinov returned and then hit him in the pickup as he came back through the gates.

But Javed watched for the next ten minutes as the blue dot moved along the Kabul-Nangarhar highway, then cut northwest toward the airport. Soon afterward it came to a halt about three and a half kilometers northwest of his current spot—at Kabul International Airport. He sat upright in alarm.

Now what? Is he fleeing? Should I head to the airport?

While he was trying to think through his options, there came the rhythmic clattering of helicopter engines. He had heard them taking off from Camp Phoenix, and now he watched as two choppers approached his location from the west, flying at no more than a couple of hundred feet above the industrial units. As it drew nearer, the engine noise vibrated in his ears.

Initially, Javed thought nothing of the spectacle. They were probably heading to Bagram.

But then the two aircraft slowed and began to hover low at the western side of Severinov's property.

The large rear door of the first chopper was open, and inside, Javed could clearly see four men, all dressed in combat gear. Three were standing next to the right side of the door, and a fourth, holding a rifle, was on the left. Behind them was a woman.

A few seconds later, the first helicopter, which Javed could now see was a Black Hawk with US Army markings, began to descend slowly and precisely and, to his astonishment, landed gently right in the center of the walled site, its nose pointing toward the house.

Through the large cloud of dust that was being thrown up by the downdraft from the first chopper's rotor blades, Javed saw the three men on the right side jump out and run swiftly toward the house. One man was carrying a sledgehammer and what looked like a circular box; the other two had rifles. The man in the door of the chopper was covering them with his rifle while the woman watched.

The second chopper landed in the road to the left of Severinov's property, and eight men jumped out, all carrying rifles. They spread out, four in each direction, around the perimeter of the site.

Javed's first instinct had been to remain still where he was. But now he grabbed the RPG launcher and his rucksack and ran underneath the only cover available, the small bicycle shelter on the far side of the roof, where he flattened himself to the ground. He hoped he hadn't been seen.

CHAPTER TWENTY-TWO

Monday, June 3, 2013
Kabul

Storey jumped to the ground from the Black Hawk and, screwing up his eyes to avoid the dust cloud billowing up from the chopper's downdraft, set off toward the house in the corner of the compound, with Thollen and Randall close behind.

He had carried out this kind of operation countless times in training, both in the US and in Afghanistan, and the skills and movements required now came as easily as dribbling a basketball, which until a few years ago had been his main sporting preoccupation back home in Charleston, South Carolina.

Once the green light for the mission had come back from the US general's office in Kabul as well as Afghan army head-quarters, Storey, Thollen, and Randall had quickly devised a plan based on the ground shots and aerial photographs of the target site received from Bagram. Now they needed to put it into practice.

The three men ran up to the dark wooden door facing out into the yard. While Storey, holding his M4 assault rifle and with an M9 pistol at his hip, stood to one side and directed operations, Randall placed a reel of detonator cord on the floor and positioned himself to swing at the door with the sledgehammer. Thollen covered the other two men with his rifle.

After four blows, the door, which looked rock solid, showed no sign of giving way.

"Blast it open," Storey shouted.

Randall unclipped a Ulisliding knot cord detonator from his belt and hooked it over the doorknob. Then he slid the two knots, to which were taped a two-inch-square piece of C4 explosive, upward so the charge was snugly tight around the underside of the knob.

This was Storey's preferred method of breaking through a firmly locked door on a target building. An explosive charge had the advantage of stunning whoever was in the room behind, giving him immediate control. There was a slight risk that Johnson might be in that room, but long experience told Storey that was highly unlikely—captives were almost invariably kept under lock and key in some other remote room, not near the main exit.

Randall picked up the reel of detonating cord, connected it, and ran it around the side of the building, where he attached a small shock tube initiator. The three men moved around the corner so they were all out of line of the planned explosion, and Randall pressed the button.

Instantaneously, despite the raucous thudding of the Black Hawk's engines behind him, they heard a loud blast. Storey indicated to Thollen to go first. The staff sergeant, holding his rifle ready, led the way around to the door, closely followed by the others.

The solid wooden door was now lying flat on the floor, the frame splintered and broken where the door had been blown inward.

There on the floor, down a hallway fifteen feet from the entrance, was a blond-haired man who was unsteadily hauling himself to his feet. He was holding a pistol in his right hand, a cell phone in his left.

"Drop it! Drop the weapon! Place your hands above your head!" Thollen screamed, pointing his M4 straight at the man.

But the man either didn't hear or understand, or he had been disoriented by the blast, or maybe he even decided to take a chance. Either way, he turned as he rose, pistol still in hand.

Thollen pulled the trigger, hitting the man in the chest and sending him flying back to the floor. His pistol fell from his hand and skittered across the tiled floor, and his head crunched hard on the tiles. Then he lay motionless.

"Let's check this way first," Storey shouted. He ran down the corridor to the first door.

"Joe, you in there?" Storey yelled. There was no response so he gestured to Randall, who kicked it open. The room behind was empty, as were the other two rooms leading off the corridor.

"Downstairs next," Storey said. "Go slowly and bring your sledgehammer, Sergeant."

After stepping outside to pick up his sledgehammer, Randall followed Thollen down the stairs into a basement corridor, Storey close behind.

"Joe, you there?" Thollen shouted. This time there was a muffled but audible shout back from behind one of the doors. "In here. I'm in here."

Randall moved forward and tried the door handle, but it was locked. He raised the sledgehammer to waist high and swung it hard at the lock. After two blows, the door smashed open, thudding back against the wall behind it, and there, standing at the far end of the room, was Joe Johnson.

* * *

Monday, June 3, 2013
Kabul

"The bird has flown, buddy," Storey said. "The only guy in the building is the stiff down the corridor. Ivan Lvov is his name, according to the name engraved on the back of his watch. Obviously Russian." He indicated toward Lvov's body, which was lying faceup.

Johnson didn't bother asking who had shot Lvov. But thankful as he and Haroon were to be released, it was a blow that their rescuers had not managed to find and detain Severinov.

"I do, however, have your chick Jayne on the chopper," Storey said, with half a grin. "She's been worried about you."

"Thanks, but she's not my 'chick,'" Johnson said.

"Could have fooled me," Storey said. "She's spent more time staring at that GPS tracker app on her phone, watching where you are, than my daughter back home spends on Instagram."

"Listen," said Johnson, pointedly ignoring Storey's army banter, "I could at least do with some proof that Severinov's been here. I'd like to nail the bastard for kidnapping, for starters. I don't know what his plan is, but he talked about some sort of negotiations."

"We'll have a quick look, but we need to get out of here as

quickly as possible," Storey said. "That chopper sitting out in the yard is a magnet for any Taliban with a grenade or an RPG."

"What are you going to do with him?" Haroon asked, pointing at Lvov's body.

"The guys at Camp Phoenix will come over and work it out with the Afghan army," Storey said. "There's a big operation going on right now against the Taliban, so it may be the morning before they get here. They'll deal with the police as well."

Johnson raised his eyebrows. "That's the normal routine, is it?" he asked.

Storey shrugged. "We don't have a normal routine. It's the best we can do under the circumstances, like so much of our work." He turned to Thollen. "Come on, we'll do a quick search, but frankly, the place looks completely clean." They headed down the corridor, stepping over Lvov's body, toward the other rooms.

Johnson looked around. He knew Storey was right. There was virtually nothing in the building apart from a few kitchen appliances, chairs, TV, blankets, and tables. There was food in the fridge and kitchen cupboards, but no papers, books, or personal belongings. The print hanging on the wall with the Stalin quote was gone.

Johnson had to give Severinov credit: for a wealthy Russian oligarch, he seemed very disciplined when it came to operational security and processes. He obviously hadn't forgotten his KGB background and training.

While Storey and Thollen were searching the rooms, Johnson and Haroon walked over to Lvov's body, which was still bleeding heavily from a bullet entry wound in his chest and a bigger exit one in his back. Johnson removed the cell phone from the Russian's hand then went through his pockets, where he found a black leather wallet containing a wad of bills but no credit cards. There was no passport or other identification document.

The phone was unlocked and had a number showing on the screen—perhaps Lvov had been about to call it when he had been shot, Johnson surmised. He flicked through the phone's contents. The number on display was the only one saved, an Afghan cell phone to which two calls had been made, and there were no messages. A burner. He pocketed it anyway; presumably the number stored was Severinov's.

Storey came back down the corridor. "The only thing we found is this," he said, holding up a plastic bag, which he put on the kitchen table. From it he removed two phones, two SIM cards, a Beretta and an H&K pistol, and two leather wallets, one black, one brown. They were Johnson's and Haroon's belongings.

"Thanks," Johnson said, as he and Haroon picked up their phones, pistols, and wallets. "That's saved us a lot of trouble."

"Other than that, there's nothing," Storey said. "Come on, let's move." He led the way out the door, followed by Johnson, Haroon, and Thollen.

From his basement room, Johnson had heard the helicopter outside but had assumed it was just another military chopper on a routine patrol. He was surprised when he had suddenly been liberated, and now, looking at the Black Hawk in the yard, was even more astonished at the precision with which the pilot had positioned the aircraft in such a tight landing area. There were no more than ten yards of space on each side between the walls enclosing the compound and the whirling rotor blades.

As they walked toward the chopper, Johnson saw Jayne jump out of the large rear door and come running over toward them, gesturing toward a block of apartments that stood nearby.

Rather than greeting Johnson with relief at seeing him

safe, as he had been expecting, she instead shouted, "There was a guy up on the roof of that building with what looked like some kind of gun or missile launcher!" She pointed at the apartments. "I spotted him while you were entering the building. I thought at first it was an RPG, but he was some distance away. Can't be sure."

"Is he still there?" Storey asked.

"I saw him move, don't know where to. Your guy has been covering the roof since I saw him," Jayne said, indicating toward the door of the helicopter, where a soldier stood with his rifle trained on the building.

Storey studied the roof carefully. "I can't see anybody up there now," he said, glancing at Jayne with a slightly skeptical look in his eye. "Must have gone, whoever they were. We'll keep a close eye when we take off, though, just in case. Thollen can give us some cover."

* * *

Monday, June 3, 2013
　Moscow

"*Dermo.* Take everything on him and get out. Now, Vasily," Severinov said. "Just check around first that there's nothing that can be linked to me."

"What? Just leave him?" Vasily asked. "He's lying in a pool of blood."

"Yes. Leave him where he is and go. Someone will find him eventually."

This was a disaster, Severinov thought to himself. Johnson and Haroon gone and Lvov shot dead in the safe house.

Severinov heard Vasily swear on the other end of the line from Kabul and decided to ram the message home, just in case. "If I find that you've done anything other than what I've just instructed, you'll go straight in the Kabul River next time I'm in town."

"Okay, boss, understood."

"And find another safe house. We can't go back to that one. You know what to do. Just make sure there's enough ground space for a chopper."

"Yes, sure," Vasily said. "I'll get something arranged as soon as I can."

"Good. Now, move. Quickly—the police are probably on the way there already. And get yourself over to Street Ten. You need to be keeping a watch for Javed there. That's your priority now."

"Yes. Although it's late now, and I'm concerned about the Taliban risk and—"

"Just get on with it," Severinov snapped. He had no time for Vasily's lily-livered concerns right now. He ended the call and swore violently.

Vasily had turned up at the safe house at half past ten in the evening on one of his routine checks and had immediately called Severinov after discovering what had happened.

Who the hell could have done it?

Severinov was as certain as he could be that nobody knew Johnson was in there. He was also certain that nobody could have traced the building back to him. He had initially doubted it was the American security forces, thinking they wouldn't just leave a dead body in the building. But when Vasily had described how the door to the building had been professionally blown in, he had started to wonder.

Either way, one thing was for sure: his plan to exchange Johnson for Andrei Fedorov had just gone out the window. That in itself was a major blow, given Putin's instructions to find a solution to the Fedorov problem he was facing. There was no other option open to Severinov.

But the other question was, how did this leave the bid for the oil and gas assets? Could he still continue? Severinov tried to think it through. In many ways, he didn't have an option. Putin and Medvedev had given their instructions, and if he didn't follow them through to the letter, he was screwed. So in that respect he had little, or even nothing, to lose by continuing.

And if Johnson and the Pakistani Haroon went public with allegations of kidnapping, they surely had no proof. There were no links to him. He could just dismiss it as another American plot to derail a Russian bid. The media had heard that kind of thing all before.

In any case, Johnson and Haroon somehow had to be responsible for the death of Lvov—there was little doubt about that. So raising their heads above the parapet would be a dangerous route to go down. The more Severinov thought about it, the more confident he was that he could ride this out.

Severinov also knew he needed to continue pursuing Javed. But Vasily had made no progress. So the best chance of achieving that was for him to get back to Kabul and to look for an opportunity as the bid process unfolded. What had happened was a setback, but he would continue.

CHAPTER TWENTY-THREE

Tuesday, June 4, 2013
Kabul

Johnson awoke in his and Jayne's villa at just after eight o'clock. He'd managed nine hours' sleep, three more than he usually needed. The first thing he did was to reach for his phone and send a text message to Peter and Carrie, giving them a quick update and telling them he was safely back in Kabul after his trip. He omitted all details of his kidnap, incarceration, and rescue. They would find out once he got home—at least the sanitized version.

After pressing send, he lay listening to the hum of the city outside and let his mind chew over the events of the previous couple of days in Wazrar and subsequently at the hands of Severinov.

His prime focus was on how he was going to pull together a war crimes case against Severinov; he was well aware that if he succeeded, it would by default deliver a large slice of what his paymaster Rice wanted.

The scraps of intelligence he had picked up left him with the clear conviction that he had to get to the root of the current conflict between Severinov and Javed. What exactly had gone on between them twenty-five years earlier?

Achieving that depended on either meeting Javed and getting him to talk—and he was struggling with that—or on finding some documentary evidence. The latter also seemed unlikely.

What to do? He reminded himself of a favorite saying often used by his old boss at the OSI, Mickey Ralph. *Never die wondering, my friend.*

He would continue pursuing Javed, who was his number one option, but it seemed worth trying to trace the KHAD archivist whom Haroon had spoken about, Abdul Akbari.

There had been no word from any of the three passport forgers they had seen the previous Friday. Haroon had received no calls, no emails, and no text messages. Johnson's strong gut feeling was that none of them would voluntarily offer up what he needed. Maybe an encouragement other than just cash would be required.

Johnson slid his legs out of bed and looked out the window. His driver, Omar, had piloted the Hilux back from Wazrar the previous night, and the vehicle now stood outside the villa.

The thought of Omar gave him an idea.

When Haroon turned up at the villa at just after ten o'clock, Johnson made him a coffee and sat him down with Jayne in the living room.

"What do you think our chances are of getting whichever forger did the job to talk?" Johnson asked.

Haroon shrugged. "They're a sly bunch of men who you're always going to struggle to pin down. Don't know—maybe fifty-fifty."

"Well, how about we try to tilt the odds a little in our favor, then?" Johnson asked.

"How?"

"Coercion," Johnson said. "Take Din Khan. I don't know if you noticed, but just before he came to talk to you at the shop, he handed a customer a brown envelope and very quickly stuffed the cash for it into a drawer. Never gave a receipt. The customer left very quickly. I'm pretty sure Mr. Khan was doing some kind of under-the-counter deal."

"So what are you suggesting, Joe?" Jayne asked.

"I'm thinking we try setting him up. A bit of old-fashioned blackmail."

"Wait a minute, Joe," Haroon said. "You think one of us can go and set him up just a few days after we asked him for a favor? Is that a good idea?"

"No, not one of us. I was thinking of using Omar. Din doesn't know him. So what about if he goes in, says that he's looking for someone to provide him with a passport, say a Canadian one, and does Din know anyone who might be able to help. Then we just see what happens. We can get Omar to record it on his phone. Then if he bites, we'll have audio of him offering to do something illegal, and—if necessary—we threaten to shop him to the NDS, unless he gives us what we want."

"But you do not know that Din is the one who did the passport for Akbari, do you?"

Johnson grinned. "No, I don't know that. But I'm fairly certain that Ali Jadoon was telling the truth when he said his machinery was broken down and he couldn't do the job for Akbari. It could have been Gul Shah, but I have a gut feeling Din might be the one. It's just one of my hunches. If it turns out not to be him, then we'll try the same trick on Jadoon. Listen, we've got to do something. Time's running out, and we can't just sit here on our hands vaguely hoping something's going to happen."

The former ISI man nodded.

Johnson called Omar's cell phone and explained what he had in mind, then instructed him to come to the villa as soon as possible. Omar, exhausted after his journey back from Wazrar, was less than enthusiastic initially but agreed after Johnson promised him an extra four thousand afghanis.

Before launching into his plan, Johnson first got Omar to drive him to Street Ten to do yet another check on Javed's house. But the property was still clearly unoccupied, and there was a gathering of street litter that had blown up against the double vehicle entrance gates—plastic wrappers, bottles, old newspapers, and other detritus—suggesting nobody had come in or out recently. Nothing had changed. Where was the man staying? Johnson wondered. He was increasingly coming to the conclusion that Javed must have another base somewhere in the city, perhaps with one of his old mujahideen friends.

An hour later, Omar, now fully briefed, set off on his mission, while Johnson settled down at the kitchen table with Jayne to try to work out a way forward and then give Rice an update on their progress.

He opened his laptop and checked his emails. The top one was from Javed, replying to the email he had sent the previous Thursday. *At last*, Johnson thought, as he hurriedly clicked on it.

Hello Joe, it was good to hear from you after such a long time. Interesting that you are back in Kabul. I would indeed like to meet you again at some stage. There is a lot to discuss. However, as you have no doubt discovered, I am managing the Afghan government's sale of a stake in its oil and gas assets. I'm busy and it will be impossible to meet until the

process is finished. I will get back in touch next week. There is much to talk about. With both Russians and Americans among the possible investors, we are in strange times. You might be extremely interested in the identities of some of the parties, but I can tell you much more when we meet.
Best wishes
Javed Hasrat

"Shit," Johnson said. He showed the email to Jayne. "Just had this from our friend Javed. What do you make of that?" Johnson asked.

Jayne also read through it. "He's dangling a carrot, but if he won't meet up it's hardly helpful."

"Not surprising he doesn't want to meet if he's trying to take out Severinov."

"Can't argue with you about that."

"This is how I remember Javed," Johnson said. "Always teasing with the promise of some big slice of crucial information—which then always seemed to be snatched from under my nose. Like that photograph of Watson with the Stingers."

"Yes," Jayne said. "At school we used to have a name for girls who were like him—prick teasers, we used to call them."

Johnson laughed out loud. "An intelligence officer's nightmare. I'll ask him again for a meeting, but if he's refusing, we'll have to put a tail on him."

He began to tap out a reply.

* * *

Tuesday, June 4, 2013
Kabul

. . .

There was silence for several seconds. Then came the low-pitched, inevitable tirade. "You bastard son of a mule," Din Khan muttered, his black eyes glittering first at Johnson, then at Haroon, from beneath a ragged mess of eyebrows. "You're trying to blackmail me?"

"No," Haroon said. "We're not *trying* to blackmail you. We *are* blackmailing you."

Johnson had to fight hard not to smirk. He turned off the voice recorder app on his phone, on which he had just played a copy of the recording made by Omar earlier that day.

"Play it again," Din said, planting his elbows on the shop countertop. "You can't prove that's me, you human cesspit."

Johnson wearily pressed the play button again, and the recording, faint but completely audible, began to run, with Omar's voice coming first, speaking Pashto.

"Mr. Khan?"
"Yes, that's me. How can I help you?"
"I understand that you might be able to help with travel arrangements overseas. Specifically passports and visas."
"It depends on your requirements."
"I need a Canadian passport and visa, but I've had huge problems with their embassy over the past two years. I desperately need to get to Toronto to—"
"It doesn't matter what you want it for. I don't need a story."
"So it is something you could help with, then?"
"Like I said, it depends. I would need you to go through my vetting process before I could discuss it much further. That could take a couple of days."

There came the sound of rustling and a slight thud, which Johnson knew was the point at which Omar had taken out an envelope full of afghanis and placed it on the counter.

"Is there an express option at all? I'm in a real hurry."

There was the sound of more rustling, presumably as Din opened the envelope and counted the bills.

"Write down on this form the personal details of the passport holder and fill in as much as you can. Date of birth, place of birth, all that. I will need photographs, of course. I can't promise anything, though. It will depend on how the vetting goes. I don't know you at all, so I'll need some references. So put them on the form as well, and don't lie. I'll be checking all of it. There is a cost, of course."
"What are the prices?"

There was a pause of several seconds.

"For a digital and machine-readable, good-quality Canadian? I don't know. Probably 250,000, maybe 300,000, approximately. It might be more. That would depend on the vetting though. I would confirm afterward if you check out 100 percent."

The conversation had continued for a few more minutes, but Johnson turned off the app and just looked at Din. "Is that enough? You don't think that sounds like you?" he asked.

Din threw up his hands in a gesture that smacked of surrender. "So what do you two snakes want?" he asked, eyeballing Haroon.

Haroon stared back at him. "You know what we asked for last week. Abdul Akbari. You were going to check in your old ledger. Have you checked?"

It was obvious to Johnson that the answer was no.

Din said nothing but walked to the back of his store and disappeared behind a curtain.

"Are we just going to let him go?" Johnson said.

"I don't think he will run away," Haroon said. "Just wait and see."

They stood there for another ten minutes. The heat in the shop was stifling, hardly made more tolerable by the four-foot fans suspended from the ceiling that turned at a snail's pace. There was nobody else in sight, either staff or customers. This was the most old-fashioned of shops, even by Kabul standards.

"Three hundred thousand afghanis for a Canadian passport," Johnson said. "That's what? About four thousand dollars?"

"Yes, probably ten years' income for most people here," Haroon said. "It's a limited market."

Finally, Din returned, carrying a cardboard-backed notebook whose cover was dog-eared and split. He put it down on the counter and opened it halfway through, then flipped over a few yellowing pages and ran his finger down a column. Then he looked up at Johnson, his eyes still at boiling point.

"So, what have you got?" Haroon asked.

"It's here. Abdul Akbari."

"Yes. What passport and where for?" Johnson asked.

"It was 1989. A French passport. And an Afghan passport."

"Two? And in what name?"

Din pointed to a line in the ledger. Johnson leaned over to look. In the first column, written in a spidery hand, it said Abdul Akbari. In the second it said France and Afghanistan. In the third was the name Abbas Ahman.

He looked up at Din. "Abbas Ahman. That's the name the passports were issued under?"

Din nodded.

Johnson looked at the ledger with a growing feeling of disbelief. "So, you keep a written record of every fake passport you have issued?" he asked, taking his phone from his pocket.

This would be dynamite for any intelligence agency.

Din scowled and jabbed his finger into the pages of the ledger. "Are you stupid? This is my insurance. If a customer tries to screw me, I can screw them."

From Din's point of view, it obviously made sense. If his customers found out, they might be less understanding. Johnson nodded to Din. "Thank you for cooperating. If what you have told me turns out to be incorrect, we will be back."

Johnson lifted his phone and snapped a photograph of the page in the ledger, then took another one of Din himself.

"What are you doing?" Din said, raising his voice. "Delete those photos. That's private. Did you hear me?"

"That's *my* insurance," Johnson said.

As the two men exited the shop, Johnson turned to Haroon. "France. That confirms what Ali Jadoon told us," he murmured. "I'm going to ask Vic to check this out."

CHAPTER TWENTY-FOUR

Wednesday, June 5, 2013
Brooklyn, New York

Watson turned his chair, looked down at Zilleman's laptop and sipped his glass of sauvignon blanc as the speech began on the screen. Across the wine bar table, Zilleman also focused on the main speaker, the US secretary of state, Paul Farrar, as the cameras zoomed in on him. Flanking him at the lectern was the Silverson Renwick chief executive, Richard Lorenzo.

The bar, 7 Old Fulton, a few yards from the Brooklyn Bridge, was a meeting place they had used a couple of times, years earlier. It was across the road from a furnished apartment Watson had taken on a two-week vacation rental, using his Dirk Leman cover name, after leaving his rented house just outside DC.

While a Yankees baseball game continued behind them on a television built into an ornate wooden frame above the bar, the two men hunched over the laptop, focusing instead on live coverage from the international security conference in Delhi.

Watson had to be careful about visiting places where he might be recognized. But he gauged it highly unlikely that he would be remembered here.

Watson had moved to New York partly because Zilleman was basing himself there for a week for meetings with investors and partly because he wanted to minimize his time in DC, where the likelihood of bumping into ex-colleagues was far greater.

The two men had spent the previous three hours in Watson's apartment poring over spreadsheets detailing projected costs for oil field development in the hydrocarbon blocks in northern Afghanistan being sold by the Kabul government. They had moved to the wine bar in order to relax a little and to listen to Farrar's speech.

The secretary of state and Lorenzo were delivering a joint address on Afghanistan that spanned business and political issues.

"Both Richard and I traveled here last night from Kabul. And I would like to reiterate, as our president has made clear, that America will complete its mission in Afghanistan, which has the key objective of defeating the core of Al-Qaeda," Farrar said, looking around at his audience. "We're committed to helping build a self-standing, unified, and sovereign Afghanistan.

"The message I gave to President Hamid Karzai at our meeting yesterday is that we intend to increasingly give the Afghan security forces more of a role in their own country. We will step back and take more of a support function, helping train the Afghan army and delivering counterterrorism measures to drive out the remnants of Al-Qaeda. That will allow us to bring thousands of our troops home. But we will need to maintain some presence to continue to support our Afghani allies. That will be important, and it is something I will be pushing for in negotiations.

"Beyond the security and military function, energy will also be a key part of Afghanistan's security—it can help provide independence in financial and business terms as well as just keep the lights on. Isn't that right, Richard?"

The secretary of state gestured with his right hand toward Lorenzo, who stepped up to the microphone.

"Thank you, Mr. Secretary," Lorenzo said. "I have been spending increasing amounts of time in Afghanistan as we step up our presence, and I can say that we are encouraged that the Afghan government is bringing private investment into its oil and gas production industry.

"However, it needs to be done in the right way so that Afghanistan maximizes the opportunity and brings in the right expertise—and that it does not allow the wrong influences to gain a foothold in the country. American and European energy companies, several of whom are clients of Silverson Renwick, are ready to ensure that happens."

There were loud cheers from some members of the audience, clearly audible over the laptop sound feed. The camera panned around the auditorium as one man yelled, "Keep Putin out!"

On the platform, Farrar looked up. "I'm making no comment, but I'm sure you know what my stance is on that."

There were more loud cheers. Watson glanced at Zilleman, who had a faint smile on his face. "Good messages," Watson said. "Let's hope Kabul is watching."

Zilleman nodded as Lorenzo continued.

"If Afghanistan can successfully develop its estimated 1.6 billion barrels of oil reserves and 15.7 trillion cubic feet of natural gas, that will utterly transform the country's energy and economic prospects. They may not be huge reserves when you compare them with, say, Iraq's 115 billion barrels of oil, but for Afghanistan, it is potentially a big deal, believe me."

Farrar stepped forward once more to conclude the address. "My message to the Kabul government today is: do the right thing, but more importantly, do it with the right people. Thank you for listening, and have a good day."

Zilleman looked around. The bar was filling up, and people were now sitting at the table next to them, whereas the place had been far quieter when they had arrived. He turned the laptop off and put it into his bag, drained the remains of his wine, and stood. "Come on, let's walk and talk. There are a few things we need to discuss."

Watson nodded and also finished his wine. He glanced up at the old clock with Roman numerals hanging from the paneled ceiling. It was nearly half past three. They walked past the crowd of afternoon drinkers huddled around the polished mahogany tables and continued through the twin half-glazed wooden doors into an open-air patio area sheltered by two huge trees. Old Fulton Street was busy with the usual crowd of tourists.

Watson took off his nonprescription tortoiseshell glasses and replaced them with a pair of sunglasses. The two men turned right, following the path beneath the high stone arches and soaring steel beams of the Brooklyn Bridge. The skyscrapers of the dramatic Manhattan skyline were laid out ahead of them across the other side of the East River.

After following the footpath round the grassy oval of Empire Fulton Ferry State Park, Watson casually looked around him, his right hand shielding his eyes from the sun like a tourist. There was no sign of any surveillance, not that he had expected it. Then he led the way to a long bench on some wooden decking next to the river, the bridge now on their left. They sat down.

"The only thing that still bothers me," Zilleman said, "is what we were discussing last time: the risk of our friend's cover being blown, but also, what if someone latches onto the fact that you're advising ZenForce and your background comes out?"

"This was all twenty-five years ago," Watson said. "There's nothing documented that would incriminate any of us. It was all paper-free at our end of the operation. The only slight risk back then was that the KGB files got into the wrong hands amid the chaos as the Soviets pulled out of Afghanistan. But when the withdrawal happened, all the files were incinerated. We've had that confirmed by moles in the Kremlin."

"Not that you could be incriminated any more than you are already," Zilleman said.

"No. You're right there," Watson said with a grimace. "Although having said that . . . " He let his voice trail away.

"Is there any word from your NDS contact on whether he's managed to track down Johnson?" Zilleman asked.

"Burhani? No. I've heard nothing from him in the past few days, which is a little worrying."

Zilleman scratched his chin. "Let's hope he comes up with something. We need to have a final meeting between the three of us to finally decide whether to go ahead with this bid, though, and at what level. I'm a little nervous."

"Agreed," Watson said. "I hope he can meet here—that's better for all of us."

* * *

Wednesday, June 5, 2013
  Kabul

. . .

The paper trail had been longer and more convoluted than Vic Walter had expected. The man calling himself Abbas Ahman and using a false French passport in that name had indeed moved from Kabul to Paris in 1989, he explained to Johnson.

"Is he still in France?" Johnson asked over the encrypted cell phone link. He had the phone on loudspeaker so that Jayne and Haroon, who were sitting next to him in the villa in Kabul, could join in the conversation where necessary.

"No," Vic said. "He spent a short period there, then he used the French passport to enter Canada, where he applied for political asylum. While that process was going on, he was able to stay in Quebec."

"And he's there now?" Johnson asked as he stirred some sugar into his tea. He pushed the sugar across the table to Jayne when he had finished.

Vic gave a sardonic laugh. "No. From Quebec, six months later, it seems he used a fake birth certificate to obtain a legitimate Canadian passport, which he then used to enter the US."

"Birth certificates are such weak documents," Jayne said.

"Yes, useless," Vic said. "No photos, no fingerprints. Anyway, when he was in the States, he applied for asylum and got it, eventually. We don't know how he persuaded the authorities. To the best of our knowledge, he's still living in the US and has been since about 1993."

There was a pause as Johnson digested the detail. "So where is he now?"

"We don't know yet. Don't worry, we'll track him down. The Canadian passport was in the same name, Abbas Ahman, and so was the US asylum."

"So he's gotten past three different immigration authorities," Johnson said.

"Clearly his fake passports and birth certificate were very good," Vic said.

Haroon leaned forward. "He's ex-KHAD and KGB-trained. Doubtless very good at maintaining a cover story under pressure, and I'd guess he knew what to do to minimize the chances of being pulled over in immigration queues. He was a complete professional. That's why I spent so much effort and took so much risk trying to recruit the worthless bastard. What a waste of time that was."

"It was obviously easier then to get through the immigration system with fake documents than it is now," Haroon added, "although it's still far too doable."

He was right, Johnson thought. Machine-readable passports, 9/11, global terror. All had combined to make things more difficult for those seeking to completely change their identity and their country. But not impossible.

Johnson shook his head. "I can't wait to find out what he's been doing in the States for the past couple of decades."

"Probably working in the White House or something," Jayne said. She grinned.

Vic didn't laugh. "It's actually worrisome that our people are not on top of this."

"Yes, well, don't raise it with your superiors yet, will you, buddy," Johnson said. "I don't want anyone sticking their nose into Akbari's situation until I've properly checked him out. And I'm not optimistic about this. The fact that he's in the US probably means he's going to be a dud, from my point of view. The likelihood that he took any old files out of Kabul, to France, and then to Quebec, and then to the States, is going to be—"

"Somewhere between zero and outer space," Vic interrupted. "Yes, unfortunately you're right. But don't worry, I'll keep our wolf pack away from his door until you've been there. Now we just need to track him down. I've got one of my guys on the case—he's good, so I think it's only a matter of time."

* * *

Wednesday, June 5, 2013
  Kabul

Javed looked up on hearing the knock at his office door to find that Safia Joya had opened it and walked in without waiting to be invited. Her lack of manners and condescending air were just two of the things that annoyed him about the deputy minister of mines and petroleum.

On top of that, he had returned to work that morning to find that someone had been in his office while he was away. A couple of the documents in his filing cabinet were in different folders. Safia was the only other person he knew of who had a key to his office.

"I hope you had a productive break, Kushan," Safia said, then continued without waiting for him to answer. "I also hope you're going to be ready for Thursday next week?"

The final presentations to the ministry team from potential investors in the oil and gas blocks were due to take place that day. The outcome depended on bidders making intelligent proposals for development of the blocks, maximizing the advantage to the Afghan state and its people, and at the right price.

"I'm ready, of course," Javed said. He deftly toggled his laptop screen away from an email from Joe Johnson that he was about to respond to and switched to a financial spreadsheet. "I'm looking forward to it. I think we should get a good outcome. There's a lot of interest—European, American, and of course the Russians."

Safia placed a folder of documents, marked Attention Kushan Mangal, on his desk. "I've had a few questions from the investment bankers representing a couple of other potential bidders. They're in the folder there. Would you be able to get answers from the team downstairs and reply?"

Javed picked up the folder and flicked through the print-outs, which were all from Safia's emails. Although highly intelligent, she was notorious for asking her secretary to print out all her emails rather than answering them on her own PC, which Javed found laughable. He suspected it was purely to demonstrate her ranking and power inside the department and not because of any inability to use technology.

"Sure, I'll answer them. Do you want me to send the answers back to your secretary, and then she can email the people back?"

"Yes, that would be helpful. Thank you."

She turned to leave.

"Oh, by the way," Javed said. "Did you come into my office while I was away? Some of my documents in the filing cabinet weren't as I left them."

Safia turned abruptly and did something of a double take. "I—well, yes, I did actually. I was looking for one of the investment bank analyst's notes on the sector, which I knew you had. I did find it. Hope you don't mind?" she said.

Javed shrugged. "Okay, no problem." He turned back to his laptop, and Safia continued out the door.

He switched his screen back to Johnson's email.

Hello Javed, yes I knew what your role is. I think I know the Russian you're referring to. Your old friend Mr. S? I have something I urgently need to discuss with you about him but not in an email. I would also like to know about the American investors you're referring to. Can we meet before your investment process is complete? I am now back in Kabul so

*can see you anytime—name your time and place and I will
aim to fit in. Please do give me a call on the number below.
Regards, Joe.*

At the bottom of the email Johnson had included his cell
phone number.

Javed gave a thin smile at the reference to Severinov.
Johnson *was* on the Russian's tail, then. That was good in
some ways, but Johnson would definitely be looking to prosecute, not kill. It confirmed in Javed's mind that any meeting
with Johnson would have to be after the deed he had planned
for Severinov was done, not before.

He wrote a quick reply to Johnson, reiterating that he was
going to be busy for several days and would get in touch.

After Javed had sent the email, he turned back to a web
page he had been scrutinizing, which showed the flight path
into Kabul International Airport for aircraft approaching to
land from the east. It went almost directly above the building
on which he had been positioned for his abortive RPG attack
on Severinov's property. He knew that was the case because
he had seen aircraft passing overhead while waiting on the
rooftop, but he had wanted to confirm it by checking the
actual airport documentation.

Javed leaned back in his chair and pursed his lips. The
rooftop was in actual fact perfectly positioned for an alternative attempt at Severinov—the next time the Russian flew
into Kabul. That would be when he would deploy not an
RPG but a Stinger missile.

He was confident that his old mujahideen friend
Mahmood, in air traffic control at the airport, would be able
to tell him well in advance when either of Severinov's planes
were heading into Kabul. Javed had provided Mahmood with
the registration details for the jets, and his role in the
Afghanistan Civil Aviation Authority, which had to approve

all flights into and out of the country's airspace, gave him access to all aircraft flight plans.

Surely the Russian's charmed life was about to end. He had somehow evaded two attempts using the RPGs. It would have to be third time lucky with the heavy artillery.

PART FOUR

CHAPTER TWENTY-FIVE

Thursday, June 6, 2013
Kabul

The encrypted text message from Vic was short and to the point.

"This is your man," it said.

Attached to the message was a screenshot from a website belonging to the South and Central Asian Studies Institute in New York City. The screenshot showed a photograph of a wiry-looking bald man with a straggly white beard and a pair of black-rimmed glasses. Underneath, it said, "Head of Research: A. Ahman."

"Well, damn me," Johnson said. He glanced across at Haroon, who was sitting on the sofa opposite. "Come and see this. Abdul Akbari, also known as Abbas Ahman, appears to be alive and well and living in New York City. Is this the same guy you remember?"

Haroon stood and came to look over Johnson's shoulder

at the photograph on the phone screen. "Don't know. It does look like him. His beard's gone white; it used to be black. He still looks thin as a rake."

"Vic says it's him," Johnson said. "So I'm trusting Vic. He's rarely wrong. The only thing that bothers me is that we could be just wasting our time."

"Because you think he won't have the files?" Haroon asked.

"That's one thing. To pin anything on Severinov, whether in court or in the media, we'll need some sort of documentary proof. Journalists won't write a story savaging a billionaire oligarch without evidence."

"You mean you're not going to bother going to New York to see this guy simply because you don't think he's got the documents you need?"

"Even if he did have them, I doubt he'll suddenly turn informer," Johnson said.

"You don't know that, Joe," Jayne said from her chair at the dining table, where she was working on her laptop.

"If he was going to be turned by the Agency or any other Western intelligence outfit, he would surely have done so years ago when he needed the money," Johnson said. "Haroon had a go at him in the '80s and got nowhere. I'm fairly certain that someone at the Agency must have done as well—it wasn't me, obviously, but I bet someone tried. And he must have had other approaches. He was a prime target—someone in his position, in charge of the entire Afghanistan KGB archive. I mean, he's probably very comfortable working as an academic by now."

Haroon and Jayne said nothing.

"I'm wondering if it might be better to stay here and concentrate on pinning Javed down," Johnson said.

"We need to do both," Haroon said.

Johnson paced up and down the room, struggling to decide. The Pakistani had a point. "Okay," he said eventually, turning to face Haroon. "I'll go to New York. You're right. The chance of meeting Akbari is too good to pass up. But—"

"While you're chasing Akbari," Jayne interrupted, "I'll stay here with Haroon and focus on Javed and Severinov. We know Severinov's back in Moscow, and we can redouble our efforts to tail Javed."

"You might need to dust off your street skills, then," Johnson said. "Try following him from his office. I'm just concerned about the security risks, though."

Jayne glanced at Haroon and grimaced. "Yes, that should be fun, with the Taliban all over Kabul looking for the next Westerner to kidnap—or blow up. But I can't see any other option. Don't worry, we'll be fine."

* * *

Thursday, June 6, 2013
Moscow

Severinov glanced out the tenth-floor window of the skyscraper office block at 42 Shchepkin Street toward the gleaming steel facade of the nearby Olympic Stadium. Then he turned to face the three other men in the meeting room.

He had been summoned by Mikhail Sobchak at three hours' notice to the board room of Russia's Ministry of Energy for a meeting with Medvedev, the energy minister Alexander Novak, and—once again, to his horror—Vladimir Putin.

Severinov had only once before seen Putin in the energy ministry headquarters—despite it being only a fifteen-minute drive from the Kremlin—and that was in 2008, not long after the ministry was formed under the leadership of Medvedev. Energy in Afghanistan, or more likely the wider strategic thinking behind it, was clearly rocketing up the president's list of priorities.

As soon as Sobchak made the request, Severinov had a rough idea of what might be on the agenda. They had made that clear enough at the previous meeting. He had asked Sobchak if he could bring along his corporate communications director to add his perspective and advice to the discussion, but the request was immediately refused. "The leadership wants to tell you what to do, not have a debate about it," Sobchak had said.

Yet again, as at Severinov's previous encounter with him at Medvedev's *dacha*, it was Putin who did most of the talking.

"We want you to deliver the message that Russia is excited to take part in a whole range of construction projects in Afghanistan," Putin said, calmly sipping from a glass of chilled water. "Oil and gas are obviously some of those— that's your key message—and backing that up, you will state that Russia is supporting and is ready to take part in the investment project to build a natural gas pipeline running from Turkmenistan, via Afghanistan, to Pakistan and India."

"Yes, I understand the importance of that," Severinov said.

"Yes, but there's more," Putin went on. "We want you to also mention that Russia is ready to make heavy investments in highways, especially the Salang Tunnel, hydroelectric projects, railways, and housing. Also civil aviation and construction."

Severinov exhaled. "My only question would be whether I'm the right man to deliver this. I'll be quite frank with you:

if I get grilled on all that at the meeting, I'm going to be out of my depth. It's not my expertise. It might be better for me just to stick to the oil and gas project, which I know well. I can touch on the pipeline too, of course."

Putin scrutinized him with a pair of ice-blue eyes, his face muscles motionless. "You are nothing but the advance messenger, Yuri. The warm-up act. Your job is to plant the seed so we get some media coverage that reflects our intention to try to create a kind of new warmth between Russia and Afghanistan. Then, further down the line, when you have sealed the deal for the oil and gas assets—note that I said *when*, and not *if*—I will travel to Kabul and sign the agreement. It will be at that point we will really make a big show of our wider plans."

Medvedev leaned forward, his elbows planted on the polished boardroom table. "Your presentation is next Thursday, correct?"

"Yes, Thursday, in Kabul," Severinov said.

"I will wish you good luck. Not that you will need it. And I will see you back in Moscow for a debriefing session, probably on the Saturday. Is that understood?"

"Yes, that's clear. Thank you."

Medvedev exchanged glances with Putin, and as if they were communicating telepathically, they rose as one. Medvedev nodded at Severinov, while Putin's face remained impassive. They both shook Severinov's hand in a perfunctory manner and left the room without a further word.

When Severinov received the call to the ministry that morning, he had somehow been hoping that the entire project might be canceled and he would not need to go through with it. No such luck. Now the pressure was significantly greater, if anything.

Severinov stood and walked to an anteroom, where his

personal assistant Zinaida was waiting. Looking serious, she stepped forward as soon as Severinov poked his head around the door. "Yuri, I've just had a call from IT about your phone. They found a GPS tracker device built into the battery."

Before he had left for the boardroom meeting, Severinov had left his main phone with his head of IT and security at his Besoi Energy offices, a three-minute drive away on Gilyarovskogo Street, in an area between the Botanical Gardens and the Olympic Stadium. The issues Severinov had been experiencing with poor battery life seemed to have been getting worse, and after returning from Kabul, he had decided to get the device checked out.

"That's why it was draining quickly," Zinaida continued. "They're replacing it immediately, of course, but they wanted you to know. It will be fixed by the time we're back to the office."

"A tracker? *Dermo*." Severinov immediately tried to think when the device had last been out of his possession. He kept it almost permanently in his pocket or in his hand, apart from when he was sleeping or bathing.

The only time he could think of was when he had attended a briefing at the Afghanistan Ministry of Mines and Petroleum, and he recalled being irritated because to remove phones on the basis that confidential information was being discussed seemed unnecessary.

"It's got to be that bastard Javed," Severinov muttered. He kicked at the leg of a coffee table that stood near the door, causing it to lurch some distance across the hard wooden floor. Maybe that was how the Afghan had managed to evade being caught in the Sulaiman Mountains.

It was time to get heavy. He needed to speak to Vasily. Before beginning their ultimately abortive and fatal operation in Afghanistan, Vasily had sent him details of the other five members of his Spetsnaz team. Perhaps he should bring them in now.

* * *

Thursday, June 6, 2013
  Kabul

Javed refreshed the map on his laptop screen for the fifth time. But still the small blue dot that had previously been showing at a location in Moscow was not there.

He was certain the tracker in Severinov's phone wouldn't have failed. They were very reliable. The only conclusion was that it had been discovered and disabled.

Javed swore and toggled the screen over to the second device, implanted into the cardboard spine of Severinov's prospectus file for the oil and gas investment project.

That, thankfully, was still operational and was showing up at the same location as it had been previously, at a large residential property near the Moscow River.

Javed was completely certain that Severinov would bring the prospectus along for his key presentation to the minister because it contained all the vital and confidential financial projections the project team at the Ministry of Mines and Petroleum in Kabul had supplied to the serious bidders. He would need to refer to the numbers frequently.

So Javed could at least still keep some track of Severinov's movements, albeit not as effectively as if the cell phone device had continued to operate.

Javed's only concern—a major one—was that if the phone tracker had been found, then Severinov would most likely not take long to work out where it had come from and who had installed it.

But what was he going to do about it, and could he prove it? It was certain he wouldn't pull out of the presentation, because the stakes were too high. And he also wouldn't be able to prove Javed's involvement. There was no forensic evidence of the tracker's origins: Javed was confident of that.

So hopefully, it might not make too much difference to the outcome Javed had planned.

CHAPTER TWENTY-SIX

Saturday, June 8, 2013
  New York City

The Turkish Airlines flight from Kabul should have taken about twenty-three hours. In the end, after delays with the connecting flight from Istanbul to New York's JFK airport, it took over thirty, arriving at after six on Saturday morning.

By ten past eleven, Johnson was sitting on a bench in Washington Square Park in Manhattan. About forty yards away, across the street that bordered the north side of the park, was the entrance to the South and Central Asian Studies Institute.

Johnson yawned and sipped the take-out double espresso Vic had just brought him from a nearby coffee shop. He still felt as though trekking to New York in the hope that an ex-KHAD man would be able to fit missing pieces into his jigsaw was overwhelmingly optimistic.

"What time does he finish work?" Johnson asked. He adjusted the Beretta M9 that Vic had given him, which he had stuffed into his belt and was concealed beneath a linen jacket.

"Don't know," Vic said. "He apparently doesn't usually work on Saturdays, but my guy tailed him here earlier this morning. Maybe he's just catching up on some work or something."

The caffeine started to seep through Johnson's veins, immediately making him feel better.

"You did well to trace him so quickly," Johnson said.

Vic shrugged. "It was easy once you got the alias. There's only a handful of Abbas Ahmans in the States. We eliminated the others very quickly and ended up with this one. His immigration records gave us all we needed. A lot of Afghan refugees came here around that time—about twenty-five or thirty thousand in the late '80s and early '90s."

"And he was one of the few illegals."

"Most were legit," Vic said.

Johnson adjusted his sunglasses. The summer sun was beating down, and the leaves of the trees in the park and along both sides of Washington Square North were already looking a little limp. A queue, consisting mainly of young students and a few kids with skateboards, had formed in front of a hot dog cart farther along the path.

A dog walker and three joggers passed along the path in front of their bench, and tourists were snapping photographs of each other. But Johnson kept his attention firmly on the five-story red-brick townhouse ahead of him, where the institute was based. Twelve red stone steps led up to a white-painted porticoed entrance with a black door.

"Should work in our favor that he's an illegal," Johnson said.

Vic glanced at him. "Gives us some leverage, definitely."

"I suggest we approach him here when he comes out of

his office, not tail him home, where he can slam the door on us."

"Agreed."

"Have you made any more headway on Zilleman's calls to burner phones?" Johnson asked.

"Some, in that there are a few of them, and they do keep changing, which is a red flag," Vic said. "I've asked the NSA team to now map exactly where the phones are that are being called. I've got a guy I've used before on this type of job working on it."

"Is that Alex Goode?" Johnson asked.

"Yes. You remember him, then. Steve's his boss. He's a bit of a wizard with this kind of thing."

"I do remember him," Johnson said. "He did the recordings of Watto's conversations last year on the Croatia job, didn't he?"

"Yes, he's the one. He's in New York at the moment. So hopefully we should get a result soon. It might be that although there's multiple phones, they're in the same locations. Then we might have something helpful."

At twenty past twelve, Johnson saw the door of the institute open, and out came a tall man with a white beard and black-rimmed glasses. He didn't need to nudge Vic, who was already picking up his bag from the ground.

As Vic had predicted, Akbari turned right in the direction of the Christopher Street subway station. Johnson and Vic headed toward the park gate at the intersection of Washington Square North and Waverly Place, arriving there thirty yards behind Akbari, who was on the other side of the street.

The two men had planned what they would do. They drew closer behind Akbari, who was walking slowly, a briefcase in his hand. When they got within five yards, Johnson called out softly. "Abdul Akbari."

The man paused in his stride momentarily but didn't turn, and then he continued.

Johnson waited until they had almost drawn level with him, then tried again, slightly louder this time. "Excuse me, are you Abdul Akbari? I think I recognize you."

This time, the man couldn't ignore him. He stopped dead and turned his head. "I'm sorry, I think you've got the wrong person," he said in clear but accented English.

"No, I don't think I have," Johnson said, fixing his gaze. "Abdul Akbari. Former KHAD and KGB archivist in Kabul. That's you, isn't it? Even if you use the name Abbas Ahman now."

Without waiting for him to answer, Johnson continued. "I'm Joe Johnson and this is Vic Walter. We're investigating two people in Afghanistan with whom I believe you've had contact in the past. We'd just like a quick word. There's nothing to be worried about."

The man scrutinized first Johnson, then Vic, his face devoid of any obvious emotion. After several seconds, he said, "I am Abbas Ahman, and I am originally from Afghanistan, you have got that part right. But that is all. I am not Abdul Akbari."

"I know that's not correct," Johnson said.

"When I lived in Kabul I was a photographer. I didn't work for the KHAD. Who are you?"

"I'm an independent investigator," Johnson said. "Listen. We know your background. But I'm not interested in that right now. I'm interested in how you might be able to help me. Can we go for a chat somewhere quieter? Not your house. Maybe a coffee shop?"

Akbari peered at Johnson through his glasses, then at Vic, appearing to weigh his options. He glanced down at Johnson's waist. "Do you always carry a gun in public?" he asked.

It was Johnson's turn to be surprised. *This guy's sharp.*

"It's for self-protection," Johnson said.

"I'm not going to be any help to you," Akbari said. "I've been out of Afghanistan since the Russians pulled out. I came here carrying nothing more than the clothes I was wearing— like we all did. I'm an American citizen now. You can go to hell."

He turned and walked off.

CHAPTER TWENTY-SEVEN

Saturday, June 8, 2013
New York City

Akbari was halfway down the steps to the Christopher Street subway before Johnson finally got him to stop again by shoving his phone under his nose, showing the photograph of the ledger taken at Din Khan's shop.

"Remember Din Khan, the passport forger?" Johnson asked, continuing to hold up the photo as a stream of people barged past them up and down the steps. He had to raise his voice above the noise from the traffic passing the subway station.

"Din remembers you," Johnson continued. "So we can either have a sensible discussion, or we can call the FBI and the citizenship and immigration service right now and let them handle this. In which case you'll be going straight to jail or back to where you came from. You choose."

Akbari grabbed hold of the steel handrail on the steps as someone bumped him in the back, almost knocking him down. He recovered his balance and stared at the photo-graph. "This is a setup. That's not genuine, it's a—"

"Yes, it is," Johnson interrupted. "We've had a trace done. Din provided you with a French passport as well as a new Afghanistan one. You came here via France and Canada, also using a fake birth certificate."

Despite the revelations, Akbari's face remained marble-like, and he continued to eyeball Johnson. He finally shrugged and looked down at the ground. "What is this all about? Explain."

Five minutes later, the three men were sitting in a quiet corner of a coffee shop on Grove Street, near to the subway station.

Akbari sipped the latte that Johnson had just bought for him. "I'm not doing this. How do I know I can trust you?" he asked.

"You don't," Johnson replied, slowly swirling his double espresso around in the small china cup. It was thick and strong, the way he liked it. "But this is the way I do business when I need to, as I'm sure you might well have done when you worked for the KHAD. I might be wasting my time—you might not be able to help. But if you can, I'm prepared to do a trade, and so is he." He indicated with his thumb toward Vic, who nodded. "Anyway, you're going to have to trust me. Otherwise I call the USCIS, like I said."

Akbari said nothing but took another sip of his drink.

"You headed the whole archives operation in Kabul at that time, right?" Vic asked.

"Yes, I did. Look, what is it you need?"

"Information about two men. Possibly more," Johnson said. "People who I'm certain the KGB and the KHAD would have kept files on. One was a Russian, a former KGB officer, who I'm guessing might have even contributed to or written some of the files. The other is an Afghan, a mujahideen."

"Names?" Akbari asked, tapping the table with his fingers.

"The Russian, the KGB man, was Yuri Severinov. He worked in Kabul on military intelligence until the Soviets pulled out. The mujahideen was Javed Hasrat."

Akbari looked out the window, then took another sip of his coffee before carefully replacing the cup on his saucer. "Severinov? Yes, I was familiar with him. I didn't like him. He was in the office periodically, adding to or retrieving files. Arrogant man who thought he was above everyone else."

Johnson exchanged brief glances with Vic. That helped, if Akbari and Severinov didn't get on.

"And Javed?"

"The name sounds a little familiar, but I don't immediately recall him. There were so many mujahideen we had listed," Akbari said. "Anyway, why are you interested in these two?"

"Because they are still, today, continuing a personal conflict between them that was very bitter and which dates back to the 1980s. I need to find out why and what the background is to that."

"Why? I don't understand."

"I've got my reasons," Johnson said. "So what happened to all the KGB files in Kabul?" Johnson asked. "Do they still exist somewhere? I'd like to trace the ones on those two men if I can."

Akbari shook his head. "No, the KGB had everything incinerated before they left Afghanistan. There were no records left behind."

It was just as Johnson had been expecting, although he had somewhere inside him a vain, slight hope that the files might have been stashed away in a cache, a vault, a basement somewhere, maybe even taken back to the Kremlin.

"So there's no trace of any of them?"

Akbari shook his head. "Correct. All the original files went."

It took Johnson only a moment to realize the significance of what he had just heard. "What do you mean, the original files?"

"Like I told you, I was a photographer—an amateur when I was in Kabul. I still am."

"And?"

"And I photographed many of the important files."

* * *

Saturday, June 8, 2013
Hell's Kitchen, New York City

Johnson stood in the doorway as Akbari walked across the darkened living room of his third-floor apartment on West Forty-Sixth Street and began pulling four long maroon curtains open.

Behind him, Vic muttered, "This could be massive." He wandered off down the hallway.

Johnson nodded but didn't say anything. While Akbari was pulling the curtains back, Johnson could see out of the corner of his eye that Vic was poking his nose around the doors of the other rooms, which led off the hallway.

The three-bedroom apartment, on the corner of Tenth Avenue in the Hell's Kitchen neighborhood, was a mess of papers, books, and magazines. They were piled on the dining table, the coffee table, and nearly every other flat surface. Two dirty soup bowls and a half-empty whiskey bottle stood on another small table next to an aged leather armchair. One wall was covered entirely by bookshelves. It was an eccentric academic bachelor's pad.

"How long have you lived here?" Johnson asked, trying to distract Akbari while Vic finished his private look around.

"I moved here in 1998, two years after I got my job with the institute," Akbari said, tugging at one curtain that was sticking. "And I have stayed. The neighborhood has really improved since."

It doubtless had. Johnson had memories of Hell's Kitchen being a slightly rough area, full of laborers, factory workers, actors, and other bohemian types. The apartment, two long blocks and about a third of a mile from the Hudson to the west, was now of the type that Wall Street financiers were probably buying and modernizing.

Vic edged through the doorway behind Johnson.

Akbari turned and stood, legs slightly apart, scrutinizing them both. "Before we go any further, we need to agree on some ground rules," he said. "The tentacles of the SVR are long. They don't know I've got these copies, and they don't know where I went to, as far as I know. If they find out what I've done, then I'm likely to get a bullet in the back of the head or a nerve agent in my tea. So I'm putting myself on the line here—I need a guarantee you're not going to tell either the US immigration authorities or the SVR."

"I fully realize that," Johnson said. "I'm a private investigator. As far as I'm concerned, I'm getting some information from a private source. Nobody needs to know where it's coming from. I'm not here, if you know what I mean. You've got my word—and that's rock solid."

"Yes, well, the question is, do I trust your word? And what about him?" Akbari said, gesturing toward Vic.

"I'm not here either," Vic said. "If you decide you want me to be here, let's have a discussion then about how I approach it at Langley. For them, old KGB files would be of huge interest, as you can imagine, and there will be ways of getting the information to them safely. A deal can be done. But for now, I'm not here."

Akbari nodded. "We would need to do a deal for the package. I can give you a taste of them now."

"Yes, as an authenticity test," Vic said.

"So tell us more about the files," Johnson said. "You're saying you photographed them. Was that officially, for backup purposes, or unofficially, for your own reasons?"

Akbari looked away. "You don't need to know that," he said.

It was obviously unofficial, then.

"But you must have had a very good reason," Johnson said. "It must have been extremely risky. What if your KGB bosses found the films?"

Akbari clasped his hands behind his head and was silent for a few seconds. "It was my insurance," he said eventually. "It was in case they turned on me, like they did many others. I saw what happened to them, and I didn't want it to happen to me. And I made sure they wouldn't find them—I had ways."

"How many did you photograph?"

"Just the important ones. Those about senior politicians, public figures, senior army and security services people on all sides, police. Some KGB officers and some mujahideen. That was enough. It ran into a few thousand, though that was just a fraction of the entire files, of course. Most weren't worth bothering with."

"How did you get them out of Afghanistan?" Johnson asked.

"I was a photographer as well as an archivist," Akbari said. "I left the undeveloped films with a friend who smuggled them into Pakistan after the Russians had gone, and he parceled them up and sent them here, by post. They were labeled as photographic supplies."

"And you developed them here?"

"Yes. I have my own darkroom in one of the rooms," Akbari said, pointing down the hallway. "I've printed them, scanned and digitized them, and then also cataloged most of them. I've been thinking of writing a book, a history, of the KHAD and the KGB in Afghanistan, using them as source material. It would be interesting, a legacy, but I'd need a way of doing it anonymously, of course. Otherwise it would amount to a death warrant."

"Yes, anonymously might help," Johnson said, trying to visualize the explosive reaction in the Kremlin and the SVR headquarters at Yasenevo if and when this came to their attention. "If you've digitized them, can we search for the files I mentioned, about Severinov and Javed?"

Akbari nodded. "Let's treat that as your taster, your authenticity test."

He now seemed fully willing to cooperate. Quite a turn-around, Johnson thought. But then, the possibility of being returned to his native country with the loss of his prized Manhattan apartment and his cushy job doubtless would focus the mind.

The Afghan led the way to one of the bedrooms, which was fitted out as an office. He had a large monitor screen on the desk with a laptop connected to it. A few minutes later, having logged onto a photograph storage application, he typed the name "Javed Hasrat" into a search box. Thumbnail images of five documents appeared.

Johnson bent over and peered at the screen. The jpeg files showed documents closely typewritten in Russian, with dates all from 1988, serial numbers, and header titles.

"Let's have a look at them," Johnson said.

Akbari clicked on the first, and a document appeared at

full size. Johnson began to read down. He found his Russian, while rusty, was still good enough to understand the text.

189/JH/46 JAVED HASRAT
January 8, 1988 r.
Kabul
Information received from GOATHERD relating to Mi-24 mission on Wazrar village on January 2, 1988, tells us that Stinger missiles which destroyed two Mi-24 helicopters nearby were fired by mujahideen Javed Hasrat from a location approximately 1.6 kilometers away. Hasrat leads the mujahideen group in that area and is responsible for other fatal attacks on 40th Army targets in and around the Khost-Gardez Pass. We are therefore prioritizing intelligence efforts on him with the intention to eliminate him and his group as quickly as possible. GOATHERD reports that Stinger missiles used by Hasrat were supplied by ISI and CIA sources over the preceding eight months.

Johnson finished reading the memo. "Who was GOATHERD?"

Akbari shrugged. "Probably a mujahideen mole."

"So Javed was seen as a priority at that time?" Johnson asked.

"Yes. I'm remembering now," Akbari said. "Severinov, the KGB officer, brought in a few memos that went into the file about him. His office was near to mine, just down the road. That was the first of them. Let's have a look at the others."

He clicked on the second.

190/JH/46 JAVED HASRAT
January 12, 1988 r.
Kabul
GOATHERD has issued a warning about Javed Hasrat

following the Mi-24 incident in Wazrar on January 2, 1988.
Hasrat's wife and youngest daughter were killed in the Mi-24
operation on the village. Hasrat now reported to be seeking
intelligence about which KGB officers authorized the attack
(Yuri Severinov). Hasrat is now also identified as the
mujahideen who killed and mutilated surviving crew
members of the second Mi-24 that was successfully crash
landed following the Stinger attack.

Scribbled in the margin in black handwriting was a short additional note: *Cross-reference see 329/AS/21 YURI SEVERINOV.*

Johnson pointed to it. "What's that?" he asked Akbari.

"I had a cross-referencing system for linking different files if there was information in both that might be relevant to a particular incident, or case, or project," Akbari said. "That's one of those. There was a file on Severinov too, of course. We can look it up when we've finished going through Hasrat's files, if you like."

"Yes, definitely, we'll need to see that," Johnson said. "It looks as though Severinov must have signed off on the attack on Wazrar. His wife and daughter—that would partly explain why Javed is on his tail now." Without going into too much detail, he briefly outlined to Akbari the recent RPG attack on Severinov in Kabul.

"I can't overstate how strong the tradition of revenge is among the Pashtun," Akbari said. "Especially if it's a blood relative involved. I do recall this case. But you said partly explain. What else is there?"

"It was Severinov who captured Javed in Jalalabad in 1988 —just after a meeting with me, as it happens—and put him into Pul-e-Charkhi," Johnson said. "He was incredibly lucky to get out alive."

"Ah, of course," Akbari said. "I think that is referenced in one of these memos too. I recall it."

"Just a minute," Johnson said. "There's another one there about the Khost-Gardez incident. Can we see that?"

Akbari clicked on the next memo. "Ah, yes, this is a copy of an internal memo that was appended to Javed Hasrat's file and also, I see, Severinov's because of its relevance to both."

Johnson peered over Akbari's shoulder. The memo, dated January 12, 1988, was also written in Russian and had a subject line that read: "*Death of 2x Mil Mi-24 helicopter crews —Flight 19.*"

It was a detailed incident report about the attack by three Hind helicopters on Javed's home village of Wazrar and the subsequent shooting down by mujahideen of two of the three aircraft. It had been written by Captain Yegor Malevich, commanding officer of the 35th OVP Independent Helicopter Regiment, based in Jalalabad, to General Lieutenant Boris Gromov, Commander of the Soviet 40th Army, in Kabul. The report included the names of the deceased crews from the two helicopters that were destroyed and the flight times.

At the end of the memo was an addendum.

SUPPLEMENTARY INFORMATION RECEIVED:
At 15:45, Aircraft 3, supported by two other Mi-24s, returned with reinforcements and landed next to Aircraft 2. The pilot and weapons system officer discovered the mutilated bodies of the crew of Aircraft 2 ten meters from the remains of the helicopter. The bodies had been decapitated and the heads placed next to the torsos. The genitalia of the crew had been severed and placed in the mouths of the deceased crew. The mouths had then been stitched shut.
The bodies were retrieved and returned to Jalalabad Airfield.

In the margin next to the supplementary information paragraph, someone had scribbled in the same black handwriting as before: *Cross-reference see 331/AS/21 YURI SEVERINOV.*

"My God," Johnson said. "Sewing their balls in their mouths. Why the hell do they do that sort of thing?"

"Why did the American Indians scalp people?" Akbari asked in a dry tone.

Johnson shook his head. "We need to look at the cross-references. Can you get to them?"

"Yes, give me a minute," Akbari said. "The testicles thing was a common torture by some of the mujahideen if they captured a Russian soldier. They used to do it while they were still alive, then kill them afterward. But frankly, given what the Russians were doing to them, who could blame them. I'm not passing judgment."

Johnson snorted but said nothing.

Abkari typed in the reference numbers into the search box. But nothing came up. He tried again, this time checking carefully that he had the numbers typed correctly. But again, there was nothing.

"That's odd," Akbari said. He scratched his head. "It may be that document is among some I'm still cataloging. I do have quite a few more to do. I can check if you like."

"Yes, please," Johnson said. "That would be helpful."

"I think I know which document it is. There is some information in there that is sensitive—very sensitive—and I'll have to decide whether to give it to you or not. I'll have to get back to you when I've been through them."

Johnson nodded, his mind whirring. "Thanks. What else have you got in these archives?" he asked. "Are there files on any other big names?" He glanced over at Vic.

"Robert Watson, for instance," Vic said. "That might be interesting, if so."

"Robert Watson?"

"Yes, he was the CIA chief of station in Islamabad," Johnson said.

"I don't know. I'd have to look. You'd be surprised what's in here," Akbari said. "I think there's a few more items on Javed and Severinov. And then we'll move on to this Mr. Watson and any others. And I'm not talking about Russians or Afghans. I'm talking about Americans—there is some material on the CIA. Give me a bit of time and I'll see what I can find."

CHAPTER TWENTY-EIGHT

Saturday, June 8, 2013
  New York City

Johnson and Vic sat on a sofa beneath the window and waited while Akbari continued scrolling through his digitized copies of the photographs taken in a dark, dusty basement in Kabul two and a half decades earlier.

Not for the first time, Johnson had the feeling that his job was just like peeling back the layers from an onion until he got to the truth within. And how often had that truth been revealed inadvertently while looking for something else?

"Come, have a look," Akbari said eventually, beckoning at Johnson with a leathery-looking index finger. "There's some more material on Javed here."

Johnson got up and walked to Akbari's computer screen.

"It appears that these items were added to the file when Javed was captured by Severinov in Jalalabad—the incident you referred to earlier," Akbari said.

On the screen was another memo.

192/JH/46 JAVED HASRAT
February 11, 1988 r.
Jalalabad
Javed Hasrat arrested by Yuri Severinov at Nadrees Accoun-
tants premises near to Jalalabad airport, after Hasrat and
colleagues met two CIA officers who had entered the country
from Pakistan. CIA officers are known to be Joseph Johnson
and Victor Walter, based in Islamabad.
Hasrat was held overnight in Jalalabad then transported to
Pul-e-Charkhi for further interrogation.
Attempts to arrest Johnson and Walter failed.
Cross-reference see 193/JH/46 JAVED HASRAT for items
confiscated on arrest.
Update will follow.

Akbari turned to Johnson. "You obviously avoided the Pul-e-Charkhi experience, then?"

Johnson grimaced. It seemed slightly bizarre to be reading an account of his own near miss with the KGB so long ago, and he was surprised that the memo did not note why efforts to detain him and Vic had failed. In a life-or-death shoot-out in an abandoned warehouse near the Jalalabad meeting location he had shot the KGB officer pursuing them, Leonid Rostov. Only then had they been able to escape back over the border into Pakistan.

"Let's have a look at the cross-referenced document, the confiscated items," Johnson said.

Akbari turned back to his screen, entered the cross-reference number into his search box, and scrolled through the thumbnails. There was an identification document, a letter from a bank, and then a photograph.

This time, Johnson felt genuine shock when the image of the photograph popped up on-screen. It was a copy of the black-and-white print that Javed and Baz had shown to him and Vic in the Jalalabad meeting in 1988.

Behind him, Vic had also seen the image. "My God, it's that photograph again. Remember that one?" he asked, his voice rising sharply.

"*Remember* it?" Johnson replied. "I still dream about it."

The photograph showed Robert Watson and another Western man handing Stingers over to some mujahideen. Presumably, the KGB had taken the photograph from Javed when they had arrested him and had then put a copy of it into his file.

Now Johnson leaned closer to the screen, focusing on the second man, a taller bearded figure standing behind Watson.

When he originally saw the photograph, Johnson had recognized the man. He was from a company called Kay Associates and had visited Watson at the CIA's Islamabad station. But Johnson hadn't found out his name.

Now, as he peered at Akbari's monitor screen, Johnson realized he recognized the man again—but not from his distant memories. The muscular shoulders and the thickset build were familiar.

Who the hell?

After a couple of seconds, Johnson remembered. He had seen another similar image of the same man very recently. It was in a profile article he had been reading in *Newsweek* magazine only a week and a half earlier on the flight to Kabul.

Kurt Donnerstein.

There was no doubt in Johnson's mind. The pieces all clicked together. Watson must have been working with Donnerstein privately to sell Stinger missiles to the mujahideen. The CIA's official routes for supplying the missiles had all been funneled through Pakistan's ISI, in line with the strict instructions from General Zia, the then president.

"Just a minute, keep that photograph on-screen. I need to get something," Johnson said. He walked to his backpack, which he'd dumped on the floor, and unzipped it. Tucked inside his spiral-bound notebook was the issue of *Newsweek*.

Johnson opened it to the profile of the US secretary of energy. There were three photographs. One showed him sitting next to Barack Obama at a White House dinner, deep in conversation. Another portrayed him giving a speech to a global energy industry conference in London. And the third, a much older one, depicted him as a young man with a beard sitting in a seaside bar, drinking a beer.

It was the third one that confirmed it. Johnson walked back over to Akbari and showed him and Vic the photograph in the magazine.

"Look at that guy in the background," Johnson said, pointing to Akbari's computer screen. "That's the same man as in this picture, isn't it?"

"*Shit!* Donnerstein. It's him," Vic said.

"They do look similar," Akbari said.

"Definitely Kurt Donnerstein, the man from Kay Associates," Johnson said. "Is there any file on Donnerstein?"

Akbari tapped the name into his search box, but nothing came up. "There's no cross-reference in the file."

"What about Watson? There must have been something on him."

"Give me a minute."

Akbari went back to the search box and typed in Watson's name. A few seconds later he had the image of another file on-screen.

Johnson peered over his shoulder and scanned down the text. It was all routine material outlining Watson's background and postings prior to Islamabad. "Go on, next one," he said.

The next typewritten document looked more relevant.

HIGHLY CONFIDENTIAL — TOP SECRET
376/RW/85 ROBERT WATSON
February 18, 1988 r.
Islamabad
Information received from agent TENOR at meeting with
Yuri Severinov in Islamabad. CIA is conducting review of
supply of Stinger missiles supplied to mujahideen, including
numbers already supplied and register of recipients. TENOR
is passing on these details. This gives an opportunity to target
the relevant mujahideen. CIA review is being conducted by
Joseph Johnson, officer at CIA Islamabad station, according
to TENOR.

"TENOR?" Vic said, tapping Johnson repeatedly on the shoulder. "Joe, do you remember? That was the code name written on the back of the photo of Watson we saw in Jalalabad. TENOR must be Watson, then, surely."

"Damn right I remember," Johnson said. "It's got to be him. It adds up. If Watson was on the KGB payroll at that time, it might explain how the bastards knew about our meeting in Jalalabad with Javed."

Vic nodded. "He tried to give us a death sentence. Nearly succeeded."

"There's another one here about Watson," Akbari said. He indicated to the screen.

377/RW/85 ROBERT WATSON
February 19, 1988 r.
Islamabad
Routine surveillance of TENOR observed him in meeting
with representative of US company Kay Associates at
Marriott Hotel. Checking identity overnight and will
confirm.

Johnson read down the short entry. "That Kay Associates rep will be Donnerstein. Is there anything that actually confirms his identity?"

Akbari scrolled down the memos below and then did a search. "No, strangely not, that's it. There's nothing more in the file about that."

"That seems odd."

"Yes, it does, although it was about that time, when the Soviets were pulling out of Afghanistan, that the KGB simply stopped making proper notes of everything. The files started getting a little thin."

Johnson shrugged. "Maybe, although that sounds unlike the KGB. But we would need copies of these files, if possible. Can I copy them onto a memory stick?"

"No," Akbari said. "I've got no control over where they go after that, have I? I'm going to be worried enough about the SVR catching up with me. You'll have to make notes if you want certain details, at least for now. I'll email you a copy of the photograph, though."

"Okay, but can I just get a photo of it on-screen as well?" Johnson said, taking out his phone. He didn't want to run the risk of an email going astray.

Akbari sighed and clicked back to the image of Watson, Donnerstein, and the Stingers, which Johnson snapped on his phone camera.

"Thanks," Johnson said. "But are you 100 percent sure there's nothing more confirming Donnerstein's identity? It said in the file that checks were being made overnight."

Akbari frowned. "There was nothing I could see." He glanced at his watch. "It's very late now. But let me do another more in-depth search tomorrow and see if anything comes up."

"Yes, please, if you can," Johnson said. "It's very important."

There was a headshake from Akbari. "It may be among the items I'm still cataloging, but I'm not hopeful. I will let you know."

* * *

Saturday, June 8, 2013
  Brooklyn, New York

Watson was not in a good mood. The day had gotten off to a good start when he had succeeded in extricating the funds stashed in his savings accounts and dispatched them electronically to an intermediary account in the Bahamas. But then he had received a text message from Mohammed Burhani in Kabul telling him there was still no progress with attempts to locate Joe Johnson, and furthermore, as he was now traveling to Pakistan for the next four days for meetings with his counterpart in Islamabad, he was putting the search on hold.

Typical goddamned amateurs, working asshole fashion as usual, Watson thought to himself.

Instead, Watson turned his attention back to an issue he had spent the previous two days mulling over: potential meeting places for the ZenForce team. It was a headache. It was essential that all three of them got together to finally decide whether to go ahead with the bid, as well as the price level if so, and to all confirm verbally they were agreed on the details, sealing it with a handshake in the absence of written documents they could sign. It was standard policy among them, given the massive amounts that were being invested. They also needed to similarly shake on details in the bid presentation and the accompanying document, which Zilleman would take to Kabul and present to the minister.

Watson's strong instinct, given the risks to himself and to

EIGER, was to meet in New York, which was more anonymous than Washington.

After decades of working for the CIA, he had a number of suitable covert meeting locations on a private list that hadn't been shared with others at the Agency. But after going through them, he decided that the best option was the vacation apartment where he was staying. It was at 8 Old Fulton Street in Brooklyn, across the street from the wine bar where he had met Zilleman the previous Wednesday.

The apartment block was an old building, originally the Brooklyn City Railroad Company headquarters, that had been converted. But because of its antiquated design, it had a myriad of external fire escapes, flat roofs, and other potential exit routes—a useful feature, if required. It overlooked Brooklyn Bridge Park just across the street, which was a strip of green parkland that ran next to the East River and beside the bridge.

The other advantage of the vacation apartment was that it had excellent access to nearby transit routes—by rail, road, and water—which was why he had chosen it. The Brooklyn Bridge and the Manhattan Bridge both gave options to get onto Manhattan Island by car or on foot. There were three subway stations and also ferry services from a pier next to the bridge, just a few yards from the apartment. The Brooklyn-Queens Expressway, Interstate 278, allowed rapid access by car to the south via Staten Island and the New Jersey Turnpike.

Watson had parked his rental car, an anonymous gray Volkswagen Golf, about 150 yards away, up Doughty Street on the corner of McKenny Street. The parking location had been chosen very carefully, and he had been forced to wait for two hours to secure a space there.

Watson went through the list of sites again but came to the same conclusion. The apartment would be the best option for the meeting, he was sure. The problem would be getting everyone available and in one place at the same time, particularly EIGER, who was always busy.

He took out his new burner phone and sent a short text message to the new cell phones acquired recently by Zilleman and EIGER. It read:

Need to make final decisions etc. Suggest 40.702684, -73.996108. Monday 17.12.

It was an old habit of Watson's to never arrange covert meetings on the hour or the half hour; picking odd times made it less obvious and less predictable for anyone who had him under surveillance. Similarly, he wouldn't send precise address details until the last minute but rather used coordinates that indicated the rough location. Ten minutes later, and somewhat to Watson's surprise, because it normally took much longer to get a response, a reply came back from EIGER.

Yes can make that. In area for meetings.

Zilleman was the last one to confirm, but he asked for a one-hour delay.

Seeing investors 17.00. Can make 18.12.

Given the tortuous processes Watson had been through on previous occasions trying to agree on meeting times and locations between the three of them, this was pain-free.

He texted back to confirm that 18.12 was fine.

CHAPTER TWENTY-NINE

Saturday, June 8, 2013
New York City

"Akbari's just a sideshow. I'm not pursuing him," Johnson said. "He's earned his keep just by giving us this stuff. But we badly need some more on Donnerstein out of those files."

"He didn't seem hopeful," Vic said.

"No, but let's see what he comes up with."

The two men were heading along Ninth Avenue toward the Fiftieth Street subway station, having left Akbari to continue sifting through more files.

Vic's phone beeped in his hand as a text message arrived. He scrutinized the screen. "Sounds like Alex is making some progress. I think we should head over and see him."

"Did he say what he found?" Johnson asked.

"No. Just said he'd made some significant headway."

"Where is he?"

"TITANPOINTE," Vic said.

The name TITANPOINTE was the cryptonym given to

the monolithic, windowless skyscraper at 33 Thomas Street, Lower Manhattan, which was officially an AT&T telecoms building but was also a critical National Security Agency surveillance site. It specialized in tapping into and monitoring all types of electronic communications, from fixed line and cell phone calls to internet, email, social media, and text messages.

The security role of the TITANPOINTE building in Lower Manhattan was not publicly acknowledged by the NSA. But its output was of critical importance to many of those who worked for the Agency.

Three-quarters of an hour later, Johnson and Vic were sitting in a small first-floor meeting room of the brown granite-clad building with Alex Goode, a cell phone security expert and cryptographer. The sandy-haired NSA man, who looked to Johnson to be in his late thirties, was hunched over a laptop.

On the screen, a satellite map showed an area of countryside about fourteen miles east of Washington, DC, just south of the John Hanson Highway, near to Freeway Airport.

"Your man Zilleman appears to have been busy," Goode said. "He's made fifty-four calls and sent forty-three text messages over nine days. Some of them have been to cell phones that don't have monthly contracts—pay-as-you-go burner phones. But we've also been logging the location of these phones he's called." Goode stabbed at the map with his finger. "We've narrowed down three of them to this spot here."

He pointed to an area where there were six large houses visible on the satellite image, all set among large grounds. "Each phone was used from this location three or four times, then no more, all of them either very early in the morning, say five thirty or six o'clock, or late at night, after ten thirty.

After that, another similar burner was used three or four times before being seemingly discarded. And so on."

"Do you know who used them?" Johnson asked.

"Not 100 percent."

"But?"

Goode hesitated. "This is the interesting bit. You're focused on this because of Afghanistan, right?"

"Correct."

"I've checked the owners of all these properties, and there's only one who has any kind of obvious connection with Afghanistan," Goode said.

"Go on, who is it?" Johnson said.

"Kurt Donnerstein, the secretary of energy, who lives in this house here." Goode pointed to the largest of the six properties visible on the screen.

There was silence for a few seconds.

"Screw me," Vic said eventually.

"My sentiments exactly," Johnson said. "Zilleman and Donnerstein. What the hell are those two doing together?"

Goode gave a thin smile. "There's been no actual calls between these phones, just a few odd text messages. My team managed to capture some of the texts. Some of them went from Zilleman to the phones at this location and also to another phone that looks like a burner, located in different places around Manhattan and Brooklyn."

"Any idea who has that one?" Vic asked.

Goode shook his head. "No. I can't apply the same methodology to New York as I have here. There's too many people. But it's clearly someone linked to Zilleman and Donnerstein. You want to see the text messages we managed to capture?"

Johnson tugged at the old wound at the top of his right ear. "Yes, let's have a look—but who the hell is it in New York, then?"

Goode shrugged and toggled to another window that showed three different blocks of text. "These are the recent messages of any significance. The previous ones were just chitchat. You know, hello, how you doing, that kind of stuff. This first one is from the New York burner phone to the other two, Zilleman and Donnerstein—assuming it is Donnerstein."

Need to make final decisions etc. Suggest 40.702684, -73.996108. Monday 17.12.

Goode pointed to the next block. "This is from Donnerstein to the other two phones."

Yes can make that. In area for meetings.

"And this is the third one, with Zilleman replying to both phones."

Seeing investors 17.00. Can make 18.12.

Johnson leaned over the laptop screen. "Can I take a photo of those?"

"Yes, no problem," Goode said. Johnson snapped a photo of the screen with his phone.

"So it's a rendezvous point," Johnson said. "Where is it?"

Goode copied and pasted the coordinates from the text message into his map app. "I did this just earlier. It's right in the middle of Brooklyn Bridge Park, next to the bridge."

The map popped up on the screen, showing the location Goode was referring to, only about a mile and a quarter southeast of the TITANPOINTE building where they were seated, across the East River.

"In a park? That's an odd location. And what is Donnerstein doing with Zilleman?" Johnson asked, turning to Vic. "It's Afghanistan-related, clearly. Is he working with his investment fund? Advising them? Investing with them?"

Vic raised his hands, palms up, and shrugged. "No idea, buddy. That's what we need to find out. We're going to have to work with the Feebs on this. They'll have to do the manhandling, especially if Donnerstein's involved. I know Simon Dover at the CCRSB from way back. We'll talk to him first."

Johnson didn't need to be told that. It was the FBI's job to make any arrests, not the CIA's. Any investigation like this would be handled by the bureau's Criminal, Cyber, Response, and Services Branch, headed up by Dover, the FBI's executive assistant director. Vic had gotten to know Dover when the latter was a supervisor in the FBI's counterintelligence division in 2002 and in charge of various espionage investigations on which Vic had also worked. Despite the tendency for CIA and FBI officers to regard each other with disdain, the two had remained friends as they each rose up the ladder in their respective organizations.

"Prepare for a bomb to go off under Obama's desk," Johnson said. "This is going to be nuclear if Donnerstein's doing what it appears and it stacks up."

"You said it, man," Vic said. "The Feebs better not screw it up. We also need to make 100 percent sure this thing doesn't leak to anyone, especially media, before we've got it nailed down and watertight. Otherwise Donnerstein will call everything off and we'll be looking like monkeys."

Johnson studied the map again. "This meeting location looks odd to me. Surely they're not rendezvousing in the park. We'll need to go check out the place beforehand."

Vic shook his head. "I presume they must have a prearranged location near to there. We'll have to stake it out —the Feebs can help us do that bit."

"Yes, fine," Johnson said. "But we'll also have to make sure they don't go too heavy too early. You know what they're like with their bull-in-a-china shop approach. We need to collect some solid evidence and catch Donnerstein and Zilleman while they're together."

"I agree, Joe," Vic said, slightly wearily.

Johnson's phone pinged as a text message arrived. It was from his son, Peter.

How's it going Dad? Where are you now? In NYC I guess. Wish I was there with you. I'm off to Old Orchard Beach with some friends this afternoon. Carrie may also come with a friend. Speak soon. Love you.

Johnson had told his kids he was in New York and had guiltily apologized for not being able to pop up to Portland to visit them. And he found himself wishing he was going to the beach with his son: Old Orchard Beach, half an hour south of Portland, was one of the family's favorites, with its amusement park, a Ferris wheel, and a pier.

He had often gone there as a kid with his mother, Helena, a Polish Jewish immigrant who had survived two years in the Gross-Rosen concentration camp during World War II before being liberated by the advancing Red Army in April 1945. She had moved to the United States two years later and had gone on to live a full life, passing away finally in 2001, nine years after his father.

Feeling suddenly stressed at the two-way tug between the need to focus on his deliberations with Vic and his son's message, Johnson sent a very quick reply, telling Peter to enjoy the beach, adding that he was fine and would send an update later. He then turned his attention back to business.

Suddenly, something that had initially been a quest for information in Kabul for Johnson's report to Frank Rice had become something of very much greater significance across the other side of the Atlantic.

But he didn't want to take his eye off the ball with regard to the overall picture. After all, the revelations contained within Akbari's documents about Severinov, given his current status, were also explosive.

And although the family-related reasons why Javed was

seeking revenge on Severinov were now clear, it wasn't so obvious why Severinov was apparently pursuing Javed.

So what would they do next? Johnson wondered. He urgently needed to check in with Jayne to brief her on what they had learned about Javed and Severinov as well as Donnerstein. His biggest concern, though, was that she and Haroon were mounting a surveillance operation on Javed on some of the most dangerous streets in the world.

CHAPTER THIRTY

Sunday, June 9, 2013
Kabul

Jayne splashed a drop of lime juice into the large vodka she had poured for herself and immediately took a large slug from it before slumping on the sofa in the villa just off Wazir Akbar Khan Road.

She definitely needed this drink—right then she wished she were back in the comfort and safety of her two-bedroom apartment in London's Whitechapel area. For the second day running, Jayne and Haroon had attempted to mount a surveillance operation on Javed and discover where he was staying. It certainly wasn't at the Street Ten address—they had checked that several times.

But on both days, their surveillance attempts had ended in failure through no fault of their own but because of incidents in Kabul city center.

On the previous day, Saturday, Haroon had worked alone with Johnson's driver Omar, on the basis that he was far less obtrusive on Kabul's streets than she was. Despite her MI6 background, Jayne felt extremely vulnerable as a Western woman out in the open.

Omar had dropped Haroon within walking distance of the Ministry of Mines and Petroleum offices, a few hundred yards south of Abdul Haq Square and just across the street from the Kabul River. The Pakistani had then continued on foot in the guise of an office worker, observing Javed in his black Toyota as he checked through the security gate on his way into the ministry in the morning, presumably to continue work on the oil and gas sale. He had carefully remembered the license plate, which he later passed on to Jayne.

Haroon and Omar had then followed Javed by car after he had emerged from the ministry at just after four in the afternoon. However, as they tracked him across Abdul Haq Square, a crowd of protesters carrying banners about poor living conditions emerged from the nearby Makroyan apartment buildings and filled the street ahead of them, blocking off the traffic just after Javed had passed through. It took Haroon another seven or eight minutes to fight his way through the throng, by which time Javed was long gone.

On Sunday, Jayne had gone with Haroon and Omar, and they had found a place near the ministry where they could park the pickup and observe together. Jayne sat in the rear seat, hidden behind the dark smoked-glass windows. They had again followed Javed from the ministry. But a car bomb that exploded on a nearby street as they shadowed him onto Sulh Road resulted in immediate traffic chaos, and they lost him again as the jam slowly unwound.

On both days, he hadn't returned to Street Ten.

"We're too old for this game, or at least I am," Haroon said, clasping his hands behind his head and wrinkling his forehead. He was seated in an armchair opposite Jayne.

"No, we were just unlucky," Jayne said. It was true, they

had simply been unlucky. In any case, she wasn't going to concede any diminution of her abilities on the street, and certainly not by using age as an excuse.

But they did need to find out where Javed was staying and to track him carefully.

Johnson had briefed her via a secure phone call on the details in Akbari's files. Given the revelations, they would definitely want to take action to expose Severinov, if not in court then certainly via other channels such as the media. The last thing they wanted was for Javed to wipe him off the planet.

Similarly, Javed too had gone well beyond the norms of warfare in the way that he had brutally tortured and mutilated the Soviet helicopter crew in the K-G Pass that day in 1988. It was only right that he too be publicly exposed for what he had done.

A few hours earlier, Jayne had tried calling the number for a senior Afghan police contact that Lieutenant Colonel Storey had given her during the operation to rescue Johnson. But his skeptical-sounding assistant had told her that the man was flat out on a major operation against the Taliban that was likely to last for the next two days and that he therefore was unavailable.

It seemed to be a familiar story across all security services operating in Afghanistan, both foreign and local—they were all utterly overstretched and overwhelmed by the battle against various insurgent groups.

"We'll give Javed's house another try tomorrow," Haroon said. "Third time lucky."

"Hope so," Jayne said, draining the remains of her drink. "I'm going to try calling Baz's family in Wazrar. They might have an idea where he's staying."

She took out her phone and dialed the cell phone number she had for Baz's wife, Nazia. *The number you are calling is not available*. Probably the Taliban had taken out the local mast again, she figured.

Then Jayne had another thought. "Hang on a minute; I could get Seb Storey or one of his guys to go to Wazrar and find Nazia in person."

Jayne knew that Firebase Wilderness was on its own military cell phone network. Sure enough, she got through to Storey almost immediately and explained what she wanted.

"We're in the middle of an operation right now," Storey said. "You're lucky I've got a couple of minutes to talk to you. But I'll try to get one of my guys to drop in there and see her as soon as we get an opportunity. I'm just not sure when it will be."

Jayne thanked him and hung up. It was just as well Johnson was making some progress in New York, because she really felt as though she were wading through dark molasses right now.

* * *

Sunday, June 9, 2013
Brooklyn, New York

Johnson pulled the cap down over his forehead and adjusted his sunglasses. "They definitely won't be meeting here," he said, looking around the park.

They were standing in the line for the ferries at the northern end of Brooklyn Bridge Park, looking out over the East River. It seemed the best place to check out the location without arousing suspicion.

The park consisted of a narrow strip of green land about a hundred yards wide with an area of grass in the center surrounded by bushes and trees. It was exactly at the spot specified by the coordinates in the captured text message.

As they looked south across the park, twenty yards to their right was the East River, with the Manhattan skyline across the water. Behind them to the north was the Brooklyn Bridge, and to their left, beyond the trees, was a building site where the beginnings of a hotel or apartment complex was taking shape.

There were a number of tourists sauntering past, cameras at the ready to snap the New York skyline. A group of four kids were throwing a baseball to each other on the grass nearby, and a couple lay flat on a blanket, smooching without coming up for air.

"No, they won't meet here," Vic agreed. "Too many people."

Next to them, Simon Dover, the FBI executive assistant director, nodded his white-haired head in agreement. "It'll be near here."

Dover, in his mid-fifties, had agreed to come with them once Vic had briefed him on the information they had collected from Akbari and the likelihood of a serious issue involving abuse of public office by someone as high up the political food chain as Donnerstein.

Wearing black slacks and a blue shirt with the sleeves rolled up, Dover slowly scanned the surrounding area with a pair of laser-like blue eyes. "Once you've ruled out the park and the building site, there's still a lot of options just a stone's throw away. Let's walk and take a look."

The three men left the ferry area just as a yellow New York Water Taxi ferry arrived at the end of Pier One behind them. From there, they walked along the waterfront, past the floating classical music venue Bargemusic and a stream of tourists licking at ice creams.

At the L-shaped junction of Old Fulton Street and

Furman Street, they halted next to the Brooklyn Ice Cream Factory. Johnson glanced at a wine bar, 7 Old Fulton, where several of the clientele already had bottles in front of them.

"I can't see them using any of these places for a confidential meeting," Dover said, gesturing toward the bars.

"Why name a place if they're not going to use it?" Vic said.

"My thinking is they rendezvous at the park, then move on," Johnson said. "There's any number of apartment buildings here or hotels down the street. If we can bust them in the actual meeting, they're screwed. Donnerstein's history."

Johnson looked meaningfully at Dover. "But we want to take a light-touch approach before they get into the actual meeting. We don't want them spotting surveillance and aborting."

"You don't need to tell me that," Dover said, slightly tetchily. "I suggest using a couple of our top surveillance guys to track people coming into and out of the park. Younger ones who'll look like locals or tourists. Then we'll use three or four others on the neighboring streets." He scanned up and down Old Fulton and Furman Street from their vantage point at the junction. "We can wait in a blacked-out vehicle just down the street here and then move when needed."

"You're going to get involved?" Vic asked Dover.

"It's Donnerstein; I need to," Dover said. "I'll also need to brief Mueller when we're finished. That'll set the cat among the pigeons, because he'll then need to brief the president." Robert Mueller was the long-serving director of the FBI, responsible for the entire organization.

Johnson nodded approvingly. It was good to see top federal agents getting their hands dirty when needed.

His phone pinged as a text message arrived. It was from Jayne, saying that local media in Kabul were confirming that potential bidders for the Afghanistan oil and gas assets were expected in the city on Thursday for final presentations to the minister of mines and petroleum and to submit their final offers. She added that the local TV news was also reporting that Donnerstein was expected back in Kabul to add his endorsement to the process.

"Listen to this," Johnson said to Vic and Dover. He read the message. "Why would he go to Kabul twice in the space of three weeks to deliver an identical message? There's definitely something going on. He's got fingers in the pie. I'm certain he must be investing in ZenForce's bid for these assets—which he's now heavily promoting. He wants to pull favors with the Kabul government and make sure the Swiss-American offer gets precedence."

Vic shook his head. "If that guy ends up getting on the plane to Kabul, I'm resigning."

"I'll be fired," Dover said.

"Well, if we're going to avoid that, we need to get eyeballs on these three guys as quickly as possible," Johnson said. "In the case of Donnerstein, he's a face lots of people recognize, so he's likely to be in disguise. Zilleman may not bother with a disguise. And then we've got the mysterious third man—the man with the burner phone who organized the meeting. And nobody knows who that is."

"Indeed," Dover said. "It's not going to be easy."

CHAPTER THIRTY-ONE

Monday, June 10, 2013
Kabul

"Is that the house?" Omar asked as he piloted the silver Hilux down Street Nine.

Jayne leaned forward. "Yes, I think that must be it."

Eventually, one of Seb Storey's men at Firebase Wilderness had gone to Nazia's house in Wazrar and had obtained an address for Javed's brother, Mohinder, in Kabul, who apparently had died two years earlier. The house was on Street Nine, not far from Javed's property on Street Ten, which ran parallel.

Nazia had told the soldier that she understood Javed had access to the Street Nine house, although she didn't know whether he was staying there or not.

The villa was a terra-cotta-colored property with a flat roof and a curved balcony on the upper floor, built ten or fifteen meters back from the street. But they could see little because of the high wall and gates that ran across the entire frontage.

"Looks like a nice, unobtrusive, typical government worker's villa," Haroon said. It definitely didn't look luxurious, but it was well maintained and had been painted relatively recently.

"Keep going," Jayne said. "Let's not advertise that we're checking it out."

Omar accelerated slightly and continued to the end of the street, which led into the chaos of Qala-e-Fatullah Road, a busy main artery almost two kilometers long that led northwest of the city center.

Jayne sent a text message to Johnson to update him on the latest development with the operation to tail Javed. She realized immediately it was going to be difficult to monitor the property without ringing alarm bells in the area. They had had the same problem with Javed's house on Street Ten.

There were few people walking up and down it. Any parked vehicle would immediately arouse suspicions, and there was nowhere for someone mounting a surveillance operation to wait unobtrusively. No cafés or restaurants or even a seated area or park. The only thing that offered the slightest cover were a few spindly trees along the curb.

"If we know Javed isn't in his office, you and Omar will just have to do occasional drive pasts," Jayne said. "It's not exactly a great surveillance operation, I know."

Haroon groaned. "It's amateurish."

"I know," Jayne said. "But tell me how we can do better, given we have no resources?"

Haroon shrugged, but she knew he was correct. It was a fifteen-minute, three-kilometer journey by car from Jayne's villa to Javed's house. Omar and Haroon couldn't check out the house more than once or twice an hour without being obvious. That left such large windows of time during which

Javed could move in and out unseen that it really was almost a waste of time.

But there seemed little option. Unlike a CIA or MI6 station chief, they just didn't have people whom they could call upon to mount an effective operation. It crossed Jayne's mind that she could exchange her *hijab* for a burkha to cover her face and surveil the street on foot, but that might be a high-risk strategy if someone worked out what was going on.

There was a very high chance of kidnap or of being killed if the Taliban or another insurgent group was tipped off that a Westerner was operating on the street. Indeed, two German women had been kidnapped and tortured in that same area the previous year. One had been shot dead, and the other had been extremely fortunate to have been eventually released alive.

"Is there anyone you can think of locally who could do this job on foot for us?" Jayne asked Haroon.

"I've spoken to a few people," Haroon said. "Unfortunately there's nobody I know in Kabul who's capable of doing the job. At least, nobody I'd trust 100 percent."

* * *

Monday, June 10, 2013
Brooklyn, New York

At six o'clock, Brooklyn Bridge Park was thronged with tourists who were shooting photographs of the skyscrapers across the East River. Obliging them, the western sky behind Lower Manhattan had remained cloudless and deep blue all day.

By contrast, Johnson was anything but relaxed. He sat, occasionally tugging at the old bullet wound at the top of his right ear, on a large rectangular block of granite outside the Brooklyn Ice Cream Factory on the corner of Old Fulton and Furman Streets.

The sheer number of people in the park and its surroundings meant it was going to be difficult to pick out their targets. That was clearly why this location and time had been chosen.

Johnson had decided to stay out in the open, wearing a black baseball cap, a gray T-shirt under his lightweight blue linen jacket, and blue chinos. He felt that at least now he could contribute something rather than put all control in the hands of others. Vic had decided likewise and was standing smoking a cigarette across the other side of Old Fulton Street, outside the restaurant Shake Shack, almost under the bridge itself.

Dover had placed four FBI surveillance specialists in the park, all of them dressed as typical tourists. One was in the grassy area in the center. Another was on the strip of concrete that ran between the bushes and the East River. A third was on the side farthest away from the river, next to the building site, and the fourth at the northern end near to the ferry pier.

Meanwhile, Dover himself was camped out in the black FBI 4x4 that was parked farther along Furman Street, controlling operations. He had placed four other FBI vehicles in nearby streets and, having reluctantly informed the New York Police Department's special operations team, there were also four of their units within four blocks.

The entire surveillance team had seen a series of different photographs of both Donnerstein and Zilleman. The unknown person, of course, was the third man, the owner of the New York–based burner phone.

Johnson subtly pushed his Beretta farther down into his belt, beneath his jacket. He kept a careful eye on the passersby. As his watch ticked around to ten past six, he could feel his adrenaline levels rising and consciously calmed himself. He needed a clear head. This was the scheduled meeting time.

There was nobody in sight who matched either Zilleman or Donnerstein's description. Forty yards to his right, near the entrance to Pier One, Johnson could see one of the feds tying his shoelaces while glancing up at three men smoking and laughing together.

Then suddenly, from behind a small clump of trees next to the Bargemusic boat, Johnson saw a man emerge. It was Zilleman, wearing a tie and with his top shirt button undone, no jacket, and gray trousers.

Zilleman walked briskly along the broad sidewalk, no more than six or seven yards to Johnson's right, and up to the crosswalk next to the traffic lights. He paused as several cars went by, until the green pedestrian light showed, and then he strode across.

Johnson stood and made to follow, but then he noticed Zilleman briefly and quickly raise his right hand, as if waving at someone. As he did so, the rear door of a gray BMW 7 series sedan parked on the other side of the street, just beyond the traffic lights, swung open, and a man stepped out, carrying a briefcase.

Despite the man's baseball hat, pulled down over graying hair, and a black polo shirt instead of his customary collar and tie, Johnson immediately recognized him as Kurt Donnerstein. There was no mistaking the muscular shape of his shoulders on top of a thickset frame and the perma-tan. Donnerstein walked without a pause in Johnson's direction, arriving at the far side of the crosswalk at exactly the same time as Zilleman.

Where are the goddamn feds?

Both men appeared to give each other a cursory greeting,

then cut right at the other side of the crosswalk, heading east along Furman Street next to a five-story block of what looked like apartments. But after about fifteen yards, they stopped in front of a short flight of five steps that led up to a red door, which had a painted sign above it reading 8 Old Fulton Street.

At that moment, the red door swung sharply open, and a white-haired man emerged onto the top step, his face unsmiling, eyes darting around.

That was when Johnson felt his jaw drop what felt like five feet in shock. The man who had come out of the apartment building had a white mop of hair and was wearing a pair of tortoiseshell-framed glasses. The glasses confused Johnson for a second, but the angular physique and craggy face were stunningly familiar.

It was Robert Watson.

He beckoned Zilleman and Donnerstein up the steps. After they had gone inside, Watson glanced up and down Furman Street, pausing for a few seconds and appearing to look and listen carefully, almost tangibly testing the atmosphere.

The old fox is checking out the street, Johnson immediately said to himself. But what the hell was he doing back in the States, and how did he get in, given the warrants out for his arrest?

Johnson's mind flashed straight back to the old photograph from 1988 of Watson and Donnerstein together with the Stinger missiles in Afghanistan.

Then Watson swiftly followed the others, pulling the door closed behind him.

* * *

Monday, June 10, 2013
Brooklyn, New York

. . .

"They've gone in?" Dover said, his tone reedy and tense.

Johnson pushed the cell phone tighter to his ear so he could hear against the noisy street background. "Yes. Gone into the apartment building on the corner. Number eight. Red door."

"Shit, what the hell are my guys doing?" Dover said.

Johnson held back from saying he had been asking himself the same question.

"All three of them have gone in?" Dover continued.

"No. One was in there already—he let the other two in. You probably know of him—Robert Watson, ex-CIA?"

"I know the Watson case," Dover said.

"He was my old boss."

"Shit. What's he doing here? Okay, wait where you are. Best if I send two of my guys into the apartment, especially if Watson's going to recognize you."

"Agreed," Johnson said, reflexively touching his Beretta beneath his jacket. He had decided to phone Dover rather than go to the FBI 4x4, just in case Watson was watching.

"Is there a doorman?" Dover asked.

"Don't know. I'll go take a look," Johnson said. "Hang on the line."

He pulled his cap farther down his face and strolled over the crosswalk, forcing himself to move slowly. Keeping his phone clamped to his left ear, which helped hide his face from the apartment building, he walked closer to the door. There was a line of doorbells running down the left side of the frame. The top one was marked Concierge.

"Yes, there's a doorman," Johnson muttered into the phone.

"Good. Move away from there," Dover said. "Go back where you were. Two guys coming in now." He ended the call.

Johnson started to backtrack, but then he had an immediate thought. Whatever Watson's role was, if he was holding
a covert meeting with a US cabinet member, Johnson's
instinct was that he would have identified an escape route
from the building in case the meeting was compromised.

If so, where was it? Johnson decided to check the front
and other side of the building first, so he was out of the way
of the FBI as they went in.

He made his way back along Furman Street toward the
corner with Old Fulton Street, past five apartment windows
at basement level, all with heavily barred windows.

Above his head, a black metal fire escape staircase was
bolted to the brickwork, providing a way out at all five floor
levels. Johnson briefly turned around. There was another
matching fire escape at the other end of the building as well.
He cursed quietly to himself. This was clearly a very old
building with a myriad of possible exits.

Johnson turned right at the corner and walked along the
front of the building. There was no entrance here, just apartment windows across the frontage, interspersed with stone
pillars. On the far side of the building was a parking lot at the
front, packed seven deep with cars, and a flat-roofed parking
garage behind them.

Johnson stopped briefly. He could follow Dover's instruction and return to where he had been across the street. But
all his instincts went against that. Almost without thinking
about it, he continued around the block, taking a right turn
onto Everit Street, only another twenty yards farther on. It
seemed to make sense to check out the side and rear of the
building as well.

CHAPTER THIRTY-TWO

Monday, June 10, 2013
Brooklyn, New York

The feeling Watson picked up from a glance up and down Furman Street when he let EIGER and Zilleman into the building just wasn't right. It was almost a sixth sense that he had developed over decades working in an environment built around surveillance, countersurveillance, lies, and subterfuge at the CIA.

Although he had not worked the street for years, Watson had been one of the Agency's slickest operators in his time: a survivor of some of the toughest tasks handed out by Langley, putting him up against the Russians, the Iranians, and the Israelis, among others. It was a capability that remained finely honed, even now that he was a couple of weeks past his sixty-seventh birthday. It was innate.

Watson had noted a 4x4 with blackened windows farther down Furman Street that hadn't been there earlier in the evening. A woman directly across the street was sitting on a concrete post, smoking, staring at him. A man in a suit was being slightly over-demonstrative in checking his watch. In the other direction, a man wearing a black baseball cap sitting on a block of granite had been on the phone, looking everywhere but in his direction and definitely avoiding eye contact.

Too many possibilities, and although they might all be "casuals," as the Agency's surveillance team called them, on the other hand they might not be. Watson's gut feeling was that they all weren't casual. But he didn't have time to check them out.

One thing was for sure: the vibe he was getting from the street outside wasn't the calm, serene one he had picked up earlier that day or in the whole time he'd been there, for that matter.

He asked himself the question he always used to carefully ask when preparing to meet one of his assets while still with the CIA. Should I abort? Then he asked himself, would I have aborted when I was at the Agency? And the answer buzzing in his head this time was yes. The problem here, though, was that it was too late. EIGER and Zilleman were already in the building.

Watson led them along the corridor and up a wooden staircase to his second-floor apartment.

The apartment looked out over Furman Street, the East River, and the Brooklyn Bridge at the west side of the building and over the narrow one-way Doughty Street, no more than an alley, at the rear.

"Take a seat, gentlemen," Watson said, indicating toward the sofa and two matching black leather armchairs in the center of the living room. The apartment had twelve-foot-high ceilings, exposed beams and brickwork, and wooden floors, giving it a classic loft look.

Watson was determined to retain a calm demeanor, even

though his mind was now racing. "Make yourselves comfortable. I just need to go get some papers from the bedroom," he said. "I'll be back in a few minutes."

He walked down a short corridor into the adjoining bedroom and edged up to the window, which looked out over the rear of the property. Now he could clearly see the black 4x4 parked on Furman Street. A man dressed in black clothing was bent down at the driver's side of the vehicle, talking to whoever was inside. Then he stood up sharply, turned, and headed back along the street toward the apartment entrance.

Shit. Watson felt a wave of adrenaline shoot through him. This did not look good.

He quickly gauged angles and lines of sight from Doughty Street to the 4x4. He could get some cover. Then he looked the other way, left of the giant sash window. The drop down to the ground below his second-floor window was at least twelve feet, a nonstarter. But there was a flat roof three feet away, positioned a little lower than the window and set up as a roof garden with a table, chairs, and potted plants.

From that roof a spiral metal fire escape led down into a small courtyard at street level. But the courtyard had a solid wooden door built into an eight-foot wall, that led to the street. There was no guarantee the door would open, Watson figured. It might be better to step from the roof garden onto the top of the wall that enclosed the courtyard and from there drop down onto Doughty Street.

It briefly crossed Watson's mind that his aging legs and ankles might not be up to all this, but he felt he had little option. He then weighed up taking Donnerstein and Zilleman with him but ruled it out. A United States cabinet member like Donnerstein would look far more suspicious if spotted climbing out of a window and down a fire escape onto a street than he would if caught in an apartment with

an investment company boss. Likewise, Zilleman had little
to run away from. Watson, on the other hand, with a fugitive tag on him, had everything to lose—most of all his
freedom.

If he could just get into the street, which was quiet and
secluded and out of eyeline of the black 4x4, he could get to
his Golf, which was only a couple of minutes' swift walk away.

It was time to decide. Stay or go. And Watson made a
decision. He picked up his passport and wallet, which were
lying on the bedside table, and pocketed them. He hesitated,
grabbed two pepper spray canisters from a plastic bag on the
floor, and stuffed one in each pocket. Then he unclipped the
sash window and raised it.

As an afterthought, he went back and took a manual
shaving razor from a bag on the bed and pushed that into his
pocket as well. He climbed with some agility for a man of his
age onto the window ledge, held onto the window frame, and
then, without any hesitation, made a jump onto the flat roof,
grabbing hold of a railing that ran right round the outside of
it at waist height. He swung his legs over the rail and headed
straight to the rear of the roof.

There Watson climbed over the railing again, grabbed an
overhanging tree branch for stability, and stepped down onto
the foot-wide boundary wall that was just below. He moved
gingerly into a sitting position, his feet dangling down the
outside of the wall, and then turned so he could hold onto the
roof tiles that topped the wall. Watson gradually lowered
himself so he only had a jump down of perhaps three feet.

A second later, wincing at a sharp pain he had felt in his
right knee when he had landed, he was on the blacktop
surface of Doughty Street and walking up it toward his
parked car.

Watson crossed the junction where Doughty met Everit
Street, but then, a hundred yards ahead of him, he spotted a

man wearing dark clothing leaning against a black car, his arms folded.

It might have been nothing, but Watson decided instantly to divert right along Everit Street and then head to his car down Vine Street, which ran eastward, parallel to Doughty Street, a block farther on.

* * *

Monday, June 10, 2013
Brooklyn, New York

Johnson turned down Everit Street, scanning the eastern-facing side of the 8 Old Fulton Street building as he did so.

This side of the building was windowless and had obviously been originally joined to another building, now long demolished.

There was no way out of the apartments there. Any exit would have to be at the Furman Street side via the door or fire escapes or windows or, alternatively, via the rear, which Johnson hadn't yet seen.

He turned his attention away from the building and looked ahead down Everit Street. Then he noticed a tall, white-haired figure, maybe eighty yards ahead, walking away from him on the far side of the junction with Doughty Street. The man had a slight limp.

Johnson stopped dead. *Shit, that's Watson.*

Johnson grabbed his phone from his pocket and, accelerating toward Watson, called Dover. The call was answered within two rings.

"I can see Watson," Johnson said without preamble. "He's heading south down Everit Street. Must have gotten out the back of the building or something."

"Right, I've got a man farther down there," Dover said. "Will alert him. My team's in the apartment building now, getting the right door number from the doorman. Thanks."

But even before he had ended the call, Johnson saw Watson cross the street ahead of him and, with surprising speed, vault over a waist-high fence that appeared to border a park full of bushes and trees.

* * *

Monday, June 10, 2013
Brooklyn, New York

His head down, Watson strode up a gentle hill to Vine Street, only to see another black 4x4, similar to the one on Furman Street, parked fifty yards ahead of him, farther up the hill. Nobody was visible next to or in it, but Watson decided against getting any nearer.

The negative feeling, the instinctive prickle at the back of his neck, felt stronger than it had when he had scanned the area outside 8 Old Fulton Street. Now he needed to get off the street.

Watson crossed Vine and walked up to a waist-high black chain-link fence that separated the sidewalk from a public park. A sign nearby read Hillside Park. He swung his left leg across the fence and climbed over.

He glanced toward the 4x4 and saw a man emerge from the back door and begin running down the sidewalk in his direction.

Sonofabitch.

Unlike many of his former Agency colleagues, Watson had made a real effort to stay as fit as possible, despite his advancing years. He visited a gym in São Paulo at least a couple of times a week, was lean and, apart from the ever-present twinge in his right knee, remained in decent condition.

Now he broke into a jog across the parkland, heading parallel to Vine Street twenty yards to his left, the snap and crackle of breaking twigs beneath his feet sounding like mini gunshots.

It didn't take long before he realized the man who had emerged from the 4x4 had also entered the park and was in pursuit, making a similar racket as he passed beneath the trees.

Watson skirted around another couple of low-hanging trees, ducking at the last moment to avoid a branch that loomed up at him. He headed toward the northwest corner of the park, where he knew, having checked out the area a couple of days earlier, that there was a pedestrian gate that led back onto Vine Street, only forty yards or so from his car.

But the rising noise behind him told him that his pursuer was gaining ground rapidly. There was no way he was going to outrun a guy who was probably at least thirty years his junior.

Watson reached into his pocket as he ran and removed one of the two pepper sprays, flicking off the safety catch with his index finger.

As soon as the man drew close enough for Watson to hear his breathing, he turned and pressed hard on the pepper spray's trigger button, squirting it hard into the man's face.

* * *

Monday, June 10, 2013
  Brooklyn, New York

. . .

After ending his call with Dover, Johnson broke into a run up the hill toward the point where he had seen Watson disappear. He grabbed his cap, which was threatening to come off in the breeze, and stuffed it into his back pocket.

Ahead of him, he saw another man sprint along the sidewalk from the opposite direction and also vault over the fence into the park in pursuit.

That must be one of Dover's men, he thought.

By the time Johnson arrived at the corner of the park, the two men had vanished behind trees and bushes. He paused and listened. He could hear the sound of footsteps and snapping twigs and then caught a few glimpses of them, now well ahead of him. He realized they were running through the trees parallel to Vine Street.

The FBI man would doubtless catch Watson easily. Instead of entering the park, then, Johnson set off down Vine Street. Maybe he could join in for the coup de grâce.

Johnson had gone about twenty yards when he heard a low-pitched male yelp, followed a few seconds later by another one, and then a squeal of metal on metal that sounded like a gate opening.

At the far end of the park, Johnson saw a dark figure topped by a white mop of hair emerge through a gate onto the street and begin running away from him.

Johnson didn't stop to think how Watson had managed to thwart a trained FBI pursuer, but he broke into a sprint down the sidewalk after him.

Watson crossed the street to the same side as Johnson, albeit some distance ahead, and continued to the corner, where he turned left, out of Johnson's sight.

Ahead of him at the end of Vine Street, high above the ground, Johnson could see a stream of vehicles flashing over the elevated section of the interstate.

Where the hell has Watson gone now? Where's the damned FBI?

Johnson turned at the corner of Vine Street and McKenny Street and stopped. Behind him was the expressway and an entrance ramp, also elevated. Watson was nowhere in sight. Neither was the FBI.

Suddenly there was the sound of an engine starting, and with an extended squeal of tires, a dark-colored Volkswagen Golf flew out of a parking spot across the other side of McKenny Street. It shot toward the junction where Johnson was standing, its rear end swaying, so rapid was its acceleration.

At the wheel was a man with a white mop of hair, wearing glasses, staring straight at Johnson. For a fraction of a second, their eyes met through the windshield. But it was enough— Johnson knew without a shadow of a doubt it was his former boss.

Watson completely ignored the stop sign at the end of McKenny Street, right next to where Johnson stood, and without braking, sped into the street beyond.

Johnson, working on instinct, pulled the Beretta from his belt, but even before he could flick off the safety, he realized there was little he could do. Quite apart from not having a license to carry the gun, blasting away at a fleeing vehicle could put him in deep trouble.

Instead, he made a mental note of the license plate, realizing as he did so that the street behind him, onto which Watson had driven, formed the on-ramp onto the expressway.

Then the car was around the corner and gone.

There was no time to even curse. Johnson grabbed his phone from his pocket and tapped on Dover's number.

"Watson's just got away onto the interstate, southbound," Johnson said. "He's in a VW Golf, gray or charcoal." He gave Dover the plate number.

"Can you get one of your drivers after him?" Johnson said. "I'd like to go too."

"Okay," Dover said. "I've got a man on Old Fulton. I'll tell him to pick you up at that Vine Street intersection with the on-ramp. You'll need to be lightning quick getting into the vehicle."

"Affirmative," Johnson replied. "I think your man chasing Watson in the park went down. I saw him go into the park but not out of it again."

There was a slight pause. "I'll check on that," Dover said. He ended the call.

Thirty seconds later the high-pitched whine of a powerful engine being thrashed in low gear echoed across McKenny Street as an unmarked black Chevrolet Suburban SUV shot around the corner from Old Fulton Street. It screeched to a halt at the stop sign, and the driver indicated to Johnson to get into the rear seat.

He climbed in and slammed the door and the driver, a younger man with short spiky blond hair, took off, the sharp acceleration throwing Johnson into the seat back. He recovered, fastened his seat belt, and stared forward.

"Golf, I was told," the driver said, focusing intently on the road. "My name's Dave, by the way."

"Yes, a dark gray Golf. He's got at least two minutes' start on us, though. I'm Joe."

"Hit the lights, buddy," Dave said to the agent sitting next to him in the front passenger seat, who was bald with a close-cropped semicircle of dark hair.

The man flicked a switch on the dash, turning on the concealed emergency lights and the siren, which began to wail loudly. Then he turned around, nodded to Johnson, and introduced himself as Ben.

Both men were dressed casually, Dave in a navy blue polo shirt and black chinos, Ben in a dark green T-shirt and blue jeans.

Dave floored the accelerator as the Suburban came off the

on-ramp and onto the expressway proper at the Cadman Plaza West entrance, then was immediately forced to brake as he navigated into a busy flow of traffic. He glanced into his rearview mirror.

"Got Pete coming up behind too," Dave said.

Johnson looked over his shoulder to see a black Ford Interceptor sedan about forty yards behind. Here the interstate was built in a double-deck configuration, with the traffic heading south and westbound on the bottom and the north and eastbound lanes on the top. The concrete expanse that formed the top deck was now stretched out above the Suburban like a canopy.

"The boss said you know this guy Watson well," Dave said. "That right?"

"You could say that," Johnson said. "He was a CIA lifer until he got caught." Johnson proceeded to briefly give them some of the background on Watson's illegal dealings.

The car radio crackled into life with a click and a hiss. It was Dover to say that an unmarked New York Police Department car was about a mile and a half farther south down 278, approaching exit twenty-six, and had slowed to a crawl.

"That's only two exits south of where you got on," Dover said. "The NYPD crew are hoping to get an eye on Watson's Golf. He'll be heading down there, no doubt about it. If they get the eye, you'll be first to know because you'll probably be there next. I'm getting two choppers airborne, and we've got two more cars coming on at twenty-six and twenty-five, in case they're needed. By the way, Malcolm got pepper-sprayed in the park—Watson hit him right in the eyes. That's why the son of a bitch got away." There was another crackle and Dover was gone.

The Suburban came up behind a truck, cut sharply left into the next lane in front of a silver Chevy, and then moved left again into the outside lane, where Dave briefly accelerated until he reached a huge RV, which belatedly moved over to allow them past.

The traffic was heavy, but at least with the lights and siren on, vehicles were making way for them. That would give them an advantage over the Golf.

With any luck, the net was closing on Watson.

CHAPTER THIRTY-THREE

Monday, June 10, 2013
Brooklyn, New York

"Always do what the opposition least expects," Watson muttered to himself. It was a mantra he had drummed into countless subordinates at the CIA over the decades. As he piloted the VW Golf onto westbound Interstate 278, he decisively abandoned his original plan to head south via the New Jersey Turnpike.

It would have worked if it hadn't been for Joe Johnson spotting him as he pulled out of his parking spot on McKenny Street. At least, he was 95 percent certain Johnson had seen him. He had definitely been standing on the corner as Watson roared past him onto the on-ramp for the BQE. Their eyes had met. There was, of course, a chance that Johnson wouldn't have recognized him, but Watson wasn't going to take that gamble.

All his instincts in the past twenty minutes had proved correct, and he wasn't going against them now.

If he had been recognized, then it was an absolute certainty that within ten minutes, the interstate would be crawling with pursuit vehicles manned by federal and local law enforcement officers, and there would be choppers filming his every maneuver until he was brought to the inevitable, crunching halt, probably somewhere around Staten Island.

Eight guns pointed at his head, special agents swearing at him at full volume, his hands in the air, cuffs snapping on. No, Watson wasn't going down in that fashion.

As the expressway curved around to the left, the giant cranes, piers, moored cruise ships, warehouses, and expanse of waiting trucks at the Brooklyn Port Authority terminals at the mouth of the East River came into view to his right. Governors Island was visible just beyond. The sign for exit twenty-seven read Atlantic Avenue, and Watson headed straight down the off-ramp.

At the bottom, he took another right, doubling back on himself, and at the intersection with Atlantic Avenue, he hesitated for a moment. Now he was less than a mile south of where he had started, near the southern end of Furman Street.

What would they least expect me to do?

Watson decided on the subway, but first he needed to dump the Golf as quickly as possible and get it well out of sight.

He took a left, then a right onto Bridge Park Drive. Ahead of him was a Quik Park garage beneath the vast concrete and glass condominium tower at One Brooklyn Bridge Park. Watson drove the Golf straight into the parking garage and to his relief found a space almost immediately.

The chances of the police quickly finding his rental car here were low, he figured.

He grabbed a blue Washington Nationals baseball cap

from the rear seat, jammed it on his head, and made his way out of the garage. He checked his watch. It was a quarter to seven. From there he strode along the street to a bus stop on the edge of Pier Six, which formed the southern end of Brooklyn Bridge Park.

From here, he could jump on a bus that would whisk him along Atlantic Avenue to the Barclays Center subway station in probably seven or eight minutes. In fact, he could see a number sixty-three bus approaching just a few hundred yards away.

And from the Atlantic Avenue–Barclays Center station, he could take a train into the ether of Manhattan Island and just disappear in any number of different directions. That was something he was very good at.

* * *

Monday, June 10, 2013
  Brooklyn, New York

The black FBI Suburban navigated through the traffic bunched up near exit twenty-seven and continued south.

Once again the radio crackled into life with a squelch break, then Dover came back on, his tone now a note or two higher than it had been before. "Good news and bad. We've got Donnerstein and Zilleman in cuffs, but the NYPD patrol at exit twenty-six haven't seen Watson."

"Not seen him?" Dave said, turning his head momentarily toward Johnson.

"No. There's been no gray Golf heading past twenty-six," Dover said.

"We're nearly at twenty-six now and we haven't seen him either," Dave said. "What the hell?"

Johnson grimaced. "He must have got there. Unless—"

"Unless he came straight off at twenty-seven. Doesn't make sense but . . ."

"It does make sense," Johnson said. "He must have seen me and knew I'd seen him. He'd probably realize I had time to see the plate. Then he would know that the game was up if he stayed with the Golf."

Johnson paused for a second, then added with a note of certainty in his voice, "He's going to dump the Golf."

"Where?" Dover asked.

"Don't know," Johnson said. "I think he'd want to put it out of sight, though, off the street. A parking garage or something. I'm guessing he'll take a bus or the subway instead. Or find another car somehow. Even steal one."

There was silence for two seconds. Then Dover spoke again. "I'll tell the NYPD to shut down the subway and bus routes. You guys know any obvious parking garages near twenty-seven?"

"I took my kids to the park at Pier Six a couple of months ago," Ben said from the front seat. "There's a big garage right there, underground, beneath an apartment building. Forget what it's called, though."

"We'll find it," Dover said. "Any others?"

"Can't think of any," Ben said. "But he could just dump it on a side street. Doesn't have to be a garage."

"Yes, true. But he might prefer it to be out of sight, like Joe says," Dover said. "Exit twenty-seven sounds like the favorite. I'll get NYPD to Court Street and Borough Hall subways. You guys come off at exit twenty-six, and I'll work out which stations you need to head to. Okay?"

"Okay, boss," Dave said.

Dover ended the call just as Dave braked hard. The traffic remained heavy, and all three lanes were moving at no more than forty. He swung the Suburban over from the outside lane to the inside and then cut onto the off-ramp for exit twenty-six, his siren still blaring and lights flashing.

"What buses go from that parking garage?" Johnson asked Ben.

"There's only one," Ben said from the front. "I know because I checked it all out when we visited. It's the sixty-three, which we used."

"Where does it go to?" Johnson asked.

"Along Atlantic Avenue to the Atlantic Avenue subway, then south past Union Street subway toward Fort Hamilton. He could get on the Long Island Railroad at Atlantic Avenue too."

Johnson tilted his head back and tried to put himself in his old boss's shoes. What would Watson do? He'd probably try to be unpredictable, that was for certain. It was his MO. So rather than running away from Manhattan, he might go back into it, using the lines from Atlantic Avenue and Union Street subways. The two big airports, JFK and LaGuardia, were too obvious and risky for Watson. But he might try to use one of the smaller ones.

"Call Dover back," Johnson said. "If there's still no sign of Watson farther down the interstate, he's definitely exited. My feeling is he'll get into Manhattan and then to one of the minor airports. He's done that before. And tell Dover we'll go to Union Street and Atlantic Avenue now. If they draw a blank, then we'll go to the other subways near exit twenty-seven after that."

"Yes, makes sense," Dave said. "My thinking exactly."

Johnson refrained from giving the thin smile he felt tempted by as Dave called up Dover and outlined the plan, which his boss agreed to immediately.

As he spoke, Dave navigated the Suburban down the off-ramp and along Hamilton Avenue, then cut left, doing a zigzag route through downtown Brooklyn and onto Fourth Avenue.

A few minutes later, the radio burst into life again. It was Dover to say that there had been a bomb scare at Union Street subway and that it had been closed. All passengers had been evacuated and NYPD were dealing with it. "So go straight to Atlantic Avenue instead," Dover said. "If that's a blank, then head to Hoyt-Schermerhorn or Hoyt Street subways. I'm still trying to get the subway trains stopped."

As Dave drove farther north up Fourth Avenue, Johnson could see the flashing blue and red lights outside the row of delis, pizzerias, and discount stores next to the subway entrances on both sides of the street. There were several police cars, two fire engines, and two ambulances. Dover had gotten that correct.

Dave cut across onto Fifth Avenue for two blocks to avoid the chaos and then continued up to the new entrance to Atlantic Avenue subway station outside the Barclays Center indoor arena.

"Stop outside the station," Johnson said.

He glanced at his watch. There was no way Watson would have been able to dump the car, take a bus, and get into the subway already.

"Turn your lights and siren off," Johnson said. "He won't be in there yet. I don't want to alert him."

"Yeah, sensible," Dave said, glancing at Ben, who flicked off the emergency lights.

The Suburban braked sharply to a halt next to a row of steel barriers next to the futuristic, brownstone-colored Barclays Center arena building. In the middle of the entrance plaza was a steel and glass subway entrance, its rust-brown facade matching the color and design of the neighboring arena that dwarfed it. There were only a handful of people on the plaza. It was a quiet time of the day.

As the vehicle stopped, a thought crossed Johnson's mind. "Do you two guys have arrest authority?"

The two men in the front looked at each other momentarily. "No," said Dave. "We're surveillance. But don't worry, we can get special agents here in no time. Or the NYPD would light up the whole area if needed."

Johnson looked at the heavens. He hoped they were correct. It would probably take Watson five seconds to work out whether they could officially hold him or not.

He let the Suburban's window down, leaned out, and looked behind. He could see a bus stop behind them and three buses in a line heading along Atlantic Avenue toward it.

As the three men exited the vehicle and walked back along the sidewalk toward the subway entrance, the three buses all began to disgorge passengers onto the plaza. Johnson scrutinized them carefully. There were teenagers with headphones clamped to their ears, grannies shuffling and carrying plastic shopping bags, professional types in suits, and mothers with toddlers. But none of them were tall with mops of white hair.

"Do all the buses stop here?" Johnson asked. He removed his black cap from his back pocket and put it back on.

"Mostly. Some stop across there," Ben said, pointing to Flatbush Avenue, the street that ran down the other side of the plaza and the Barclays Center at forty-five degrees to Atlantic Avenue. "There's a sixty-three, arriving now."

Sure enough, a bus coming from Pier Six was pulling into a stop where Ben was indicating. Again the three men scrutinized the passengers getting off, but none of them remotely matched Watson's profile.

"Why don't we wait and observe for a few minutes," Johnson said. "What about the outdoor table at Starbucks there? We don't have to order." He pointed toward an empty table on the plaza, in front of the coffee shop.

Dave nodded, and the three of them walked over and sat down. There were a few empty coffee cups from the previous occupants of the table, which made it look as though they had been there for some time.

"You got a MetroCard?" Ben asked Johnson.

Johnson nodded, patting his wallet in his pocket. "Yes." He had bought a seven-day pass for the New York transit network on arrival.

"Good. Don't want to have to announce ourselves at the subway barriers if we need to go in."

Realistically, what were the chances of Watson using this station? Johnson asked himself. Where else would he go? His conviction that Watson would have dumped the Golf and taken a bus had hardened. So if he didn't head to this subway, then it would be another, most likely.

After he and Johnson had eyeballed each other, Watson must have known that every police car in the borough would be on the lookout for him.

* * *

Monday, June 10, 2013
  Brooklyn, New York

Watson waited until the number sixty-three bus was within a couple of blocks of the Barclays Center, then got off at a stop on the corner of Third Avenue. The last thing he wanted was to be dumped right outside the subway station only to find himself in the middle of a bunch of NYPD officers and cars.

If, as he assumed, Joe Johnson had informed the FBI and police about his getaway in the Golf, they would most likely be targeting all transit stations in the vicinity on the assumption that he would bail out of the vehicle sooner rather than later.

So he wanted to approach Atlantic Avenue cautiously on foot. But to do that, he needed to do something else first.

Watson stood on the sidewalk and looked around. Immediately he saw what he required: Hank's Saloon, said the sign on the wall, with flames painted around it. It looked rough as hell from the outside, but his long experience in New York bars told Watson it would probably be characterful inside.

He pushed open the door and, lowering his head to avoid colliding with the low black-painted ceiling, made his way past a heavy, battered old wooden bar where drinkers were sitting on a row of red stools. The clock read ten minutes past seven. It was indeed very characterful and also very dark. The posters advertising various upcoming shows told Watson it was a beer-and-a-shot music joint.

Watson made his way straight to the bathroom, where he removed his cap and glasses, took out the razor from his pocket, and proceeded to shave his head. Three other drinkers came in while he was doing it. Two ignored him completely; the other, a stocky man in his thirties, stood staring after he had finished using the urinal.

"I lost a bet," Watson said. "Can you just check the back to make sure it looks okay?"

"Sure, buddy," the guy said, examining it. "Looks good to me. Nice job." He walked out, and Watson cleared up the clumps of white hair in the sink and on the floor and threw it all in the trash can.

He replaced the glasses and Washington Nationals cap on his now shaven head and headed out the door. It wasn't exactly a foolproof disguise but probably the best he could do in the circumstances.

Watson took a right out of the bar along Atlantic Avenue and walked past an old post office building and a series of food shops until he was drawing near to the distinctive brown and green shape of the Barclays Center ahead of him.

As he walked past an electronics superstore, Watson slowed down, scanning the sidewalks and the traffic methodically. There were no flashing lights ahead near the subway entrance, no sirens, and no obvious sign of a police lockdown. The only thing that rang an alarm bell was a black Suburban parked about sixty or seventy yards past the subway entrance, against the curb. Watson looked at it carefully for several moments. Was it a federal vehicle? It was difficult to tell from this distance, but there certainly weren't any officers near it.

Pulling his cap lower, he went over the crosswalk at the forty-five degree corner of Atlantic Avenue and Flatbush Avenue and sat on a concrete seat next to a pickup zone, positioning himself so he could continue to monitor the Suburban. However, the subway station entrance with its grass-covered roof and the much larger arena building behind it were the main point of his focus. There were a few people on the plaza, mainly in groups, and some others were sitting at the tables in front of Starbucks, but all of them looked like casual customers.

Everything looked good. But Watson wanted to wait until there were more people on the plaza before heading down to the platforms. It didn't take long. After a few minutes, two buses drew up on the Atlantic Avenue side of the arena building, followed by another two on the Flatbush Avenue side. Within thirty seconds, the plaza was swarming with scores of people, most of them heading for the subway.

Watson stood. Now was the time to make his move.

CHAPTER THIRTY-FOUR

Monday, June 10, 2013
Brooklyn, New York

From behind the empty take-out Starbucks cup, Johnson was keeping a close eye on the ebb and flow of people moving across the Barclays Center plaza. There was no event currently being staged at the arena, so the vast majority were either getting off buses and heading into the subway or vice versa.

Behind them, a giant video screen that was visible to all in the plaza was running footage of the Brooklyn Nets, the National Basketball Association team based at the arena.

Dave and Ben had temporarily turned off their radios, not wanting hisses, crackles, and squelch breaks to give them away and attract the attention of passersby.

"How long do we give it here?" Ben asked.

"A little longer," Johnson said, glancing at his watch. It was a quarter to eight. "Dover's got cover at the other subways nearby, hasn't he?"

"Yep," Dave said, scrolling down a text message on his phone. "He has, and he's just messaged me saying there's three NYPD cars heading here right now. So that takes care of the arrest authority."

Two buses drew up at the Atlantic Avenue side of the arena, one following the other as if somehow joined together. At the same time, another two pulled up at the bus stop across the other side of Flatbush Avenue. A large crowd of passengers was disgorged from all four vehicles, jostling and jockeying for position in the rush to get through the subway entrance and down to the trains.

Clearly Dover's efforts to have the subway closed had not yet borne fruit.

Again Johnson watched carefully as the crowds crossed the plaza. There were a couple of men with white hair among the throng, but the body shapes and the gaits were all wrong. A man with iron gray hair ran awkwardly from the second bus on the Flatbush Avenue side toward the subway. And another tall man wearing a blue cap and glasses appeared from behind the station entrance building and made his way around to the front.

Johnson scratched the old bullet wound on his ear. His eyes flicked from one person to the next. His attention was grabbed by a group of young kids who ran out from the station entrance, forcing the tall man with the blue cap to stop in his tracks. Then he resumed his onward path.

As the man walked, Johnson watched. His cap appeared to be resting on a bald head, as far as Johnson could make out. But then, as the man drew nearer to the escalators, Johnson's attention was caught by something else. It was the angular shape of the man's shoulders and his limp.

It was Robert Watson. He was certain of it.

Johnson jerked to his feet. "That's him, walking in now. Let's move."

The two FBI men stood as one, and the three of them ran across the plaza, just as Watson disappeared from sight.

While they were running, three NYPD cars, their sirens turned off, braked to a halt on the Atlantic Avenue side of the arena.

"Don't stop, they can catch up," Dave said, without breaking his stride.

As they reached the entrance, Johnson caught a glimpse of Watson in the entrance hall below, going through the row of turnstiles.

The three men, seeing the escalators crowded with people, diverted at the last second down the stairs instead.

As he descended, Johnson could see Watson striding at surprising speed down the left side of the hall, following the signs for trains toward Manhattan and the Bronx.

Johnson took the steps two at a time, keeping to the left side, hoping he wouldn't slip. To his right, three tattooed men climbing the stairs stopped dead, blocking the FBI duo, who were forced to dodge around them.

Johnson, now several yards ahead of Ben and Dave, grabbed his MetroCard from his pocket, swiped it, and pushed through the barrier just in time to see the blue cap disappear around the corner into a tunnel at the bottom of a ramp. Watson was heading toward the center platforms for lines four and five, the express services running north into Manhattan and south to New Lots Avenue and Flatbush Avenue.

He was certain he saw Watson breaking into a run just as he rounded the corner and moved out of Johnson's line of sight.

Johnson sprinted down the ramp, lined by white-tiled walls with maroon stripes, catching a glimpse in his peripheral vision of Dave and Ben behind him, their footsteps thudding.

He rounded the left-hand bend at the bottom of the ramp into the tunnel, almost slipping as he sidestepped to narrowly avoid an old lady carrying shopping bags. Two teenagers, earphones clamped to their ears and walking side by side, reactively parted at the last second to let Johnson through between them.

Watson was nowhere in sight: he must have already gone up the stairs to the express train platforms.

Johnson reached the bottom of the staircase just in time to see Watson clear the top step. He could hear the rumble of an approaching train on the platforms above.

The old bastard's fitter than I expected, Johnson thought.

He took the stairs two at a time, knees now twinging, and reached the top, heading onto the eastern end of the plat-form just as a silver steel Manhattan-bound train pulled into the station alongside him, a couple of yards to his right. The train, its twin headlamps beaming bright in the gloom, was slowing quickly but still traveling with some momentum as it continued toward the far western end of the platform.

Now Watson was visible well ahead of him, running along the platform at a speed that belied his age, the train coming up behind him.

"This is an Express Five train. The next stop is Nevins Street . . . " boomed the automated public address system.

While the Barclays Center entrance to the subway, opened only the previous year, was sparkling new, the plat-forms below were part of the much older original station, dating to 1908. Archaic, chunky square green supporting pillars ran down both sides of the central island platform, a few yards apart and close to the edge of the platform.

As Watson continued running, Johnson could see a fat man in a brown leather jacket, who was focusing intently on his cell phone screen, meandering toward him, not looking where he was going. He veered to his left just as Watson drew level, forcing Watson to try to sidestep to avoid him.

But Watson barged hard into the man's left shoulder, causing the CIA veteran to lose his balance and lurch to his right, where he crashed with some force into one of the green pillars.

Watson bounced off the pillar and went sprawling head-first to the ground. Johnson could see he was trying desperately to recover himself, both arms flailing, but in a flash, he tumbled over the yellow hazard markings and fell off the edge of the platform into the path of the number five express train that was approaching behind him.

Instantaneously there came an ear-piercing screech of steel on steel as the train conductor slammed on his brakes. The squealing continued as the train slowed, but it was still sliding onward toward Watson, who Johnson knew must be on the tracks right in front of it.

Johnson continued running at full tilt, although he knew it was too late to do anything. A group of teenage girls standing near a stairwell down to the lower level platforms, just a few yards from the impact, began screaming and wailing, as did two older women waiting with young children.

Finally, the teeth-jarring noise stopped as the train came to a halt. It was only when Johnson finally overtook the driver's cab that he saw Watson's body sprawled at the front of the train, his head lying at an odd angle over the rail nearest to the platform.

The disgraced former CIA veteran wasn't moving.

CHAPTER THIRTY-FIVE

Monday, June 10, 2013
Brooklyn, New York

The three paramedics finally picked up the aluminum stretcher on which Watson was lying. His body was secured by three orange safety straps, his face was still contorted with pain, and there was a bloodstain on the white sheet beneath his hip. His shaven head and face had a distinctly gray, slightly unreal pallor.

As the stretcher rose, Johnson caught Watson's eye. His former boss lifted his head a little and turned it to look fully at Johnson.

"You stupid asshole," the ex-intelligence chief groaned. "You don't know what you're doing. You never did." His head sank back onto the stretcher again. Watson had a broken shoulder, a broken femur, a deep hip wound that had required the paramedics to insert emergency stitches right there on the platform, extensive bruising and a large gash on his temple. But despite the injuries, there was no mistaking the look of hatred on his face.

Johnson folded his arms and stared at Watson. "It's been a long time coming, Robert," he said. "You've deserved what's coming to you. You're a disgrace to your country and yourself."

He would have said a lot more, but the paramedics carrying the stretcher set off past Johnson and along the island platform back toward the eastern end of the Atlantic Avenue station. A powerful emergency police floodlight cast an eerie deep shadow ahead of the stretcher as it moved.

The three NYPD officers, who had been supervising proceedings and who had formally arrested Watson as soon as he had been stabilized, followed the stretcher. The FBI duo Dave and Ben tucked in right behind them, and Johnson, together with Vic, who had joined him on the platform, did likewise.

"Where are you going to take him now?" Johnson asked the senior of the three police officers.

"I'm still waiting for confirmation, but I think Langone Hospital. It's the nearest," the officer said. "We'll stay with him and process initial charges once the medics have finished with him."

As he had fallen, Watson had been whacked by the front of the train just before it came to a halt, throwing him forward and knocking him unconscious.

It had then taken considerable time for the police and paramedics team to bring him around, treat his injuries, lift him off the tracks, and prepare him for transit to the hospital. In truth, Johnson knew he was fortunate to still be alive.

All northbound express train services and most of the slower local northbound services had been canceled since the incident, and it was expected to take another half an hour at least to get them running again. Police and subway staff had rapidly evacuated all the platforms in that area of the station and closed them to passengers. Those trains that were allowed through on the southbound local line did not stop.

As they walked, Johnson felt a sense of elation come over him. He had been relieved that Watson had not been killed by the train—death would not have represented justice. Now he had the opportunity to help bring Watson to court, something he had been dreaming of for years.

They followed the stretcher team down the stairs into the exit tunnel and then up to the plaza outside. The whole area outside the Barclays Center was lit up blue and red by the flashing lights on the roofs of an array of police, ambulance, and fire service vehicles. Two black FBI Suburbans and three Dodge Chargers, also black, were parked next to the curb near the NYPD vehicles.

The paramedics placed Watson's stretcher on a trolley and began wheeling it toward one of the ambulances, followed by the three NYPD officers.

Eight TV crews were waiting in the far corner of the plaza, their lights and reflector panels creating a pool of brightness. Another TV van was pulling up across the far side of Flatbush Avenue. They had all requested interviews with Dover. A large bunch of other journalists brandishing note-books and hanging on their cell phones was also gathered in the same area, which had been cordoned off by the police press information team.

"I nearly screwed up there, Vic," Johnson said. "We nearly lost him."

"No, you didn't," Vic said. "He's gonna get what he deserves, like you told him."

"Yes, but it was a close thing. I should have seen him more quickly outside on the plaza," Johnson said. "I should have positioned us nearer the entrance, not at the Starbucks, so we could move quicker. And then I should have acted more subtly, somehow. I didn't think he'd seen me, but he started running, so maybe he did."

"Joe, just stop it, buddy," Vic said. He stopped walking, turned, and put a hand on Johnson's shoulder. "What the hell are you talking about? We've got him in the bag. They'll fix his injuries. He'll go to prison. End of story."

Johnson smiled at last. "I know, I know. But it wasn't ideal. What's the latest on Donnerstein?"

Vic pulled Johnson away, out of earshot of Dave and Ben. "The Feebs are still questioning him at Federal Plaza," Vic said. That was the FBI's main New York office, just off Broadway, near to city hall in Manhattan. "Could be an all-nighter. He's finished. The media are already going crazy with it, but frankly, they've heard nothing yet. It's not even begun. The Feebs are having difficulty getting right to the bottom of his investments over the years—just wait until all that comes out into the open. All the cash originally came from his arms dealing in Afghanistan and elsewhere."

"Yes, but we need the proof of the original arms dealing," Johnson said. "That's the critical thing. And that's got to come from Akbari. Nobody else is going to come up with anything on that."

"True."

"And Obama's going to have to make a statement," Johnson said.

"Yes, probably about Watson as well as Donnerstein, and sooner rather than later," Vic said. "He's coming under pressure from all directions."

Johnson paused. He knew he needed to think about the bigger picture and keep his focus on the war crime elements of his investigation, and on Severinov and Javed, which had been difficult with everything that had gone on in the previous few hours.

He urgently needed to speak to Jayne, and then to Frank

Rice, to keep them briefed. He glanced at his watch. It was just after ten. Three in the morning in London and seven thirty in the morning in Kabul, he calculated. He'd better call Jayne as soon as he could.

Johnson felt a wave of exhaustion slip over him. It had been a long, demanding day. But he knew that if he took his foot off the gas pedal, only half the job would be done.

Vic's phone beeped loudly. He took it from his pocket and scrutinized the message. "It's our station chief in Moscow. They've picked up that one of Putin's four planes has just filed a flight plan to go to Kabul, leaving at nine tomorrow morning Moscow time, arriving three in the afternoon Kabul time."

He showed Johnson the message, which went on to say that the plane was an Ilyushin Il-96-300PU, registration RA-96016.

"Interesting," Johnson said. "But is it significant?"

"It could be just one of their routine decoys. They file all kinds of flight plans for Putin's jets, and nobody knows which of the four he's on until takeoff. But nevertheless, the timing is significant."

Vic's phone pinged again. He read the message. "Hmm. The plot thickens. There's a second Putin jet also filed to fly to Kabul at the same time. Another Ilyushin."

"My God," Johnson said, as a thought struck him. "You don't think Putin's going to be flying in to join Severinov for the oil presentation, do you? Can't just be a decoy, with two flight plans for two jets."

Vic shrugged. "No idea. But we need to try to find out. You'd better get yourself back to Kabul. I can deal with things on this end."

Two more pings sounded, this time from Johnson's phone as text messages arrived. He glanced at the screen and read the first, from Dover.

Well done on Watson. Can you come to Federal Plaza ASAP. I need you to assist with questioning of Donnerstein. Thanks.

He flicked over to the second message, which was from Akbari.

I have been through the uncataloged files and found the missing cross-reference document about the killing of the helicopter crews in the K-G Pass. It's the sensitive information I mentioned. I've decided to show it to you. Can you come to my apartment tonight? You will find it very interesting.

Johnson groaned and showed the messages to Vic. "What do you think? I'm feeling exhausted, buddy."

"Better do both," Vic said. "Dover first, Akbari second. We can't afford to screw around, even if we're all in." He pointed at Dave and Ben. "Let's see if we can persuade these guys to give us a ride. They've got nothing better to do. We'll get a drive-through coffee on the way."

* * *

Monday, June 10, 2013
Manhattan

"Tell me about Kay Associates and what you, or they, were doing in Afghanistan in the 1980s," Dover said to Donnerstein.

Johnson sipped his espresso, folded his arms, and waited to hear how the energy secretary was going to respond. Dover had told him before the meeting began that Donnerstein had denied all wrongdoing and had even declined to call in his lawyer.

Johnson wasn't surprised at the denials but was stunned that Donnerstein didn't want his attorney present while he was being questioned by federal agents. Maybe the energy secretary was so arrogant he felt he could handle the situation himself.

The men, together with a couple of Dover's top investigators and the FBI's special agent in charge of New York, Rod Blyth, were sitting in Blyth's office on the twenty-third floor of the steel and glass skyscraper at 26 Federal Plaza.

The floor, housing the FBI's main New York field office, was buzzing with agents, analysts, secretaries, and other staff, despite it now being quarter to eleven at night.

Hardly surprising, Johnson thought. It wasn't every day a cabinet member was brought in for questioning.

"I've never heard of Kay Associates," Donnerstein said, leaning back in his chair. "Means nothing to me, and I'd bet my last dollar you have no proof that I've ever had any connection with them."

"I suppose you've never heard of Robert Watson or Rex Zilleman, either?" Johnson asked.

Donnerstein said nothing. He had a quizzical expression on his face, his iron gray hair still immaculate. After a short silence, he sighed. "I think you would be well advised to just stop this game and let me go."

Dover impatiently held out his hand to Johnson. "Joe, can we see that photograph, please?" he asked. "Maybe that will persuade the energy secretary to cut the crap."

Johnson took his phone from his pocket, tapped on the photograph that he had discussed with Dover before entering the meeting, and enlarged it so it filled the screen. Then he put it down on the table in front of Donnerstein.

The energy secretary leaned over to view the photo. His face visibly tensed and blanched. His lips moved a little but he didn't speak.

The photograph clearly showed a younger Donnerstein holding a Stinger missile, standing behind Watson, who was presenting another Stinger to some mujahideen.

Donnerstein stared at the photograph for a few moments. "I don't want to answer any further questions until my attorney is here," he said eventually. "Can I call him, please?"

* * *

Monday, June 10, 2013
Hell's Kitchen, Manhattan

Akbari had a pot of brewed coffee ready when Johnson and Vic finally turned up at his apartment at nearly midnight after a twenty-five-minute journey from the Federal Plaza offices in an FBI Dodge Charger.

They had left behind a very satisfied Dover, who was convinced he was about to checkmate Donnerstein and also seemed particularly happy at the demise of Watson. "I tell you, these top CIA guys, you can't trust a single one of them," he had said as Johnson had left.

The arrest of Watson was on the rolling CNN news that Akbari had on in his apartment when Johnson and Vic arrived. The anchor was running through a list of some of the corrupt activities that the former CIA chief had been involved in. CNN had clearly been carefully briefed by someone—probably inside Dover's section at the FBI, Johnson surmised. The Feebs never missed an opportunity to land a punch on the Agency.

"Thank God for that," Johnson said as Akbari poured a coffee and handed it to him. "You don't know how necessary that is right now." He decided not to go into details of what they'd been up to in Brooklyn earlier in the day.

The closest thing to a smile that Johnson had seen since he had met Akbari appeared on the Afghan's face. "Just take a look at this. I think this will give you more of a jolt than a cup of coffee, frankly. I had to think long and hard before deciding to show it to you."

A few moments later Akbari had a short memo up on-screen. "This relates to the helicopters shot down in the K-G Pass and the incidents that followed."

Johnson nodded and began to read the Russian text.

HIGHLY CONFIDENTIAL — TOP SECRET
KGB RESTRICTED LIST ONLY
331/AS/21 YURI SEVERINOV BACKGROUND FILE
January 12, 1988 r.
Kabul
FOR INFORMATION ONLY: Reference incident 2.1.1988
Wazrar, Khost-Gardez Pass, shooting down of two Mi-24
helicopters by mujahideen.
YURI SEVERINOV, born November 10, 1957
Parents: Sergo Severinov and Olga Orlov (married name
Olga Severinov)
Sergo Severinov's parents: father Josef Stalin, mother Irina
Severinov
IOSEB GRIGOROVICH, born October 16, 1947 (pilot of
second Mi-24 helicopter shot down)
Parents: father Josef Stalin, mother Olga Orlov

Johnson read through the memo slowly, his stomach turning over, and then reread it twice more to make sure he had understood what it was saying. He felt initially confused as he tried to get the relationships clear in his mind.

"This can't be right," Johnson said slowly. "Or is it? Tell me. It's saying Severinov's grandfather—his father Sergo's father—was Josef Stalin. Presumably Sergo was the product of some affair he had, and he took his mother's surname, not Stalin's?"

Johnson looked up at Akbari, who nodded.

"And Severinov had an older half brother, Ioseb, who was also fathered by Stalin," Johnson continued, his eyebrows raised.

"Yes," Akbari said. "It seems Stalin spread his seed quite widely. He had an affair with Irina Severinov in 1912, and she gave birth to Sergo."

Akbari paused. "Stalin then for a short time in early 1947 took Olga Orlov as his mistress while she was working as a cook at his *dacha*," he continued in a level, matter-of-fact tone.

Johnson's eyes widened as he digested the detail. "Stalin had an affair with his *son's wife?*"

"It seems so," Akbari said. "Typical of the bastard. He was in his late sixties at that time. He probably terrified her into it. Put a gun to her head or something."

"My God," Johnson said. "That's disgusting." He had known since studying Stalin at university that he was reputed to have had several affairs and illegitimate children during his lifetime. But *this?*

"It happened just after she got married to Sergo, who worked in security for Stalin. She then gave birth to Ioseb. It seems Sergo believed he was the father for a long time before the truth emerged. Yuri was born later."

"But why the hell did Sergo stay there, working for Stalin, after that?" Johnson asked. "Why stay married to Olga?"

Akbari pressed his lips together. "You need to understand what life was like in the Soviet Union under Stalin. His power was absolute. Anyone who crossed him and his desires, his orders, was killed immediately. Everyone was dispensable. These people, Sergo and Olga, were servants, but they might as well have been slaves. They had no choice but to keep their mouths shut and carry on. They had no money. They couldn't afford to leave."

Johnson exhaled. What Akbari had said made absolute

sense. He felt momentarily incapable of saying anything. "Why hasn't all this emerged before?"

"Stalin made Sergo, Olga, and everyone else who knew sign confidentiality agreements. They all knew what the price of breaking them would be," Akbari said. "I and other KGB employees who had access to these top secret files in the '80s also had to sign agreements promising never to disclose this information, anywhere, to anyone. That was why I wanted to have a long think before disclosing all this to you. But frankly, I've decided I no longer care. It should be known."

Johnson turned back to the memo. "And then also, Ioseb was a helicopter pilot who was shooting the shit out of the Afghans before he was shot down and killed by Javed and his men in the K-G Pass."

He looked up at Akbari again. "If I remember correctly, Stalin's birth name wasn't Josef or Stalin. He adopted those later. His birth name was Ioseb something, I can't remember."

"You are correct," Akbari said. "Stalin's birth name was Ioseb Besarionis dze Jughashvili. Which accounts for why the name Ioseb was given to Severinov's half brother."

"I'll be damned," Johnson said. "This is dynamite. It also accounts for why Severinov has been out to get Javed as well as vice versa—it's all in the blood, the family, I mean. And if it's Stalin's blood, well . . ." His voice tailed off.

"Yes," Vic said. "They are both trying to wreak revenge on each other for things that happened twenty-five years ago."

"And the seeds of which were planted a century ago," Akbari added.

There was a pause in the conversation while they all contemplated this startling twist to the legacy of Josef Stalin.

Finally, Johnson broke the silence. "You know, as kids, every time we talked about getting revenge on someone who'd wronged us, my mother would say: love your enemies and pray for those who persecute you. It was from the Sermon on the Mount. So I'm not having that. I'm all for justice but not for revenge. It needs to stop."

Akbari shrugged. "What are you going to do about it?"

"Not sure yet," Johnson said. "But I'm heading back to Kabul tomorrow as soon as I can get a flight and if at all possible, I'll try to make sure they answer for what they've done. If not in court then in the media. I'm sure the Afghans will have a view on all this—I'm sure they'd love it if they found out someone like Severinov was planning to buy up their oil and gas industry."

Another thought struck Johnson. He had been wondering why Severinov had called his company Besoi Energy. There seemed no obvious reason for the choice. But now he realized. "The name of Severinov's company—Besoi."

"What about it?" Vic asked.

"That's *Ioseb* spelled backward."

"Damn me. You're right," Vic said. "He really must have strong feelings for his half brother."

"The other thing we urgently need is the KGB files on Donnerstein to confirm him as the man from Kay Associates," Johnson added. He turned to Akbari. "Have you found those yet?"

Akbari looked impassively at Johnson. "It would be the final piece in your jigsaw, unless I'm mistaken," he said.

Johnson nodded. "Yes, it would." He knew instinctively what Akbari's next line would be.

"If I provide it and complete your puzzle," Akbari said, "you both need to undertake to walk out of here and forget we've had any of these conversations. Forget you ever came here or met me."

Johnson glanced at Vic, then turned back to Akbari. "And if we were unable to provide that?"

"If you caused me trouble, I would make it known that

these documents were of dubious origin and certainly could not be relied on as evidence in any court. I might add that the levels of corruption among the KGB officers compiling these files was extremely high. I'm good at muddying the waters when I need to do so."

I bet you are; years of practice makes perfect, Johnson thought to himself. He again caught Vic's eye, and the two men held each other's gaze for a few seconds. Vic eventually shrugged and gave a slight nod.

"Okay," Johnson said. "We're not having this conversation. We both give our word that we will not push for any action with regard to your US citizenship, as you are asking. Neither will we highlight publicly the source of our information or where the documents came from." It seemed that Akbari had mentally summed up both of his visitors and somehow knew that neither were the type to go back on their word.

Akbari indicated with his thumb toward his darkroom. "Follow me. I've a print that I ran off just earlier."

Akbari walked to his darkroom, with Johnson and Vic following. He flicked on a light switch and went straight to a length of washing line, strung across the far wall, to which were clipped six photographic prints, hung up to dry.

He removed the print at the far right of the string and handed it to Johnson, who began to read the text, written in Russian.

381/RW/85 ROBERT WATSON
February 20, 1988 r.
CROSS REFERENCE 377/RW/85 19.2.88 (ADDI-
TIONAL INFORMATION)
Islamabad
Result of overnight identity check on representative of US
company Kay Associates, seen in meeting with TENOR at
Marriott Hotel.

Identity confirmed as Kurt Donnerstein, US citizen. Further check confirmed Donnerstein involved in missiles and weapons sales, non-approved by US government. POSSIBILITIES FOR BLACKMAIL AND RECRUITMENT? OPTIONS SHOULD BE URGENTLY INVESTIGATED.

"Bingo," Johnson said. "This is the torpedo that's going to finally sink Donnerstein." A smile inexorably crossed his face as he took out his phone, photographed the document, and immediately sent it to Dover with a quick translation.

CHAPTER THIRTY-SIX

Tuesday, June 11, 2013
Moscow

News of the arrest of Kurt Donnerstein in New York and his supposed links to Rex Zilleman and ZenForce Group had come in to Severinov from one of his SVR contacts at the agency's Yasenevo headquarters in a call during the morning. Soon afterward, he had received confirmation in a second call from the same SVR source that his onetime CIA mole Robert Watson had been arrested after falling in front of a subway train, also in New York, while apparently being pursued by FBI agents.

Both pieces of news almost put a smile on Severinov's face. Anything that was going to terminate or even damage ZenForce's bid for the Afghanistan oil assets was hugely helpful. His strong suspicion was that the arrest of Watson on the same day in the same city had to be linked to Donnerstein. It was otherwise too coincidental.

The temptation to smile didn't last long, though. His SVR

contact also said that the Donnerstein arrest was thought to have stemmed from inquiries that Johnson had made into events in Afghanistan dating to the late 1980s.

Maybe the Watson arrest had similarly been somehow linked to Johnson's inquiries as well, Severinov wondered.

It was worrying in the sense that Johnson might also turn his investigative spotlight on Severinov. There were too many risks, too many skeletons hidden away, of all kinds—personal, KGB, and business-related. Given his incarceration in the Kabul safe house, Johnson was hardly going to hold back if he found some usable ammunition. And what if the story about his family came out, the true details of the Stalin lineage? The leadership would set the SVR's pack dogs on him.

Yet there was no option to pull out of the Kabul trip. That would be akin to signing his own death warrant, given President Putin's orders.

Severinov went back to finalizing his preparations for his planned flight the following morning to Kabul, ahead of Thursday's presentation to the Afghan minister of mines and petroleum. Rather than use his luxury villa in the Sherpur district, he was planning to sleep at Kabul Airport in his own plane, which was equipped with a bedroom and bathroom at the rear as well as office space for him to work.

He told Zinaida his choice of suit, shirt, and tie, then instructed her to have the packing completed by that evening and to ensure Vasily was at the airport when he arrived in Kabul. They needed to discuss a new plan to eliminate Javed.

He returned to his desk, flipped open his laptop, and opened the PowerPoint presentation that he was going to deliver to the ministry on Thursday. A couple of the slides required tweaking to reflect changes received from international energy analysts just the previous day in fore-casted oil prices over the following decade, all in a downward direction.

Many executives in his position got others to make such changes in their slide decks, but Severinov liked to fully understand the numbers if he was going to be in a position where he could face serious questioning on assumptions he was presenting. So, in close cooperation with his finance director, he generally chose to go through everything person-ally, especially for such a high-level ministerial presentation and briefing as the one scheduled in Kabul.

Once he had finalized his slides and was happy with them, he copied the file to a small flash drive as a backup and placed it in an envelope, which he tucked inside the copy of the asset sale prospectus he had obtained from the ministry in Kabul. There was a lot of vital information in the prospectus, and he needed to take it with him in case he had to refer to some of the production forecasts or other data.

Severinov placed the prospectus and his briefcase next to his suitcase in his dressing room. Zinaida could pack it all up for him.

His phone rang. It was Mikhail Sobchak, Medvedev's energetic assistant.

"Yuri, the president called just a short while ago for a conference call with Dmitry," Sobchak said. "He's changed his plans. He's now going to Kabul tomorrow for a private one-to-one dinner meeting with Karzai."

Severinov's spirits dropped just as surely as if they had been weighted with lead and dropped into the sea. The last thing he wanted was Putin breathing down his neck while he was trying to focus on the oil and gas presentation.

"Why's he doing that?"

"It's a meeting about future investment in Afghanistan. And the president also wants to speak with you further to discuss again what you might say at a press conference following the petroleum ministry presentation. He would like to use you to deliver some important messages about our intentions in Afghanistan while keeping himself distant from it all at this stage."

Severinov swore to himself. "When does he want to do that?"

"You need to be at the VIP terminal at Vnukovo at eight in the morning. We'll send a car for you at seven."

"Yes, that sounds fine," Severinov said. "My plane's due to leave from there at nine o'clock. No problem."

"Yes, well, regarding your flight, there's one other thing the president wants you to do," Sobchak said.

Severinov hesitated. "What is that?"

He listened carefully as Sobchak ran through the set of instructions Putin had given him, then ended the call.

Severinov put his phone down on the table and looked up at the ceiling. "*Dermo*," he said to himself. "Shit, shit, shit."

CHAPTER THIRTY-SEVEN

Wednesday, June 12, 2013
  Kabul

It was the third time Javed had seen the same silver Toyota Hilux drive slowly down Street Nine outside his brother's house and disappear. It never stopped, never pulled up outside anyone's house. Nobody ever got out. He wondered if it had been past other times too while he was in the office. It was one too many visits, and there seemed no obvious reason for it.

His antenna for surveillance had been on hyperalert since his return from Wazrar with the Stingers, which remained in a concealed cupboard in his basement. The Hilux had been the only anomaly he had spotted near his office or his home.

If the vehicle was surveillance, then although there had been an Afghan or Pakistani at the wheel, Javed's guess was that it belonged to either Severinov or to Joe Johnson, given the latter's interest in meeting him again.

Since Javed had emailed Johnson a week earlier,

expressing a willingness to meet after the oil and gas asset sale was complete, he had heard nothing more from Johnson. But the man had worked for the CIA and was an investigator.

It didn't matter much, anyway. Javed was certain that in Kabul, he could easily throw off any tail, whether CIA, SVR, or whatever. He had a few stair-step, zigzag anti-surveillance routes from the old days that still worked very well, using side streets, alleys, and tracks across disused land and through industrial units. He had absolutely no doubt that the Taliban used similar routes, enabling them to get around the city and avoid security checks by Afghan police or army or by international forces.

Javed went to a desk, which was placed on the second floor near to a window so he could keep an eye on the street, flipped open his laptop, and for the umpteenth time toggled over to the window showing the location of the GPS tracker he had installed in Severinov's prospectus pack.

Since the previous Thursday, when the tracker in Severinov's phone had vanished entirely from his monitor screen, the one in his prospectus had not moved at all. It had remained at the same extensive *dacha* near the banks of the Moscow River. Javed had been able to zoom in with his maps app in satellite mode and see its exact position in the Gorki-8 area.

The thing that worried him was that Severinov certainly would not have remained in the house all that time without moving. So would he actually take the prospectus with him when he flew to Kabul for the presentation to the energy minister? Javed had been assuming he would have to, but there remained a nagging uncertainty at the back of his mind. Or had he discovered the tracker and removed it from the pack?

Javed refreshed the screen and waited for it to load. It always took some time.

When the screen did load, Javed sat straight up. The blue dot marking the position of the tracker was now eleven miles to the south, in a building very near to the main terminal at Vnukovo International Airport. Given Severinov's status in Russia, Javed was certain that the building where the tracker was located would be a special VIP terminal. He found an airport map online that told him he was correct.

If Severinov was on the move, he was going to need to act more quickly than he thought.

Javed grabbed his phone and sent a text message to Mahmood Marwat, his old friend in air traffic control. *Can we speak now? Urgent.*

Mahmood would know exactly what it was about. The two men had discussed the Severinov case in some detail, and he was expecting to hear from Javed at any time.

A couple of minutes later, Javed's phone rang. It was Mahmood.

"Is he moving?" Mahmood asked, without any preamble.

"Yes, he's at Vnukovo right now," Javed said. "Can you check flight plans from there?"

"One minute."

There was the sound of fingers tapping on a computer keyboard and then a long pause, followed by more tapping.

"Strange," Mahmood said. "Can I just check the aircraft registrations you gave me again?"

He read out the two numbers that Javed had supplied for Severinov's Bombardier Global Express and Cessna Citation.

"Yes, that's them," Javed said.

"The Bombardier is listed to come in at three in the afternoon from Vnukovo. But there are two other aircraft also with flight plans filed coming from Moscow at that same time. And listen to this—I'm certain the other two are Putin's planes. Consecutive registration numbers, both flying from Vnukovo to Kabul."

"*Putin's?*"

"Yes. Both of them."

"Putin can't be going to the presentation," Javed said. "That's way below him. He must have some other business in Kabul. Maybe with Karzai."

"I agree. Don't assume he's even coming," Mahmood said. "The Russians always do this. Multiple flight plans, different aircraft, try to keep people guessing. It's the normal routine. Fools nobody in the business. Although of course you don't actually know which of the planes Putin will be on."

"No, but two planes makes it look more likely that he actually is coming," Javed said. "These are the Ilyushin 96-300s, right? Do those jets have any anti-missile protection?"

"I'm certain they do. I heard lasers or something. But how well tested they are, how effective, I don't know. Could just be bullshit, for all I know. Why? You're surely not going to—"

Javed was silent for a second. "Just make sure you tell me if there's any late changes to those flight plans," he said.

* * *

Wednesday, June 12, 2013
  Kabul

A long delay at JFK prior to takeoff and then another holdup with the connecting flight in Dubai meant that, frustratingly for Johnson, his plane into Kabul arrived only at twelve thirty in the afternoon.

His aggravation at the delays and his sense of urgency both deepened dramatically while he was in Dubai, when he managed a short phone conversation with Jayne, who had made some good progress in Kabul.

Jayne had received from her friend Alice Hocking at

GCHQ in Cheltenham some flight plan data for that afternoon, picked up by an electronic trawl of air traffic control communications in Kabul. When Jayne had made the request to Alice, it had seemed a slightly circuitous way of trying to obtain the information she needed, but as was often the case, GCHQ's tentacles ran deep and swiftly into areas that were generally otherwise inaccessible.

She reported to Johnson that there were three flights involving nonscheduled airlines due into Kabul from Moscow that afternoon, all at three o'clock, according to plans filed. One was Severinov's private Bombardier jet; the other two belonged to none other than the Russian president, Vladimir Putin.

There had been a slight pause while Johnson had digested the implications of what he had been told. Severinov, it was obvious, was flying in for the presentation the following day to the minister of mines and petroleum. That was expected, and it nailed down the time at which any attempt on his life by Javed and his Stinger missiles was likely to take place.

The flights involving Putin's aircraft, though, were completely from left field. What the hell was that about? Common sense told Johnson that Putin wouldn't be involved in a petroleum ministry presentation, so he must be heading to Kabul for some other higher-level meeting, presumably with Hamid Karzai.

The odd thing was that the flights were all scheduled for the same time of day.

"Jayne, you need to get on the phone to Seb Storey and tip him off," Johnson said. "I'm sure the army will know about Putin coming in; they're probably working with the Afghans on it. But maybe they won't have put two and two together and realized that Severinov's plane is due in at the same time and that the risk from Javed could apply to all the aircraft."

There was a short silence. "I've already called him and I've been trying the local police chief," Jayne said tersely.

Idiot, Johnson said to himself. *Of course she has. She's always one step ahead of the game.*

"Good, sorry, I thought you probably had already. What did they say?" Johnson asked.

"I haven't managed to speak to either so far. They've got another big operation underway out of Wilderness—there was a huge Taliban attack last night. Storey's calling me back as soon as possible. The police chief here is also tied up with the Taliban and is also manically busy organizing security for the Putin visit. His assistant just brushed me off. What a joke."

Johnson heard nothing more from Jayne before boarding his connecting flight from Dubai to Kabul. The circumstances combined to make it among the most nerve-racking journeys he had ever undertaken. For the first time, he felt a sense of relief when he breathed in the familiar Kabul smell of hot sticky tarmac, diesel fumes, cooking oil, grilling meat, burning charcoal, and sweat the second he walked off the plane and onto the aircraft steps.

Thankfully there were no delays going through the terminal building. Forty minutes later, Johnson had greeted Jayne with a hug and was walking with her and Haroon through the crowded pickup zone with its array of stern-looking armed security officers to the silver Hilux, where Omar was behind the wheel. Nearby, business executives were being rapidly ushered by their bodyguards toward waiting armored cars.

"Great that you got the flight details, but what about Javed?" Johnson asked.

"Haroon saw him go into his office early this morning, about seven o'clock, and then he headed back to his brother's old house at eleven," Jayne said.

"And now?"

"Presume he's still there."

"But you're not sure?" Johnson asked.

"No. We still haven't found a way of tracking him effectively from the house," Jayne said. "His part of the street is bloody difficult. There's no cover to speak of, other houses are all hidden behind tall walls and gates, and there's rarely cars left parked outside. So any surveillance vehicle or person on foot stands out like a policeman in a pub. I can't operate there alone because of the kidnap factor, and Haroon can't spend his whole time there."

"I know. It's difficult. It would be nice to put people at either end of his street," Johnson said.

"Yes. And before you ask about a tracker, he never parks it unattended anywhere in public. Not had a chance, so far."

"We're out of time now, anyway," Johnson said as he loaded his bag into the back of the Hilux. "He's going to make a move today, with Severinov's plane coming in. We know he's got Stingers. It must be now."

"It could be when Severinov leaves," Jayne said.

Johnson shrugged. "Doubt it. I think he'll look to do it on the way in. Then the return flight will be the backup option if that fails."

He climbed into the front passenger seat while Jayne got into the rear seat.

Johnson looked across at Omar. "Take us to Javed's street. Quick as you can. But this time we'll wait on the street near the bend, just along from the medical center." Johnson had spotted the center on previous visits, and although there was very little traffic in and out—it was a small private clinic, not a large hospital—it was the only possible source of cover. At least if needed they could drive the Hilux into the clinic entrance, which had a U-shaped driveway, and pretend to be dropping off or collecting a patient.

Omar swung the Hilux out of the terminal and west onto the busy Airport Road, a divided highway hectic with speeding taxis and heavy trucks, around the traffic circle at Shahid Square, and then south down Forty Meter Road before entering Qala-e-Fatullah Road, past Cheragh University and the hospital.

Omar drove straight past the house on Street Nine, but as usual, the gates were closed and there was no sign of movement.

"Turn around near the medical center and face the car the other way," Johnson instructed. "My guess is he'll head out that direction."

Omar nodded and glanced in his mirror. Then he visibly stiffened, which Johnson immediately noticed. "Seen something?"

"Yes, he's just driven out of his gate and headed the other way," Omar said.

"Shit," Johnson said, turning his head around 180 degrees. Through the rear window, in the distance, he could see a dark pickup heading away from them. "Turn around. Go into the medical center driveway, then out again. Quick."

Omar accelerated into the medical center driveway, with its white-painted concrete gateposts and red-brick paving, startling the crew of an ambulance who were getting into the vehicle near the entrance. He shot around the half-circle driveway, his tires squealing on the bricks, then out the other side into the street, turning back the way they had come, the engine whining in second gear as he pushed the gas pedal down.

He barreled back toward the intersection with Qala-e-Fatullah Road. But Javed's pickup had already disappeared.

* * *

Wednesday, June 12, 2013
   Kabul

Javed accelerated out of Street Nine and up Qala-e-Fatullah Road for about two hundred meters, overtaking a fuel truck, a yellow rickshaw, and two taxis. He cut a sharp right followed by a stair-step route through the backstreets of the Taimani and then Qala-e-Fatullah districts, taking one corner after another. He glanced in his mirror, although he knew instinctively that the silver Hilux wouldn't be visible.

The timing couldn't have been better. He had been preparing to leave his house but was still concerned about the possibility of surveillance at either end of Street Nine. Then, from his second-floor window, he had seen the Hilux heading slowly toward his house. He knew straightaway that the car wouldn't stop nearby—that would have been far too obtrusive.

So the moment it was down the street in the opposite direction, he had a window of opportunity to get out. And he had taken it. He had run down the stairs, flung himself into the driver's seat, and exited his property just as the Hilux was rounding the bend near the medical center.

That had given him at least a thirty-second head start, which was all he needed.

Now Javed relaxed a little, continuing on his backstreet route eastward. Normally, he would have taken a route around the north side of the airport, through the Khaje Bughra area until he came to Tajikan Road.

Today, however, he was certain that if Putin was heading into the city, there would be a huge security operation in place on all the obvious routes around the airport.

In that, he was correct. At almost every turn that took him across or near to a major street, he caught sight of

Afghan National Police checkpoints, flanked by green Ford pickups. At most there were long lines of vehicles waiting to pass through.

But with their restricted budget, Javed knew for sure there was no way in which the hard-pressed security services could cover all the rat runs as well.

So he opted for a tortuous route that ran through the suburbs south of the airport but north of the city center, through Wazirabad, Deh Sabz, and Khwaja Rawash. It was a route that certainly would not show up on any satellite navigation device, involving a shortcut through a scrap metal yard, across a bombed-out factory unit, and along dirt roads with potholes almost deep enough to swallow a person. The open sewers running alongside many of the streets were another constant hazard.

Within three-quarters of an hour, he was parking his black pickup in the same alley he had used on his previous visit to the apartment block overlooking Severinov's property.

In the back of the pickup, safely stashed under the false bed, were three Stinger missiles. He pulled them out, placed them in a large backpack, and put the gripstock, the sight, and six battery coolant units into a black carry case.

Javed glanced at his watch. It was ten minutes to three. He pulled the large backpack rain cover over the top of the missiles, concealing them as best he could. Then he slung the backpack over his shoulder, picked up the carry case, and set off down the alley toward the apartment building across the road.

CHAPTER THIRTY-EIGHT

Wednesday, June 12, 2013
Kabul

The barrier of roughly painted red and white concrete barriers and plastic orange cones stretched halfway across the northbound side of Forty Meter Road, funneling traffic into a police checkpoint, where officers went through all drivers' and passengers' passports and identification documents before searching their vehicles. The checkpoint was flanked by two green twin-cab police Ford pickups, with machine guns mounted on the back, manned by nervous-looking officers.

It took ten minutes to get to the front of the line and then another few minutes while a solemn policeman checked all their documents and had a quick look in the cab and the back of the Hilux.

By the time they were finally waved through, Johnson, in the front passenger seat, had given up on all chance of successfully tailing Javed. Behind him, Jayne's phone beeped.

"I've just had a message from Seb," Jayne said from the rear seat behind Johnson. "Police and army checkpoints have had no luck so far."

Johnson stared out the windshield as the Toyota headed east along Airport Road. That was no surprise.

"We're not going to tail him or outrun him," Johnson said. "And I doubt the police will pick him up. He probably knows these streets like his way to the toilet on a dark night. We'll have to outthink him."

Jayne's phone beeped again. "That's Seb saying the first of the flights in is expected at ten past three now," she said, reading the screen. "He doesn't know which one."

Johnson turned to Haroon and Jayne in the back of the Toyota. "Where would he do this job from?"

"I would say the hills," Haroon said, pointing out the window at the khaki-colored mounds that rose into the azure sky a mile and a half north of the runway. "That's the obvious spot."

Johnson glanced at his watch. It was five past three. "Yes, the hills are the obvious spot. But the army and police know that. They'll be up there."

Haroon nodded. "I hope so."

"And the airport is guarded like a fortress," Johnson went on. "So he won't be able to do anything from around there. I'm thinking it has to be somewhere farther out but still on the flight path coming into land."

Suddenly Johnson's mind went back to his rescue from Severinov's property in eastern Kabul by Storey and his US Army helicopter. He recalled the sound of planes passing low overhead as they droned in to land and then the comment that Jayne had made.

"Jayne," he said, swiveling around. "When you were in Storey's chopper pulling me out of the Severinov shack east of the airport, you said you thought you saw a gunman on the roof of an apartment building."

Instantly Jayne banged the back of the driver's seat with the flat of her hand.

"Shit, that's it," she said, her voice rising sharply. "The guy with the missile launcher, an RPG or whatever it was. Standing on the roof when I glanced up. By the time that door gunner tracked on the roof, he was gone."

"Well, let's get down there," Johnson said. "Nothing to lose." He turned to Omar. "Get us down to the Nangarhar highway; it's about two kilometers beyond Camp Phoenix. I can't even remember the damn road name, but I'll know it when I see it."

Omar accelerated along Airport Road to the end, then cut a zigzag course through the backstreets of Khwaja Rawash, just south of the airport. He hammered past a series of massive apartment building projects that were midway through construction, the back of the pickup bouncing over potholes and ruts in the road. He then steered through an industrial area with its fuel and chemical tanks and lines of trucks waiting to load before finally getting onto the highway.

As they drove eastward past Camp Phoenix to their left, Johnson could see ahead of them in the distance a plane coming in westward toward the airport, its landing gear down, its lights on.

* * *

Wednesday, June 12, 2013
Kabul

As soon as the tiny black outline of the plane appeared in the distance, Javed knelt on his right knee and screwed the battery coolant unit into the base of the green gripstock. He glanced around him one more time from his semi-concealed spot beneath the small shelter on the roof of the apartment block. There was nobody else there: he had the place to himself.

Then he checked the screen of the laptop that lay on top of its case next to him. The screen showed an aerial satellite view of Kabul, with the airport runway visible in the top left, the long straight line of the Kabul-Nangarhar highway below it, the wiggling snake of the Kabul River, and the distinctive bicycle spoke outline of Pul-e-Charkhi prison and the mountains to the bottom right.

A blue dot, visible just over Pul-e-Charkhi, was moving slowly but steadily toward Javed and the airport.

This was it. The chance he'd been waiting for since 1988.

Javed placed the long, slim Stinger missile tube in position on his shoulder, then put his eye to the sight and focused on the incoming plane, which he could see now was the white Bombardier Global Express that he knew Severinov owned, with its distinctive T-tail and twin rear engines.

He glanced down one more time at the laptop. The blue dot, representing the position of the tracker device built into the spine of Severinov's prospectus file, had advanced farther and was now on a path that looked as though it would take the aircraft almost directly overhead. His plan was to let it pass over, then trigger the Stinger just as the aircraft approached the airport—that way, the Stinger's infrared tracking mechanism would shove the missile right up the Bombardier's engine exhausts. Javed almost smiled at the thought.

The plane would then, in all likelihood, crash on the airport site or very near to it. That would be the most spectacular outcome, which would hopefully avoid wreckage smashing into residential housing.

Javed stepped out from beneath the shelter and watched as the plane drew gradually closer, its outline clearer as it emerged from the haze that hung over Kabul, its drone growing louder.

The roar reached a peak as the Bombardier passed over him, and then as it continued toward the landing strip, Javed lifted his Stinger. The plane was now filling the sight. He activated the missile against the blue sky by pressing on the safety and actuator switch and realigned it with the aircraft, which resulted in a loud beep as the infrared mechanism locked on to the Bombardier.

Javed clicked on the uncage button at the front of the device, allowing it to automatically track the plane. There was little need to compensate for gravity here, given the relatively short distance between him and the aircraft.

Now was the time. He pulled back the trigger and a second later there came an explosion as the launch motor ejected the missile from its tube. With a loud whoosh, the missile's flight motor activated, and the weapon flew directly over Kabul's eastern suburbs toward the retreating Bombardier—a slim tube of death, arcing toward Severinov's jet at a speed of about 2,500 miles per hour, its direction dictated with minute accuracy by the infrared detector that was locked onto the aircraft's engine exhaust heat.

Instinctively, Javed punched the air with his left fist. *Yes!*

He almost felt a sense of shock that the Stinger had operated the way it was intended—his biggest fear had been that the missile itself or, more likely, the BCU simply would not function after such a long time in storage in the cave.

Seconds later, and just a short distance from touching down on the Kabul runway, the Bombardier exploded in a deafening white and orange firework display.

Most of the tail section, housing the engines, fragmented

and was catapulted away in a cloud of debris in all directions, away from the rest of the aircraft, while the nose of the plane turned upward but then fell along with the main body of the fuselage vertically onto the tract of land that formed the approach to the runway. There it exploded as it landed, throwing up a cloud of black smoke and dust that drifted up into the air like a giant mushroom.

Javed stood and stared at the exploding aircraft in awe. His plan had worked spectacularly well. Severinov was dead. Finally, he had extracted his revenge.

He jerked himself out of his semi-trance and began to place the spent Stinger tube, the gripstock, the sight, and the remaining BCUs back in their bags. He flipped the laptop lid down and stowed it in a small carry case. He now needed to get out of there, as quickly as possible.

* * *

Wednesday, June 12, 2013
Kabul

Johnson caught a glimpse of the white vapor trail scorching westward against the brownstone mountain backdrop just a second or two before the Stinger struck the aircraft. The ensuing explosion and fireball physically rocked the pickup in which they were traveling.

"Shit . . . that goddamn plane's just been hit," Johnson said, his shoulders tensing as he craned his neck to get a view. "It's gone down."

"We're too bloody late," Jayne said as a dark mushroom cloud of smoke and dust began steadily rising up into the atmosphere from the direction of the airport, about a mile and a half northwest of where they were driving along the highway. There was another distant bang, presumably from a secondary explosion.

"Looks that way," Johnson said. But he had seen enough of the vapor trail to confirm the direction it had come from. "Keep going," he shouted at Omar, who had put his foot on the brake and was pulling onto the side of the highway. "Quick, give Storey a call and put him on loudspeaker. We need to tell him what's happened and say we're heading toward where the missile came from."

"Where did it come from?" Jayne said, grabbing at her phone.

"There, where we were heading," Johnson said, pointing ahead of them toward the east. "Not the hills. I think that apartment building. Can he get a unit from Camp Phoenix?"

Jayne nodded and began tapping on her cell phone screen.

Johnson knew they probably had a matter of minutes, perhaps less, to cut Javed off before he vanished from his firing position and into the labyrinth of backstreets in the northern suburbs surrounding the airport.

Then he remembered there were two other aircraft coming in at the same time.

Putin.

Surely Putin's pilot would have realized what had happened to Severinov's jet—he could hardly have missed it if coming in behind on the same flight path—and would have headed out of the danger zone, although Stinger missiles had a long range, he knew that.

Storey answered the call. "Colonel Storey."

Jayne spoke first. "Seb, if you've not heard already, we've got a major incident here in Kabul. A jet, we believe belonging to Severinov, has just been shot down on the way into land and—"

"I know," Storey cut in. "I'm at Camp Phoenix. I came in

on a chopper an hour or so ago. So I'm aware of what's going on, but we have no more details yet."

"Two things," Johnson said. "We saw roughly where the missile came from. We suspect the same apartment where Jayne saw a gunman when you got me out of Severinov's place, and we're certain it's Javed Hasrat. We're heading there right now. Can you get a team from Phoenix there?"

"I'll get it done. Good thinking. I'll join the team and come with them. What vehicle does he have?"

Jayne gave Storey details of Javed's black Toyota Hilux and the license plate.

"Thanks," Storey said tersely. "And the other thing you wanted to mention?"

"You know Putin's plane is due in at the same time—right now," Johnson said. "It needs to be diverted. Might be a follow-up attack."

"Yes, they'll know what's going on—I'm sure they'll take action. But I will double check anyway. Anything else?" Storey asked, his voice level but strained.

"No, that's it," Johnson said.

Storey ended the call with a brief instruction to keep him updated.

While Johnson was talking, Omar had accelerated down the highway, about three-quarters of a mile past Camp Phoenix. Now he braked hard and swung a left into a potholed side road heading north, just as the sound of wailing sirens began in the distance.

After about five hundred yards and a couple of left and right turns past industrial units, Johnson recognized exactly where they were. Ahead of them, on the left, was the building where he had been incarcerated by Severinov. On the right, on the opposite side of the road, was the apartment building where Jayne had spotted the gunman.

At the intersection two blocks ahead of them, a cloud of

dust blew up as a dark-colored pickup truck sped across it from right to left without stopping, heading southward toward the Kabul-Nangarhar highway.

Before Johnson could open his mouth, Jayne spoke from the rear seat. "That must be him. He's got a black pickup."

Without instruction, Omar accelerated toward the intersection where the truck had crossed, the silver Hilux bumping across the heavily potholed surface. He turned sharply left, and immediately they saw the black Toyota speeding away from them, halfway down the long straight street, throwing up dust behind it.

As Omar gave pursuit, the unmistakable bulky shapes of two US Army Humvees, painted in khaki and green camouflage, turned the corner at the bottom of the street, right in front of the black pickup. The truck veered at the last moment to avoid colliding with them, appeared to skid on gravel, and smashed into the perimeter wall of a house on the left of the street, where it flipped over and came to rest on its roof in a drainage ditch, wheels spinning in the air.

Three soldiers carrying rifles jumped from the first Humvee and ran up to the stricken pickup, pointing their weapons at the driver's cab. Storey got out of the second Humvee and walked up to join them.

Omar braked to a halt twenty yards from the Humvees, and Johnson, Jayne, and Haroon jumped out.

One of the soldiers was pointing his rifle and screaming and swearing at the driver of the pickup to get out. Slowly, the door of the inverted Toyota swung open and the driver crawled out onto the gravel and dust, blood streaming down the right side of his face from a cut on his forehead, his clothing disheveled. It was Javed.

Javed raised his hands in the air in a token gesture of surrender. At the same time, a green Afghan National Police pickup appeared from around the corner and headed toward them, its siren wailing, headlights on, blue emergency roof lights flashing.

The police vehicle braked to a halt and an officer wearing a blue-gray uniform and a peaked cap and carrying a pair of steel handcuffs got out and walked over to the group.

Johnson moved closer and caught Javed's eye. The Afghan just looked blankly at him and shook his head.

"The bastard deserved it," Javed said. "For what he did. You know he killed my wife, my daughter. He had it coming to him."

"I was going to greet you with that old phrase, *salaam alaikum*. Peace be upon you. But it's not appropriate—is it?" Johnson said. "And I know what Severinov did. But nothing can justify what you've just done, shooting down that aircraft. I had plans to bring Severinov to justice my own way. And I had hoped to meet with you to discuss all that—but you've been running and ducking. You didn't give me a chance."

Storey took a couple of steps toward Johnson. "We need to get him taken into the police headquarters," he said. "Maybe you can talk to him in depth later. But I don't want to hang around here. We're going to attract attention, maybe Taliban attention. We need to move."

Johnson nodded reluctantly. "We never do seem to quite complete our meetings as intended, do we?" he said to Javed. "I feel we have unfinished business."

He would have liked to grill Javed in more depth there and then. But after a quick conversation between the police officer, Johnson, and Storey, it was agreed that the police should take charge of Javed and drive him to their headquarters for questioning, as Storey had suggested. The officers pushed Javed into the back of the green Ford, his hands now cuffed tightly behind his back.

As he watched the police unit drive off, Johnson found himself with mixed feelings.

Javed had been caught, and Watson would now be prosecuted for his illegal activities over the years. But death in a plane crash had robbed Johnson of his chance to deliver at least some form of justice to Yuri Severinov for all the evil that the Russian had done during the Soviet occupation of Afghanistan and, it had to be assumed, during the years since.

Rather than being jubilant, Johnson suddenly felt as though he had been cheated in a major way.

Storey walked over to Johnson. "I've just had a message about the Putin flight. There was only one of his planes in the end, not two. They diverted it to Bagram, and he's on the ground safely there."

Bagram was the largest US military base in Afghanistan, about twenty-five miles north of Kabul, with two long runways and a sprawling mass of support buildings, housing for soldiers and aircrews, and offices.

Johnson nodded. "Okay, good. I don't think having an American Stinger missile disappear up Putin's backside while the US is more or less in charge on the ground here would have done much for Russian-American relations, and definitely not for Russian-Afghan relations. Looks like Severinov was the sacrificial lamb in this case, then. Not that Putin will care about that."

"Actually, he wasn't the sacrificial lamb," Storey said.

"What do you mean?" Johnson asked.

"I've just heard that Severinov wasn't on his own plane—the one that got shot down."

Johnson felt a jolt go through him, and there were a few seconds of silence before he replied.

"You *what*?" Johnson said.

"He was on Putin's plane. The only people on the

Severinov jet were the pilot, the copilot, a couple of crew, and one of Severinov's assistants."

Johnson stared at Storey. "You're joking."

But it was very clear that the US lieutenant colonel was not joking. "No. Severinov's on the ground at Bagram right now."

CHAPTER THIRTY-NINE

Thursday, June 13, 2013
  Bagram Airfield

The meeting room at Bagram Airfield fell silent as the TV news bulletin began. Johnson leaned back in his chair to watch the large screen on the wall, as did Sally O'Hara, sitting opposite him, and Jayne, to his right. A fan standing on a table whirred away behind them in a vain attempt to keep the room cool.

"Following President Obama's dismissal of Kurt Donnerstein yesterday, speculation is mounting that the former energy secretary will face a series of as-yet unspecified charges relating to alleged corruption and abuse of public office involving using his position to make substantial financial gains," the TV newscaster said. "Sources close to the White House and to the House of Representatives indicate that it is possible Donnerstein could even face charges relating to alleged arms deals in Afghanistan involving Stinger missiles that were carried out as long ago as 1988, as well as more recent breaches of federal law."

The bulletin went on to state that Donnerstein remained under close questioning by senior FBI agents in New York City following his arrest three days earlier at a rented apartment in Brooklyn.

"It has emerged from FBI sources that the downfall of Donnerstein followed the unearthing of secret documents from files compiled by the KGB, the former intelligence service of the Soviet Union, that were held in Kabul. It was previously thought that all such files had been destroyed in the late 1980s after the Soviet withdrawal from Afghanistan," the newscaster said. "The sources indicated that a private US investigator was behind the sourcing of the documents, but his identity is not known at this stage."

Johnson fought to stop a wry grin from spreading across his face. A media and political storm had erupted following the arrest of Donnerstein and the details that had emerged from the photographs of the KGB files that Abdul Akbari had spirited out of Afghanistan.

The CNN bulletin continued with a separate story about Vladimir Putin's jet having a narrow escape after the plane landing ahead of his at Kabul Airport was shot down in what was believed to be another Taliban attack. The reporter detailed how the wreckage of the plane, a privately owned Bombardier Global Express, had narrowly missed a residential area and had smashed into the southeastern end of the runway. Attempts were ongoing to determine the identities of those on board, including crew, all of whom had died. To Johnson's relief, there was no link to the previous story about Donnerstein. Doubtless that would all emerge in time, but it was too soon now.

Meanwhile, Robert Watson had been formally charged at his hospital bed with a series of offenses, historic and more current, spanning espionage, corruption, illegal arms trading, and the theft of federal funds and property. His case too had generated worldwide news coverage and widespread condemnation that reflected badly on those at Langley who had supported him for so long. Some of the background material and footage was rehashed from when Watson had initially fled the US following Johnson's Yugoslav war crimes inquiry the previous year.

Latest indications from the FBI, via Vic, had been that Watson was likely to be in the hospital for another week and would then be taken to Federal Plaza, where further charges could follow. It was almost certain that Watson would be refused bail while waiting to be arraigned in front of a judge. "If Watson isn't a flight risk, then I don't know who is," Vic had said.

O'Hara turned to Johnson and winked. "The ripples from the stone you threw into the pond seem to be spreading far and wide," she said calmly. "From Manhattan to Moscow."

"It looks that way," Johnson said.

Johnson, Jayne, Haroon, and O'Hara, along with Seb Storey, had been ferried in a US Army Osprey helicopter on a short flight from Camp Phoenix to Bagram to assist with interviews taking place with Severinov. Now they were waiting for the Russian to be brought to the meeting room.

Clearly he's being spared some of the more extreme interviewing techniques, Johnson thought to himself. *A pity*.

A couple of minutes later, Storey took a call giving him an update on Javed Hasrat, who continued to be detained at the Afghan National Police headquarters, a little farther along Bibi Mahru from the US embassy.

Johnson had requested a meeting with Javed, just for the purposes of closure more than anything. But Storey told him that the police were not going to cooperate given that they had their own interrogation process well underway—a successful prosecution was inevitable.

Johnson had felt a great deal of empathy for Javed in the late '80s, when their anti-Soviet agendas had been aligned, but certainly did not envy him now. Javed's fate was a grim one, and ironically, it was quite possible he would end up back at Pul-e-Charkhi, from which he had so fortuitously escaped in 1988, but this time for a much longer stint.

The price of revenge.

Johnson knew that soon he would have to brief media and senior US political investigators on what had happened and on some of the findings he had uncovered about all the players in this complex historical web of events. Already there had been interview requests from Kabul correspondents of *The New York Times* and CNN after someone at the US embassy had pointed them in his direction. It would be interesting to see what journalists—especially Russian ones—made of the twin tales of revenge involving Javed and Severinov.

Even more interesting might be the impact of the news that Stalin's oligarch grandson had been following firmly in the family tradition of barbaric behavior—and had almost succeeded in buying up a large chunk of Afghanistan's oil sector.

"I've received one interesting piece of information back from the police interrogation team holding Javed," Storey said.

"What's that?" Johnson asked.

"Apparently Javed told officers he couldn't understand why Severinov was not on the plane that he had shot down. He explained exactly why he had done it: it was revenge for the killing of his wife and youngest daughter by a Soviet helicopter unit operating under Severinov's orders in 1988. He also told them he had installed a tracker device in Severinov's prospectus document or file or something and that his tracker app had indicated clearly that Severinov was on the plane he had hit with a Stinger."

"Except he obviously wasn't."

"Indeed. It will be interesting to find out why."

The door opened and in walked Severinov, wearing a heavy cotton white shirt with gold cufflinks, black slacks, and deeply polished brown shoes, flanked by two US Army officers. He took two steps, then stood and glared first at Johnson, then at Storey and Haroon.

The tables are turned, Johnson thought. It was exactly ten days since he had escaped from Severinov's property in eastern Kabul. He would love to see the Russian taken into custody by Afghan police and properly prosecuted.

"Sit down," Johnson said. "So nice to see you again," he added, with as much sarcasm as he could muster.

Severinov didn't reply but just walked, almost in slow motion, to a chair on the opposite side of the long table and sat, folding his arms as he did so.

"So, you had a narrow escape, it seems," Johnson said.

"It seems so," Severinov said. "Just like you."

Johnson withheld the temptation to guffaw. "We can talk about our previous encounter at your shack later. But I'd like to know why you weren't on your own plane coming here. Why were you on your president's jet?"

"I didn't invite myself, you asshole," Severinov said. "He wanted me. I was instructed to join him."

"Right. So what happened to all your papers, documents, files?" Johnson asked, ignoring the insult. He wasn't going to directly mention the tracker. "Why weren't they with you?"

Severinov looked slightly nonplussed. "I had some with me. My assistant, Zinaida, took the others on my plane."

That explained that. Zinaida had died along with the crew.

"Good thing you followed your leader's instructions, then," Johnson said. He paused, then added, "Just like your father and your mother followed Josef Stalin's instructions—your grandfather's instructions."

Johnson needed to let Severinov know that he was aware of his family situation and that none of his secrets were secret any longer.

Severinov's face froze momentarily. "What are you talking about?" he said.

"Was that why you were after Javed?" Johnson asked. "Because of your half brother?"

Severinov's face visibly tensed and went red. He clenched his fist, and after a second's pause, banged it down on the table, rattling the drinking glasses that stood next to a jug of water, and swore in Russian. "How the hell do you know about my family?"

Johnson shrugged. "Old KGB files."

"Bullshit. *Bullshit!* They were all destroyed. I know that for a fact." He stood suddenly and lurched toward Johnson, only to be pulled back by the two US military men standing behind him, who with lightning speed grabbed him by the collar and jerked him back into his chair.

"He is the one who deserves to die," Severinov spat, "not Zinaida or my flight crew. That Javed is an animal, like all the other *dukhi*. My father always told me, be a bee that stings for the Motherland. That's what I've always done. It's about the Motherland, not about me."

Privately, Johnson had to agree that what Javed had done to Severinov's half brother was indeed animalistic.

Johnson shook his head. "So what about those helicopter attacks you ordered on the villages in the Khost-Gardez Pass, the ones that killed Javed's family and others," he said. "How would you characterize those?"

Severinov leaned back and gazed at Johnson with a look

of pure contempt. "What do *you* know? My orders were the orders given to me," Severinov said. "I had no choice. It was that or the Lubyanka."

The usual KGB operative's defense, albeit probably true.

"Speaking of bees stinging for the Motherland, I saw that quote on the wall of your shack in Kabul," Johnson said. "But it was attributed to Stalin, your grandfather, not your father."

"Josef Stalin gave the original print to my father," Severinov said. "It was a little private saying. He taught it to me."

"So all this was inspired by Stalin, then?" Johnson asked.

"In one sense, yes," Severinov said.

Jayne folded her arms and turned away. "Stalin's final sting," she murmured under her breath, just loud enough for Johnson to hear.

"What's that?" Severinov said, turning to her.

"I said, the gunship attack on Wazrar was Stalin's final sting," Jayne said, turning back to him. "Or was it the killing of Baz, who you also murdered there a couple of weeks ago? I have to say, Stalin taught your father and you very well. Chips off the old block."

"You're talking complete shit," Severinov said.

"You're a real credit to your grandfather," Jayne continued. "He would have been proud of you. I guess it's all in the genes. A triumph of DNA."

The sarcasm seemed to wash over Severinov almost unnoticed. Rather than responding, he leaned forward, eyeballed Johnson, and said menacingly, "And *you* and the rest of your CIA scum deserve to be stung for what you did, supplying the mujahideen with missiles and weapons."

Severinov paused and appeared to collect himself. "I would like to request that you keep my historical family situation private," he said. "The leadership does not want it made public because of the Stalin connection. It reflects badly on him."

This is laughable, Johnson thought. "I'm not going to even comment on that. Anyway, perhaps you can tell me why you continued to admire Stalin despite his atrocities—quite apart from what he did to your family."

Severinov shrugged. "He was a strong leader. He saw off Hitler and modernized and industrialized the country. Simple. He actually inspired thousands. Inspired me."

Johnson found it difficult to think of an appropriate retort and instead let his silence do the talking.

"How did your family cope with what he did?" Johnson asked eventually. "It would have finished off most."

Severinov pressed his lips together. "We forgot and we moved on. My mother never spoke of it and my father hardly ever did. I don't think of it."

"I can understand that," Johnson said. "But how did you find out, if they never spoke of it?"

Severinov screwed up his face, as if in some pain. "One night, after my father had been drinking again, he told me. I was eighteen years old by then. I was utterly shocked—of course, until then I had believed Ioseb simply to be my older brother. But I'm not going to talk about that with you."

Johnson sighed inwardly, finding himself sympathizing with Severinov on the issue, if on nothing else the Russian had done. Further questioning could wait. There would be other opportunities.

"Look," Johnson said. "You need to know I'll be pushing the ICC as hard as I can to try to get you into court. Either way, I will be telling the story as fully as possible. Maybe someone, somewhere, might learn from it."

Severinov clenched his fists tightly on the table, his knuckles white. "I will be crucified by the Kremlin," he said. "You have no idea."

"That's the general idea," Johnson said in a disinterested tone. He could see that Storey was reading a message on his phone and was wanting to interrupt. "What do you have, Seb?" he asked.

Storey indicated toward Severinov. "You may not want to hear this, but he'll be flying back to Moscow in another couple of hours. He's got another jet coming to pick him up."

Johnson felt as though he had just been kicked in the guts. "*What?* Afghanistan isn't going to prosecute him?"

Storey shook his head. "I'll tell you later, but seems they just want the bastard out of the country as quickly as possible. Not sure if Putin's been pulling strings or making threats." He indicated with his thumb toward Severinov. "They've declared him persona non grata in Afghanistan, though, for what he did during the occupation, I've just been told."

His phone beeped again as another message arrived. He read it. "The government is citing the destruction of villages and their populations through helicopter attacks and arranging the systematic torture of prisoners at Pul-e-Charkhi and other detention centers," Storey continued. "They'd probably like to declare Putin persona non grata as well but can't."

Johnson felt a little dizzy as the news sank in. How could Severinov get away with it? This was a joke.

He tried to look for the positives. The episode marked the end of Severinov's ambitions regarding the Afghan oil and gas assets, anyway—Johnson was certain of that—just as surely as Zilleman and Donnerstein's ambitions had been quite rightly thwarted. The Ministry of Mines and Petroleum had already announced they were canceling the bid presentations scheduled for that day, and indeed the whole process, in view of what had happened—two of their main bidders had disappeared.

Johnson nodded at Storey. There was no point continuing the interview. "Okay, I'm finished with questions here. There's nothing much more to ask. At least, not that will make a difference," he said. "You can take him away."

One of the two soldiers flanking Severinov indicated to him to stand, which he did, eyeballing Johnson.

"You will regret this," Severinov said. "Remember my words."

Johnson shrugged again. "I doubt it. My only regret is that you're getting a lot less than you deserve, unless your man Putin suddenly does something sensible for a change."

Severinov narrowed his eyes and glanced alternately at Johnson and Jayne. "One piece of advice, both of you, don't come to Russia. I have friends deep inside the FSB and SVR —I will make sure you are both on their list."

Severinov turned on his heel and walked toward the door, one soldier on either side.

After the door had closed behind them, Johnson turned back to Storey. "Any news on what is happening with Putin?" he asked.

"He's flying back to Moscow shortly as well. Karzai's canceled the meeting." He smiled.

"Some good news at last. Excellent," Johnson said. The story of Putin's rebuke by Karzai, a minnow in world politics by comparison, would provide a great backdrop and justification for the story he wanted to tell to the media.

"The only downside is Putin lives to fight another day as well, then," Storey said. "What a pity."

"Indeed," Johnson said. "It is."

CHAPTER FORTY

Friday, June 14, 2013
  Moscow

Severinov paused at the door that led from his house onto the expansive granite patio with intricate inset patterns that spanned the front of the property. He gazed down over his carefully manicured lawns and the swimming pool to the Moscow River beyond, all bathed in sunlight.

He knew he was lucky to be back home rather than incarcerated in some cell beneath the deceptive blue skies of Kabul, a city that, in the past twenty-four hours, he had come to dislike intensely.

From his seat beneath a white canvas canopy to his left, Vasily called out in a growly voice. "Yuri, are you all right, comrade?"

Severinov jumped a little. "Not really. We need to talk." He walked over to his colleague, who had accompanied him back from Kabul, and sat down. He picked up the ice-cold glass of his favorite Beluga vodka that one of his house staff had placed on the table for him and took a sip.

After his excruciating interview at the hands of Johnson and company and his subsequent release, Severinov had gone straight to Putin's aircraft, which was on the tarmac at Bagram, for a debriefing.

Putin had initially appeared to view the entire episode as something that should be blamed on the ex-mujahideen Javed Hasrat, the American investigator Joe Johnson, and Karzai's Kabul government.

Karzai's decision to cancel his meeting with Putin seemed to have focused the president's anger firmly on the Afghan leader rather than on Severinov. He hadn't even mentioned the Fedorov prisoner exchange issue, to Severinov's relief.

However, just as Severinov was about to leave Putin's aircraft to return to his own Cessna Citation X, the president had casually switched tack—a not unfamiliar strategy.

There was a complex set of clauses and options in the sale and purchase agreement under which Severinov had obtained the three original oil and gas fields in western Siberia that allowed the Russian government, under exceptional circumstances, to claw back rights to all of the output from those fields.

Putin told Severinov he was unilaterally declaring an exceptional circumstance and would exercise one-third of those options as a penalty for the failure to secure the Afghan investment. It would deal a hammer blow—albeit not a terminal one—to his cash flows and his ability to repay debt obtained from banks to finance other acquisitions.

It was impossible to argue: Severinov undoubtedly had Putin to thank for the Afghans' decision not to detain him. Karzai's security forces had taken the view that they had probably irritated the Russian leader enough already without adding fuel to the flames by imprisoning one of his oligarchs and former KGB colleagues.

"I don't know where all this is going," Severinov said, glancing across at Vasily. "I have visions of losing all this." He indicated with a sweep of his hand the house and land that stretched out in front of him.

"I think it will be okay. The dust will settle," Vasily said.

"I'm not sure. It's embarrassing."

Already *The New York Times* and CNN had run stories about the destruction of his plane in Kabul, referring to Severinov as Stalin's secret grandchild—the cat was out of the bag. Johnson must have briefed them. There had been a wave of follow-up calls from other journalists to the Besoi Energy offices, which his communications director was so far ignoring. It was a matter of time before it became known that his late half brother was Stalin's illegitimate son.

His defense with the leadership would have to be that it hadn't been him who had talked about it—something he had been expressly forbidden from doing.

The problem was that nothing that tarred the memory of Russia's leader during the Second World War was to be tolerated. Severinov himself didn't want to do such a thing.

He feared that if the coverage got out of hand, the penalty imposed by Putin might rise dramatically, and he could lose the entirety of the three oil and gas fields.

It was also to be hoped that whoever had supplied the nuggets of information about the Stalin connection to Johnson did not have access to any other of his secrets.

The big concern that Severinov had was the risk that Johnson might actively stir up a storm against him in the way that he appeared to have done in Washington against the US energy secretary Donnerstein, who had been very publicly hounded out of his job.

"What do you want to do?" Vasily asked, picking up his own drink.

"We need to make a plan," Severinov said. "I'm not going to reach Javed now, I accept that. But I'm not going to let Johnson get away with what he's done. I'll need your help with that."

"You want to do something now?"

"No, not now. That would be too obvious. We'll look at it in the future."

Severinov sank back into the plush cushions of his patio armchair, clutching his vodka.

"Well, here's to the next operation," Vasily said. He raised his glass.

"Yes. To the next operation. To the Motherland." Severinov reached over and clinked glasses with Vasily, then downed the Beluga in one swallow.

EPILOGUE

Saturday, June 15, 2013
Bagram Airfield

"What did you say?" Johnson shouted, the blistering roar from the F-16 fighter jet's engines gradually fading as it climbed into the blue above the mountaintops surrounding Bagram Airfield. The planes had been taking off in close succession for the previous ten minutes, making conversation difficult.

"I was saying, three and a half out of four isn't bad," Jayne said as she clinked her can of Coca-Cola against Johnson's. They were standing outside a Burger King kiosk at the base's PX shopping area, waiting for Seb Storey and Frank Rice, whom they had arranged to meet for a farewell chat.

"What do you mean?" Johnson asked.

"You've nailed Watson and Donnerstein—they will certainly go to prison, and you're already getting the credit for that. You've nailed Javed, who'll be in a hell pit at Pul-e-Charkhi. And you've destroyed Severinov's chances of doing that massive oil and gas deal," Jayne said. "That's three and a half."

"Yes, Watson—what a huge relief that has been," Johnson said. "I never thought I'd get the chance, and then I thought he'd gone under the train. I've got mixed feelings about Javed, despite everything he's done, and it's something of a disaster that the Afghans aren't going to put Severinov behind bars too. That would have been four out of four. He's now going to be spitting blood. Free to come back at us."

Jayne shrugged. "I don't know."

"I'll bet he tries," Johnson said.

There was another deafening roar as yet another F-16 took off from the nearby runway, forcing them to put their conversation on hold again. A group of US troops walked past and headed into the nearby grocery store, doubtless looking for a few home comforts to compensate for having to spend extended periods away living in hot, uncomfortable, and dangerous conditions. Most servicemen seemed to be coming out of the store with arms full of energy drinks, chocolate bars, and cigarettes.

Johnson felt a tap on his shoulder and turned around to find Storey and Rice standing there, a grin on both of their faces.

When the noise from the jet abated, Storey put one hand on Johnson's shoulder. "I just wanted to say thanks before you fly home," he said. "You did a good job."

"Thank you," Johnson said, shaking Storey's hand. "I wouldn't have been alive to do any job if it hadn't been for you and your team pulling me out of that building."

"Yes, agreed," Jayne said to Storey. "I would have been left completely stranded without you guys. We both owe you."

"Let's call it teamwork, then," Storey said, turning to Johnson and indicating toward Jayne. "You owe a lot to this lady, Joe."

"You're right there," Johnson said. "Not for the first time."

"People forget quickly," Storey continued. "With all the current battles going on against the Taliban and the Haqqanis, they forget about the horrendous things that happened during the Soviet occupation and how bad the Russians really were. Nice to see at least some justice being handed out."

"Not quite what I wanted," Johnson said.

"I know. But almost. Keep it in perspective. I think you're the kind of guy who's never satisfied."

"True," Johnson said. He knew it *was* true—he hated seeing anyone who deserved justice walking away free, especially when it involved the kind of large-scale genocide perpetrated by the Soviets on the Afghan people.

"I need to go," Storey said. "I need to get on a chopper flight back to Wilderness soon. Keep in touch. I'll leave you with Frank here." He shook Johnson's and Jayne's hands, flashed them a salute, and with a nod of the head, disappeared around the corner.

Johnson turned to Rice. "I guess we've cleared out the opposition for you when they restart the bid process—the Russians and the Swiss Americans," he said with a grin. "You've got to be happy with that."

But Rice wasn't smiling. "Not quite, unfortunately."

"Why, what's happened?" Johnson asked.

"You haven't heard what happened, obviously. The Afghans are handing the bid to the Chinese, without an auction. So we're out of it too."

Johnson tried not to roll his eyes, and he could see out of the corner of his eye that Jayne had her hands on her hips.

"Sorry to hear that," Johnson said.

"I guess Karzai must have just felt hugely embarrassed by the US and Russia and looked in a different direction?" Jayne asked.

"Yes," Rice said. "I heard Karzai was in a complete rage

and ordered the mines minister to sign the deal with the Chinese." He sighed. "They got it for over a billion dollars less than we would have bid. It's a travesty—not least for the Afghan people. A billion dollars would build a lot of hospitals and schools. But never mind, the circus moves on. We'll find another deal."

Rice took a folded sheet of paper from his pocket and handed it to Johnson. "The payments for you and Jayne have gone through. I've added bonuses for you both for all the additional work you've done and for the danger you put yourself into. It was much appreciated, even if we didn't get the result we wanted. And it's not every day you scalp a US cabinet member."

"Or a top CIA officer," Johnson said. He unfolded the paper and read it, then pulled back in surprise. Rice had almost doubled the promised fees.

Jayne leaned over and looked the sheet. "Wow," she said.

"You didn't need to add that much," Johnson said. "It's really—"

"Take it and run," Rice interrupted, with a wink. "My client's paying. We're investment bankers, remember?"

Their conversation was interrupted yet again by the low-pitched raucous drone of another plane, this time a C-130J cargo turboprop, as it took off behind them.

"What's your plan?" Rice asked, when the C-130's engine noise had faded. "Have you heard back from the ICC yet about that contract?"

Johnson still hadn't heard from the ICC. But it was something he had been mulling over in his mind for the previous several hours. Given events over the past couple of weeks, did he now actually want to spend longer in Afghanistan and do the job?

In that moment, he suddenly decided.

"No, I haven't heard, and I don't want the contract now

anyway," Johnson said. "I'm heading home." He glanced sideways at Jayne. "I need to see my kids. And I think we've done well enough with nailing 1980s war criminals here in the last couple of weeks. Someone else can deal with the post-2003 inquiry."

Jayne nodded. "We've done our bit," she said. "The ICC will have their work cut out with the more recent allegations."

Johnson knew she was right. One of the biggest problems would be the unwillingness of Hamid Karzai's government to fully support the ICC's work and make information available, not least about the wartime activities of many senior politicians and military leaders. Some of them were seen as potential candidates for president and vice president in the elections due to be held the following year, 2014. That seemed like a bureaucratic nightmare.

Suddenly, Johnson found the idea of a four-and-a-half hour flight to Dubai from Bagram, and then on to JFK and back home to Portland, very appealing. He would take a break, and maybe use some of Rice's bonus payment to book a holiday somewhere with Carrie and Peter. Then he would think about finding another project to work on, maybe somewhere less dangerous. Afghanistan had been a fascinating place to operate, but he had remained constantly aware of his own mortality, every minute of every day. As a single father, he found it difficult.

The list of incoming work inquiries had continued to flow. His interest had been piqued by a couple of Nazi-related proposals in particular, which would take him back to his old stomping ground, but there were other options too. Hopefully Jayne could join him, if the right project came up. He had found himself enjoying working with her yet again. She was professional, tough, resourceful, and yet had a sense of humor about her that helped get them through the most difficult of situations. Johnson felt he owed her a lot.

"I need to go now," Rice said. "My flight leaves in fifty minutes."

Johnson pocketed the payment note that Rice had given him and shook hands. "Thanks very much," he said. "You've helped me bury a few ghosts from my past."

"Yes. Just a pity about the Russian," Rice said.

"Don't worry. I feel there will be another chance," Jayne said.

Johnson gave a thin smile. "Hmm. You're probably right," he said. "You usually are."

* * *

BOOK 5 IN THE JOE JOHNSON SERIES: THE NAZI'S SON

If you enjoyed **Stalin's Final Sting** you'll probably like the fifth book in the Joe Johnson series, **The Nazi's Son**, which is another investigation into dark crimes from the past.

If you liked it so much you want several other books from the series, you can buy various bundles of my paperbacks from my website shop at a significant discount to Amazon. I can only currently ship to the US and UK though. Go and visit:

https://www.andrewturpin.com/shop/

Otherwise if you only want a single copy of **The Nazi's Son**, or if you live outside the US or UK, it is best to use Amazon—just type "Andrew Turpin The Nazi's Son" into the search box at the top of the Amazon sales web page.

To give you a flavor of **The Nazi's Son**, here's the blurb:

A deadly legacy of the Cold War . . . A mysterious Nazi source. A desperate escape bid through northern Russia. And life-threatening secrets being leaked by a mole at the heart of Western intelligence.

In the fifth book of this thriller series, ex-CIA war crimes investigator **Joe Johnson** heads to Berlin to assist with the supposedly straightforward debriefing of a Russian defector. The defector knows the background to the terrorist bombing of the city's famous La Belle nightclub in the 1980s as well as the identity of a Russian agent who is funneling American and British military secrets to Moscow.

But things go wrong. Johnson is pursued by his nemesis, the vengeful Russian oligarch Yuri Severinov. And subsequent events turn out to be vastly more complex and terrifying than he expected.

Why are ex-KGB and Stasi intelligence chiefs so anxious to prevent Johnson from getting to the heart of what really happened? And what are the Kremlin connections that suck him into a life-or-death chase in St. Petersburg?

Johnson and his ex-MI6 colleague Jayne Robinson find themselves battling against the odds to dig out truths that have been concealed for almost thirty years.

At the same time, the pair find themselves inexorably drawn toward resuming the brief love affair they once had in Islamabad.

The key to solving the conundrum around the Berlin bombing comes from an unlikely direction, and the identity of the Russian mole who is wreaking havoc in the West turns out to be equally surprising.

The story works its way to a climax in London and

Leipzig as Johnson battles against overwhelming odds to outwit the forces arrayed against him.

The Nazi's Son is a thriller with many unexpected twists that will keep the reader guessing right to the end.

* * *

ANDREW'S READERS GROUP AND OTHER JOE JOHNSON BOOKS

If you enjoyed this book, I would like to keep in touch. This is not always easy, as I usually only publish a couple of books a year and there are many authors and books out there. So the best way is for you to be on my Readers Group email list. I can then send you updates on the next book, plus occasional special offers. There's no spam and you can unsubscribe at any time.

If you would like to join my Readers Group and receive the email updates, I will send you, **FREE**, the ebook version of another Joe Johnson thriller, **The Afghan**, which is a prequel to the series and normally sells at $2.99/£2.99 (paperback $9.99/£9.99).

The Afghan is set in 1988 when Johnson was still in the CIA. Most of the action takes place in Afghanistan, then occupied by the Soviet Union, and in Washington, DC. Some of the characters and story lines that emerge in the other books have their roots in this period. I think you will enjoy it!

The Afghan can be downloaded **FREE** from the following link:

https://bookhip.com/RJGFPAW

If you only like reading paperbacks you can still sign up for the email list at that link to get news of my books and forthcoming releases. Just ignore the email that arrives with the ebook attached. A paperback version of **The Afghan** and all my books is for sale at my website, where you will find large discounts on bundles of my books. I can currently ship to the US and UK:

https://www.andrewturpin.com/shop/

You should also enjoy the other thrillers in the Joe Johnson series, if you haven't read them yet. You may find it is best to read them in order, as follows:

Prequel: *The Afghan*
1. *The Last Nazi*
2. *The Old Bridge*
3. *Bandit Country*
4. *Stalin's Final Sting*
5. *The Nazi's Son*
6. *The Black Sea*

I also have a separate spy conspiracy thriller series, albeit with strong connections to the Johnson series—the **Jayne Robinson** thrillers. So far the books in this series are:

1. *The Kremlin's Vote*
2. *The Dark Shah*
3. *The Confessor*
4. *The Queen's Pawn*
5. *The Dam Keeper*

To find the books, just type "Andrew Turpin thrillers" in the search box at the top of the Amazon page — you can't miss them!

IF YOU ENJOYED THIS BOOK PLEASE WRITE A REVIEW

As an independently published author, through my own imprint The Write Direction Publishing, I find that honest reviews of my books are the most powerful way for me to bring them to the attention of other potential readers.

As you'll appreciate, unlike the big international publishers, I can't take out full-page advertisements in the newspapers or place posters on the subway.

So I am committed to producing work of the best quality I can in order to attract a loyal group of readers who are happy to recommend my work to others.

Therefore, if you enjoyed reading this novel, then I would very much appreciate it if you would spend five minutes and leave a review—which can be as short as you like—preferably on the page or website where you bought it.

You can find the book on the Amazon website by typing 'Andrew Turpin Stalin's Final Sting' in the search box at the top of the Amazon website.

Once you are on the book's page, scroll down to 'Customer Reviews', then click on 'Leave a Review.'

Reviews are also a great encouragement to me to write more.

Many thanks!

THANKS AND ACKNOWLEDGEMENTS

Thank you to everyone who reads my books. You are the reason I began to write in the first place, and I hope I can provide you with entertainment and interest for a long time into the future.

Every time I get an encouraging email from a reader, or a positive comment on my Facebook page, or a nice review on Amazon, it spurs me on to press ahead with my research or writing for the next book. So keep them coming!

Specifically with regard to *Stalin's Final Sting*, there are several people who have helped me during the long process of research, writing, and editing.

I have two editors who consistently provide helpful advice, food for thought, great ideas, and constructive criticism, and between them have enabled me to considerably improve the initial draft. Katrina Diaz Arnold, owner of Refine Editing, again gave me a lot of valuable feedback at the structural and line levels, and Jon Ford, as ever, helped me to maintain the authenticity of the story in many areas through his great eye for detail. I would like to thank both of them—the responsibility for any remaining mistakes lies solely with me.

As always, my brother, Adrian Turpin, has been a very helpful reader of my early drafts and highlighted areas where I need to improve. Others, such as Martin Scales, David Cole, David Payne, and Warren Smith have done likewise.

But I also have a growing team of advance readers who go through my books at a later stage, just prior to publication, and have been able to give me a few useful pointers and have spotted the odd error. If you would like to join my Advance Readers team, send me an email at andrew@andrew turpin.com and let me know. Make sure to tell me a little about yourself — including what part of the world you live in and the type of books and authors you like.

I would also like to thank the team at Damonza for what I think is a great cover design.

AUTHOR'S NOTE

The conflict in Afghanistan during and after the Soviet military occupation from 1979 to 1989 has been a rich feeding ground for fiction and nonfiction authors alike.

As with all the books in the Joe Johnson war crimes series, much of the historical backdrop to **Stalin's Final Sting** is factual, including details of the atrocities inflicted on the Afghan population during that time.

The Khost-Gardez Pass was the scene of many bloody battles during that period between the Soviet army and the mujahideen forces who managed for almost all of those ten years to control the pass and keep them at bay.

In particular, the deployment by the Soviets of Mil Mi-24 helicopters—dubbed Hinds by NATO—and the use by the mujahideen of Stinger missiles to combat them has become the stuff of legend.

During all of this, the ongoing duels between the Soviet intelligence service, the KGB, on one side, and the CIA, MI6, and Pakistan's ISI, who were supporting the mujahideen on the other side, were critical to the outcome.

As with all the books in this series, because my protagonist Joe Johnson is from the United States, and most scenes are from his point of view, it seemed to make sense to try to use American spellings and terminology wherever possible, rather than my native British.

Finally, on a lighter note, I should mention that the one thing that keeps me going through all the long months of research, writing, and editing before I can publish each book is coffee. I do enjoy a good latte—it is essential brain fuel!

So when I was invited to join **Buy Me A Coffee**—a website you might have heard of that allows supporters to give the providers of their favorite goods and services a cup or two—I thought it sounded like a good idea.

Therefore, if you enjoy my books and would like to buy me a latte, I would be extremely grateful. You will definitely be playing an essential part in the production of the next book!

You will find my online coffee shop at:

https://www.buymeacoffee.com/andrewturpin

Many thanks.
Andrew

RESEARCH AND BIBLIOGRAPHY

My research for *Stalin's Final Sting* and for its direct prequel in the Joe Johnson series, *The Afghan*, was all carried out as part of the same process. Both books are set mainly in Afghanistan and I researched, wrote, and edited both of them in parallel. The biggest difference lies in the timeframe: *The Afghan* is set in 1988, when Johnson was still working for the CIA, and *Stalin's Final Sting* in 2013, but there are many references in the latter book to events and situations in the former.

For this reason, the following notes that I have put together on my research sources are very similar for both titles.

Across both books the research proved to be so interesting that I often found myself immersed in some book or article online and had to remind myself to get on with it, collect the information I needed, and focus on the writing of my story.

The whole saga of the Soviet occupation of Afghanistan really is a classic case study of the CIA at work to try to further the interests of the United States in an under-the-radar manner. As the Soviet army marched in during December 1979, the Cold War was running strongly, and there is no doubt that the US feared what the next move would be if it proved successful.

As it happened, the Soviets ended up being bogged down in an attritional war against the mujahideen that lasted for nine years before they finally pulled out in 1989—just before the Eastern European revolutions of that year, including the fall of the Berlin Wall, that led to the collapse of the Soviet Union.

That certainly did not seem the likely outcome during the

first few years of the occupation, when over 100,000 Soviet troops took control of the country, backed by the KGB.

The CIA, which together with Pakistan's ISI intelligence agency assisted the mujahideen in their fight, can take a large amount of credit for the eventual victory.

The CIA's Operation Cyclone proved a critical turning point. This program funded and arranged the supply of Stinger missiles from September 1986 onward, which finally gave the mujahideen the weaponry they needed to combat the terrifying Soviet Mil Mi-24 gunship helicopters—dubbed the "Hind" by NATO.

These Hinds had been used by the Soviets to destroy villages and to kill a lot of the two million Afghans who died during the war. Another three million fled the carnage across the border into Pakistan.

Anyone who would like a colorful and racy account of how the Stingers were deployed by the CIA, and the politics behind those decisions, should look no further than *Charlie Wilson's War*, by George Crile, available on Amazon.

A 2007 film of the book, under the same title, and starring Tom Hanks and Julia Roberts, is also available. There is no doubt that the late Charlie Wilson, a Democratic congressman, was a driving force that championed the use of Stingers and cajoled and pushed his colleagues in Congress to support Operation Cyclone with ever-increasing levels of funding. It seems likely that without the energy of this larger-than-life character, they may not have been deployed at all.

Another extremely insightful book is *Ghost Wars*, by Steve Coll, a *Washington Post* journalist. The book covers the CIA's operations in Afghanistan from 1979 through to 2001 and includes sections on Bin Laden. It is available on Amazon.

Milton Bearden, a thirty-year CIA veteran, was station chief in Islamabad from 1986–89, during which time he was very heavily involved in Operation Cyclone. He subsequently wrote a vivid and technically detailed thriller about the battles between the Soviets and the mujahideen entitled *The Black Tulip* (1998), which is still available on Amazon. I found it very useful as background reading and as an inspiration for some of my plot lines.

Before anyone asks, my fictional CIA Islamabad station chief during the 1980s, Robert Watson, is NOT based on Bearden, who I'm sure would be appalled at most of the things Watson did during his career.

For the story of the KGB archives photographed by Abdul Akbari, I drew inspiration from the Mitrokhin Archive, a collection of notes put together by former KGB archivist Vasili Mitrokhin, which he brought to the UK in 1992 when he defected.

Steve Coll wrote an excellent article in the *The Washington Post* about the role played by intelligence agencies in Afghanistan and the importance of the Mitrokhin Archive in deciphering this activity. See: https://www.washingtonpost.com/archive/opinions/2002/02/24/spies-lies-and-the-distortion-of-history/7469fae7-4859-495b-959d-42eccdb38fbe/?utm_term=.8bc1189b2e60.

There is a Wikipedia entry about this at: https://en.wikipedia.org/wiki/Mitrokhin_Archive. There is also a book by Christopher Andrew, entitled *The Sword and the Shield*, available on Amazon.

For more color about the impact of the Soviet occupation on the Afghan people, I would recommend a book by ITN journalist Sandy Gall, *Agony of a Nation* (1988) which is available on Amazon.

On the genocide committed by Soviet forces against the Afghan population, there is a good article by Michael Reisman and Charles Norchi that details the extent of depopulation and atrocities committed. Entitled "Genocide and the

Soviet Occupation of Afghanistan," it can be found at: http://www.paulbogdanor.com/left/afghan/genocide.pdf.

A good summary of the Soviet-Afghan war, including the extent of the genocide perpetrated by Soviet forces, can be found in Wikipedia, at: https://en.wikipedia.org/wiki/Soviet%E2%80%93Afghan_War#Destruction_in_Afghanistan.

The degree of international interest in investing in Afghanistan's oil and gas reserves is well documented. For example, *The Daily Telegraph* reported in 2011 how China National Petroleum Corp secured a joint-venture deal to invest in oil exploration in Afghanistan's northern provinces. See: https://www.telegraph.co.uk/finance/newsbysector/energy/oilandgas/8979038/China-begins-scramble-for-Afghanistans-oil-reserves.html.

In January 2013, *The Atlantic* carried an article entitled "The New War for Afghanistan's Untapped Oil" about the attacks carried out by the Taliban on various energy installations. See: https://www.theatlantic.com/international/archive/2013/01/the-new-war-for-afghanistans-untapped-oil/267010/.

My prologue about Javed's escape from Pul-e-Charkhi prison is entirely fictional but was inspired by real-life accounts of escapes from the prison, albeit in a much less dramatic fashion than Javed's. For a report on one such escape, involving fifteen Taliban commanders, see this article in Tolo News: http://www.tolonews.com/afghanistan/taliban-commanders-death-row-escape-central-prison.

The legendary Khost-Gardez Pass may need little introduction. However, there are some excellent videos on YouTube about this region, including a few about the lengthy and controversial construction project to pave the highway. For example, there is this one produced by USAid: https://www.youtube.com/watch?v=-ciitRebvuA, and another by the same organization: https://www.youtube.com/watch?v=pdYAR3C6uJg.

These two films give a good illustration of the type of terrain through which the highway passes and the small villages en route, similar to my fictional village of Wazrar. I could have chosen a real village as the backdrop for the scenes in the K-G Pass, but I decided that the sensitivities of the situations I was writing about made it perhaps better to come up with a fictional one, albeit closely based on reality.

One of the themes that runs through *Stalin's Final Sting* is that of revenge. This concept is one that is deeply rooted in the Afghan culture and is tied to the idea of honour, particularly at the family and tribal level. This lifestyle is known as Pashtunwali, or Pushtunwali, depending on your choice of spelling, and is an unwritten code adopted by the Pashtun people.

An excellent article which explains the principles of Pashtunwali can be found in *The Economist* here: https://www.economist.com/special-report/2006/12/19/honour-among-them.

Expat life in Kabul is a challenge, whether as an embassy employee or in a private capacity, due to the constant threat of Taliban attacks and kidnappings. A good article that captures the essence of daily life in what amounts to a war zone has been written by Bill Bent on the American Foreign Service Association website. It can be found at: http://www.afsa.org/serving-embassy-kabul.

Life at the various US army outposts around Afghanistan were similarly hazardous. Forward Operating Base Wilderness, in the K-G Pass, features in *Stalin's Final Sting* and some of the detail was inspired by a CBS News Sixty Minutes feature entitled "Afghanistan: Fighting in a Hornet's Nest." It can be found at: https://www.cbsnews.com/news/afghanistan-fighting-in-a-hornets-nest/.

Also helpful with regard to life at FOB Wilderness was an article in *The Huffington Post* by journalist Franz-Stefan Gady, which can be found at: https://www.huffingtonpost.com/franzstefan-gady/a-deadly-artillery-duel-i_b_3824468.html.

All these books, articles, and videos are simply a flavor of the many I read and watched while researching *Stalin's Final Sting* and *The Afghan*. However, they do give you the basis for some further reading should you be so inspired.

ABOUT THE AUTHOR AND CONTACT DETAILS

I have always had a love of writing and a passion for reading good thrillers. But despite having a long-standing dream of writing my own novels, it took me more than five decades to finally get around to completing the first.

Stalin's Final Sting is the fourth in the **Joe Johnson** series of thrillers, which pulls together some of my other interests, particularly history, world news, and travel.

I studied history at Loughborough University and worked for many years as a business and financial journalist before becoming a corporate and financial communications adviser with several large energy companies, specializing in media relations.

Originally I came from Grantham, Lincolnshire, and I now live with my family in St. Albans, Hertfordshire, U.K.

You can connect with me via these routes:

E-mail: andrew@andrewturpin.com
Website: www.andrewturpin.com.
Facebook: @AndrewTurpinAuthor
Twitter: @AndrewTurpin
Instagram: @andrewturpin.author

Please also follow me on Amazon, using the following link. That way they will keep you informed about the next book.

https://www.amazon.com/Andrew-Turpin/e/B074V87WWL/

Do get in touch with your comments and views on the books, or anything else for that matter. I enjoy hearing from readers and promise to reply.

Manufactured by Amazon.ca
Bolton, ON

37154485R00245